A
DANGEROUS
PLACE

ALSO BY JACQUELINE WINSPEAR

Maisie Dobbs

Birds of a Feather

Pardonable Lies

Messenger of Truth

An Incomplete Revenge

Among the Mad

The Mapping of Love and Death

A Lesson in Secrets

Elegy for Eddie

Leaving Everything Most Loved

The Care and Management of Lies

A DANGEROUS PLACE

A Novel

JACQUELINE WINSPEAR

HARPER
An Imprint of HarperCollins*Publishers*

HarperCollins books may be purchased for educational, business, or sales promotional use. For information, please e-mail the Special Markets Department at SPsales@harpercollins .com.

FIRST EDITION

Library of Congress Cataloging-in-Publication Data is available upon request.

ISBN: 978-0-06-222055-4

15 16 17 18 19   OV/RRD   10 9 8 7 6 5 4 3 2 1

To Kas Salazar

Dear friend, this one's for you.

The world is a dangerous place to live; not because of the people who are evil, but because of the people who don't do anything about it.

—ALBERT EINSTEIN

The world is getting to be such a dangerous place, a man is lucky to get out of it alive.

—W. C. FIELDS

A
DANGEROUS
PLACE

CHAPTER ONE

Gibraltar, April 1937

Arturo Kenyon stood in the shadows of a whitewashed building opposite a small guesthouse known locally as Mrs. Bishop's, though it had no sign to advertise the fact. He was waiting for a woman who had taken a room under the name of Miss M. Dobbs to emerge. Then he would follow her. She had, after all, been instrumental in not allowing the dust to settle on the death of one Sebastian Babayoff, a photographer of weddings and family events, and contributor of photographs to the odd tourist pamphlet. Not that there were the usual number of tourists in Gibraltar at that very moment. Refugees—yes. Government officials—yes. Increasing numbers of soldiers and sailors—yes. Black-market profiteers—of course. And to top it all, more than a few like himself, working on behalf of their country in a role not specified on any identification documents, but considered important all the same. In fact, the town was crawling with men—and, he had no doubt, women—with a similar remit: to be the eyes and ears of their government's most secret services in a place seething with those dispossessed by war across the border. This place of his birth wasn't a good place to be.

Kenyon's father had been a navy man stationed in Gibraltar when he'd fallen for a local girl of Maltese heritage named Leonarda. Such a love affair was not an unusual occurrence—Gibraltar was, after all, a military garrison. An only child, Arturo had grown up on tales of Lord Nelson and the Battle of Trafalgar, and the strategic importance of his home. His father had been killed in the war, but his loss at the Battle of Jutland in 1916 did not deter Arturo from following in his footsteps and joining the Royal Navy, albeit under the name Arthur Kenyon. It wouldn't have done him any favors to be an Arturo on board ship. An injury sustained while at sea should have mustered him out of the senior service, but instead he was—as his commanding officer termed it—"reassigned" to another role. Which is how Kenyon found himself working for naval intelligence, now back in Gibraltar under the name by which he had been known until he left his mother's house at sixteen on a quest to follow in his father's footsteps. Fluent in Spanish and English, and the strange hybrid of those two languages that could be heard in Gibraltar, he was a good man to have at their disposal as far as the government was concerned. Especially now, when the Spanish were killing each other across the border.

The body of Babayoff, a Sephardic Jew, had been discovered by the Dobbs woman when she was out walking one evening. That was another thing about her; she walked alone at night, despite curfews in place to protect the citizenry. At first it appeared as if she would not pose too much of a problem—Mrs. Bishop had informed a policeman that Miss Dobbs would likely book a passage to Southampton soon, based upon what had happened. But instead she remained and began asking questions and visiting Babayoff's people, one of the older Gibraltarian Jewish families. She wasn't doing these things in a hurry,

Kenyon had noticed. It was as if each day she took it upon herself to make an attempt to tidy an ill-kempt room—dust a little here, sweep there, remove a cobweb or two.

Dobbs was a strange one, thought Kenyon as he lit a strong French cigarette and drew until the tip almost enflamed. He'd followed her a couple of times since receiving orders. She was tall, her chin-length hair almost jet black, though he'd noticed a few gray hairs at her temples. And those eyes—she almost caught him looking at her once, and he thought then that those eyes might see right through a person, though the person in question might not see anything in return. If eyes were windows into the heart of a human being, then hers were locked tight, as if a portcullis had come down across her soul. Kenyon—whose hair was almost as black as that of the woman for whom he waited, though his eyes were the pale blue of his blond father—was used to watching people, well versed in discovering the truth about someone just by observing them about their daily rounds. He thought this woman, Maisie Dobbs, carried something inside her, as if she didn't really want to be involved in the death of Sebastian Babayoff but could not help herself. It was as if she felt a responsibility to the deceased, having found his body. What was it she'd said to the police at the time? He'd read her statement in notes acquired from his man at the police station. *His death deserves our attention, so his family can be at peace. There is a duty here, and it cannot be ignored.*

Peace? That was a fine word—everyone who entered Gibraltar now wanted nothing more than to be enveloped by peace. Perhaps this Maisie Dobbs was looking for something too. According to a report he'd received from Whitehall, she might have been traveling under another name; Dobbs was not the name on her passport. She'd begun her journey in India, bound for Southampton, yet had disembarked in Gibraltar three weeks ago. She should have continued on to her final destination, but for some reason she'd decided to remain, having left the ship against the advice of the captain. More interesting to Arturo Kenyon, a man named Brian Huntley, from one of those nameless government departments in London, seemed pleased to know where she was, and had given orders for her to be accounted for. Not intercepted, not approached and questioned, or even—he dreaded the word— "eliminated." His brief was to keep an eye on her.

Kenyon was watching the whitewashed house, its window boxes trailing geraniums, when the door opened and Maisie Dobbs stepped out into the sunshine. Though her clothes were made of cotton and linen, she was not dressed for fine weather as a tourist might. A black blouse and a narrow black skirt to mid-calf emphasized her slender shape, and she wore plain black leather shoes with a peep toe. She wore no stockings, which was something of a surprise to Kenyon. That woman could do with a bit of fat on her, he thought, and as he watched, Maisie Dobbs looked up at the sky, took off her hat, and put on a pair of dark glasses. Replacing the narrow-brimmed hat, she glanced both ways before setting off along the narrow passageway toward Main Street. It was clear that she was not short of funds—something about her demeanor suggested a confidence that attended the well-heeled. The guesthouse proprietress had informed him—in return for folding money—that Dobbs had paid one month in advance.

Kenyon waited just a moment before stepping out of castellated shadows cast by late-morning sunshine against mismatched buildings, and kept her in view as she went on her way. He wondered why a woman of means would not be staying at the Ridge Hotel. Only a few years old, the luxurious hotel had become a mecca for the rich. And he wondered what had come to pass in her life, and why she'd chosen not to continue on her journey—for surely being safe at home in England would be more desirable than lingering in a town overrun with people running from hell.

Darjeeling, India, March 20ᵗʰ, 1934

Maisie Dobbs sat at a desk of dark polished teak set in a bay window, looking out across terraced tea gardens that seemed to sweep up into the foothills of distant mountains. She held her pen over a sheet of writing paper, but was distracted by converging thoughts as she watched a cadre of women pick young "first flush" tea shoots. Their hands moved across the bushes with speed as they snatched at the soft, rubbery leaves of *Camelia sinensis*, more commonly known by the name for the place in which it now grew across the vast estate. She continued to watch the women as they filled the deep baskets resting on their backs, held steady with a belt across their foreheads.

Soon she would leave this place where she had found a measure of calm. March and April brought spring to Darjeeling, days of crystal light and pearls of dew on rhododendrons of peach and magenta, and on flora she had never seen before and might never see again. There were light breezes filled with a sweet fragrance, and days when she turned her face to the sun and felt its warmth flood her body. A chance meeting in Bombay, where she had spent several weeks helping a man named Pramal set up a school in honor of his dead sister—a woman whose killer Maisie had found—had led her to Darjeeling, and an opportunity to rent this bungalow for some three or four months. The journey had been long and arduous, by train for the most part, and then all manner of transportation, including her first—and to this point, only—passage atop an elephant. But it was worth it for the peace. In London—how many months past, now? Was it six, even so soon?—she had begun to doubt herself, to question what she had believed for so many years to be her vocation. On behalf of those who came asking for her help, it was her task to uncover the truth and lies that stood in the way of their personal contentment. Sometimes the truth and lies were held within one tormented individual, who sought out Maisie in her role as psychologist to unravel the contradictions underpinning his or her turmoil. Some had simpler problems—a missing piece of jewelry, or a profligate business partner who had hidden evidence of funds misplaced. But among the clients who came to the Fitzroy Square office of Maisie Dobbs, Psychologist and Investigator, were those touched by the unresolved and perhaps mysterious death of someone dear, someone whose memory was tightly held. Maisie had brought every element of her training, every ounce of her character, and every last ache in her soul to the task of restoring peace to the bereaved—but then it had been her turn to find peace.

Amid the tea gardens and mountains, in the solitude she craved—a different solitude, away from even those she loved—she felt the war was truly behind her. All her wars were now behind her. It was as if the laundry had been washed and aired, ironed and folded, put away in a cupboard and locked. She had accepted what she considered to be her failings, had come to terms with her powerlessness against fate itself. Now, with the sleepless nights of dark thinking consigned to the past, she felt as if she were walking along a road that kept narrowing until it reached the vanishing point. She had come to a juncture where she could consider what might come next. And she knew the responsibility awaiting her: she had promised a decision. On March 31 she would send a telegram to James Compton: YES STOP, or NO STOP.

Darjeeling, March 31ˢᵗ
Miss M. Dobbs to James Compton

YES STOP

Miss M. Dobbs to Mrs. Priscilla Partridge:

HAVE ACCEPTED JAMES STOP WANT VERY SMALL CEREMONY STOP JUST US STOP WILL WRITE STOP

Mrs. Priscilla Partridge to Miss Maisie Dobbs

HOPE THIS ARRIVES BEFORE DEPARTURE STOP WONDERFUL NEWS STOP RE-CONSIDER CEREMONY STOP DO NOT DEPRIVE YOUR FATHER OF WALK DOWN AISLE STOP I WANT CHAMPAGNE STOP

The *Times*, London, April 1934

The engagement is announced between Margaret Rebecca, only daughter of Francis Edward Dobbs and the late Mrs. Analetta Phyzante Dobbs, and James William Maurice, Viscount Compton, only son of Lord Julian and Lady Rowan Compton.

The *Times*, London, August 1934

A fine summer's day greeted guests last Saturday at one of the year's most anticipated weddings, when the Viscount James Compton, son of Lord Julian and Lady Rowan Compton (the former Lady Rowan Jane Alcourt, daughter of Lord Jonathan Alcourt), was married to Miss Margaret Dobbs, daughter of Francis Dobbs, Esq. Following a service at St. Joseph's Church in Chelstone, a reception was held at the Dower House, Chelstone Manor, the bride's home. While honeymoon details are held secret by the groom, it is expected that the happy couple will be leaving for Canada within the month.

May 1935
Maisie Dobbs to Priscilla Partridge

Dear Priscilla,

I cannot believe I have been married now for over six months! I doubted ever coming to enjoy the life of a wife, but I have found a certain delight in marriage, and though I might have had my doubts when I walked up the aisle (holding on to my father's arm as if my life depended upon it), I made the right decision. We spend Monday to Thursday in northern Ontario, in a sizable leased house on the edge of a town named Dundas. James is very busy with what I can only call "Otterburn business" during those days. I worry about the work, which as you know involves his skills as an aviator (that's all I can say, really), but he assures me he is more of an "on the ground" man. You may wonder what I do all day, now that (for the first time in my life) I do not have a job. I am going through Maurice's papers with great care and am learning much about him and his work. It is illuminating. Suffice it to say, he had so much more to teach me, and I sometimes feel as if he were here at my side offering words of advice, and his own inimitable wisdom.

At week's end we generally return to Toronto—not a short journey by any means, but we enjoy our apartment (the one where James lived in bachelor days), which is very large, I must say, and we have so much fun sailing on the lake. Sometimes we remain in Dundas, however, we end up seeing more of the Otterburns at those times because they like to remain at their farm, and of course they have lots of guests and we are always expected to be at their parties. Fortunately, we can avoid them with more ease if they're in Toronto—they have a rather grand house in an area called Rosedale—and as you know, I still would rather avoid Otterburn.

I cannot believe Thomas is fifteen now, Timothy thirteen, and dear Tarquin eleven (and with a full set of teeth! I still remember him losing those front teeth!). At least my middle godson is no longer bound and determined to be an aviator—sailing, you say? Well, it's lucky his pal Geoffrey comes from a family with a boat, otherwise you would be on your way to the coast every Friday evening.

My father and Brenda are well. They moved from the Groom's Cottage to the village two months ago and now live in a new bungalow they've purchased on the Tonbridge side of Chelstone. Brenda loves what she calls the "mod cons" that the cottage didn't have, but they come back to the Dower House twice a week to make sure all is well, though I have tenants moving in on a year's lease at the end of the month. Dad is establishing a rose garden at the new house, though he checks the gardens at the Dower House, which are looked after by Mr. Avery.

Finally, to answer your question—please continue to keep our news under your hat. The doctor advised me to take care, so I don't want to tempt fate.

With love to you all,
Maisie

The *Times,* London, September 1935

James Compton, son of Lord Julian and Lady Rowan Compton, was killed in a flying accident in northern Ontario, Canada, on Sunday. Details of the tragedy have not been revealed, but according to early reports the Viscount Compton, chairman of the Compton Corporation, was a keen aviator and enjoyed the hobby whilst working for his company in Toronto. Viscount Compton's wife, the former Miss Margaret Dobbs, has been admitted to hospital in Toronto, though she was not involved in the immediate accident. It is understood that Viscount Compton's parents have sailed for Canada, along with his wife's father and stepmother. Viscount Compton was with the Royal Flying Corps during the war and received commendations for gallantry following an attack during which he sustained wounds. Details of a memorial service in London will be released by the family in due course.

Toronto, November 1935

Dear Priscilla,

This will be a short letter. Everyone has gone home now. I did not want to return to England, but I do not want to remain here. There are too many memories for me to encounter every single day, not least James' study—which looks as if he might be home at any moment—and a beautiful nursery that haunts me each time I pass the door. I had never expected marriage to James to make me so content, but it did.

I will be in touch again, in good time. You know and understand me, Pris—I have to be alone, and I need to go away, perhaps even back to India. I think traveling might be the best idea. If I am on the move and not in one place, then I can perhaps outrun myself. If I linger, then like dark flies on a dead deer, the memories and thoughts land and terror seems to fester and pull me in. I cannot bear to be at Chelstone or even in London, where too many people will be watching me, waiting for something to happen, waiting for me to sink or swim, when all I want to do is float, as I did in hospital when the present was held at bay by ether and morphia and whatever else they put into me. The thought of return bears down upon me and renders even my home unsafe.

Please keep in touch with my father and Brenda. I know they will

*worry—it was all I could do to get my father to leave, but Brenda
understood. She once lost a baby too.*

Love, as always,
Maisie

January 1936
Lady Rowan Compton to Priscilla Partridge

My dear Priscilla,

*I find it so strange, yet heartwarming, that I have come to know
you since my beloved son died, and our Maisie has been all but lost
to us. Though I feared for them when a romance seemed to be in the
offing, it seemed that they had so much going for them as a couple,
and had settled into a very happy marriage—I think it surprised them
as much as it did me! But now I grieve, for I have lost them both. You
may not know that James' older sister died in an accident when she was
a child, and though the years softened the hard edges of my anger—for I
was angry at my loss, there is no other way to describe the utter pain—
Maisie became like a daughter to me. There was talk about her station,
yes, but to be honest, when you have grieved as a mother, such things
matter not. Once you've decided not to sink into the dark caverns of
your aching heart and die yourself, only life matters—and as I am sure
you know, you feel more able to tell the world what to do with itself if it
doesn't "approve" of you or your family. And Maisie was such a light.
Of course, she had her days of sad reflection—the war did that to so
many of our young, as you know yourself—but she was always so spir-
ited. Stubborn at times, yes, but she gave her all to her work. And once
she was married, she gave her all to James. That's the sort of person she
is. And now we don't know where to find her.*

James' father still has contacts where contacts count. I never ask him about it, because to be frank, I don't want to know. When she had her business, Maisie would telephone him on occasion, you know, to squirrel some information from on high when she was working on a case. I think he rather liked it, being of service to someone in that line of work. In any case, he has not been himself since James' death—none of us have—but I think it's time for him to call upon his old chums in Whitehall. They always seem to be able to find someone who appears to have vanished into thin air. I'll tell him the last letter you received came from Boston, though she did not mention where she was staying, or give a return address. I vaguely remember that Simon Lynch had a wartime doctor friend there who Maisie kept in touch with—she might have gone to him and his wife to seek solace. Or she might be alone, which always worries me, and I know it does you, too. I don't like the idea of her without company, not after all she's lost. And I am sure her health is not what it should be, especially after everything she's gone through.

I will be in touch as soon as I hear something.

With affection,

Rowan

Boston, February 1936

Dr. Charles Hayden to Priscilla Partridge

Dear Mrs. Partridge,

We met briefly when I was over in London a few years ago, and then again at the wedding. If you remember, I knew Simon Lynch during the war, and he introduced me to Maisie. When I first met you, you'd assisted her with some information on a case concerning the son of family friends, the Cliftons. She helped them discover a few things about their son, who was killed in 1916. Considering the horrors that happened during their stay in London, it is a miracle that Mr. and Mrs. Clifton are still alive and enjoy fair health. However, this letter is not about them. I wanted to let you know that Maisie has been staying with my wife and me at our home here in Boston. I believe she has not let anyone in England know her whereabouts—not an unusual response from someone who has experienced such a tragedy. I am a neurosurgeon by profession, and though I have an understanding of psychological trauma, my field is brain disease and injury—but I know deep shock when I see it, and I believe Maisie is in a very vulnerable position.

The purpose of this letter is to inform you that Maisie has now left us. Pauline begged her to stay on, to no avail. My wife is very good with people, and she managed to bring Maisie out of herself, but in the end Maisie said she felt she had to go back to India, that she had found peace there, and she believed it was the best place for her to stay for a while. She said she had to "unpick the knitting" and start all over again. I guess you might know what that means—and I suppose in my heart of hearts, I do too. She needs to go back in order to go forward in life. God knows, she's done it before, and if anyone can do it again and rise from the flames like a phoenix, then it's the Maisie we both know and love.

I hope this letter finds you and your family very well. Your boys were an impressive trio, I must say. I have a daughter about the same age as your eldest—if Patty ever comes over there, I'll have to warn her about those darn good-looking Partridges!

We will let you know if Maisie gives us a forwarding address.

With best regards,

Sincerely,

Charles D. Hayden, MD

October 1936
Mrs. Brenda Dobbs to Maisie Dobbs

Dear Maisie,

First of all, per your instructions, we have not told anyone that you're in India, even though Lady Rowan sends a message to the house at least once a week. I think she's even been to see your tenants to find out if they know where you are, but of course Mr. Klein deals with them directly, and I know he would not tell a soul of your whereabouts—he's your solicitor, after all.

Maisie, I'm not one for writing long letters, but there are things that need to be said, and if you know this already, then consider it a reminder. Your father and I both understand what you've gone through—your dad watched your mother die of that terrible disease, and I lost my first husband and child. Between us women, we all know that the death of a child, even one not born, is a terrible thing to bear—and you were so late on, really. Then on top of seeing your dear James lose his life, well, that's just beyond my imagination. My heart aches for you, Maisie, really it does. But that doesn't stop me saying what needs to be said now. Your father wouldn't want me to write this letter, so this is between you and me. Frankie isn't getting any younger. He'll be eighty years old next year, and though his only complaint is that limp from the accident a few years ago, time is written across his face, and he misses you. We all miss you.

It's time to come home, Maisie. I know you must be scared, imagining how difficult it will be seeing the places where you and James courted, and having to face the grief all over again. Not that I think grief is something you put behind you in the snap of a finger. But come home, Maisie. If for nothing else, come for your dad. You'll

be safe at home, dear love—we're family. We'll look after each other.
I promise you that.

Yours most truly,
Brenda

Bombay, January 1937
Maisie Dobbs to Mr. and Mrs. Francis Dobbs

COMING HOME STOP LEAVING END OF WEEK STOP DO NOT TELL ANYONE
STOP PLEASE STOP

On board the SS Isabella, *off Gibraltar, March 1937*

"But, Lady Compton, I—"

"Miss Dobbs, if you don't mind, Captain Johnstone. I've had to correct you once already. If you would just let me go about my business without argument, I would be most grateful. I have decided to disembark and remain in Gibraltar. I can join another ship bound for Southampton at any point."

"My good woman, you are clearly unable to grasp the situation. I doubt you will find adequate accommodation, and even if you do, this is not a safe place. People are swarming across the border from Spain—all sorts of people, and not all savory. Any location in close proximity to war presents an element of risk, especially for a woman."

"Yes, I am most abundantly aware of that particular fact, Captain—I was a nurse in the war, and closer to battle than you might imagine. Now, if you will just follow my instructions—the leather case, the carpetbag and my satchel will disembark with me, and I would be obliged if you would be so kind as to have the remainder of my luggage delivered to this address once the ship has arrived in Southampton." Maisie handed him a page of ship's stationery. "The details are on that slip of paper. Send care of Mr. Francis Dobbs. And it must go to exactly that address in Chelstone, and no other."

The captain sighed. "Very well." He pulled a folded piece of paper from his pocket. "I have a note for you, too. I suspected you would not relent, so here's a list of hotels and the like where I believe you might secure accommodation. I would suggest the Ridge Hotel for someone of your station—I have already made inquiries, and they have informed me that a room is available. It will be held until further notice."

Maisie reached out her hand and grasped the small sheet of paper. "Thank you, Captain Johnstone. I am most grateful."

The ship's captain raised an eyebrow. "Please take care, Miss Dobbs. I wish I could urge you to remain with the ship—I repeat, this is not a safe place for a woman on her own."

"It's safe enough for me."

Maisie held out her hand to Johnstone, who took it in his own.

"I will ensure a taxi is waiting to take you to the hotel," said the captain, who held on to her hand a second longer than necessary, as if he might be able to keep her aboard ship after all. "And please, be very careful. There is a war not very far away, and battle can wound people. Not all injuries are visible to the naked eye, and they can render the most human of beings volatile. That is what you are facing here; an element of instability."

"I understand very well, Captain Johnstone. And I know very well that not all wars are between countries—are they?"

She turned and left the cabin.

After Maisie had disembarked, Captain Richard Johnstone made his way to the ship's telegraph room—he had not asked a cabin boy to run this errand—and ordered a message sent to a man named Brian Huntley. He did not know exactly what office Huntley might hold in Whitehall, but he knew the man worked in a department cloaked in some secrecy. The message was that Margaret, Lady Compton, widow of the late Viscount James Compton, was disembarking the ship and would soon be en route to the Ridge Hotel. There was something Johnstone did not add, though: his doubt that the woman would remain even one night in the hotel. If she did, he suspected, she would be gone by the following morning. He had no solid evidence for such a supposition, but as his crew knew only too well, he was a man who trusted his gut. He'd been known to temper the rate of his vessel on no more evidence than the swell of the waves, or a certain texture to the air. In any case, the fate of this particular passenger was out of his hands now. Whatever these people wanted with the woman who preferred not to use her title by marriage—and in his experience, most women would love a title other than Miss or Mrs.—well, they would have to find her themselves.

For her part, though she had sent word that she was returning to England, with every mile closer to her destination, and at every port along the route, Maisie's sense of dread had grown. It was akin to sickness, a fear that she could not bear to step onto home soil. When only two ports remained on the journey—Gibraltar and Cherbourg—the urge not to return to the ship but instead seek refuge where she knew no one, where she might be invisible, unknown, had strengthened like a fast-approaching storm. Cherbourg was too close to England. When she imagined leaving that port of call with only Southampton awaiting her, she knew she would have little choice. No, she would remain ashore in Gibraltar. She was not ready to face a familiar world in which something so precious was missing. The very thought of returning to Chelstone without James made her feel as if she were looking over the edge of a precipice into the void.

CHAPTER TWO

April 1937

Maisie Dobbs sat inside the small café on Main Street, having taken a seat on a banquette underneath an embossed mural of Gibraltar in earlier days, when there was no such thing as an airfield, little in the way of a port, and when almost all inhabitants were army, navy, or marines. Sailing ships floated offshore, sails furled, and one could almost distinguish small figures clambering up the mast of the vessel closest to shore. She knew that in choosing this particular seat she might not be quite so visible to anyone walking by; the busyness of the painting at her back was a distraction to the eye. There was one pair of eyes she was determined to deceive if she was to have anything resembling quietude for a few hours.

She had discovered already that his name was Arturo Kenyon, and that he lived in the upper rooms of a whitewashed house in one of the oldest streets flanking the Rock of Gibraltar. He was known in the town as a jobbing carpenter; apparently he'd been mustered out of the Royal Navy due to a shoulder injury, and had taken up a trade on home turf. She was willing to bet he was working on behalf of her father-in-law, no doubt through someone else, but she could not be sure. In all likelihood he would not know who, along the chain of communicants, had assigned his remit.

There were those, she knew, who would not understand or sympathize with her decision to adopt her maiden name once again. But there was comfort in hearing herself say "Maisie Dobbs." Her surname carried a sense of belonging, now that James was gone. It had her father's down-to-earth roots in its very sound, reminding her of the way even his footfall seemed grounded with meaning. It was as if the name were stamped on her very being, like a brand. Her father was the most stalwart person she had ever known, perhaps even more so than her late mentor, the famed forensic scientist and psychologist Dr. Maurice Blanche. And as much as she knew her deceased husband's parents loved her, she did not feel as if she were a Compton. Her eyes filled with tears as she tried again to banish the images from her mind, images that came to her often and unbidden, with no warning of their imminent arrival. There it was again, the aircraft gaining speed, swooping low across the escarpment. Once more the memory was so strong that she might have been swept back in time, to the day John Otterburn's cadre of engineers, designers, and a selected aviator were due to test a new weapon on board the aircraft. James was not meant to be flying. He was to be making notes, having discussions on the ground, and peering into the sky through his binoculars. She was sitting on a rocking chair on the wraparound porch of the old farmhouse used as headquarters for the engineers and aviators, where lunch had been laid out. One hand rested on her rounded belly, while the other shielded her eyes from the sun. John Otterburn had come back to the house twice to see if his indulged daughter—indulged, as far as Maisie was concerned—had arrived for the flight. Elaine Otterburn had claimed the piloting of this particular test for herself, arguing that a woman with her expertise could handle the craft just as well as a man. Otterburn had cursed when Maisie informed him that Elaine had yet to appear, then left to walk back to the other men, clustered alongside the landing strip. Maisie stood up as she watched James meet Otterburn, still shielding her eyes with one hand. The two small figures in the distance appeared to be in some discussion. She left the farmhouse and began to walk across the field toward her husband and the man he had agreed to help in his quest to provide a new fighter aircraft to support Britain's air defense, should war come once more. They had waited and waited at the airfield—a most secret airfield on Otterburn land—and still there was no sign of Elaine. Then, as Maisie reached the men, a messenger came along on a motorcycle. He brought a note from Otterburn's wife, informing her husband that Elaine had been to a party the night before, and could not even construct a sentence that morning, let alone fly. She was spending the day in her bed, sleeping off too many champagne cocktails. Maisie remembered thinking that only this spoiled young woman could have found a party in such a rural area.

Then James offered to fly the test. Just one flight, just one test. A takeoff and landing, and in between a burst of gunfire to make sure everything worked, after which he would report on the aircraft's stability, the effect the gun had on trim when firing, and how changes in weapon emplacement affected handling. Once again James was stepping forward in the service of his country. The thought crossed Maisie's mind, though, as she watched her husband don the padded overalls and his sheepskin aviator's jacket, then pull a leather balaclava over his head, that if push came to shove, his country would know nothing of his work. On behalf of his friends in high places, Otterburn would deny that James Compton had been anything more than an enthusiastic aviation hobbyist. She regretted ever having had that thought, but James had gone back on his word that morning. He'd promised her he would not fly, not now, with a child on the way. He'd given her his promise that from now on he would only ever be an observer, working in an advisory capacity; his feet would not leave the ground. With the baby coming, he had too much to look forward to, and too much to lose. After all, the doctor had instructed them that, given problems she'd already experienced, Maisie should do everything in her power to have a calm final month before the child was born.

Arturo Kenyon walked past the café and finger-combed his hair in the window's reflection. Maisie could see him trying to peer into the café. Why didn't he just come in, sit right next to her? She put her head down so her hat shielded her face, and waited. Glancing up at last toward the window, she saw Kenyon walk to the other side of the road, and look both ways.

She called the proprietor over to her table. "Mr. Salazar, would you mind if I left by the back door? There's a man lingering outside who's been bothering me, making a nuisance of himself, and I want to avoid him."

The proprietor looked around. "You tell me who he is, señora, and I'll give him something to look at. You're a good lady, a good customer—there's too many bad men on the streets now, so I have to watch out for my lady customers. Here, come with me."

Maisie left by the rear entrance, following Salazar along an alley that snaked around to Main Street. There she thanked her guide and slipped out onto the hot stone thoroughfare behind Arturo Kenyon. As she watched, he approached another man waiting in the afternoon shadows, just as Kenyon had waited for her. Looking into a shop window, she could see reflected in the glass a piece of paper changing hands—it might have been money, it might not. Kenyon nodded at something the other man said.

She recognized the man Kenyon was meeting, though he'd pulled his hat down at the front, perhaps to avoid identification. His name was Michael Marsh, and he was an inspector with the Gibraltar Police. Inspector Marsh had taken her statement after she found Babayoff's body. She had thought then that he was a good man, though he'd been annoyed by her insistence that perhaps it was not a simple case of robbery, not when the man's Zeiss camera was still on a strap around his neck. It was Marsh's conviction that the case was cut-and-dried—one had to remember the sheer numbers of broken ne'er-do-wells entering Gibraltar, he'd said—that had inspired Maisie to do something later, something that she knew was a crime in itself. It was as if she could not help herself, as if she were at the mercy of her own reflexes.

Maisie had revisited the scene in daylight, after the pathologist had left, after the police had allowed the path to be used again. It seemed that someone had poured bleach on the gravel in an attempt to clean it, should guests wish to meander. She stood for a while, inspecting the ground, retracing her steps from the hotel, looking at first for something the police might have missed and then simply admiring the blooming shrubs, which seemed so uplifting on such a day. It was as she moved that something glinted, catching her eye. Setting one foot on the low wall, she leaned forward, moving a branch to one side. A Leica camera lay on the ground underneath, obscured by foliage. It did not seem to be a professional camera, though she knew it was expensive. It was the sort of camera used for speed, for catching a scene before it changes, not, perhaps, for a more formal portrait. She reached for the camera and put it in her satchel.

There was no reason now to follow Kenyon. He would look for her, and then send a report to whoever was instructing him—yes, it must be Lord Julian, perhaps through Huntley. She sighed. That was all she needed—Brian Huntley of the Secret Service keeping tabs on her. She just wanted to be alone, with more time to steel herself for her return. She needed more time to be strong, more time to prepare herself to settle once again in England, and to face Chelstone. She had not been back since she'd departed for her honeymoon, a precious time when she believed all that awaited her was a contentment she'd never before imagined. Now it would never be again. It was as if she could feel her blood running colder, hardening her heart.

Maisie watched as Kenyon and Marsh parted, and the agent—she had no doubt he was someone's agent—went on his way, walking along Main Street toward Grand Casemates Square as if he had not a care in the world. But Maisie had a care—though she knew it might be a means of deflecting her thoughts away from her father and Brenda, from the expectation of others—and the care at that moment was Miriam Babayoff, the dead man's sister. Miriam, too, was being watched. The poor woman was scared, and she had every right to be: she knew something that others wanted kept silent. The trouble was, as far as Maisie understood it, Miriam Babayoff had no idea what that something might be. And Maisie could not protect the woman unless she, too, had such knowledge at her fingertips.

She continued on her way toward a cluster of houses where Gibraltar's Sephardim lived. Maisie reached into her satchel for a packet of cigarettes, lit one, and drew upon it as if she had been smoking her entire life. Now she knew why Priscilla smoked. It calmed her. Holding a cigarette was something to do with her hands when she began shaking. It sharpened her mind while dulling her emotions. And at least it wasn't morphia.

As she walked back along Main Street away from Grand Casemates Square, with its Moorish buildings and their ornate arches built by Moroccan invaders centuries past, Maisie considered, again, the evening she'd discovered the body of Sebastian Babayoff. She'd been staying at the Ridge Hotel at the time, where she'd remained longer than anticipated, given the difficulty in finding simpler accommodation. Earlier in the day she'd noticed Babayoff in the hotel, taking photographs of the interior and then moving out into the gardens. Was he recording a wedding party? She hadn't really paid much attention, though by instinct she avoided anyone with a camera. Later—after what might have been suppertime had she felt like eating—she'd wanted to walk, to be outdoors in the dark. There was something comforting to her about darkness, about being shrouded only by that which she could smell, touch, and hear. Without light her eyes became accustomed to shapes, sounds became more acute, and as she ambled along some distance from the hotel, she became aware of an unfamiliar noise.Was it a curious, treat-seeking monkey? She'd been told about the Barbary macaques that infested Gibraltar, making a nuisance of themselves. Or perhaps a stray dog, or a cat? Then another noise, and footsteps receding along a narrow alley—human footsteps in heavy boots, running away. After a moment she continued, but took only a few steps before she tripped over something. Her heart leaped, for even before she knelt down to touch the thing in her path, she knew it was flesh and bone.

In the dark, by feel, Maisie distinguished an arm, and then the wrist, searching for a pulse. She reached toward the man's chest—by the size of the wrist, it must be a man—and then his neck. She fingered his skin for the carotid pulse, but there was none.

Miriam Babayoff lived along a narrow cobbled street that resembled so many other streets in Gibraltar. The terrace houses on either side were like ill-kempt teeth, their roofs uneven, their foundations having shifted with the years. The whitewash was dingy, though window boxes planted with summer blooms demonstrated evidence of care by a few of the residents. Maisie Dobbs came alongside the house—it was not numbered—that she knew to be the home of Miriam Babayoff, her sister and, until recent weeks, her now deceased brother. Maisie had met Miriam once before, at a time when the woman was still so shocked she could barely speak. It was a meeting during which she sat on the very edge of a chair at the kitchen table—the front door opened into the small square kitchen, the only room downstairs—her eyes darting to the bolt drawn across to lock the door, as if it might fly back at any moment and the house be invaded. Maisie had offered her condolences, a basket of fruit, and some flowers. She had remained with the dead man's sister for some ten minutes—long enough to sense the woman's unease, to observe her movements, and to know by the cast of her eyes that there was cellarage below the house, and that something of importance was held there.

Now Maisie was visiting again, by invitation, having sent a note to request a little of the woman's time. She would not push too hard for information; in fact, she wasn't sure why she was doing this. Perhaps she should leave well enough alone, especially when she felt so very fragile herself, as if she were made of the finest glass and could shatter at any moment. But she wanted to find out more about the photographer, and why he was killed. It was as if the act of searching, of fingering the facts and mulling over suppositions, would help her excavate something inside herself.

She knocked at the door.

Miriam Babayoff was not a tall woman, probably just over five feet tall. Maisie found it difficult to guess her age, as her sallow skin and the way her lustrous dark hair was pulled back in a tight bun might have made her seem older than she was. Sebastian Babayoff, she knew, had been thirty years of age at the time of his death. There was also another older sister, confined to a wheelchair, or more likely to her bed, now. Maisie suspected Sebastian had been the one who'd helped her out of her room and pushed her up and down the street in her wheelchair. Maisie could not imagine Miriam having the strength to carry her sister down the narrow stairs she suspected lay beyond the curtain-draped door across the kitchen. Miriam must have been the youngest of three, around twenty-five. She had probably not married because she was needed at home.

"Hello, Miss Babayoff." Maisie spoke slowly. Miriam Babayoff could speak English, but with hesitation; she sometimes squeezed her eyes shut as she struggled to remember a word, though her vocabulary was quite good. "Thank you so much for letting me come to see you again."

"Come, señora." Miriam extended her hand in welcome, but closed the door again as soon as Maisie had crossed the threshold, pulling across two bolts and a chain for good measure. The second bolt was new, as was the chain. Miriam must have been waiting for her, peeping through lace curtains so she wouldn't need to open the door on the chain.

"Please sit down, Miss Dobbs." Miriam pulled back a chair for Maisie. "Would you like tea?"

"That would be lovely."

Maisie's attention was drawn to a wooden box at the side of the table, with a spool of silks poking from under the lid. "Oh, Miss Babayoff, I didn't know you were an embroiderer." She picked up the bright embroidered cushion on the chair Miriam had pulled out. "Is this yours? It is exquisite. Do you sell your work?"

Miriam blushed as she poured scalding water onto tea she'd had measured into a china teapot. The face of Queen Victoria stared with imperious displeasure from the side of the pot.

"Yes. It is an important income for my family." She put the kettle down and rubbed a hand across her forehead. A tear trickled down her face.

Maisie put the cushion back down and came to Miriam's side, putting her arms around her. "I know, dear child. I know—"

And as if she understood that knowing, Miriam Babayoff leaned into Maisie's embrace and wept. Maisie bit her lip, remembering that Maurice had always cautioned against reaching out to assuage grief, arguing that such sadness needed room to emerge and be rendered powerless by the elements of light and understanding. He would have suggested that in the rush to embrace, the tide of emotion is stemmed just when it requires expression. But in that moment, she pushed aside her training and held Miriam until her tears subsided, until any reticence on the part of the dead man's sister was washed away and she was ready to talk.

Maisie pulled out a chair for Miriam before seating herself. The two women sat at the table, each with a cup of tea and a slice of sweet bread. The tea was served in tall glasses, with sugar cubes set on the saucer. There was no milk on the table, nor did Maisie look for any.

"Tell me, Miss Babayoff, will your embroidery suffice to keep you and your sister?"

Miriam wiped her eyes and nose with a handkerchief pulled from her apron pocket. She shrugged. "At the moment, I am not under water." Her eyes filled again. "My sister paints. She is in bed now, but she has her watercolors, and we sell her work, though there aren't so many tourists. And she embroiders too."

Maisie nodded. "Did your brother have savings? Was he owed money by anyone who could be approached for payment?"

"He had some savings, Miss Dobbs. And we are owed for some photographs—there is a shop at the end of the street where he had set up a small area for portrait work. The owner of the shop is Mr. Solomon—he sells our needlework and other, um . . ." Miriam closed her eyes, searching for a word. She opened them again. "Other haberdashery goods." She nodded, then paused to sip her tea, though Maisie suspected she needed to rest—speaking in English was tiring for her.

Miriam began again. "And the hotel sent an envelope with money—some from recent work Sebastian did for them, and a little extra to help us. It was very kind. And our people here, we are—how do you say? Close-knit? Like a cardigan? They have helped." She nodded toward the door. "The new bolt and the chain."

Maisie said nothing, staring into her tea for a moment. *I could help her. I could give her money.* She shook her head, remembering the trouble such largesse had caused in the past. She had learned that to give money did not always serve the recipient. But she knew she had to help the Babayoff sisters.

"Miriam, may I ask some questions about Sebastian?"

The woman swallowed, as if bile had come up in her throat, but she nodded.

"Your brother's death was as a result of a dreadful attack in the dark. The police believe the culprit to have been one of the many newcomers to Gibraltar—a refugee, or a black marketeer. I have to tell you that I have my doubts, and—"

Miriam looked up, her brow knitted. "But how would you know? Who are you, Miss Dobbs, that this suspicion would enter your head?"

Maisie sighed. "I'm sorry—I should have explained. Until about three years ago, I was a private investigator in London. My training is in medicine and psychology, and I had the honor to work for many years with one of the world's foremost forensic scientists. I took on his practice when he died, and though I am not a forensic scientist, he taught me that the dead have stories to tell—that even following the most dreadful passing, there is evidence to suggest what had happened to that person. More than anything, he taught me about duty, about doing all in our power to bring a sense of . . . a sense of rest and calm to those left behind. I was—I am, I suppose—an advocate for the dead." She paused and fingered the cuff of her blouse. "You and your sister are bereaved following the brutal death of your brother. I found his body. It is ingrained within me to follow my instinct, and my mentor's training—and, if I can, to bring about something resembling acceptance of what has come to pass, for the sake of you and your sister. That is who I am."

Miriam Babayoff regarded Maisie and nodded. Then she looked away. "There is no peace to be had in this household, Miss Dobbs. There is only fear. There is only sadness and worry. It would have been better if they'd killed us in our beds."

Maisie waited, this time allowing the woman her moment. Then she asked a question.

"Who are 'they,' Miriam?"

Miriam Babayoff shivered, clutched her arms as if to protect herself, and looked down at the untouched sweet bread. Maisie leaned forward and picked up the teapot, refilling the thick glasses.

"It's stronger now—it'll do you good. Now, eat something," she said.

Miriam sipped the tea, then cut the slice of bread into four smaller squares. She ate one square, coughing as she swallowed, sipped her tea again, and set the glass on the table.

"Who do you think wants to kill you, Miriam?" asked Maisie.

"Miss Dobbs—"

"Maisie. Please call me Maisie."

Miriam nodded, and then looked up into Maisie's eyes, her own dark eyes like coals against the pallor of her skin. "I don't know. I just know that over the past two months, Sebastian had become very . . . very . . . oh, how would you say? Very . . . not scared, not as if he could not sleep—well, not at first, though that came. But he was, um, *wary.* Yes, wary. He started being wary. Then it increased, as if it were a heavy stone right here." She placed her hand on her chest. "Yes, and he worried me. You see—" She leaned closer, as if the trickle of words were about to become a flood. "Before this time he would try to come home in the afternoon, and he would lift my sister and bring her down and we would take chairs outside here to the front of the house—there is nothing at the back, just a gully. It was good for her to get a little sun. And if people walked by, she would talk to them and show her work—and if it was a visitor, maybe sell something. But then—then he stopped doing that. He said that with the war across the border, it was not safe. I argued with him—we are all Sephardim along this street, and we've lived here all our lives. We will die here." She nodded. "Yes, we will die here."

Maisie sipped her tea and set down the glass. "You say his behavior changed about a couple of months ago."

"I cannot be exact, but yes, about that."

"Can you remember anything that happened around that time? I would imagine as a photographer, every day might be different. But if you consider the change in his demeanor—his way of doing things— can you remember anything else?"

"Well, it was probably around the same time as Carlos died," said Miriam.

Maisie looked up. "Who was Carlos?"

"Carlos was a friend of our father's, though a little younger. My father died ten years ago, and my mother soon after—they were joined, you see." She crossed the forefinger and middle finger of her left hand. "One could not live without the other."

"I'm very sorry, Miriam. I know what it is to lose a parent at an early age." Maisie paused. "But tell me about Carlos, how he died."

"Carlos was a fisherman, about seventy years old. He was not one of our people, but my father and he had become friends and liked to go out in the boat together, early in the morning, as the sun rises. They would talk enough to change the world, I think. And Carlos was very good to us—he made sure we never went without. He was alone, you see. His sons had left Gibraltar, and his wife had died anyway, so he visited once a week and would bring fish and always leave a few coins to help us. We knew his health was not the best—he said his sons had broken his heart long ago—but it was very sad when he died. A navy patrol vessel discovered his fishing boat, drifting. Carlos was dead— there was no wound, nothing visible. At first it was thought the boom might have swung around and caught him off guard, but in the end they said it was his heart. He left only enough money for his burial. Then his sons came and took any possessions he might have had, and they sold his boat, which had been his home."

Maisie chewed the inside of her lip. "So, when Carlos died, it was as if Sebastian—as if you all—had lost your father all over again, in a way."

Miriam nodded.

"And you think that was when Sebastian became more fearful?" asked Maisie.

"I think so, perhaps." Miriam sighed and looked toward the window, though the lace obscured her view. "He last saw Carlos a couple of weeks before he died. They went out on the boat together, very early in the morning. Sebastian liked to go every now and again, if he could. He would take his cameras—he liked the light. He said it skimmed off the water and made it look like jewels. And I think it brought back my father to him—he and Carlos would talk about him, out there in the morning." She shrugged. "They came in early that day, I remember. I remarked on it—I said, 'So soon you're back?' He never said anything, just went to his dark room." There was a pause. "I've wondered, you know, whether he didn't get a . . . a . . . what do you call it? When you see something that has not happened?"

"A premonition?"

Miriam Babayoff nodded. "Yes, a premonition. Of Carlos dying on the boat. He was a bit quiet, you see, for a few days. Then when Carlos died, he became different."

Maisie was about to ask another question when a hammering sound came from the floor above.

Miriam pushed back her chair. "Oh, look at the time. I must go to her, Miss Dobbs—Maisie. I must look after my sister, make sure of her. She may need to . . . you know . . . personal things."

"Would you like some help?" asked Maisie.

The woman shook her head, then looked up at the ceiling as the *thump-thump-thump* continued, and several flakes of plaster fell on the table.

"I'll leave you to get on then, Miriam." Maisie picked up her satchel and turned toward the door. Miriam drew back the bolts and the chain, opening the door just enough to allow Maisie to slip out onto the street.

"May I come again, Miriam?"

Miriam nodded. "Perhaps tomorrow."

Maisie lifted her hand to wave, but already the door was closed. She could hear the bolts being shot home, the chain drawn across, and the key turned in the lock.

And as she walked back toward Main Street, Maisie thought about dear Carlos, an elderly fisherman who had lost his wife, who had not seen his sons for years, and who—she had no doubt—had come to consider his old friend's son as his own. She had a strong feeling that Carlos might not have been felled by a bad heart, and that Sebastian Babayoff knew the why of it, even if he did not know exactly how the old man might have lost his life.

CHAPTER THREE

Shadows were beginning to lengthen across the rooftops as Maisie returned to the guesthouse, and the late sunlight shimmered rose-pink on the water. Fishing boats had returned to their moorings, and those seeking refuge who had not already found rest looked for shelter. She was weary, now—fatigue seemed to come more readily than it had before, and there was a dull ache across her abdomen. She'd been told that the scar would heal, that the place where her lifeless child had been taken from her body would cease to give her pain, yet some discomfort remained. She was reminded of her tenure as a nurse during the war, working close to the front, a terrible time when soldiers screamed with the pain of limbs no longer there. A man would clutch the stump of amputation as if to soothe the violence to his flesh and bone, and she wondered if that same ghost of what was and could never be again had been haunting her. It was as if every day her child cried to be held, and she thought she would die, wishing she could reach out and envelop the small body with her love.

She sat in the armchair next to the open window, looking out toward a sliver of sea. If she were an artist, she might try to paint that fragment; the color and subject seemed so intense. In the frame a fishing boat crossed before her, and a naval vessel lay at anchor, as if watching. Of course there were people watching and waiting on that ship, guarding the sovereignty of Gibraltar's waters.

Maisie reached for a packet of cigarettes, turned it upside down, and shook one free. She looked at the slender roll of tobacco in its thin paper shell. How could she do this? She had always hated smoking. She would take Priscilla to task for the habit: *You smell like a chimney, Pris—I'm sure it's not good for you.* And Priscilla would point out that advertisements extolled the virtue of the cigarette, that it was said to be excellent for the health. Maisie doubted that very much. Yet Maurice had smoked a pipe, and she had loved to walk into his home—now her home, though she was loath to return—and smell the fragrant rich tobacco he favored. Still, she'd never imagined she would take up smoking. Perhaps this cigarette would be her last.

She inhaled and thought about the murder of Sebastian Babayoff. In truth, she felt ill equipped to investigate his death—ill equipped, yet compelled by the very fact that she had discovered his body. Had she bitten off more than she could chew by getting involved? After all, she could have walked away, could have just given a statement to the police. But she hadn't. Her instinct had pressed her to keep the Leica and the film it held. Why had the larger camera been left behind? Unless she had disturbed the killer in the midst of attack—likely enough, after all. Or perhaps Babayoff's murderer had no interest in a camera.

Maisie felt at sea; she realized this sense of inadequacy was due to her lack of knowledge about Gibraltar, about the conflagration across the border, even about the Sephardic community. What did Maurice always say? That the commencement of an investigation was akin to entering a dark room, where there were no shadows, no familiar shapes to guide the person who wanted to cross from one wall to the next, or find the door. She closed her eyes and tried to summon the image of her mentor. He was not a tall man, and not one who carried weight, though there was a strength to him, a substance demonstrated when he walked—even in later years, when he depended upon a cane to provide balance. His suits were tailored to fit shoulders that were broad but not overly muscular, and without exception his trousers had turnups, fashion or no fashion. Always he had seemed old, even when he must have been a younger man. From their very first meeting she'd sensed a deep wisdom within him, as if he held at his fingertips all the knowledge a person might need to navigate the waters of life—yet he too was a student when he visited Khan, his own mentor, who had advised her on many an occasion. Was Khan still alive? At the thought, she felt herself sink farther into the chair.

We must bring light to the darkened room, Maisie. Maurice's voice echoed down the years, and it was as if he were with her. *Knowledge is the light. Information is the light. Come out of the darkness one lamp at a time. Paint your picture of what came to pass question by question— and remember, some are never meant to be answered because the response closes the door to knowledge you most want and need.*

Pressing her hardly smoked cigarette into the ashtray, Maisie clutched the arms of the chair and drew herself to her feet. But as she moved toward a writing table at the corner of the room, the pain crossed her abdomen again, and she doubled over. *It should have gone by now.* She began to weep. She knew she should probably see a doctor, just to be on the safe side. But she was in the dark room in more ways than one. Yet there was a light—only a temporary light, but it gave her a means of escape more potent than the occasional cigarette. Refuge came in the form of a small pill. She had first been given the medicine by her doctor at the hospital in Toronto, then again in Boston. After she was rushed away from the airfield—after she'd run toward the fallen aeroplane, tripped on rough ground, and run again—she was taken to a local doctor before being transferred to the hospital in Toronto. She remembered holding on to her belly after she'd witnessed James' aircraft plummeting to earth, as if to protect her child from the terror. The doctor had given her the drug via a syringe, and then at the hospital, it had been administered through a line into a vein in her arm. She'd tried to stop them, but the ether had done its job, and soon it seemed she was drifting above herself, looking down at the melee in the operating room, at her body and the other small body, and then that tiny perfect being rose up to be cradled in her arms before she heard her name and had to follow the sound, releasing her child—her dear sweet child—to the hereafter.

Morphia. It had often brought terrible images into her mind's eye, but it took away the pain, and she had some in a small bottle, right there in her leather case.

M aisie woke the following morning still dressed, her clothing crumpled as she lay on top of the bedcovers. The curtains were still open from the day before, and already she could hear midmorning sounds on the street. She sat up and rubbed her eyes, then dragged her legs to the side of the bed and pressed her knuckles down on the mattress as she rose to her feet. At first the room seemed to swim before her, so she steadied herself, reaching out to the bedside table. The carafe was still half full of water; she filled a glass and quenched her thirst. The physical pain had gone, for now. She picked up the bottle of pills and walked across the room toward her leather suitcase. She lifted the lid, placed the pills inside a small silk bag containing a few items of jewelry, which she secreted in a pocket inside the case. She closed the lid and secured the lock and then the straps. She was not trying to hide the bottle of morphia. She was making it harder for herself to take the drug at will.

Maisie made her way to the window, her legs finding their strength and balance. Kenyon was across the road. Another person might not have seen him, leaning against a wall just inside a narrow alleyway commanding a good view of the front door of the guest house, but Maisie spotted him at once. She observed his stance. He was leaning, his right leg bent with the sole of his shoe against the wall. He smoked a cigarette and read a newspaper, though his eyes moved from the page to the door, from the page to the door. He was vigilant, of that she had no doubt. But as she watched, Maisie set her upper body in the same position, her shoulders hunched just so, mirroring the man who waited for her in the shadows. Then she knew that Arturo Kenyon held within him a feeling of inadequacy. She was sure this was his emotion, not her own sense of worth seeping into her observation. Maisie was willing to bet that he had no real interest in his remit, that no matter what he'd been told about her, it made him feel less than a man, having been tasked with following what appeared to be a very ordinary, if perhaps meddlesome woman, albeit a woman who was able to lose him with ease. Kenyon must feel he was capable of much more, and wish he were embroiled in an investigation of greater importance. But perhaps he had not been told everything. And perhaps today would be the best day to approach him, to let him know that she had his number. She would have to see.

Maisie rubbed her forehead as the room began to move again. She knew she needed to eat, and it had to be something substantial. The dose of morphia would have left its imprint on her thinking—it had tempered the physical pain, but now she had to get it out of her system—and she could not let it prevent her from achieving something in the hours to come. If she had nothing to show for herself, then she might as well be with her husband and child. Dead.

Having bathed and breakfasted at the guesthouse, Maisie made a mental list of two or three things she wanted to accomplish before her energy was spent. First of all, she would visit Mr. Salazar—he would know where she could buy a large sheet of paper. It was time to begin a case map; she needed to focus her mind on the murder, and she needed to see before her the threads linking everyone she met—if such connections existed. She needed colored pencils to mark her steps on the map, and to see where gaps were revealed in the story. And she wanted to find someone who would tell her more about the territory she'd chosen as a refuge. She added Mr. Solomon to her list, as well as Inspector Marsh. She still had the Leica with a roll of film inside, and had yet to discover what images it might hold. Who could she trust with developing the film? And what could she find out about Carlos, the fisherman? Already she could see that each item amounted to a fair amount of work for one day—she admitted to herself that she would not be moving at her accustomed speed—thus it might not be the best day to approach Kenyon. Perhaps, like certain important questions, he should be left alone for the time being, after all, he might have much to tell her by his very presence.

Arturo Kenyon flicked down the half-smoked cigarette and folded the newspaper into the pocket of his linen jacket. He pushed his frame away from the wall with his foot and emerged from the alley as

Maisie Dobbs left the guesthouse and began walking down the street. Today she was wearing a white blouse with the black skirt and the same black sandals. She'd clipped her hair back with a comb on one side of her head, and though she wore dark glasses, she did not wear a hat. She carried her leather satchel with a long strap over her shoulder. Kenyon sighed. Another day of tedium, following this woman who someone surely must have been been wrong about. Yes, she'd managed to lose him yesterday, but he hadn't been paying as much attention as he should. It was not as if she was doing anything worth remarking upon. He'd returned to the guesthouse, and watched as, at six o'clock in the evening, she entered again. Back in her room, she'd stood by the window, looking out—he imagined she was trying to view the sea through spaces between the buildings. She'd allowed the lace curtains to fall, but as it grew darker, the light inside never came on. Had she just sat in darkness, this Dobbs woman? Had she gone downstairs to her landlady to ask for supper, only returning after night fell, perhaps? And did it really matter what she'd done?

Kenyon maintained a working distance behind the woman as she walked once again toward Salazar's little restaurant. Perhaps he'd have to go in for a word with Salazar, see if there was anything on those old bones ready to be picked off.

Ah, my good lady, Miss Dobbs—very kind of you to come again," said Salazar, wiping his hands on the white apron he wore, day in, day out, though each day the apron was fresh and crisp with starch. "A cup of my best coffee? A little something to set you up for the day, perhaps?"

Maisie smiled. There had been a lull in the stream of customers, and only two others were present, a man and a woman at adjacent tables, their heads bowed over a newspaper and a book, respectively.

"Good . . . day, Mr. Salazar. Of course, I was going to wish you a good morning, but it's getting a bit late for that, isn't it?" Maisie looked up at Salazar. "I think I'll have a cup of milky coffee, if you would be so kind. And a pastry—not too sweet. Could you pick something for me?"

"A plain croissant, perhaps? I know they're French, but our customers like them—though a Frenchman came in and said ours were not light enough."

"I'm sure they will go down well with butter and a little jam or marmalade, if you have some."

"I'll be just a moment."

Salazar left, pushing his way through a door behind the serving bar. The door swung on its hinges a couple of times, and Maisie could hear him shouting to the kitchen staff, which amounted to a member of his family. It was not an aggressive order, but loud all the same, as if he had an army to command. Maisie liked Mr. Salazar; she liked his manner, the way he bustled, and his good heart. Sometimes she thought she could see that good heart beating, and realized that more often now she looked for goodness in a person, sought it out and found it comforting. She had been so practiced in looking for that which brought ill, yet Maurice had taught her to look for the duality in everyone. Her success had depended upon an ability to see the innocent within the guilty, the monster within the angel. More often she looked for the victim within the perpetrator of a crime. Perhaps that's what she had to do with the death of Sebastian Babayoff—look for another victim. But of what? So far Babayoff was the only victim, though Carlos, the fatherly fisherman, might also have met an unnatural fate.

Kenyon waited outside. How does he not know I am aware of him? thought Maisie. The doors swung open again; the voices in the kitchen became loud and then muffled as the doors thumped into each other and closed.

"Lovely, miss, a good coffee and a heavy Gibraltarian French croissant. With English marmalade."

Maisie felt her stomach lurch, but smiled at Salazar. "Won't you join me just for a moment, Mr. Salazar?"

The man looked around, held up one finger, and moved across to the bar, where he poured a cup of coffee, bringing it back to the table. He pulled out a chair and sat down, running his fingers across his almost bald head. "The best invitation I am likely to have all day, Miss Dobbs." He lifted his cup and sipped, setting it down on the tablecloth—he had not brought a saucer. "Now, then. I think you might have something to ask me, no?"

Maisie sipped her coffee, soothing, strong with warm milk. She grasped her cup as she spoke. "I've walked around Gibraltar for several weeks now—I'm just staying a while before I sail back to England, though I am not sure when I will be able to leave. It occurred to me that I know so little about Gibraltar. There are so many people here from across the border—and I am not even sure I understand what has happened there. How did it start? I find it so hard to believe that here we are, safe, to a point, and yet just a few miles away, people are killing each other."

Salazar nodded. "It is a—how would you say? A contradiction, no? That our town here was taken by the British as the spoils of a war centuries past, and yet we have refugees from war here. And not only that—we are many rolled into one, we Gibraltarians." He seemed to sit up, clearly proud of his heritage. "My own people—my ancestors—come from Spain, Malta, the Azores, even Morocco. Yet we all lived here under a British flag. It is as if this rock were a great big pot on the stove, and each one of our ancestors an ingredient mixed in." He paused. "By the way, Miss Dobbs, speaking of mixed ingredients, did you know that Arturo the carpenter has been following you like a puppy?"

Maisie raised an eyebrow. "Arturo the carpenter?"

Salazar pointed to the figure of Arturo Kenyon, reading a newspaper across the street.

"Oh, is that his name, Arturo? I thought he might be someone up to no good."

Salazar shook his head. "No, just a local man with a trade, though I don't know why he is not at his work."

Maisie sipped from her cup and set it down on the saucer, then took up the croissant and began to spread a thin film of marmalade on it as she spoke. "Tell me, Mr. Salazar, about the war in Spain."

Salazar shrugged, opening his palms as the line of his mouth curved down and his chin jutted out. "It is very bad. That brother fights brother, that innocents are killed. There are volunteers coming from your country, from America and across the world—to fight for the, how do you say it? The man in the street? Well, I do not know who he is anymore, just that many want to leave, but are caught in a funnel at the border. Those with relatives here in Gibraltar are trying to stay—and remember, many of our people here have had jobs across the border for years, but now those jobs are lost. We are safe, but so much goes on here." He pointed to his eyes. "I keep my eyes open."

Maisie dipped the croissant into her coffee cup and took a bite. She looked at Salazar again. "And what do you see?"

"I see many new people here, and that is of no surprise. We have always had visitors to Gibraltar. But I also see people who are watching, as Kenyon watches you."

"Did you ever know a fisherman named Carlos?" asked Maisie. "Or a photographer—Sebastian Babayoff?"

"I knew Babayoff. He came in with his camera once, to take a photograph of the inside of my restaurant. Then he wanted to charge me—and I'd never even asked him for a picture." He shrugged. "But I know he was a good fellow, though he tried to fool me. He was like anyone, just trying to get by." He looked at Maisie with bloodshot eyes. "I understand that his life was taken—by a refugee, most likely."

"It would seem so," said Maisie. "At least, that's what I read in the newspaper."

Salazar nodded. "And I knew Carlos to buy fish from—but they keep to themselves, the fishermen. They speak the same language—fish. Are the fish biting? How many did you catch? Not much meat on them, eh? Fish, fish, fish. But I cook good fish here, if you want some."

Maisie raised a hand and shook her head. "Not today, thank you."

A bell chimed above the door. Salazar looked around as it opened and a customer entered. He lifted his cup and drained it. "Funny you should mention Carlos, though. He seemed troubled last time I saw him—only a day before he died. It must have been his heart bothering him even then—he kept rubbing his chest. He was a good friend to the man with the camera, by all accounts. They both liked the early morning—good light, and a good time to catch a fish."

Maisie looked out toward the street, where Kenyon waited.

"Good morning, sir—please, sit wherever you want," said Salazar to the new customer, a short man wearing a linen suit with an open-necked shirt and cravat. The man removed his Panama hat and nodded, moving toward a seat at the bar. "As long as it's not on that good lady's lap!" added Salazar as he turned back to Maisie, nodding toward the window and Kenyon. "You want my back way into the alley, miss?"

"Thank you, Mr. Salazar. I think I'll take you up on that."

M aisie made her way into the shadows to consult her map. She was looking for Catalan Bay, from which most of the fishing boats left Gibraltar each morning. She had stopped to ask a street vendor, a woman who looked down at Maisie's sandals and then back into her eyes before raising her eyebrows and informing Maisie that it was a good two miles to the bay. Maisie thanked the woman and went on her way, having considered her footwear to be adequate for the hike. It would give her time to gather her thoughts, which—she conceded—were still thick, as if cotton wadding had been pressed into her skull.

A good time to catch a fish. She allowed herself to linger on the café owner's comment—not that she imagined Salazar to have knowledge he had failed to impart during their conversation, but people often made observations borne of an intuition they would never lay claim to, and would not even know existed within them. Sebastian Babayoff and Carlos the fisherman—what was his surname? she wondered— had returned early from a dawn sail into the waters around Gibraltar, and since that time both had died. Coincidence? Perhaps. A tragedy? Of course it was, though the older man had seen his three score years and ten. But what if something else had come to pass? An altercation with another fisherman? She knew from a past case that had taken her into the fishing community in Hastings that although the men were in fierce competition, they shared their knowledge and supported each other when help was needed. Though Mr. Solomon had been next on her list, she continued her walk toward the boats. The fishermen would be back now, for the most part, setting out their nets to dry and talking about their morning. She knew they were a closed people, but perhaps there was a shell she could pry open.

She turned around. Arturo Kenyon was nowhere to be seen.

CHAPTER FOUR

U pon first disembarking in Gibraltar, Maisie had struggled to understand the different dialects and cultures that made up the population. She'd asked Mrs. Bishop—who seemed less than British herself, despite her name—and was treated to an account of immigration to the Rock over the centuries. There were Jews from North Africa and Maltese traders. Most of the Spanish had left when the British took control of Gibraltar following the Treaty of Utrecht in 1713, but there were Portuguese as well as fishermen from Genoa among the first settlers, and of course the British, with their own peppered history of immigration. "But we're all Gibraltarians, my darling," said Mrs. Bishop, as if assuming an intimacy. It was later that Maisie heard the word—pronounced "dahlen"—in certain quarters, and realized it was akin to adding "my dear" at the end of a sentence.

Now she walked toward Catalan Bay, home to fisher families of Genoan descent, though the British had mistaken their land of origin for Catalonia—thus the given name of their village home. By the time she reached the fishing boats, her feet were a little swollen, though the walk had been good for her. Perhaps tonight she would sleep without the aid of any draught or pill. She pictured the leather case, locked, with straps drawn across and secured.

She held her hand to her brow and squinted as she watched the men on their boats, some lifting baskets of fish, others pulling nets and laying them out on the sand. A few women in black—the uniform of the fisherman's wife, a mark of anticipated losses at sea, of a collective widowhood—had gathered to one side, busy with long needles and sturdy thread. For a moment Maisie felt as if she could walk among them and be comforted, held by fleshy arms as she sank into soft folds of compassion. She took a handkerchief from her pocket and wiped her eyes, telling herself it was only sunlight and heat. She'd come out without her hat, after all.

Approaching the women, she spoke in English, asking if anyone spoke her language. At first they looked at her and then at one another. She suspected they all understood her very well. A younger woman came to her feet, smiling.

"Can I help you, miss?" she inquired.

Maisie inclined her head. "My name is Maisie—Miss Maisie Dobbs. I wanted to know if anyone could tell me about Carlos. He was one of the fishermen here, and he died a little while ago. About four or five weeks, perhaps."

The younger woman nodded and looked around at the others, who were already talking among themselves. Yes, they know exactly what I've said, thought Maisie. The woman turned back to her.

"I am Rosanna. You are asking for Carlos Grillo. He had a heart attack on his boat."

"Yes, that's right," said Maisie. She waved her hand in front of her face to cool her skin.

Rosanna looked at Maisie, then back at the women, one of whom flapped her hand as if to chivvy them along. Rosanna nodded and invited Maisie to walk with her, away from the women and from the men and their boats.

"Why do you want to know about Mr. Grillo?" asked the younger woman.

"He died shortly before another man—only a couple of weeks separated their deaths. It's that man I'm trying to find out more about, and I know he missed Carlos very much. He had known his—"

"The Jew? Is that the man you speak of? The Jew whose father was a friend to Carlos Grillo?"

Maisie turned to the girl. "Yes—his name was Sebastian Babayoff. You knew him?"

Rosanna nodded, staring out across the water, almost as if she could see the men again. "Mmmm, yes. He came here to go out on the boat with Mr. Grillo. Before his father died, it was the three of them sometimes; then Mr. Grillo would take just the son out."

"Mr. Babayoff helped Carlos Grillo with his catch?"

The girl laughed. "His catch! The Jew had not the arms for pulling in a net, but he brought his camera with him. And I suppose he helped—but that depended upon the haul." She paused, as if unsure whether to say more.

"What do you mean, Rosanna?"

"Nothing." She shook her head and looked at the other women, then back at Maisie. "I must return to my aunts—there is work to do."

Maisie did not move, but she touched the young woman on the arm. "Do you believe Carlos Grillo suffered a heart attack, Rosanna?

You knew him." She pointed to the men on boats, on the beach. "The fishermen here all seem very hearty fellows—strong, though not all are young men."

"Not all men follow their fathers now." She sighed, and shrugged. "His heart had broken when his sons left, so it surprised no one."

Maisie watched the girl as she folded her arms, rubbing her hands against the cloth of her blouse. Now she was protecting herself, putting up a wall against the temptation to say more. It occurred to Maisie that the girl had spoken with little governance over her thoughts, and had been given leave to do so by the women, who in their manner—working in a circle—were a tight group.

"Rosanna, I have one more question for you, if you don't mind." Maisie did not wait for a response. "You have spoken quite freely, considering you do not know who I am and have been offered little explanation as to why I've come here. Perhaps there is something else bothering you, among the answers you've given."

The girl glanced seaward, curls of jet-black hair escaping from the ribbon she had tied at the nape of her neck. "We wish Carlos had not spent so much time with the Jew."

"I've heard he was a nice man, a good man," said Maisie.

"He was a Communist. Carlos was his donkey." She looked back at Maisie. "I have to go now, back to my work."

"But wait," said Maisie. "Tell me, why did you agree to talk to me?"

The girl looked up along the path behind them. "You're from the police, aren't you? We do not refuse the police. And Carlos was my uncle."

Looking where the girl had set her gaze, Maisie caught sight of a man in the distance, watching. She could not be sure, as she narrowed her eyes, better to see against the afternoon light, but she thought it might be Arturo Kenyon. The man turned and walked away.

"I am not with the police, Rosanna. But I had the misfortune to find Sebastian Babayoff's body, and it has disturbed me enough to find out what happened to him."

"Then good luck to you, Miss Dobbs." The girl bore an accusatory look as she nodded towards Maisie's wedding ring, shrugged again, and walked away.

Maisie held her left hand to her chest and massaged the ring—now on a chain around her neck—with the thumb and forefinger of her right hand. The gold did not exhibit the marks of long-worn jewelry, though she had never removed it from her hand when James was alive, not even to wash. She remembered her mother, when she was dying, refusing to let anyone remove her wedding ring from her swollen finger. "A woman should never take off her ring," she said. "It's binding, and it stays on my finger." She was buried with her wedding ring in place, as she had lived.

Maisie made one stop on her way back to her room at Mrs. Bishop's guest house, to purchase a large sheet of paper and some colored pencils. She also bought a book about Gibraltar and a postcard. As she walked along the narrow path to the guest house, she was aware, without looking into doorways or along an alley here and a rough path there, that she was being watched. Was it Kenyon again? Or someone else? No matter. She would know soon enough. In the meantime, she'd learned something else about Babayoff: in one person's estimation, at least, he was a Communist. If that were so, what were his feelings about the conflict across the border, so very close to home? He could hardly ignore it.

She turned the key in the large, rusty lock and stepped into the cobblestone courtyard.

I n her room, Maisie poured herself a glass of water, drank it, and poured another. As she sipped the second glass, she kicked off her sandals and sat on the bed. Looking up at her reflection in the mirror, she could see she had caught the sun—her cheeks and nose were red, and her lips felt dry. She felt tired, but in a good way, the way she'd felt when, as a child, she'd been all the way to Covent Garden and back with her father. She closed her eyes, remembering the darkness as they came finally back to the small house in Lambeth, and how her mother would be in her chair alongside the stove. She would open her arms and Maisie would run to her and bury her head in the blankets. How would it be to feel enveloped by such love, so secure, once again? But had she felt safe, really? She went with her father to market so her mother might rest, so she could settle by the fire or in her bed and perhaps sleep. At once, Maisie realized something that had never occurred to her: that even then her mother must have been taking morphia, otherwise the pain would have been intolerable. Money they could ill afford had gone to doctors and medicines; Frankie had worked so hard to give his beloved wife a serene passing and a decent burial.

Maisie shook her head as if to dislodge the memory, surprised that it had ambushed her now, when her mother's death was so far in the past.

M aisie moved a vase of paper flowers from the table, along with a lace doily which had left a stencil of dust across the wood—the surface had not seen a cloth for some days. She used the towel that hung next to the washbasin in the corner of the room to wipe the table clean. She set down the large sheet of paper, smoothing it with her hand, and drew up a chair. As she looked at the clean white paper before her, she smiled. Yes, this was what she needed. Work. Perhaps that was why she had taken the camera, why she had held on to the discovery of Sebastian Babayoff's body as if it were a lifeline, involving herself in the investigation when most people would have been glad to have the police tell them that there were no more questions, and they were free to leave.

With the red pencil, Maisie wrote "Sebastian Babayoff" at the center of the sheet of paper, then circled it twice. She drew lines from the circle, adding names: Miriam Babayoff, Carlos Grillo, and the other Babayoff sister—what was her name? Yes, Chana. There was the young woman, Rosanna, and of course, farther from the center, Mr. Salazar. Looking up from her work, she walked to one side of the window, where she moved the curtain just enough to see across the road. A small pinprick of light glowed as the man drew upon his cigarette. Would now be a good time? Perhaps. She would wait a little while, see if he was still there when she had finished with her case map.

Again she smiled. *Case map.* She was at work again. There might not be a client, no person coming to her door with a request to find someone, or to investigate a loss dismissed by the police, but her curiosity would serve as her reward. How many cases had she solved that Scotland Yard had labeled open-and-shut? More than she could count on the fingers of both hands. Open-and-shut meant business for her, though this time it was something she was hanging on to. She'd been feeling as if all meaning in her life had perished when she discovered Babayoff's body. Perhaps she would find the person she used to be, before tragedy struck her a second time, cutting deeper into her soul, a still-open wound more livid than anything left by the war. Now she was in business—and that responsibility to another would give her a reason to live.

Maisie worked on her case map for another twenty minutes or so, adding questions to which she wanted answers. What did it mean to be a Communist here in Gibraltar? And to be Jewish *and* a Communist? It seemed people of different faiths and origins lived respectfully together here—but what about politics? And how had the refugees affected life on the Rock? As far as she could see, people were treated well, had been given food and shelter—the winter food kitchens, originally set up for children in the harsh cold months, had been extended to ensure that those crossing the border in search of refuge had a good meal inside them every day. Many had returned to Spain, but a good number remained, or were trying to move on to North Africa, to France, or even Britain. Was there really the kind of trouble that would have led to Babayoff's death at the hands of a penniless robber refugee? She rolled the case map and placed it in the wardrobe. The leather case tempted her. She closed her eyes. No. Not tonight. She felt the familiar ache across her abdomen—perhaps from her long walk today, perhaps from sitting at the table, working—but she could bear it.

Maisie stepped to the window again. The glow of the lighted cigarette was gone, though it did not prove Arturo Kenyon had ended his surveillance. Only that he might not be smoking. But Maisie no longer felt his presence. He had gone, she was sure—perhaps to Mr. Salazar's for a late-evening drink. Perhaps home. She turned away, toward her bed. No matter: he would be back in the morning, of that she was sure.

For the first time in months, Maisie slept well, and though dreams came to her, they were not of blood-soaked terror. Sometimes she was a girl again, in France during the war; in other dreams she was running with a kite on Box Hill with James. Then the kite would spiral and spiral, and she would try so hard to keep it aloft. And then the dream would change again, and she would be with her father, listening to him as he taught her to ride. *Don't worry, my little love, I won't let you fall.*

I won't let you fall. Don't worry, I won't let you fall. . . . Maisie woke to those words, as if her father had laid his hand with a light touch upon her shoulder. A needle of light pierced through the curtains; from the angle, she judged it to be about ten o'clock in the morning. She had slept for almost twelve hours.

She remained in her bed, listening to the sounds of the street—a vegetable vendor calling out along the alley, children skipping along the cobblestones. *Coffee.* At once she craved coffee as Maurice used to make it—real coffee, delivered from an importer's in Tunbridge Wells. She remembered how he would grind the coffee himself, in a small wooden box with a handle on top. It came from Dominica, he said—a place she could not imagine, nor imagine why he would have been there in the first place, but there were many such unanswered questions about Maurice Blanche. When the handle turned easily against the grounds, he would pull out a small drawer in the front of the box and tip the fragrant milled coffee into a pot. He'd lift a kettle just off the boil and pour hot water over the grounds, allowing it to sit for at least five minutes. Then he would fill her cup halfway, topping it off whisked hot milk. "Your café au lait, Maisie. Now we must work— there is no time to be lost."

Swinging her legs off the side of the bed, Maisie grabbed her dress- ing gown, opened the door onto the corridor and, assured that she would not run into any other guests, tiptoed along to the bathroom. She wanted to bathe away the sleep and step out into her day as soon as she could.

Today she wore a white blouse and a pair of wide navy-blue linen trousers. She had blisters where her sandals had rubbed, so she pulled out her case, unstrapped the leathers, and found a pair of espadrilles she had bought at a market during one of the stops on her first voyage to India, and hardly worn since. She grabbed her hat and her satchel, making sure she had a notebook and pencil, and left Mrs. Bishop's guest house, though not before spending a little time with the landlady, who was at work pinning out laundry on a line across the courtyard. Mrs. Bishop informed Maisie that she would be putting clean sheets on the beds, and having a "good go" at the rooms.

As she stepped out onto the narrow street, Maisie noticed the man in the alley opposite, his face obscured by a newspaper. He wore cream trousers and black shoes—and, she suspected, no jacket, as the only other part of him visible was his arm, covered with the sleeve of a white shirt. She went on her way toward Mr. Salazar's café on Main Street.

The main thoroughfare was already crowded with street vendors, locals walking to and from Casemates Square, and visitors hailing the distinctive horse-drawn taxicabs, with curtains at each corner. Groups of sailors meandered, looking in shop windows, some holding bags, perhaps with gifts of embroidered linen for a sweetheart, wife or mother. She wondered if business might be picking up for the housebound Babayoff sister. Tables were set up outside Mr. Salazar's café, and he was already busy running to and fro, holding four cups of coffee—a cup and saucer in each hand and two balanced on his left arm. He did not spill a drop before setting them down in front of his customers.

"Ah, miss—lovely to see you this morning." He waved to her and opened the door.

"I'd like to sit outside this morning, Mr. Salazar—how about over there, near the window?"

"To watch the world go by, Miss Dobbs?"

"Oh, yes. And I would like you to do something for me, if you wouldn't mind."

"For you, miss, anything."

"You flatter me, Mr. Salazar. Would you mind walking across the road to Mr. Kenyon, and telling him I would like him to join me for coffee? I'd like mine very strong, with hot milk. And some of that lovely pastry—what is it called? I know you told me you make it all the time, but it's what people eat at Christmas. *Pan* something or other?"

Salazar looked across the road toward Kenyon, who was looking in a shop window. He turned to Maisie. "Kenyon?"

"Yes, please, Mr. Salazar. I would like to talk to him. And some of the—what is it called?"

"Pan dulce." He gave a short bow. "Mine is the very best."

Maisie nodded and stepped toward a table under the awning, alongside the window, outside yet partially in shadow. She watched as Salazar crossed Main Street—it wasn't wide—and tapped Arturo Kenyon on the shoulder. He began to speak, and Kenyon leaned forward to better hear amid the noise of passersby. The younger man looked up, then around at Maisie. She thought that if she were closer, she would have seen him redden to the roots of his hair. He followed Salazar back to the café and walked toward Maisie's table, where he gave a short bow.

"You wish me to join you, madam?"

"Yes, please, Mr. Kenyon. And let's not start off on the wrong foot—you know my name very well, you know where I am staying, and I daresay you know an awful lot more about me."

Kenyon took a seat.

"I don't know what—"

Salazar returned with two cups of coffee and two plates of the sweet bread, which he set down in front of Maisie and her guest.

"Thank you, Mr. Salazar," said Maisie.

Kenyon nodded.

Maisie watched as Salazar walked away, then turned to Kenyon. "You know exactly what I'm talking about. Please—I have neither the time nor the energy for us to wallow in contradicting each other. Now, then, are you working for Julian Compton or Brian Huntley?"

"I don't—"

"You do. Please do not insult me, Mr. Kenyon."

The man sighed, pushing up his sleeves. "Huntley."

"Good, that's a start. Have you heard the name Compton during your communications?"

"Only as far as you're concerned."

Maisie nodded. "I am using my maiden name here in Gibraltar. For personal reasons, not for reasons of security, though that possibility has only just occurred to me—surprisingly." She paused, lifting the cup and sipping the coffee. "How often do you communicate with Huntley?"

Kenyon fidgeted in his chair, leaning back and crossing his legs, leaning forward again. He took a packet of cigarettes from an inside pocket of his black waistcoat, tapped out a cigarette, and held the packet toward Maisie.

She shook her head, biting her lip.

"Do you mind if I smoke?" he asked.

"If it makes you a bit easier to talk to, go ahead." She set down her cup and pushed back her chair a couple of inches. Reaching for the *pan dulce*, she pulled off a piece of the bread, which she dipped in her coffee before eating. She wiped the corners of her mouth with her fingers—there were no table napkins—then picked up the cup and took another sip.

"So—it's Huntley. How often do you send in a report, and how do you communicate?"

Kenyon shrugged. "Every two days. I go to the garrison—I have a pass—and send my report from there."

"I see. And you receive your orders at the same time?"

He nodded.

"But you're also in contact with Inspector Marsh, yes?"

"How do you know all this?" Kenyon leaned forward, his voice low, though he still looked around to see if anyone had overheard.

"Calm down a bit, Mr. Kenyon. We wouldn't want to attract attention." Maisie sipped her coffee, again holding the cup with both hands. "It seems you know a fair bit about me—or perhaps you don't—but I could tell you exactly when you began following me, and exactly when I first saw you with Inspector Marsh. I wonder you have time to lift a hammer and chisel, Mr. Carpenter Kenyon, given the energy you've dedicated to being on my tail."

"Why did you want to talk to me?" Kenyon leaned back. He placed his cigarette on the ashtray, tore off a strip of the bread from his plate, and dipped it in his coffee before eating it. He smiled. "I've never done that before. It tastes good."

Maisie looked up at other customers eating and drinking, at those who passed by. Her eyes lingered on sailors being moved on by a shore patrol.

"I want you to help me," she said.

Kenyon laughed, shaking his head.

"I'm not making a joke, Mr. Kenyon. I want to find out who killed Sebastian Babayoff, and I've realized I need help. I do not know Gibraltar, and it's hampering me. I don't quite understand the people yet, though I'm getting by. But I don't have time to undergo a cultural education, so I need some assistance, and I've decided you're my best bet. In return, I will give you information to feed back to Mr. Huntley—

who I know very well, I might add. I don't want him—or anyone else in England, for that matter—meddling in my life." She paused, gauging his response, alert to any movement. Then she smiled. She knew his next question, even before he opened his mouth.

"And if I agree, what will you pay me, Miss Dobbs?"

She waited a moment, sipping coffee, dipping bread, eating it and brushing her hands together to be rid of crumbs.

"What do you think is fair? You tell me."

Salazar watched from the window as his much-respected customer and Arturo Kenyon stood up at the same time. She pulled a bank note from her wallet and left it on the table under the plate, then turned to Kenyon, and they shook hands. Kenyon glanced at his watch, and Miss Dobbs did the same. They both nodded, as if they were traders satisfied by a transaction. Kenyon stood back for her to pass him, and as they stepped out onto the street, they exchanged a few more words before she turned in one direction, and Kenyon went on his way toward Casemates Square. Salazar watched as Miss Dobbs lingered to look into a shop window, then another, before stepping out into the street. He thought she might be checking her clothing, then realized she was looking at her own face, smiling at her reflection as if she were contemplating at a photograph, trying to identify the subject. He wondered if he had seen her smile in such a way before. There was still that sadness about her, but it was as if something had changed, something he could not put his finger on. For the moment at least, she seemed lighter.

CHAPTER FIVE

M aisie stood outside Mr. Solomon's shop, studying the window display—tablecloths, small cocktail napkins, handkerchiefs, doilies, nightdress cases, cushion covers, all manner of embroidered and lace-edged goods, plus haberdashery supplies. There were some framed crewel-work pictures of the sea and the Rock, the natural edifice that defined the town, giving the impression of fortification even if there were none—but Maisie knew Gibraltar was arguably one of the most protected places in the Empire. She set her gaze on a set of fine white linen handkerchiefs, the lace so intricate, it might have been woven by a spider to drape across a rosebush on a spring morning. Brenda, her stepmother, would cherish these, would wrap lavender soap in each handkerchief and set them in the chest of drawers where she kept her "delicates."

Maisie opened the door. A bell rang above her head as she crossed the threshold.

Jacob Solomon reminded her of a thinner version of Mr. Salazar.

He was somewhat taller, and lacked the girth of the café owner, but each wore black trousers and a white shirt with sleeves held at bay by black garters above the elbow. Solomon was balding, and though he spent no time outside—unlike Salazar, who seemed to always be running back and forth, inside and out, the door constantly in motion as he served customers—he wore a shade to shield his eyes from the light, and a pair of wire-rimmed spectacles on the end of his nose.

"May I be of service?" Solomon spoke in another dialect—a hint of North Africa, thought Maisie. He clasped his hands together, bowed his head, and came out from behind the glass-topped counter, which also displayed a number of pairs of women's gloves.

"I should like a set of lace handkerchiefs, like those in the window."

Solomon frowned, his deep-set dark eyes appearing to close a little. "Let us go outside—you show me," he said.

The man followed Maisie onto the street, where she pointed to the handkerchiefs. He nodded, and they stepped back inside the store. Solomon turned to a series of wooden drawers behind the glass-topped counter and pulled out a drawer at eye height, so he had to stand on tiptoe to reach in for the handkerchiefs, a set of three tied with a narrow white ribbon.

"Will this be all?"

Maisie looked around, at linens draped across the walls and hanging just so from the ceiling. A series of mounted photographs had been exhibited on the wall closest to the counter. There were families seated, posing together: a mother with a child on her knee, or a man with his son. A woman, her skin sallow, her eyes dark and deep, seemed to stare out at Maisie from another photograph. A group of sailors had been captured for posterity, laughing as they looked toward the lens.

"Do you have a studio here?" She turned to the shopkeeper, smiling. "Sorry—it's Mr. Solomon, isn't it?" She gave him no time to reply, but looked back at the portraits. "These are very good—you seem to capture more than just the physical features of the subjects, Mr. Solomon."

"They're not mine, madam. They are the work of a photographer who no longer works here. I allowed him to set up a small studio in my stockroom. It was to his advantage and to mine—a little rent, and of course, more sales. Mainly people have a photograph to remember a special day, and then they buy something as a gift." He looked at Maisie. "But I am afraid he works here no longer, though I am hoping another photographer will take his place." His glance moved to the images on the wall. "It would be hard to get someone as good as Mr. Babayoff. Customers said you could almost see the sitter's thoughts in his photographs."

Maisie's eyes turned once again to Sebastian Babayoff's work, lingering on the eyes of a mother holding her child. She looked away, pressing her lips together.

"Indeed, you're quite right, Mr. Solomon. May I ask—do you have more examples of his work? I am interested in photography. I had a camera but gave it away—I always ended up frustrated that I couldn't quite capture what I was aiming for. Instead of a couple of friends on horseback, I would cut off their heads! Or when I tried to photograph my father with his dog, I managed to get the dog and not my father. I just don't know how people do this." She held out her hand toward the photographs, aware that she was chattering to distract herself from the image of the child in her mother's arms.

Solomon nodded. "Just one moment." He walked to the door, turned the sign to inform customers that the store was now closed, and returned to the counter. "If you would like to come with me, Miss Dobbs?"

Maisie smiled. It came as no surprise to her that Solomon knew her name, though she would bide her time with the shopkeeper.

Solomon pulled a chain with a set of keys from his trouser pocket and opened a door set between the rows of drawers behind the counter. Maisie expected the door to lead to another room, but instead it opened onto a small courtyard, a door on each of its four sides apparently leading to a series of dwellings. Turning immediately to their right, Solomon led Maisie up a stone stairway to a room above the shop. Piles of boxes appeared to have been pushed against the perimeter of the room to clear a space in the middle. On one side two chairs were positioned before a wooden frame covered with a heavy dark velvet cloth, with a potted plant to either side—rather grand and mature shrubs. Maisie looked around the room. Behind the screen a chaise longue was barely visible under a pile of linens and embroidered cushions.

She stepped toward the plants, reaching out to touch the leaves. "Oh, my—they aren't real."

Solomon smiled, shaking his head. "The stems are made of wire and silk or satin ribbon, as are the leaves. They look real enough in the photographs, though. Sebastian had a way with light."

"I can see that. Did he leave any more examples of his work here?"

"Only more portraits to be collected by customers—you may see them if you wish. Most have gone now—only a few remain to be claimed, and those are mainly of army and navy men. They could have left the garrison, though—sometimes they are filled with drink when they see the photographer is here, so they forget. It's a shame, because they pay after the sitting."

Maisie nodded, turning to Solomon. "So you know my name."

"I do, yes. You have visited Miriam Babayoff. You discovered Sebastian." He rubbed his chin. "I would imagine that most people would try to forget such a discovery, but I have the impression you're not that sort of person."

"If Miss Babayoff has spoken of our meeting, then she would have told you about the job I used to do. I had a business conducting private investigations—that's the best way to describe it—until several years ago, when I left England. Let's say it is ingrained in me to ask questions."

Solomon rubbed his chin again. "Be careful, Miss Dobbs. Questions can get you into trouble—especially here, and especially now."

"Who do I have to fear, Mr. Solomon?"

The man walked to the door, opened it, looked down into the stairwell, and closed the door again. He stepped toward the window, moving a box out of his path, and then lifted two brown paper-wrapped packages atop a crate. He shook his head as he reached for a blind and covered the window, then turned on a dim light.

"It's a wonder the whole lot hasn't gone up in smoke before now. Whenever I come up here, I swear I will sort out every box, parcel, and wrapping." He held his hand toward one of the chairs. Only after Maisie was seated did he take the other, rubbing his chin, as seemed to be his habit.

"The truth is, Miss Dobbs, I cannot be more—" He drummed his fingers on his forehead, as if to wake up his words. "What can I say? I cannot be more—yes, specific. But know this—Sebastian would put his nose in a wasp's nest if he thought he could photograph the queen. He was always after something more. He wasn't happy with just a mother's face and the child's face—he tried to photograph love itself. He would not be content with a photograph of the fisherman with his catch—he wanted to find the pain of toil in the image." Solomon wiped the back of his hand across his mouth. His words had not come with ease, and the effort of communicating was evident in the furrow of his brow.

Maisie nodded. "Had he been in some sort of trouble?"

Solomon shrugged. "A curious man with a camera in his hand—

what do you think? I cannot tell you who and why, but I do know that since he first picked up a camera, that boy was everywhere, shooting this or that. First on glass, then in rolls. He would starve to keep a camera running."

"I see." She paused. "Can you tell me about his politics, Mr. Solomon?"

"His politics? I don't know that he had any. He only cared about whatever he was pointing his camera toward." He rubbed his chin again and then removed the shade above his eyes, pressing his fingers back and forth along the indentation it had made in his forehead. The lines between his eyebrows appeared even deeper. "Why do you ask about his politics?"

Maisie sighed; fatigue was claiming her. The dark window blind and locked door conspired to accentuate the musty smell of packed linens, rendering the air stagnant and oppressive. She was at once aware of the dust on boxes, of cobwebs across the dark wooden ceiling and along the soft leaves of satin at her side. She wondered, then, how she might look if Sebastian Babayoff were training his lens on her face at that moment. Mirroring Solomon, she rubbed her hand across her forehead, feeling not only her thirst but something of the lassitude emanating from the man beside her.

"I spoke to a young woman yesterday, the niece of the fisherman, Carlos Grillo. Apparently Mr. Babayoff would go out to sea with Mr. Grillo, who had been a friend of his father." She rubbed her head again. The atmosphere in the room was bearing down as if a boulder were being rolled across her chest. "She also said that the photographer was a Communist."

Was it the atmosphere that made Solomon's appearance at once become like wax, whitening as she looked at him, waiting for his answer? He pulled on the black eyeshade once again and pressed down on his knees as if to stand. He shook his head.

"As far as I know, Sebastian was interested only in his work, and in keeping hunger and want from the door of the house. Family is our strength, Miss Dobbs—and the Sephardim are all family. His sisters were his first concern, that is why we hold them close." He smiled. "Now I must return to the shop—I too need to feed my family, my mother and sister."

Maisie pulled a handkerchief from her bag and wiped her forehead as she came to her feet. "Yes, I could do with some air, Mr. Solomon."

The shopkeeper opened the door to a rush of warm air and light that flooded across the bottom two steps into the courtyard.

"Please be careful as you go down, Miss Dobbs."

Solomon locked the door behind him, and they returned to the musty coolness of the shop. He wrapped the set of handkerchiefs for her, tying the package with string, and was about to bid her farewell when Maisie pointed to the photograph of the woman with a baby on her lap.

"Why is that for sale, Mr. Solomon?"

He shook his head. "Sebastian said he would wait for payment from the family, and he developed the photograph anyway, but I cannot be so generous—and neither could he, if truth be told. So when they have the money to pay for it, they can have the portrait—unless someone else buys it. And not before."

"I suspected as much," said Maisie. She reached into her bag for her wallet, pulling out a handful of coins, which she held out toward Solomon. "Please take what is owed and have the photograph delivered to the family, if you would be so kind?"

Solomon's eyes widened, and he took three coins from her hand, then closed it around the remaining money. "I will deliver it myself. You are most generous."

Maisie smiled. "I have another question or two for you, Mr. Solomon. Where did Mr. Babayoff develop his photographs? Was it in the cellar of his home?"

Solomon reddened, as if the heat of the day had assailed him. He started to speak, and then faltered. Maisie suspected he was struggling with the question of whether or not to tell the truth.

"Yes, he had a darkroom set up in the cellar—an obvious place, for it is without light already."

"Thank you for your time, Mr. Solomon. I daresay I will be back to purchase more of your lovely embroidered linens before I leave Gibraltar."

Solomon took her proffered hand and gave a small bow in reply. He escorted her to the door and waved as she departed, closing the door behind her.

Maisie crossed the road and went into another shop, this one selling leather goods. Once inside, she stopped to look at a pair of shoes from a vantage point that afforded a view of Jacob Solomon's shop. The sign on the door had not been flipped over from Closed to Open, she noticed. Within minutes Solomon departed, a broad-brimmed black hat upon his head and a parcel under his arm. He locked the door and went on his way at some speed—a pace that did not seem required for the simple act of delivering a wrapped, framed photograph, though she suspected it provided a useful explanation for his hurried almost-run along the street.

For her part, she left the leather shop and made her way back toward Mr. Salazar's café. She considered the conversation, and planned her next move. And she thought of the photograph of the woman with her baby, and the essence of absolute love that surrounded the pair despite the formality of a straight-back chair and a plant made of wire and satin. She held her hand to her waist as she walked, a feeling of light-headedness enveloping her as the dull throbbing returned to her abdomen. She was not so taken with pain, though, as to miss the fact that she had been watched as she left the shop. This time the man's silhouette seemed to bear a strong resemblance to a certain policeman she'd known in the past. At first she shook off the idea of the resemblance, then wondered: If she had not been mistaken, what on earth was a man from Scotland Yard's Special Branch doing in Gibraltar?

Though she had only accomplished two things—bringing Arturo Kenyon under her wing, though his loyalty was in question, and visiting Solomon—Maisie was tired. And she was fearful, anxious again about the night ahead. She felt hungry and light-headed, but she also wondered if the listlessness would usher her into a dreamless sleep, or whether nightmares would return. Or would she succumb to the precious tablets in the small brown bottle, now hidden and locked in the leather case; locked against her desire to be lifted above the responsibility for living a life.

She opened the door into the courtyard and stopped to speak to Mrs. Bishop, who was bringing in the dry laundry.

"Miss Dobbs. How was your day?" asked the woman.

Mrs. Bishop was in her mid-sixties, in Maisie's estimation. She was well-built, with wide hips and an ample bosom, and though she was a good head shorter than Maisie, she gave the impression of muscular strength about the arms. She picked up the wicker laundry basket and set it upon one hip, her right arm holding it steady as she shielded her eyes from a shaft of sunlight with her free hand.

"Very good, Mrs. Bishop—thank you for asking."

Mrs. Bishop nodded toward the door leading into her private quarters. "Come along and have a cup of tea with me. You look tired."

"Oh, that's not nec—"

"Come on, no arguments. A cup of tea brings your temperature down. Why people drink cold beverages on a hot day, I'll never understand. Hot tea is the ticket."

Maisie smiled, thinking that Mrs. Bishop sounded a little like Lady Rowan, and at that moment, a sudden affection for the guest-house landlady caught her unawares. "All right," she said. "A cup of tea would be lovely, thank you."

As they stepped onto cool tiles and made their way along a narrow corridor, Maisie's eyes adjusted to the shadows. Mrs. Bishop opened a door on the right and put the laundry basket inside, then with her thumb indicated that Maisie should follow through another door, which opened into a small kitchen. It was not unlike the kitchen in the Babayoff house. A kettle was already boiling on the stove, and on the table a cake had been turned out onto a cooling rack. Mrs. Bishop pointed to a chair, instructing Maisie to sit down while she brewed a pot of tea. While she made tea and placed the cake on a plate, cutting two slices, she asked questions about what Maisie had seen in Gibraltar, not always waiting for an answer before commenting on what she should not miss.

"But this war over there, it's a terrible, terrible thing. And right on our doorstep—though I can't say I haven't been glad of the business. A lot of them have gone home now, though. It's not like it was on fair day in La Linea; I thought everyone would die. There was such a rush across the border to get home to Gibraltar when the firing started—we love fair day, you know, there were a lot of people from the town there. I didn't breathe again until I was through that door." She pointed across the courtyard. "I locked it tight and hardly slept that night."

"I was lucky you had a place for me," said Maisie. "And such a large room—it's perfect."

Mrs. Bishop looked at Maisie as she pushed a cup of tea toward her—she had added milk and sugar without inquiring if it was to

Maisie's taste—and then placed a plate with a slice of cake in front of her guest. "Eat that up—it'll do you good."

Maisie sipped the hot tea and looked up at Mrs. Bishop. The woman held her cup to her lips but did not drink, nor did she speak for a second or two.

"Is something wrong, Mrs. Bishop?"

The woman shook her head and took one sip of tea, holding the cup as if she was grateful for the warmth on her hands.

"You know, Miss Dobbs, you've probably wondered why my English is good, so let me tell you. I was married to a military policeman who was stationed here, and I went back with him to England. I lived there until he died, and then it was time for me to come home. Both my children were born there, and they decided to stay, but I wanted to come back to my roots." She shrugged. "I miss seeing the grandchildren grow up, but as you English say, 'You make your bed, and you have to lie in it.' I've made my bed here." She shrugged again. "I bought this place ten years ago." She cleared her throat and leaned forward, picking at the cake on her plate but not lifting the crumbs to her mouth. "When my husband left the army, he became a policeman. Scotland Yard. He never talked about his work much—I don't think it was that thrilling, not at his end of things anyway. But I learned one thing, Miss Dobbs, having seen his mates come to the house and watching policemen at work—I can tell a copper a mile off. They all have to start somewhere, you see, and I think that walking the beat gives them a way of holding themselves—you can see it in the shoulders."

Maisie reached for the tea she had set down as Mrs. Bishop began speaking. "I'm not sure I'm following you, Mrs. Bishop." She took two sips of the now-lukewarm brew. "Why are you telling me this?"

The landlady raised her eyebrows and sighed. "I'm telling you because a man came here asking for you today, and though he didn't introduce himself, I know he was a policeman—and not from here, either. He wasn't in uniform, and he seemed . . . serious, if you know what I mean." She folded her arms. "Now, I didn't pay much attention to that scallywag, Artie Kenyon, hanging around. I thought he might be keeping an eye on you because you were the unlucky one who found Sebastian Babayoff. Anyway, you knew he was there—I watched you go down the street once, with him on your tail like a lost pup, and I could tell you knew he was following you. It was the way you seemed to glance sideways, checking your hair or your hat long enough to see him out of the corner of the eye. Anyway—"

"Tell me about this man," Maisie interrupted. "The man who came to the door asking for me. What was he like?"

"Big." She sat up and pushed back her shoulders, as if to suggest the size of the inquirer. "Tall, a bit of a belly, but not too much. Seemed no-nonsense, as if being cordial wasn't a natural talent."

"He didn't identify himself? No name? No identification?" asked Maisie, who had decided that subterfuge or feigned surprise would cut no ice with Mrs. Bishop.

"No. I asked if I could pass on a message, and he shook his head."

"Anyone with him?"

"I looked down the street as he left, but I couldn't see anyone waiting—but that's not to say he works alone."

Maisie nodded. She rested her elbows on the table and her head in her hands, feeling tears prick her eyes.

"Are you all right, Miss Dobbs? Not in any trouble?"

Maisie gave a half-laugh and then raised her head and sighed. "No, not in any trouble, Mrs. Bishop—though I suppose finding a dead body counts as trouble."

"You could leave it alone—you don't have to go sniffing around." Mrs. Bishop reached for Maisie's cup, and poured more tea.

Maisie's eyes met those of her landlady, and she smiled. "But I do. That's the trouble—I do have to sniff around, as you put it. The police believe the man's life was taken by a refugee or some ne'er-do-well robber. But, you see, he wasn't robbed. And because I found him, I believe it's my responsibility to bring truth to the matter of his death—for the sake of his family, if nothing else."

"And the man who was here? Who is he?"

"If he's who I think he is—and because you know Scotland Yard through your husband and you've spoken your mind to me, I will tell you—his name is Robert MacFarlane, and he is indeed a policeman."

"With one of those special offices they have there?"

Maisie sighed, as if chagrined to be revealing so much. But she was tired, and there was some comfort in sharing a secret with this woman. "Yes, he's with a special office."

"And why does he want to speak to you?"

"Because someone wants me back in England, and I'm not ready to go, not yet."

Mrs. Bishop nodded, slowly. "You must be important, Miss Dobbs."

Maisie laughed. "No, not important. But there are important people who worry about me. And a few other important people who worry what I might say." She stood up from the table. "Now I must go, Mrs. Bishop."

"Would you like me to bring you some soup in an hour or two? And a little glass of wine? You've got to eat, and I notice you don't go out for supper, come evening."

"Yes, why not? I love soup. What kind do you have?"

"Chicken and lemon. Hearty and a little tart."

"I could eat that—thank you."

"What shall I do if the man comes again, Miss Dobbs? I know he'll be back, even though I said I didn't know you."

"Don't worry, Mrs. Bishop, MacFarlane will find me when he's good and ready. At the moment he's like a cat with a mouse. He thinks he's playing with me."

"What will you do, then?"

Maisie pushed her chair back in under the table. "Oh, I'll just play him for the mouse myself, just for a while." She smiled, thanked her landlady for the tea and cake, and left the kitchen, making her way across the courtyard and up the stairs to her room, and set the key in the lock.

As she opened the door, she saw a plain brown envelope on the floor. Picking it up, Maisie noticed it had been used before, the previous address struck through so it could not be read and her own name penciled in above. The flap had been glued in place, but she raised a corner, tore across with her finger, and lifted out the note. It was from Arturo Kenyon. It informed her that a policeman from Scotland Yard had joined Inspector Marsh, and was interested in speaking to her. He would find out more and report back to her. He also said that he had some information for her about Sebastian Babayoff, and suggested they meet—but not at Mr. Salazar's café. He indicated another place, close to the American Steps, the memorial to a collaboration between the US and British navies in the Great War. He would meet her tomorrow morning. She sat down on the bed, set her bag down beside her, and tore the envelope and letter into tiny pieces, which she sprinkled into the ashtray on the bedside table. She took a match and lit the shredded paper, and once it was destroyed, she picked up the packet of cigarettes alongside the ashtray. She shook out one cigarette, placed it in her mouth, and struck another match. Before she could light the cigarette, she blew out the flame, took the cigarette from her mouth, and pushed it back into the packet, which she took to the wardrobe. She released the straps on the leather case and pressed down on the lock to open the case. Slipping the packet of cigarettes inside, she wavered, touching the bottle of morphia tablets. Just one to get her to sleep. Just one to help forget the scar on her belly, to let her rest without the image of a crashing aeroplane in the distance, then the explosion. She closed the case, snapped the lock, and buckled the leather straps. Soon Mrs. Bishop would bring her soup, and a glass of wine. Then she would lie back on her bed, hoping a dreamless sleep would claim her until the morning. She would deal with "little Artie Kenyon" tomorrow. She was beginning to think that Mrs. Bishop herself might have been a better choice of assistant. Time would tell if her faith in the local runner for the British Secret Service had been well placed.

CHAPTER SIX

Maisie was restless, waking every hour or so, then slipping into a half-sleep before she began to dream again, as if she had fallen through a fissure in consciousness and was aware of herself sleeping. In the end she opened her eyes. She would struggle, toss, and turn no longer. But she did not rise from the bed. Instead she stared at a crack in the ceiling, allowing her gaze to follow it. She thought it looked like a river on a map, or a mountain path. It was a scar on otherwise perfect white rendering. She knew about scars.

She planned her day in her mind as she felt the room grow warmer, and watched dust motes dance in shafts of sunlight beaming through the window. She had opened the curtains again after undressing and slipping into her nightgown last night. She wanted to be woken by daylight, to hear the gulls above the rooftops; she wanted to know as soon as her eyelids lifted that she was not back in the past. She hated waking up only to experience the jolt of remembering why her heart felt heavy in her chest. The light might allow the ache of recollection to enfold her gently.

First she would meet Kenyon at the American Steps memorial. It was still considered a new fixture in the architectural mishmash of Gibraltar, not yet inaugurated in ceremony. She would wait at the bottom of the steps, looking for all the world like another tourist. Then she would go to the Babayoff house, this time taking the Leica. She had no idea how to make a raw film into a print, but she hoped Miriam Babayoff might put her in touch with someone; she wanted to look at the cellar darkroom anyway. When she had accomplished these tasks, she would go to Mr. Salazar's café. It felt like such a haven each time she took her customary seat inside, camouflaged with her back against the mural. Was she ready to confront the person she knew might come? Or would she draw back and avoid meeting?

Her plan was made; it was time to begin. She pulled the covers aside and stood up, drawing her hand across her nightclothes. It was habit, now, as if one day she would feel the child she had lost, as if the turmoil would end and all would be well again.

Maisie remembered seeing a photograph of Thiepval's new memorial to the missing of the war that ended in 1918—a stark, imposing edifice that held the names of those men for whom no remains had ever been found, and who lay under farmland still marked by the scars of battle. She was reminded of it now as she looked up at the American Steps. Though not as grand, nevertheless it bore the same broad, deep, square design with a rounded arch, and it had the same sense that this was a place of remembrance and reverence. She stood at the bottom of the steps, her hat low across her eyes, protected by dark glasses with round metal frames.

Looking up, she knew she appeared as if she were any other interested tourist, marveling at an example of modern architecture. Gibraltar was a place of memorials, it occurred to her; a military town where so many who left its shores had been lost. Here women waited for a widowhood that came too soon, and black was the color of both fisherfolk and garrison families. It was a place where men had been brought from the bloody fighting in Gallipoli, to recover or die from their wounds. Yes, it was a place of memorials—that very fact alone might have been at the heart of her desire to stay; perhaps there was a comfort in belonging here. Perhaps someone who felt the depth of scars across her heart every day could be at home in a place with so many reminders of war, with war still so close, across the border.

Hearing steps behind her, she turned to see Arturo Kenyon, holding a cigarette as if to inquire whether she had a match to light it. She shook her head, and he smiled and began to speak. A couple walked past, arm in arm, so he asked Maisie if she were enjoying her stay. She pulled a map from her bag and leaned toward Kenyon, unfolding the paper and pointing. He nodded and motioned to a bench underneath the wall alongside the steps. Resting the map on her lap, she turned to him.

"You said you had something to tell me," she said.

He nodded. "There is a man here, from London—his name is Mac-Farlane."

"Yes, I know that—he's been looking for me. But surely he's not here because a photographer was murdered. That's not his bailiwick. I can't see why Babayoff would interest him."

Kenyon raised his eyebrows—his default countenance when surprised, it seemed. "You have seen him?"

"I know a man who fits his description has been asking after me," she said. "But I cannot imagine what he might be doing here. MacFarlane is with Special Branch."

"That's not what I've heard. He might be with special something, but no more with the Special Branch. He's been transferred, and is now the linchpin between the police—all branches, but admittedly mainly Special Branch—and the Secret Service. Their work overlaps, and apparently he's done this before on a case-by-case basis, but now it's official—but hush-hush."

Maisie smiled, giving a half-laugh.

"What is it?" asked Kenyon.

"You saying 'hush-hush.' Even though you don't have an accent, it's amusing. I'm sorry."

"I was told you never laughed, that you had no sense of humor."

"Really? Well, I haven't had much to laugh about recently, but I'm quite able to see the funny side of things." She sighed. "I suppose I also take murder seriously—it's a death, after all, which means that usually someone, somewhere, is grieving. Someone is feeling their heart ripped out with the ache of loss. So no, you don't usually get me laughing about that."

Kenyon apologized.

"That's all right. Now then, do you know what MacFarlane is doing here?"

"The official story is that he's here to look at how the flow of refugees from Gibraltar to England might be stemmed, and where the others might be going, and how it affects Britain's security. But many have gone home, and the fighting is not so close to Gibraltar now. A good number have gone across to North Africa, to Morocco. It's about that, mainly."

Maisie looked at Kenyon. "I see. And is that it? Do you have anything more about Mr. Babayoff?"

Kenyon shook his head. "Not yet, but I do have some news about Carlos Grillo."

"Yes?"

"I've heard he left letters for both his sons, as if he knew he was going to die."

"If he was ill, that would not be unusual, would it? A note to sons who never come to visit? A last word in case he never sees them again? That doesn't surprise me, Mr. Kenyon."

"But what if he were afraid, if he knew his days were numbered?"

Maisie nodded, folded the map, which had remained open on her lap, and stood up. "I should be on my way, Mr. Kenyon. Yes, you're right—the letters are somewhat suspicious." She paused, looking up at the monument to collaboration. "The note you poked under my door was a good idea—you should have been a cat burglar. Let me know if you have anything else I might be interested in."

"Where will you go now?"

Maisie looked at Kenyon and smiled. "Well, I'll tell you this—I may have an opportunity to see Robert MacFarlane today, though I may also decide I don't want to see him. I doubt he'll be calling himself 'Chief Superintendent' or any other title at the present time—not if he doesn't want anyone to know who he is." She sighed. "I suspect he won't be able to wait any longer before he approaches me, so I may have to be nimble on my feet if I decide to avoid him."

Kenyon nodded. Maisie saw his feigned nonchalance. She slipped her hand into her bag and touched a bank note, folding her fingers around it until it was firm in her palm. Withdrawing her hand from the bag, she held it out toward Arturo Kenyon. He took the note with the handshake.

"Thank you for helping me with the directions, sir. So I go this way, if I want a taxicab?" asked Maisie, her voice raised.

"Of course, madam. Just along there."

She took a step as if to take her leave, and Kenyon began to walk in the opposite direction. She turned and watched him for a moment, then continued on her way on foot.

Now the game would begin. Kenyon would give her information fed to him by the Secret Service, and she would rattle their cage when he gave them an account of his meetings with her. But at least Kenyon was out in the open now, and she could get on with her job. Her job? Yes, it was her job. She wanted it to consume her as it had in the past, when she had first worked for Maurice and struggled to forget the war. She didn't want to lie in bed until late morning anymore, nor to linger over the straps and lock of a leather case, drawn by the promise of half-consciousness held within. She wanted to work until she felt herself raw from thinking, weary from trying to answer questions that could hardly be framed. *Work.* Investigating the death of a Jewish photographer was her sword, and at that moment, it was the only way she knew to slay the dragon of memory.

Lace curtains twitched a half moment after Maisie rapped her knuckles on the door of the Babayoff house. She leaned closer, her lips almost touching the wood.

"It's Miss Dobbs, Miriam. I'm alone, and there's nothing to fear." Her voice was loud enough to be heard by the woman on the other side of the door, but low enough not to be discerned by neighbors.

She heard the bolts slide back, and the door opened.

"Come in, please—quickly."

Maisie felt the woman's nerves taut, pulled to the extreme, as she closed the door and pushed home the bolts, then turned a key in the lock for good measure. It was as if a coil inside her wound tighter with every noise from outside, every footfall on the flagstones or voice heard on the street, and then released just a little as the source was revealed, and deemed safe.

"You've come again. Is there news?" Miriam Babayoff pulled out a chair for Maisie. She folded a dress that had been spread across the kitchen table and pushed it to one side, along with her needlework box. She nodded toward the now-neat pile. "I take in mending too." She shrugged. "Clothing repairs and alterations. I'm very quick, and I charge a good price, so word gets around." She began to tap her finger on the table. She still wore her thimble, so the rhythmic sharpness of the sound seemed to exaggerate her tension.

"There is no news from the official sources," said Maisie. "Nothing from the police, and I don't think they'd be telling me anyway. But I have talked to a few people, and I have some more questions for you—if that's all right, Miriam?"

The woman rubbed a hand across her forehead, the thimble leaving a mark in its wake, as if another worry line had formed in an instant. "So many questions, and so few answers about my brother."

"I understand, Miriam. Truly I do. But questions are a means of discovery—they may take us down a deceiving path or two, but they're like stepping stones, a way to break down the wall to find a door, perhaps."

Miriam nodded. "What do you want to know?"

"I've been told that Sebastian was a Communist, Miriam. Was he? Did he have political beliefs that might have upset someone?"

Miriam shook her head. "This is a British colony. The British want everyone to stay in their station, never to—how does the saying go? They don't want anyone to upset the apple cart. You should know that, Miss Dobbs."

Maisie nodded. "That doesn't answer my question, though I agree with your summation, to a point. Was your brother a Communist?"

83

"My brother believed in equality—we all do. Our father and mother believed too. Go to the big new hotel—see the people there, high above the rest of us. The rich always like to live on the top of the mountain, don't they? Perhaps they think they are God, able to look down on their earth." She began tapping her thimble on the table again. *Tap, tap, tap, tap.*

Maisie touched her right temple with her fingertips. "But Sebastian made money out of those people. He photographed them at the hotel. They paid him."

"Hmmph." Miriam turned away, then back to Maisie. "Yes, my brother had the political beliefs of a Communist—we all do—but he would take work where he could. I will work my fingers to the bone until I die, caring for my sister." She looked up at the ceiling, as if the woman were floating above her. "No man will look at me—I will never marry, never have children—because I am here with a burden. I have no money to speak of, and I have my station—I cannot rise, even with the help of my neighbors. And we are strong together, we look after each other."

"I understand, Miriam."

The woman made a show of looking at Maisie's shoes, at her clothing. She leaned forward and took the hem of Maisie's skirt between thumb and finger, as if to measure the quality of the fabric. She let it go and leaned back.

"Yes, I am sure you do." Her words had the edge of spite.

Maisie held Miriam's gaze. "Miriam, I wonder if you wouldn't mind showing me Sebastian's darkroom. It's down in the cellar, I believe."

"Why do you want to go there?"

"I'm interested in seeing his work—and he must have spent a lot of time down there."

"It was not my place to go to his cellar, Miss Dobbs. It was his private room where he worked. I haven't been down there since he died."

"Did the police ask to see the darkroom?"

Miriam shook her head. "They probably didn't even think to ask. Not all the houses have cellars, only a few."

"Didn't they ask where he developed the film?"

"No." Miriam Babayoff paused. "I wondered about that, to tell you the truth. I mean, I wasn't going to tell them, but I wondered where they thought he had the film developed. Or maybe it didn't occur to them, especially as they thought he was murdered by a desperate refugee."

"Perhaps." Maisie nodded toward a narrow door to the right of the stove. "May we?"

Miriam Babayoff pushed back her chair, the feet screeching against tile. She took a key from the mantelpiece above the stove, and opened the door. Maisie followed her onto a small landing. Directly in front of them a staircase led to the upper floor, where Maisie imagined there were two rooms, and perhaps another smaller set of stairs to the roof. One room would have been occupied by the sisters, and one by Sebastian. Did Miriam still sleep in the same room and even the same bed as Chana? Or would she have moved into Sebastian's room? Maisie made a mental note to ask later, another time, perhaps.

To her left a stone staircase led down into a barely visible chasm. Carrying a lantern, Miriam led the way. Selecting another key on the ring, she opened an unpainted wooden door and stepped into the cellar.

It took a second or two for Maisie's eyes to become accustomed to the lack of light before Miriam flicked a switch, and an electric bulb in the ceiling came on. Maisie blinked.

The walls were of rough stone, though wooden shelving had been set against the far wall. The shelves held demijohns of various liquids, which she assumed were used in the development of photographs. Maisie also noticed a shade set to one side, made of a transparent dark red material, which she suspected might be used to change the light in the room when Babayoff was processing his film. There was another light fixture close to the wall, where Maisie could imagine the photographer holding up negatives to choose which he would print. It was a simple, unsophisticated studio; Maisie imagined Babayoff had furnished it over the years as his income afforded new equipment and materials. Though it was more cramped, this photographic lair reminded Maisie of another similarly converted cellar at a house in London. She had been investigating the death of an American soldier in the war, a mapmaker who had joined the British army because his father was born in England. Her visit to that studio had resulted in her identification of the man's murderer. She shivered and moved toward a set of narrow drawers, on top of which were stacked wooden boxes that she suspected held photographic equipment. She opened the top drawer, stopping for a moment to look around toward Miriam, who was still holding the lantern, watching her.

"Do you mind, Miriam?"

The woman shook her head, tears forming in the corners of her eyes. "I'll go back upstairs. Bang on the ceiling when you're ready to leave, Miss Dobbs, and I will come with the lantern." She pointed to a broom leaning against the wall in the corner. "I am the only one who ever used a broom for sweeping in this house, after my mother died. My brother used it to summon me to help him, and Chana bangs on the floor with a broom handle by her bed."

After Miriam left the cellar, Maisie stood for a moment, listening to the woman's footfall ascend the stone staircase, as if each step were a mark of her bitterness. It was the resigned march of the put-upon, to a theme of one deep sigh. Maisie turned back to the chest of drawers. One drawer was filled with negatives, one with processed prints, and others with film that had yet to be developed, each dated. It was clear that Sebastian Babayoff had needed to be parsimonious with chemicals, so he was selective about the films he chose to develop. Maisie went through one pile of prints, mainly portraits, each with a scrap of paper folded around it, bearing a name and the amount of money still outstanding, after the deposit was paid before the sitting. The print would only be handed over when he received the balance owed.

Based upon the number of prints ready for collection, the photographer was owed a pretty penny. Maisie wondered how she could help facilitate their final sale to the advantage of Miriam and her sister.

Another collection was possibly taken in the company of Carlos Grillo while out on the fishing boat. Maisie squinted at these images, then moved closer to the light to better view them. The Rock of Gibraltar—the northernmost of the two Pillars of Hercules guarding the entrance to the Straits of Gibraltar—loomed large in several photographs; others showed ships coming into port. Another half dozen, taken on ship, were of men and women in evening dress. Since the war ended, travel had boomed by road, rail, sea, and air, and Gibraltar had seen more visitors as a result. Decommissioned naval vessels had been bought on the cheap, reconditioned, and sent on their way with cruise passengers, who enjoyed visiting a little piece of England that was at the same time so very foreign, and relished the sunshine. Oh, how the younger set had yearned for sunshine, especially those who had suffered the bitter cold mud of Flanders. Maisie suspected that Babayoff earned a tidy sum from photographing the new breed of traveler. He had just enough time to go on board when the ship docked, take orders for photographs and then deliver prints before the ship sailed again. He probably took hundreds of images in this manner—if a dozen or so didn't sell, it was probably not a huge loss.

There were photographs of fishing boats and, surprisingly, a few of Carlos Grillo's niece, hidden in an envelope at the back of the drawer.

Instead of the black clothes she'd been wearing at Catalan Bay, in these photographs Rosanna wore a flounced skirt and a ruffled white blouse that was slipping down from her right shoulder, its bareness concealed only by her hair, which, instead of being tied back at the nape of her neck, was carefully styled to cascade to one side, brushing her neck in a suggestive manner. The photograph had been taken outside, possibly on a secluded stretch of rocky beach. Maisie replaced the photographs in the envelope, committing the images to memory, though she was not sure of their significance at this point.

Rummaging toward the back of the drawer, she drew out another envelope, this time thicker. More photographs taken at sea. Maisie looked at each in turn—there were about half a dozen—and then again at the ones she'd studied first. There was a difference. The previous batch were taken looking out to shore from on board a vessel—she assumed Carlos Grillo's fishing boat; in fact, in one photograph, Carlos was smiling directly into the camera, having looked up while hauling in a full net. But which shore? It was not Gibraltar; the Rock would have been evident, even from a distance. Was this the shoreline of Morocco? Or somewhere along the Spanish coast? How far would the boat need to go before her skipper received a warning from the Spanish that she was in their territorial waters? Or another patrol boat, instructing them to leave the area? She looked at the second set of coastal photographs, squinting. There was another fishing vessel close by, and in the distance something else, though she could not quite ascertain what it was. Land? An illusion caused by waves? Or the coast? She went through the photographs, sighing in frustration. She needed a magnifying glass.

Maisie searched the drawers, ran her fingers across the dusty shelves, and then looked around the room.

"Oh, there it is," she said out loud. She stepped across to the chest of drawers and reached along the side, where a magnifying glass was hanging on a hook from a piece of string looped around its handle. As if to Sebastian Babayoff's ghost, she said, "Well, I can see why you'd hang it there—if you put it down, you'd never find it again!"

Maisie held the magnifying glass above the photographs, leaning to one side under the light to better view the images.

"Oh," she said, and looked up. She took another photograph and looked at it through the glass. "Oh, dear Lord, Sebastian, what on earth did you see?"

Maisie collected the photographs and slipped them into the envelope. Should she take them with her? Yes, she would ask Miriam if she could have the photographs, take them to her room, and hide them somewhere—they would not be safe here, in this house. She wanted to look at the images in better light, where she could study them in greater detail. And she wanted to know about that coastline. Where was it? Perhaps Carlos Grillo's niece could help her. She had a feeling that the disdain the young woman had shown for Sebastian Babayoff was meant to disguise her affection for him.

She still had her satchel with her, and there was enough room to slip the envelope into the bag. It would be better, after all, she decided, for Miriam Babayoff if she had no knowledge of the photographs. But now Maisie was even more intent upon having the film from the camera she had lifted from the flower-filled rockery, above the path where Sebastian Babayoff lost his life, developed. She could not ask just anyone to do it, though. The images held on the film *could* be innocent enough, but they could also be the catalyst for increased danger. And that danger would not only compromise her own safety, but that of the two sisters, one of whom was scared enough anyway.

She looked around the darkroom once more, then picked up the broom and banged on the ceiling with the handle. Miriam Babayoff's footfalls moved across the kitchen, then down the stairs toward her.

Five minutes later Maisie was sitting at the table, a cup of tea in front of her. Miriam was sewing, her thimble-capped finger pressing the needle through the fabric, then pulling on the other side. She looked up as Maisie asked a question.

"Miriam, do you know anyone—perhaps a friend of Sebastian's—who can develop film? Someone discreet, someone who would not reveal the source of the film to anyone, or—more crucially—what was on the actual film."

"Sebastian's film?"

Maisie nodded. She explained about finding the camera.

"His Leica?"

"Yes, I think it must be his."

"It was secondhand. He saved for a long time for that camera—he liked it because it was easy to take with him. He said it was good for quick photographs, for the newspaper and such like. He sometimes saw famous people at the Rock, and would snap photographs and take them down to the editor of the newspaper, so they could write about them—Errol Flynn, people like that. And he was there when HMS *Hood* tested a new gun offshore. He rushed up there with that Leica to take photographs last year, after it was hit by a bomb."

"Do you know someone who could develop the film, Miriam?"

The woman paused and set her sewing down on the table. She resumed tapping her thimble before looking up at Maisie, whereupon she began pulling her thimble off and pressing it quickly back onto her finger, over and over again.

"I can, Miss Dobbs." She blushed. "I know the cellar better than I admitted."

"You know how to process film?" Maisie looked at Miriam. "I mean, forgive me, I'm not questioning your ability, but I thought Sebastian seemed such a perfectionist, he would want to do everything himself."

"Oh, that was Sebastian, Miss Dobbs. You're not mistaken there. But when he went to the ships, or up to the Ridge Hotel to do photographs, he had to process them in a hurry, before people left—he needed to come home, develop the film, make the prints, and get back there so he could get his money. He could not have done that on his own, so he taught me how to get the job done."

"Would you do it for me?" asked Maisie.

"I may be filled with fear at times, Miss Dobbs, but I would do anything to find my brother's killer."

Maisie opened her mouth to say something else, but the sound of a broom handle on the floorboards above—*bang-bang-bang*—drew her attention.

Maisie looked up at the ceiling, then at Miriam. "Thank you, Miriam—thank you so much. I will be back soon with the camera. Would that be all right?"

"Yes. Yes, please bring it to me."

Maisie nodded. "Of course."

As they stepped toward the door, Maisie placed her hand on Miriam's arm. The young woman stopped, looking at her arm as if expecting to see an imprint of Maisie's fingers branded onto her skin.

"Miriam, did Sebastian travel into Spain in the weeks before his death?"

Miriam nodded. "Yes—he wanted to photograph the war. My brother wanted to be important. He wanted people across the world to recognize his work."

"Do you think he took unnecessary risks?"

Miriam shrugged. "He considered himself an artist, whereas others mostly saw him as Babayoff, who took a portrait of your new baby, or went on the ships to photograph the rich. But he wanted to change the world with his work, so yes, I suppose he took risks that others might not."

"And how about the people he photographed? Not the ones who posed in Mr. Solomon's shop, but others, perhaps those caught up in a scene your brother wanted to capture." Maisie paused. "It's just a thought, having looked at his work in the cellar."

Miriam shrugged, then motioned Maisie to the door. She slid back the bolts, turned the key in the lock, and opened the door just enough for Maisie to slip through. Once out in the street, Maisie turned to say a final good-bye, but the door had already closed. She could hear the bolts being rammed home and the key turning once again.

As she walked away across flagstones that led to another alley and finally onto Main Street, Maisie felt the weight of the photographs in her shoulder bag. Why, she wondered, was something that looked very like a submarine, floating in the waters between Spain and Gibraltar, of interest to Sebastian Babayoff? A photographer might be curious about such a thing, if that's what he thought he had seen in his view-finder. Perhaps the increased shipping, the neutral countries keeping tabs on the situation in Spain, was of interest to the press overseas. But why had he then hidden the envelope at the back of the drawer? And why were Carlos Grillo and Sebastian Babayoff in waters that seemed so far from the coast of Gibraltar? She would have to show the images to someone more familiar with the neighboring seas if she hoped to identify the location.

And that—perhaps unfortunately—brought her back to Arturo Kenyon.

CHAPTER SEVEN

t was early evening by the time Maisie approached the café. It would not be long now before Mr. Salazar began to bring in chairs and tables from outside, then sweep the flagstones and close up for another night. A few soldiers were sitting at the bar, talking in low voices. A couple sat by the window, sipping coffee. As Maisie closed the door behind her, she saw the man pull a handkerchief from his pocket, lean across, and dab the side of his wife's mouth. Was it his wife? His fiancée? Or perhaps they were lovers seeking privacy in the shadows.

"Miss Dobbs!" Salazar emerged from the kitchen, approaching Maisie with both hands held out to grasp hers. He bowed and then extended one hand toward her usual seat underneath the mural. "There, I've saved it for you."

Maisie wagged a finger at him. "Oh, you are flattering me again, Mr. Salazar—it's almost closing, and most of your customers have gone on their way."

"For once. At least I don't have to throw anyone out onto the street and point them in the direction of their hotel or the port." He had pulled out the table so that she could take her place, and shifted it back again. "A coffee with lots of milk? Cocoa? Or something stronger?"

"I'd like some milky coffee—quite hot, please."

"As good as done."

She leaned back on the padded banquette and closed her eyes.

"It seems you are one of Salazar's favorites."

The voice was unfamiliar. Maisie started, and looked to her right. A man was smiling at her and raising his glass—whisky or brandy, something smooth and golden, reflecting dregs of light in the shadowed café.

"I'm sorry—I did not mean to startle you." The man reached across to offer his hand. "Antonio Vallejo. I am a regular here at Mr. Salazar's café when I am in Gibraltar."

"Maisie Dobbs," she introduced herself. "And I don't think I'm a favorite—Mr. Salazar knows how to woo his customers so that they come back again."

Vallejo laughed, then seemed more serious. "And you are out alone at this hour?"

Maisie was about to respond that it was still barely twilight when she saw Salazar approaching. He set the coffee in front of her, and a plate with what looked like a sugar-covered doughnut placed on a doily.

"A little something extra for you, Miss Dobbs—it would not last until tomorrow." Salazar waved his hand. "On the house. It's *japonesa*—we fry sweet dough and then fill it with our own special-recipe custard."

"It will be lovely with this cup of your wonderful coffee—thank you!" Maisie wasn't sure she really wanted anything sweet, but she didn't want to disappoint Salazar.

"And you have met our professor? Miss Dobbs—the Professor." Salazar bowed toward Vallejo.

Maisie looked at the man who had just introduced himself to her. "Professor?"

"He knows everything," said Salazar. "Together we rearrange the world to our liking here in my café, in the evening, when other customers have gone. But this evening, well, you have the lady to talk to, Professor." He bowed again and left the table.

Maisie lifted the coffee to her lips, blew across the foam, and took a sip.

"You really should have some of the *japonesa*—it is delicious, and a local delicacy," said Vallejo.

She took the knife set alongside the *japonesa* and cut off a small wedge, lifting it to her lips. Its sweetness caused her tongue to tingle, the sugar crunching along her teeth as she chewed the dough. She took another sip of the coffee.

"You need some of the custard with it—it smooths out the sugar," offered Vallejo.

Maisie nodded and took a handkerchief from her bag to wipe her lips. She turned to Vallejo. "You are a professor. I wasn't aware of a university here."

Vallejo shook his head, setting down his drink on the table, though his right hand still held the glass. "Across the border. I work in Madrid, but my family came from Gibraltar, so I return when I can."

"For a short visit? Isn't it difficult to cross the border at the moment?" Maisie asked the question while cutting another piece of *japonesa*. The smooth yellow custard oozed out, and she used the knife to sweep it back across the slice. She lifted it to her mouth, leaning forward in case the custard slipped. She took up her cup once more and looked at Vallejo.

"Sometimes a short visit, and sometimes not—and it is not difficult for me to cross the border. I am not required at my post for a little while, so I decided to come for a few days." He stared at the liquid in his glass, and sipped again. "If I had my choice, I would stay here until Spain becomes, well, quieter, if you will."

"I have been struggling to understand the war. I have asked different people, but I still can't grasp who is on the side of good. It seems to be confusing."

"There are many oppressed people across the border, people who are dirt poor and have little chance in life. Then there are those who don't want them anywhere near the table, let alone sitting at the feast. In 1931 the people of Spain voted in their first free election in sixty years. Until that point the country had been controlled by the rich— the landed aristocracy, the church, and the industrialists. But the new Republic had its problems, though the poor saw more in the way of education and public money. So if you are looking for the roots of the war, they lie in discontent—and discontent always rises up like froth on beer. Look at Russia. The revolution is a fine example of what might happen in such a society."

"And what about the Communists?"

"Communism is the anger of the people—but if not tempered, it is an anger that turns on itself. It must be managed with care, or it can result in an oppression that could be as bad as the all-powerful rich pushing those who have nothing into the ground." He set down an empty glass. Maisie watched as Salazar approached with the bottle, but Vallejo held up his hand: *No more.*

Maisie leaned forward as if to ask another question, but Vallejo began to speak again.

"And Britain is complicit in the bloodshed. Your country walks a narrow path. The British government is happy to have Communists banished from their doorstep, and they are not sorry to see the poor kept in their place—your British and their classes; the last thing they want is a powerful peasantry too close to Gibraltar. They'll appease Germany, and Italy too. They're turning a blind eye to Germany's collusion with the Nationalists—yet Germany would love to get her hands on Gibraltar. What a coup that would be! The gateway to the Mediterranean, an impermeable rock to protect interests in Europe and Africa, and then on to the rest of the world."

"Please, Professor Vallejo, I'm afraid I don't quite see how Britain is turning a blind eye to Germany and Italy—are they involved? Please forgive me, I have been here in the town only a matter of weeks, and—"

"And you haven't seen the German or Italian aircraft given the freedom of the skies overhead? And you don't know that there are rumors they have refueled here? That they are supplying arms to Franco's Nationalist armies? Your politicians are tap-dancing on the fence while trying to protect their own interests."

Maisie held her cup in both hands for the heat it offered. She seemed to be seeking comfort everywhere she went, yearning to be tightly held by warmth. A heavy fatigue enveloped her, and she felt the urge to leave. She was about to speak again, to offer her apologies and then depart from the café, when Vallejo leaned forward.

"May I ask, Miss Dobbs—have you recently suffered a loss? You use the title of an unmarried woman, yet you have the bearing of a widow."

Maisie flinched.

"I apologize," continued Vallejo. "But I could not help but feel that you wear the cloak of the bereaved." He paused. "And you wear a wedding ring on a chain around your neck."

Maisie felt for the ring. When she dressed each morning, she took pains to ensure it was close to her heart, but never visible above her clothing. She lifted the chain and dropped it under the collar of her blouse, feeling it brush against her skin once more.

"I am sorry for your loss—you are young to be a widow, and you must surely miss Mr. Dobbs very much." Vallejo looked away, then back at Maisie.

"Dobbs is my maiden name, Professor Vallejo. Mr. Dobbs is my father. My married name is Compton. My husband's name was James. James Compton."

She wondered how callous she might seem, abandoning her husband's name, though the choice was in part to protect herself.

"It must be balm for the wound across your heart," said Vallejo. "Using your father's name."

Maisie nodded, but moved to change the subject. "Do you know a man named Sebastian Babayoff?" It was a question without preamble.

Vallejo shook his head. "No, the name is not familiar to me. Why do you ask?"

"He was a local man, a photographer—a yeoman, if you like, taking work where he could; weddings, tourists, portraiture, some for the press. And he was murdered several weeks ago. There is a suspicion that he was a Communist."

Vallejo inhaled audibly, the sound underlining his opinion. "If this man were a Communist, then he would be in a difficult position here in Gibraltar. Why are you interested in him?"

"He was murdered recently. I discovered his body—in fact, I probably disturbed the killer, though there was no chance of saving Mr. Babayoff."

Vallejo gave a slow nod. "What do the police say?"

"That his life was taken by some ne'er-do-well, a poor refugee in difficult circumstances. Apparently, even though many had returned to Spain, there was another influx after the fall of Malaga—more people who were left with nothing."

The man's expression changed, his bottom lip jutting out as he shrugged, demonstrating his doubt. "It could have been so. But had the man, this Babayoff, been putting his hand among the vipers?"

"The vipers?"

Vallejo sighed. "This is what troubles me, Miss Dobbs. I wonder how any man professing to be a Communist could ignore what is happening in Spain. I wonder if Babayoff might not have become involved in something too big for him to manage."

"What do you mean? How could he have been involved?"

He shrugged again. "To wage a war, both sides need money, arms, sustenance, medical supplies, a place of refuge. Sympathizers must be courted. People who can supply these necessities of battle, even a guerilla battle, must be brought into the fold. Many could be termed tea boys, runners—the little men and women who contribute here and there, perhaps sending food, perhaps offering a place to sleep, or blankets. There are men and women coming from your country, from America, Italy, and France, Russia too, and from other places, to fight with the International Brigades. More help, more support for Republicans who fight Franco—and a good number of those men and women were recruited by Communists overseas to help those of us who fight for the Republic."

Maisie felt herself shiver, and rubbed her arms.

"Does what I say scare you, Miss Dobbs?"

"War always scares me," said Maisie. "People swarming together to kill each other scares me, even when they are fighting for their freedom."

"Freedom always has a high price. Look at your war of 1914. I wonder how people who have borne such loss can ever be free."

"The cloak of bereavement always around them?"

"Yes, exactly," said Vallejo.

Maisie raised her hand to catch the eye of Mr. Salazar, who stepped from behind the bar to approach the table. She reached for her bag.

"Please, Miss Dobbs—allow me." Vallejo pulled a handful of coins from his pocket.

Maisie hesitated and then said, "Thank you—that is most kind of you, Professor Vallejo." She moved to stand as Vallejo waved Salazar to his table, then added, "Tell me, Professor Vallejo, what subjects do you teach, at the university?"

"Politics and philosophy—subjects that many students are drawn to, until it comes to the actual work."

Maisie smiled. "I taught in a college once. I enjoyed it very much."

"I am sure you were a very good teacher," said Vallejo, waving away Salazar's offer of change.

"I hope so—I did my best. In any case, Professor Vallejo, I must leave now." She held out her hand.

"Until we meet again, Miss Dobbs."

"Indeed. Until then."

Maisie smiled at Salazar, who held open the door and bowed as she stepped out onto the street. As she walked away, she looked back and saw the lights go dim and hear Salazar push home the bolts at the top and bottom of the door. She and Vallejo had been the last customers, and Vallejo had not left with her.

It was not far to Mrs. Bishop's guest house, and Maisie's step was light across the flagstones as she made her way to the front door, slipped in the key, and closed it behind her. She was sure there was no one in the shadows waiting for her, though when she arrived at her room, she stepped across to the window without first turning on the light, just in case. She gave a sigh of relief, closed the curtains, and lay down on the bed. It was too late now to ask for soup, but as she switched on the light, she noticed a sandwich on the side table, and a small carafe of wine, together with a note from Mrs. Bishop to the effect that she was sure Miss Dobbs would like a "little something" when she returned.

Maisie did not reach for the plate, not at first. She closed her eyes to marshal her reflections upon the day. Instead of feeling closer to finding Sebastian Babayoff's killer, she felt as if the landscape from which she could pry her evidence was becoming broader and deeper. And now there was one more thing, something she had not alighted upon with a comment during her conversation, but let pass like a cloud in the sky. It was the look on Vallejo's face when he said, "and many of those men and women recruited by Communists overseas to help those of us who fight for the Republic."

Us. Many of *us.* If Vallejo considered himself a fighter, then what was he doing in Gibraltar? And did he remain in the café to talk long into the night because Mr. Salazar was an old friend, or was there something else for them to discuss? And really, could he have known Babayoff? There was no surprise in his voice when she mentioned that she had discovered the man's body, a shock that needed no stretch of the imagination. It was as if he knew.

Of course, it could have been nothing more than the chance meeting it seemed at face value. But what if it were more?

Maisie sighed. Was her intuition off? Had the months of retirement diminished her ability to think strategically? Had settling into the comfortable life of an expectant mother allowed her senses as a psychologist and investigator to lie so fallow that she could no longer separate the wheat from the chaff? She pressed her hands to her eyes. It was so long ago. So long ago that she was Maurice's student, then his assistant. She remembered how, in the early days, he would only allow her to toil over the case map after she had meditated, had spent time alone in silence. He had advised her that later, when she was ready to work independently, her need for that time would lessen, though he would expect meditation in the morning and evening.

Maisie sat up, threw her pillows on the floor, and sat upon them with legs crossed. She clasped her hands together, her thumbs just a rice grain width apart. It had been a long time since she'd had the courage to return to her practice—how would she ever tame her mind? How would she control the images she knew would assault her senses? As if he were there with her, she heard Maurice's voice. *Watch the image, and let it go. Take note of it, know that it is there, and allow it to move away, across the landscape of your mind's eye. Allow yourself to see connections, Maisie. Then go to the case map, and plan your next move.*

She closed her eyes. It was time to go back to her training, to become a student again. The student and the graduate, at the same time. She would immerse herself in the sacred silence of the next two days. There was little she could do; Shabbat had already begun, and for the town's Catholic and Protestant congregations, Sunday, with its tolling bells and church services, was sacrosanct.

Maisie woke early on Monday, April 26th. There was no heaviness in her limbs, no weight of nightmares to leaden the morning. She swung her feet onto the floor, pulled down the pillows, and slipped into meditation again. *Still the mind, if only for five minutes. Then open your eyes—and your heart—and consider what needs to be done.* Maurice's voice was louder now, and she had followed his instructions to the letter. She washed, dressed in a dark skirt and white blouse, her black sandals, and a straw hat. She unbuckled her leather satchel, took Sebastian Babayoff's Leica from its hiding place at the back of the wardrobe, and placed it in the satchel, along with a notebook and pencil she slipped into the front pocket. She folded a cardigan on top of the camera, then looked around the room for anything she might have missed. Picking up a fresh handkerchief, her wallet, and her sunglasses, she added them to the satchel. She would ask Mrs. Bishop for a small flask of water to take with her, and perhaps a few biscuits. She left the room and found Mrs. Bishop once again pegging out laundry in the courtyard.

"I'll get you a bottle of ginger beer, much better than plain old water on a hot day—though, as you've heard me say, a cup of tea is best. Fight heat with heat."

"That's what people told me in India—until it came to the afternoon gin and tonic!"

Mrs. Bishop laughed and set off into her inner sanctum, returning a few minutes later with a corked bottle of ginger beer and a small paper-wrapped snack. "There, I've half-pulled the cork for you, so all you have to do is give it a little tug and it'll come out. And I don't know if you like this sort of thing, but I made some Eccles cakes yesterday—I used to make them for my husband, and just fancied setting up a batch."

Maisie's eyes widened. "Oh my, what a coincidence! Eccles cakes are my favorite!"

Mrs. Bishop nodded toward Maisie's satchel. "There you go, then—put them both in your bag to keep you going today. Make sure that bottle is upright—it shouldn't leak, but you never know."

Maisie thanked her landlady and went on her way, heaving open the thick oak door and stepping out into the alley. She wondered where Arturo Kenyon was today, and if she would hear from him later. Thoughts of MacFarlane skimmed over the surface of her mind. Today she would take the camera to Miriam Babayoff, and afterward she would make her way to the fisherman's beach for another visit. She wanted to speak to Rosanna, Carlos Grillo's niece.

The sun was shining, and a soft yet determined breeze was blowing; there was a dampness to the air. A large cloud seemed to linger overhead, casting shadows across the Rock, and Maisie wondered if this was the Levanter, a weather phenomenon she had heard about but not as yet experienced—it was more likely in May, but it was almost the end of April, so there was always the possibility. If it was the Levanter cloud, there might be showers. Perhaps she should have brought an umbrella. In any case, she might be grateful for her cardigan before nighttime claimed the day.

She continued on her way towards the Babayoff house, and was only a little surprised to see Jacob Solomon leaving as she approached. Maisie suspected that Miriam had already locked the door following his departure; upon seeing her walking up the cobblestone alley, he banged on the door again, and though his voice was low, Maisie heard him say, "Miriam. Miriam, you have another visitor." By the time she came alongside the house, the door was open, and Solomon was making a small bow in greeting. He did not raise his black hat, though he bowed again to Miriam, who, Maisie thought, seemed more than a little flustered. Perhaps having two visitors in succession was more than she was used to. Without doubt, though, Solomon trusted Maisie—why else would he have heralded her approach?—the woman was on tenterhooks as she closed the door and went through the ritual of pushing home bolts and locking the door.

"I hope I have not come at an awkward time, Miss Babayoff," said Maisie.

"No, though I have laundry to do, and mending that must be returned to my customer this evening."

Maisie unbuckled the flap on her leather satchel and took out the Leica. She held it out toward Miriam, who did not move for a few seconds. Tears welled in her eyes as she wiped her hands on her apron, her fingers shaking as she reached for the camera. She looked at Maisie as she held it to her heart.

"He loved his Leica, you know." Miriam turned the camera in her hands, then squinted at the top. "It looks like he'd used the entire reel. I'll begin immediately."

"Don't you have work to do, Miriam?"

"I can do it all. When can you come back?"

Maisie looked at her wristwatch. "Let's say this afternoon—how about three o'clock? Would that be time enough for you to provide something for me to look at?"

Miriam nodded. "Yes—I can do this."

Maisie stood up and walked to the door, followed by Miriam, who was still holding the camera to her chest.

"One thing, Miriam." Maisie paused and regarded the woman directly. "Please remember that every single image on that roll could help me. Know that even if there is something there that you do not care for—I don't know what it might be, but let's say it was something that did not throw a good light on your brother—it could hold a key to the identity of his killer, or the person who wanted him dead."

Miriam nodded.

"Are you sure you understand?" asked Maisie.

The woman nodded again. "Yes, Miss Dobbs. And I even understand that his murderer might not be the person who ordered him killed."

Maisie smiled. "Good."

Yet again she heard the bolts slam home as she left the house, a sound that seemed angry and final, yet signaled fear. Miriam had grasped that the man—or woman—who wields the weapon is often not the person who wants a life ended. It was almost as if she expected such an outcome.

The fisherman's beach at Catalan Bay was busy when Maisie arrived, keeping her distance to observe the scene before her. For the most part it seemed the morning's catch had been unloaded and was already on its way to market, but a couple of the boats were pushing back out to sea again. It was apparent that, for the fisher folk, there was always something to do—nets rinsed and checked, then brought to the women to mend, though some fishermen repaired their own nets. And there were decks to be sluiced and rigging to be inspected. As before, the women sat farther back along the beach. Maisie took out her binoculars to scan the scene. Rosanna Grillo was not there among the women, but as she watched, she saw one of the older matrons turn around, call out, and beckon. The gesture seemed to express annoyance.

Moving the binoculars in the direction of the woman's wave, Maisie saw Rosanna walking toward the net-mending circle. She thought the girl held anger within her as she stepped across the beach, revealed by a tightness across her shoulders, and in the way her arms were crossed. Maisie lowered the binoculars, then lifted them again. Rosanna was being followed by a man—a man she turned to face and then moved her hand as if to direct him away. She was asking him to leave. Maisie adjusted the binoculars, pursing her lips. She could not get a better view of the man, though she suspected she knew who it was.

Rosanna approached the women and sat down among them. It seemed they had not seen the girl with the man, and went about their business, passing her a section of the fishing net to work on. Maisie directed the binoculars toward the man, watching as he turned and walked away. He did not look around, did not check to see whether he had been observed, though she suspected he might be aware of her presence. His walk suggested a man carrying a burden; his shoulders were hunched. He stopped once and looked back at the gathering of women, then went on, cupping his hands to light a cigarette as he went. When he was out of view, Maisie returned the binoculars to her bag and sat down on a rock. She wanted to speak to Rosanna, but at the same time, she wanted to think. At first glance the drama played out before her might have been one of a lover spurned. Or was the man pressuring the young woman for another reason? But she was settled upon one thing—that Carlos Grillo's niece knew Arturo Kenyon very well indeed.

CHAPTER EIGHT

C ould Maisie be sure that Kenyon had not seen her? He had departed with only the briefest glance back in the direction of the women. Although he had made errors, he was no fool. But the question remained—what was he doing with Rosanna, and why had she been so angry?

She sat watching the fisherfolk for some time without making her move, weighing the possibility of having a productive conversation with Rosanna. But she had to find out more about the woman's relationship with Babayoff—which Maisie suspected had been a romantic one, if only on the part of Babayoff, who may have had designs on his friend's niece. Coming to a decision, she rose and made her way across the beach, smiling as she approached the women. Rosanna looked up at her.

"Hello, Rosanna." Maisie addressed the girl, but nodded at the women. She brought her attention back to Rosanna. "May I speak to you? In private?"

Rosanna stood up and motioned with her head, indicating that they should walk away from the cluster of women, out of earshot of the fishermen.

"What you want from me, Miss Dobbs?"

The girl's hair was drawn back and her clothing was as before, a black skirt, black blouse, and a shawl across her shoulders despite the heat. Maisie remembered the photograph and the smile she had for the photographer who had revealed the vitality within her. Maisie thought it was like a fairy tale in which the prince releases his love from her prison—and perhaps is given freedom in return.

"I wonder if you can help me again. Sebastian Babayoff—" Maisie allowed the name to hang in the air, watching the girl's response. Just a flinch at the corners of her eyes gave her away. Maisie continued. "I believe you were friends."

"I told you—he knew my uncle, Carlos Grillo."

"Yes, I know that. But I've seen some photographs he took of you—and it occurred to me that you might have been quite attached, and not just because he was a friend of your uncle."

The girl pressed her lips together and turned away. She wiped away tears with the back of her hand.

"Rosanna, did you love him?"

The girl nodded.

"But it was not to be—is that it?"

Rosanna shrugged by way of an answer, and pointed to a place in the shade where they could rest. They sat on the sand, their backs against solid rock. Maisie brought out the bottle of ginger beer and offered some to the girl. She declined, but Maisie took a sip, wiping her mouth with the back of her hand.

"Will you tell me what you know about Sebastian?" asked Maisie.

The girl pulled a handkerchief from her pocket and opened her mouth to speak, but stopped short and looked up. Maisie was already on her feet, having heard the same sound, a deep whining, as if something were falling from the air. It was an aircraft engine, coming closer. Both women looked up as Maisie pressed her hands to her ears and hunched her shoulders. From beyond the cliffs, a flight of aircraft flew at speed overhead; she closed her eyes and fell to her knees on the sand. Rosanna knelt beside her as she doubled over, weeping.

"Miss Dobbs. Miss Dobbs, are you all right?" Rosanna asked, her voice raised above the noise.

The two women watched as the aircraft appeared to change direction over the sea, a cluster of small dots becoming smaller, then larger again, only to be joined by more aircraft overhead.

"Where are they going? What are they doing?" Maisie looked across to the fishermen, who stood with their hands shielding their eyes from the sun so they could watch the aircraft. The women had instinctively gathered their children and run for cover in the lee of the cliffs.

"I don't know, Miss Dobbs—but listen, they're going now."

"They're flying back across Spain, aren't they? Did you see the insignias? They weren't Spanish—they were German, and I saw another I think was Italian." Maisie was calmer now, holding her hand to her chest. She was aware of Rosanna holding out her handkerchief.

"Thank you. Yes, thank you very much." She took the proffered cloth and wiped it across her eyes and temples.

"The aeroplanes make you sad, Miss Dobbs," said Rosanna

Maisie nodded. She sat on the sand again, leaning against the solid rock and closing her eyes against the sunshine. She could still feel her heart beating inside her ribs as she leaned forward, her head in her hands. The girl sat beside her and began to rub her back, as if she were a child fearful of imagined ghosts in a darkened room.

"Do you feel better now?"

Maisie nodded. "Thank you. It was a shock. I didn't expect those aircraft to come flying out of nowhere, without warning. It took my breath away." She turned to Rosanna, but waited, her eyes closed. Then she spoke. "May I ask you the question again? About Sebastian Babayoff?"

The girl looked out to sea, but kept her hand on Maisie's back. "I adored him, and he adored me, Miss Dobbs. But it was a difficult love." She shrugged. "He was a Jew, you see, and my family is Catholic. It did not matter to us, but, well, this is not a very big place. There would have been difficulties—and of course, he had his sisters to think about." She shook her head. "But we were trying to find a way to be together, though neither of us could imagine leaving Gibraltar. It is home."

Maisie looked at her. "And Arturo Kenyon?"

She shook her head. "He's like a mosquito that keeps you from sleep." She patted Maisie on the back, a gentle touch that was more of a question, as if her fingers were asking, *Are you all right now?*

Maisie put out her hand to steady herself as she came to her feet. Rosanna followed, and both women brushed sand from their skirts.

"Was Sebastian a Communist?" asked Maisie.

"His family held that there should be equality, that we should all have the same chance, whether peasant or prince."

Maisie studied the girl as she answered, then pressed her again. "Was he doing anything dangerous, do you think?"

Rosanna sighed in response, rubbing her hand across her forehead, revealing fingertips angry and red from mending fishing nets. "I don't think he would have done anything he thought might bring harm to his sisters."

The fisherman's beach was quiet again, though in the distance Maisie could see specks in the sky she believed to be aircraft. She wondered what it meant, to have these aeroplanes flying overhead. And she knew enough by now—after months in Canada, often privy to long conversations about new aircraft design, when John Otterburn and James would talk of such elements as air speed and lift, of trim and maneuverability—to know that the German aircraft were bombers. She looked at her watch and decided to leave Catalan Bay now. She would walk back to Main Street—with any luck she would find Vallejo there. He might have the answer.

Maisie watched Rosanna as she in turn looked out to sea, and to the fishing boats being pushed out, perhaps to gather in another catch.

"Thank you," said Maisie. "For your honesty."

Rosanna smiled. "I'm glad someone is trying to find out who took Sebastian's life. The police are too busy with refugees to bother."

Maisie took her hand. "I'll find out who wanted him dead. Time is not on my side, but I will not leave Gibraltar until I discover the truth behind Sebastian's murder."

The walk back into town seemed longer, even though Maisie felt as if she were walking faster. She was anxious to see Miriam Babayoff again, to see whether she had managed to develop her brother's last roll of film. Perspiration ran down her temples and between her shoulder blades. Approaching Grand Casements Square, she stopped and closed her eyes. In her mind's eye she saw the aircraft above her head, then making their way out across the straits and looping back again. To do what? Were they en route to an airfield, perhaps in North Africa? And why fly over Gibraltar? *Because they can.* She sighed, another image coming to mind, this time a small fighter aircraft unknown outside the cadre of aviators and engineers John Otterburn had gathered around him. The aeroplane swooped low over the escarpment, followed by a retort from the guns on board. The wings tilted this way and that, and the engine spluttered, coughing as if fuel were blocked. The pilot struggled to keep aloft, and then it was over, the small aircraft spiraling down, down, down, and blown into tiny pieces on impact.

Maisie held her hand to her mouth and began to weep anew. She would be happy never to see anything other than a bird in the sky for the rest of her days. Walking on, half stumbling, she recalled seeing a church nearby. Though all faith had left her during the war, she half staggered into St. Andrew's Church. She wanted to feel the touch of prayers fanning around her like butterfly wings, and she wanted to be held safe in the still coolness of the familiar building—it could have been a church anywhere in the British Isles, though there was a certain Moorish influence. She took a seat in a pew at the back of the church and closed her eyes. *Help me*, she whispered. *Please help me.*

The sound of the door opening and closing caused her to look up, and she realized that others had entered the church, their footfall light and voices low before slipping into silence as they knelt with bowed heads. There was no service, yet the minister was present, in prayer at the altar. Most visitors did not remain long in the church, as if they wanted only to petition the Lord and then be about their business once again, yet they had come, and perhaps for the same reason as she had sought a place inside—the aircraft overhead had unsettled her.

Half an hour later Maisie stepped out into the shadows cast by the church, and walked in the direction of Main Street. She was only half surprised to see Professor Vallejo walking toward her. She forced a smile as he approached.

"Miss Dobbs. How are you?"

"I went into the church to . . . to be in a cool place for a while. I have been walking, and I'm rather warm."

"Did you see the aeroplanes? German and Italian?"

"I did, yes, and they seemed rather low—I thought they were German and Italian. Not that I am an expert on aviation, by any means," she added as an afterthought.

"I am troubled by them," said Vallejo. He looked up as if he had heard the distant drone of an engine aloft, but only seagulls swooped and called.

"You said they fly over Gibraltar."

"Aircraft such as those have only one purpose, and that is to cause damage—to wage war. In any game there is a winner and a loser, and the purpose of those planes is to increase the chances of winning. But in war there are no real winners—too many lives are lost, too much pain to endure. How can we look back at any war and say, 'We won'?"

They began to walk toward Main Street at a slow pace. Maisie fell into step with Vallejo, and focused on the way he carried himself as he put one foot in front of the other. His shoulders were hunched, just a little; as if he had caught a glance of his reflection in a mirror, he began to draw himself up, pulling his shoulders back. *There's something he wants to tell me,* she thought, though it occurred to her that anything the professor might choose to tell her had a very definite purpose, and she wondered how she might respond to whatever he had to say.

"Spain was neutral in the war, wasn't it, Professor Vallejo?" asked Maisie.

He nodded. "As much as any country can be neutral, when such terrible fighting is going on across the border. I was here in Gibraltar in 1915 and saw the hospital ships coming from Gallipoli, and we knew about the disasters not only in the Dardanelles, but in France and Belgium. That was when I decided that I could not stand by and do nothing. I went to Belgium as a volunteer, and I drove an ambulance, back and forth to the front from hospitals and aid stations. Never have

I seen so much pain, so much blood. I gave up my position at the university to serve."

"That was brave of you, and good." Maisie felt the anger emanating from Vallejo. *The dragon is alive inside him. And if I allow it, he will bring me down further.* It was an idle thought, tagged on to the realization of Vallejo's memories, red-hot like coals fallen from a fire.

Vallejo shrugged. "There were many who came—as they have to Spain. People with good hearts and worthy intentions, but alas, most of us could never have been prepared for such hell on earth."

They walked in silence for a minute or two before Vallejo spoke again. "Miss Dobbs, it occurred to me, when you said you had been a teacher at a college in Cambridge, that you might have met an old friend of mine who also taught there."

Maisie shrugged. "Well, there are many colleges in Cambridge—it's teeming with students and lecturers, with teachers who only come in for one term or even a day or so a week."

"Yes, of course. But in any case, it occurred to me that you might know Professor Francesca Thomas—that's her name now."

Maisie caught her breath, trying to hide any sign that she recognized the name. Should she admit to knowing Dr. Thomas? She decided to feign ignorance.

"I'm afraid it doesn't ring a bell, but I'll rack my brain and see if I can shake anything out." She laughed, then looked at her watch. "Oh, dear, I have to run—I'm due to see someone in about five minutes, so I had better crack on."

Vallejo gave a half bow. "I hope we meet again—perhaps at Mr. Salazar's little café."

"I'm sure we will," said Maisie. She waved her farewell and turned up a narrow street she had not taken before, feeling for her map in the leather bag as she stepped along the flagstones. Dipping into a doorway, she sighed with relief. "What just happened?" she said aloud, though there was no one on the street to hear her. She leaned against the stone wall to catch her breath. She was thirstier than ever, and would have loved to go to the café, but she had to get away from Vallejo.

"Blast!" she admonished herself. "Damn and blast!"

She knew her mind had not been limber enough. She had lied, and she was sure he knew she had lied. But perhaps she had to give him the benefit of the doubt. Perhaps he was uanware his arrow in the dark had hit a bull's-eye. Maisie remembered, once, laughing with James as she read out part of a letter from Brenda. Her stepmother had asked if, now that she was in Canada, she had ever come across an uncle of hers who had crossed the ocean in search of his fortune, finally to settle in Alberta. "It's always the way," said James. "People just cannot fathom how big this place is. They think we all know each other, expats from the mother country—but we'd be hard-pushed to bump into him if he lived in Toronto, let alone Alberta!"

Had Vallejo made a similar leap, assuming a teacher from one college in Cambridge must know all others? But no, that was not an error; Maisie was sure she had never mentioned that she had been in Cambridge, let alone the college where she had worked. *He knows.* And there was much to know—her position had been a cover for an investigation on behalf of the Secret Service and Special Branch, during which time she reported to none other than Robert MacFarlane. The same Robert MacFarlane who was biding his time in Gibraltar, probably waiting for just the right moment to approach her.

But more than anything, it was the mention of Dr. Francesca Thomas that had taken her aback. A senior professor at the same college—the College of St. Francis—Thomas had been educated at Oxford University and the Sorbonne, in Paris. Maisie remembered taking the woman's file from the college office so she could read it at her lodging. There had been precious little to support the feeling she had at the time that there was more to the professor of French literature and philosophy than met the eye. When Maisie visited one of the woman's former professors at Oxford, she had been described as passionate, an expert with languages, a woman who had worked in something "hush-hush" during the war. And there it was again, that phrase. *Hush-hush.* Maisie smiled to herself. If Maurice had been with her, he would have said, once more, that she should pay attention to coincidence, that coincidence was a shadow cast by truth.

It was Thomas who had in the end taken Maisie into her confidence, having seen her outside a building belonging to the Belgian Embassy. Francesca Thomas had worked for the British Secret Service during the war, before moving on to Belgium, where she became an agent with La Dame Blanche, a resistance network supported by the British. La Dame Blanche—"the White Lady"—was an organization of mainly women and girls involved in sabotage, assassination, and reconnaissance in occupied Belgium. Their bravery was beyond measure. Thomas had proven her mettle time and again, and bore a deep scar across her throat where she had fought the Hun in hand-to-hand combat—and won, though it almost cost her life. She considered herself a soldier, perhaps no more than on the dark night when she murdered her husband's killer with her bare hands.

Now, as Maisie made her way along the street, following the map's zigzagging directions to Miriam Babayoff's home, she remembered Francesca Thomas' parting words to her as if they had been spoken only yesterday. *They won't let you go, you know. And we will meet again, Maisie.*

"They" were the British Secret Service, and they had found her, Maisie knew that much. But were they playing her as if she were a fish on the line, teasing her in any direction they pleased? Perhaps it was time for her to find MacFarlane. Perhaps it was time for the fish to pull on the hook.

As Maisie approached the house shared by Miriam Babayoff and her sister, it was evident that something was wrong. A cluster of four men, all without jackets and with sleeves rolled up, appeared to be inspecting the door and its frame. She could see that Jacob Solomon was one of them. Each of the men was wearing a black broad-brimmed hat, and one had curling earlocks that reached his collarbones. Miriam stood to one side, holding two of the jackets, while a woman seated in a chair outside rested her hands on another two jackets laid across her lap. Miriam held her hand to her forehead, and appeared to have been crying, while the other woman—Maisie assumed it was Chana, the sister—stared at the flagstones.

"Miss Babayoff," Maisie called to Miriam. The young woman turned to face Maisie, revealing her reddened eyes. "Miriam, whatever has happened?"

The men continued to work, giving each other instructions as one stepped aside to rest a piece of wood on a small trestle and began to smooth it using a folded piece of sandpaper. Another worked on the door, removing a broken lock and fitting a new one. The two others measured the glass, and all agreed that the pane in the upper part of the door should be replaced with wood, and made very strong.

"But Miriam won't be able to see who's there," said one of the men.

"She can look out of the window," said another.

"She shouldn't open the door to anyone unless they call out to let her know who's there first—we'll spread the word so people identify themselves. She must not open the door to anyone else." The man looked at Maisie, as if to appraise whether she was friend or foe.

Solomon glanced up from sanding the frame. "Miriam and Chana should not be alone, two women on their own in this house. It is not good, and—"

Miriam began to weep. Maisie put an arm around her shoulder and the woman leaned in to be soothed. Chana looked up from holding the coats and, seeing her sister upset, also began to whimper, holding out her hands toward her sibling, making little fists, opening and closing her fingers as a child might reach out to her mother. Miriam went to her sister and wiped her tears with a handkerchief she took from her pocket. Maisie noticed Chana tapping her feet, one after the other, up and down in her distress.

"She should go to her room and rest," said Miriam. "She only gets like this if she's very upset. I thought that with the men helping, it would be good to get them to bring her down to see some sunshine. But now she's tired." She looked up. "Mr. Solomon, would you help me?"

Maisie watched as the man left his task and came to Miriam's side.

"I can help, Miriam," he said. He knelt in front of Chana Babayoff and spoke to her in a low voice. "I'm going to take you up, Chana. Now then, give the jackets to this lady, and then reach up with your arms and put them around my neck."

Maisie took the coats and stood back as Chana clasped her arms around Jacob Solomon's neck, allowing him to lift her up and carry her to the door. The men stood back as he stepped through, followed by Miriam. Maisie looked at the men. "I'll put these on the kitchen table and then make tea—would you like tea?"

Maisie set out the thick tea glasses on saucers, and placed cubes of sugar to the side of each cup. She measured several spoonfuls of the fragrant black tea from the caddy into the pot, and poured in the boiling water. She allowed it to steep and began to pour as Miriam returned to the kitchen and the men came for the refreshment, each of them setting a cube of sugar between their teeth and drinking the strong brew through the sweetness of sugar.

"How long will it take?" asked Miriam.

"Not long," said one of the men. "Another hour, maybe a little more. Do not worry, Miriam, you will be safe in your home tonight. And we will make sure one of us walks by the house every hour, to check that you're safe."

"Solomon will probably sleep outside the door," said another man, looking toward the shopkeeper, who, having taken Chana upstairs to her room, now continued with his task.

Miriam blushed.

"Can we talk somewhere private, Miriam?" asked Maisie.

"Come with me," she replied. "We'll go down to Sebastian's darkroom—I have something to show you in any case."

The women left the men to the task of strengthening the door and replacing the lock. They stepped into the darkroom, and when Miriam switched on the light, Maisie turned to her.

"What happened? And when did it happen?"

"I was down here, Miss Dobbs, working on the film you brought. I had locked the door, and the bolts were across. But I heard a crash, and a noise upstairs, so I ran up—I was worried about Chana, you see. If it were just me, I would have locked myself in down here, but Chana . . ."

"It's been a dreadful shock for you, Miriam. It's such a violation, and you cannot expect to feel safe yet. Did you see anyone? A face at the window, perhaps?"

Miriam Babayoff shook her head. "I came to the kitchen as a hand was coming through the window. The fingers were groping around for a lock, for a way to open the door, so I screamed. And it was a very loud scream, and it started Chana off, so whoever it was ran away, down the alley. Then help came. Mr. Solomon was first to arrive—I think one of the women called out to him—many of the men were still at work, you see, but Mr. Solomon is just down the street." She blushed. "It is not accepted for these men to be alone with an unmarried woman, but who else could help?"

"You were lucky," said Maisie. "But it seems as if you will be in safe hands."

There was an hiatus in the conversation. Finally Maisie spoke again. "Did you manage to get anywhere with the film?"

"Oh, forgive me, Miss Dobbs—but yes, I have developed the film. It's not quite dry yet—but handle carefully, and you can look. It seems very ordinary to me, photos taken at a party at the hotel. Just people."

Maisie stepped over to a darker part of the room, where a collection of photographs had been pegged to a line that ran along one wall.

"Just people?" Maisie smiled. "I have discovered that there is no such thing as 'just people' when a man's life has been taken."

She began scrutinizing the photographs, then shook her head and reached for her leather bag, which she had set on the floor. She took out her own magnifying glass, which she had brought with her.

"Sometimes I need a little help," she said, and began scrutinizing the prints once more.

They were indeed, for the most part, images of a party. It seemed that everyone gathered was holding a cocktail, and some of the women were grasping cigarette holders. Maisie thought of her dear friend Priscilla, of the way she would flourish the cigarette holder when she was making a point, waving it around like a wand to emphasize her opinions. She missed Priscilla, missed her bossy caring, her informed comments, her knowing. Many thought Priscilla light, as if she were some sort of sparkling dust invited to a party to infuse people with joy. But Maisie knew another side to Priscilla, the deep wounds that war had left upon her soul, her fears about the future—especially for her three sons, who seemed to be growing ever faster toward manhood. Maisie missed Priscilla perhaps more than anyone else, aside from James.

Maisie brought her attention back to the photographs, still damp on the wire. There were compositions taken outside, as well as inside. They seemed very much the sort that might appear on society pages in the newspaper. She recognized a film starlet of the moment, and a man she seemed to recall was a millionaire. Then she started, leaning closer, bringing the magnifying glass in toward the black, white, and shades of gray that made up the picture before her. There, in a corner, apparently in conversation with a woman she thought might be in her sixties, was Professor Vallejo. She moved to the next photograph, and the next. In each he had moved just a little, so by the time she reached the fourth print, his head had turned, though his companion in conversation was—it seemed—still talking to him. Maisie went to another image, this time from farther back in the room. She followed the line of Vallejo's gaze, and it was clear he was looking straight at a man in the foreground of the shot, a man with either blond or gray hair, swept back from a high forehead. He had what might be termed a Roman nose and was smiling at the young woman facing him. They were in evening dress, the woman in a silk gown that caught the light in such a way that the fabric shimmered like water rippling across the curves of her body. The man wore a dinner suit, a bow tie, and a heavy watch on his wrist—Maisie noticed the watch because it was quite obvious that it was not an everyday timepiece. There was something different about it. She considered the man's face; his demeanor suggested he had an easy and elegant way about him. She moved on to the next image and held up the magnifying glass. She gasped and again drew in closer. Could it be? Something—perhaps the flash from the previous shot—must have caused the man and woman to turn to face the photographer. The woman's thick, lustrous hair was swept to one side, revealing a single faux diamond earring—it had not the luminescence of a real gem. Her full lips were enhanced by lipstick, and her eyes had been made more expressive by kohl. It was almost a dated look, yet the sweep of the hair, the cut of the dress, suggested a modern and exciting glamour. She was younger than the man by about ten years, thought Maisie, which would put him at about thirty or thirty-five. She brought her attention back to the woman, then to the man. He seemed put out by the disturbance, or perhaps . . . could it be he was afraid? No, not afraid, but he did not want his photograph taken. His eyes, animated in the previous photograph, seemed cold.

Maisie scanned the rest of the image and saw that in the background, Vallejo was also looking in the direction of the camera, though his eyes were focused on the distinguished man with the unusual watch. The man who had been in animated conversation with Carlos Grillo's niece—though Maisie suspected that no one at the fisherman's beach would have recognized her at first glance.

CHAPTER NINE

Maisie returned to her room at Mrs. Bishop's guest house, and was met by her landlady as she stepped across the courtyard.

"Had a nice day, Miss Dobbs? You look like you've caught a bit of sun again." Mrs. Bishop smiled. "Care to join me in a glass of wine? I thought I would just sit out for five minutes and rest my legs, and then it crossed my mind that a little tipple wouldn't go amiss."

Maisie hesitated for a few seconds. "I think that would be very nice indeed. Thank you, Mrs. Bishop."

The woman smiled, holding out her hand toward a round table with two chairs. "I shan't be a moment. I just have to nip down to the cellar—the wine keeps cool there."

The chair Maisie settled into was old and rickety, and would have been quite uncomfortable without a cushion. A fresh cloth had been laid across the table, and Maisie wondered if Mrs. Bishop had been anticipating her arrival, waiting for her to set foot across the threshold so that she might waylay her with an invitation to enjoy a glass of wine together. Perhaps she welcomed the company of another woman, someone also alone in the world. Or she might be a nosy one, looking for a bit of gossip. But Maisie could not help but feel that almost everyone she'd met since arriving in Gibraltar had his or her own agenda, and that they were all connected to Sebastian Babayoff's death. And when she thought of the investigation, she felt as if she were trying to hold on to jelly with her bare hands.

"There we are. It's from Italy, this one. Not very cool, but enough for us to enjoy a drop or two." She closed her eyes and wrenched the cork from the bottle, her exertion audible. "I thought I'd have to knock the top off for a minute there!" She poured the wine into glasses, pushed one toward Maisie, and set the bottle between them before sitting down. "Chin-chin, my dear."

Maisie clinked her glass against Mrs. Bishop's and took a sip of the wine. She tried hard not to wince.

"It's a little tart, isn't it? Not as smooth as I prefer, but I don't suppose I shall notice by the second glass."

"It goes down very nicely, Mrs. Bishop."

"So what did you do today, my dear? You seem to be walking a lot, I must say."

Maisie smiled and took another sip. "Yes, I like to walk. As long as I keep my hat on, I find it, well, restful, in a way."

The woman regarded her for a few seconds, then leaned forward, narrowing the space between them. "Are you feeling better?"

"I'm feeling very well, Mrs. Bishop. Very well indeed."

"Oh, I almost forgot. I saw that man again today—the one who came before. He was just walking into Mr. Salazar's café. For a moment I thought he had seen me, and I was about to give a little wave, but he just walked in. Funny that, isn't it—when people seem to look right through you without noticing that you're there?"

Maisie thought that MacFarlane would not have missed a trick, and would have known Mrs. Bishop was within striking distance of accosting him in conversation on the street.

"I am sure I will bump into him, Mrs. Bishop. This is a small place, after all."

"It might be small, but people flood into Gibraltar in waves—off the boats, across the border, sailors, soldiers. One minute it's quiet and then there'll be a *whoosh* and you wonder what's been washed up. They say most of the refugees have gone back now, but I wonder about that—there still seem to be a lot more people around than before. I wouldn't want to go over to Spain, not with all that business going on."

"I would imagine it's quite dangerous in places." Maisie took another sip of her wine, and when Mrs. Bishop reached across to replenish her glass, she shook her head and covered the rim with her hand. "Oh, better not. I will never get up in the morning if I drink any more!"

"Well, I think I'll sit here and enjoy the shank of the day, Miss Dobbs, then I'll get myself a bit of something to eat. I have some chicken—would you like some on a plate, with a little salad perhaps?"

"I would indeed—I'll come down and pick up a tray, in about an hour, if that's convenient for you."

"Right you are. I'll have it ready for you."

Returning to her room, Maisie put down her bag, kicked off her shoes, and lay on her bed. Images converged in her mind's eye—Arturo Kenyon at the beach with Rosanna, then the aircraft overhead, and the sickening fear that rose inside her—oh, how she hated that sound, the engine coming closer, droning on like a hornet loose from the nest and intent only upon harm. Next the break-in attempt at Miriam Babayoff's house, in broad daylight. The assault on her home had failed, and a community had gathered to protect the two women who lived alone.

Maisie sat up, dragged her bag onto the bed, and took out the photographs, placing each carefully atop the counterpane so as not to damage the images. Three people were shown clearly, only one of them not known to her. As the shutter closed in the last photograph, Vallejo was captured moving toward the camera—toward Babayoff. To stop him, perhaps? But why? Did he not want to be in the picture? Or did he not want someone else to be photographed? Was he scared for himself, or for Grillo's niece? He could have been trying to warn Babayoff. Was that it? Or was it simply that he had been a gate-crasher, and did not want to be discovered as such? Maisie remembered that Sebastian was at the time earning his money by attending social engagements, selling prints later to party guests or to the press. But might he have been at this particular party in another capacity?

She went to the wardrobe and lifted the other photographs from her case—the ones Babayoff had taken while out on the fishing boat with Carlos Grillo. She wished she had a means of enlarging the print—she believed it could be done, indeed, she remembered asking for a similar process once before, while on a case in London. But that was in London—she was sure such a procedure was beyond Miriam Babayoff's capability.

Maisie took up the magnifying glass. What was it that Babayoff had caught in his viewfinder, that day out at sea? A fishing boat low in the water? An ocean creature? No, though she had read that there were cetaceans in these waters, whatever had attracted Babayoff's attention seemed inorganic, not a giant of the natural world. She flicked through the photographs and with the magnifying glass squinted again at one of them. Yes, she was right. It could only be a submarine. And though she could only see part of a marking, she was sure it was not British.

Maisie pored over her case map the following morning, with sun streaming through the window and a gentle breeze flapping the lace curtain back and forth. She was surprised not to have seen or heard from Kenyon for a couple of days. Perhaps his superiors had discovered his alliance with Maisie—though, on second thoughts, she was sure they had known of the arrangement from the start. Then again, here was the fact that the job was done—Lord Julian had received word of her whereabouts, and whoever he had asked for a report may well have considered the remit complete. Of course, there was still MacFarlane to consider, and to see. Today might be the day. In fact, she knew it. His presence had at first been like a small irritation on the skin. Now it was becoming a welt.

She continued to work on the case map a little longer, using the colored pencils to link names and write out questions as she phrased them in her mind. She made a mental list of tasks she wanted to accomplish in the course of the day, and then leaned back to look at her work. It satisfied her, this challenge, though there was something missing. She would have liked another person to talk things over with, someone to echo her thoughts or contradict them. She had entertained a fleeting hope that Arturo Kenyon might have been a worthy companion, though she understood that he was playing the game with two racquets, bouncing a ball between her and the Secret Service.

There was something about Miriam Babayoff as well—a feeling that there were elements of her recounting of events that did not quite fit—like a door that seems closed but then clicks open as one walks away, for the lock is not true.

Maisie realized she had felt a frisson of connection with Vallejo. Had she been seeking a mentor since Maurice's death, someone who seemed wiser, who possessed a greater understanding of the world? Her mind drifted to Dame Constance, the Benedictine nun who had counseled her on many occasions, and then to others in her circle, those she loved, though perhaps she had never voiced her affection.

Minutes later she realized she had been daydreaming, staring into the whiteness outside the window. She was thinking of Billy and Sandra, and the office in Fitzroy Square. The daffodils would be gone by now, but she imagined the trees resplendent in their canopy of cooling green. She walked across to the window as if to recall the many times she'd stared out of the floor-to-ceiling windows in the office, allowing herself to simply gaze at those trees in the square while she thought about a case, considering the next steps to take. How was Billy? What had happened to the Compton Corporation, now that James was dead?

She put her hand to her mouth but could not stem the tide of tears. What was she going to do with herself, now that the future—a future she had finally embraced—was gone? Was she pursuing a wild goose chase to deflect her thoughts from what had become of her life? Yes, she admitted, of course she was. She sat down on the bed. Well, perhaps it wasn't exactly a wild-goose chase, but without doubt she had latched on to the death of Babayoff as if it were a line thrown across the turbulent waters of early widowhood, a line she would use to pull herself through the pain of a terrible loss, onto land. And what was that land, if not a reason for staying alive, for putting one foot in front of the other? She looked toward the wardrobe and the bag with the leather straps and lock, and she knew it would be so easy, so simple, to swallow the pills one by one, until the bottle was empty. Then it would be done. She would drift away, held aloft in her dreams until she reached the heavens.

She rested her head in her hands. Such a thing was not the solution. Apart from anything else, there was Frankie to consider, her beloved father. No, she had to keep going, to cast out her line to the next island, and the next, and the next, until the ocean was crossed and she found herself once more on firm and steady ground. But in the meantime, anywhere she might find herself seemed to be a dangerous place. Yet she felt no fear. Surely the very worst she could imagine had already happened.

M r. Salazar greeted her in the usual manner when she entered the café, taking her hand in both his own, asking her about her morning, telling her the weather would be good, with no wind today, though perhaps a little cloud. He pointed out which pastries were the most delicious, one sweet delicacy after another. Then he drew closer to whisper.

"Your usual seat is taken, Miss Dobbs."

The interior of the café was usually shaded, but it had seemed even darker when Maisie first came in from the street, her eyes slow to adjust after the bright sunlight outside. She looked across to the seat below the mural.

"I think the gentleman is expecting me. My usual coffee with hot milk, please. And you can choose which pastry I'll have for breakfast—it'll be a surprise."

Salazar gave a short bow, and Maisie turned toward the mural. A tall, heavyset man stood up to greet her.

"Maisie Dobbs. It's been a long time, hasn't it?"

"Robbie MacFarlane—it has indeed. I have heard that I should no longer use a Scotland Yard title, so I presume plain mister will do."

MacFarlane stepped aside to allow Maisie to sit on the more comfortable padded banquette, while he took a chair on the other side of the table. He unbuttoned his jacket for comfort. "Mister, perhaps, but please, Miss Dobbs—never *plain*."

Maisie smiled, though it was brief. "What can I do for you, Mr. MacFarlane?"

"What can you do for me? Well, for a start, you could leave this place and return home. People are worried sick about you—people who care and who happen to be in places where they can make my life a bit of a misery."

"I think that's something of an exaggeration, don't you think?"

MacFarlane sighed. "Margaret—Lady Compton, if I may—"

Maisie cleared her throat, shook her head, and nodded toward Salazar, who was approaching the table with a tray. He set down the cup of coffee in front of Maisie, and the plate with two pastries between them.

"Oh, heavens, I don't need any extra sweetness, do I, Miss Dobbs?" MacFarlane patted his stomach and smiled up at Salazar.

"On the house, sir, but only because you're with the lady," joked the proprietor. He smiled, then turned to greet another customer.

"Well, Maisie, here you are, staying in a less than salubrious area, in a small guest house when you can well afford to stay at the Ridge Hotel, and into the bargain getting yourself involved in the coshing of a two-bit purveyor of snapshots."

Maisie sipped her coffee, determined not to be goaded. She had worked with MacFarlane on several occasions, and their conversations had always been akin to a tennis match, the quips volleying back and forth. It seemed that even in her bereavement he would allow her no quarter.

"As you know very well, I discovered the body of Sebastian Babayoff, and—"

"And why didn't you bloody leave well enough alone?" interjected MacFarlane.

Maisie raised an eyebrow. "Oh, that'll do wonders for Mr. Salazar's business, I'm sure—and it'll look very pretty on the front page of the *Times*: 'Former Scotland Yard Man Disgraces Britain, Shouting in Gibraltar Café.' "

"How about 'Peer's Daughter-in-Law in Garrison Lockup'?" It might have been a quip had MacFarlane not been frowning, his words uttered with a cutting edge.

"For what crime, Mr. MacFarlane?"

"I don't need one. Neither does Brian Huntley."

"Oh, I might have known. And is Professor Vallejo one of your happy little trio of musketeers too? Or perhaps with Dr. Francesca Thomas you're a quartet." Maisie picked up her coffee and sipped, looking over the top of the cup at her companion.

MacFarlane's jaw tensed, and he pressed his lips together. His complexion became chalklike. He stared at her as she set down her cup and tore off a piece of the pastry.

"This isn't a game, Maisie. This isn't a game, and you shouldn't even be in the ring. Leave now, while you can."

"And what does Huntley say?"

MacFarlane looked away, as if to control his temper.

Maisie nodded slowly. "Right, I think I understand. Huntley wants to let me have my head, and to just follow on and see where I might end up—danger or no danger. But you don't think it's a good idea, because you have come to the conclusion that I am a loose cannon bereft of all good sense and focus because I'm a woman in an emotional—what . . . state?"

"You're grieving, Maisie. You're vulnerable. You were pegged for work with Huntley even before you knew who he was, and I can see why—you've proven yourself to me, dear girl, on more than one occasion. But not now. Go home. Rest. Spend time under your father's wing."

Maisie blushed, and tears sprang to her eyes. She looked down until she felt them subside, then looked up at MacFarlane.

"No. No, I will not leave. There's a grieving family, and they cannot rest until they have answers. I know something else is going on, and I know who's involved."

MacFarlane leaned back in his chair. "I knew that would be your answer."

"Then why did you even ask?"

"I had to make sure."

There was a silence between them.

"Had to make sure of what?"

MacFarlane sighed. "I don't know, Maisie. I had to make sure you had at least some semblance of a plan, of a clear purpose for doing this—though you can't fool me, lass. This interest is to deflect your attention from widowhood."

Maisie looked down at her hands, clenched before her on the table. "I lost more than my husband, you know."

"Aye, I know, lass." MacFarlane reached across and placed his hand on hers. It was large, broad, the fingers long and thick; one hand covering both of hers, as if he were bestowing a benediction.

After a moment, MacFarlane withdrew his hand, and they reached for their coffee and sipped. He put down his cup and picked up one of the two jam-filled pastries. "None of this cutting off little bits here and there—this is how I do it." And with two bites, he had finished the pastry and was wiping a handkerchief across his chin and hands.

Maisie could not help herself; she laughed. "You don't change, do you, Robbie?" They had slipped into first-name terms. She held her open handkerchief to her chest and picked up the remaining pastry. "I don't want to get the jam all over this clean blouse."

"That's the way, lass. You get that down you—you could do with a bit of weight on those bones." MacFarlane paused, then leaned forward. "So give me a thorough account of what you've done and what you know."

The sudden direct question took Maisie aback, though she did not give herself away. Instead she took up her coffee cup and finished the beverage. MacFarlane looked at his watch. Maisie cleared her throat and recounted her investigation, with one omission. She did not want the policeman to know about photographs taken by Babayoff just prior to his death—as much as she respected him, she knew the man before her was working for the Secret Service now, with the threads of connection to Scotland Yard remaining unsevered.

"And I haven't seen Mr. Kenyon since," she concluded.

"No, you wouldn't have," replied MacFarlane, looking at his watch again.

"Do you have a prior appointment?"

He shook his head. "No, but as I always say, the sun must be over the yardarm somewhere in the world, so I think it's time for a wee dram." He turned and summoned Salazar, who came to his side at once. "Have you by any chance got an eighteen-year-old malt whisky languishing behind that bar of yours?"

Salazar smiled and nodded, placing a hand on MacFarlane's shoulder in a conspiratorial fashion as he laughed.

"Good man. I don't believe the lady will partake, so if you could bring me a good two fingers' worth in a glass, I will be a happy laddie." MacFarlane looked at Maisie, raising his eyebrows as if daring her to comment. Salazar walked at a clip toward the bar.

"What about Kenyon?" she asked.

"I do believe he was no longer quite as useful as he had been—he had found you, reported back to the necessary quarters, and was poking here and there, not getting anywhere and on the verge of upsetting the local bobbies. He was playing above his rank, Maisie—though the death of this photographer fellow seems to have that effect on people. Mr. Kenyon is at the moment engaged in some carpentry work at the garrison. Windows, I believe. It necessitates him staying in quarters there."

"I see." She paused. "I've told you about Babayoff and Carlos Grillo—but what do you think was going on? You haven't told me why you're here."

"And I don't have to, either."

Salazar approached, holding the bottle of single-malt whisky and a glass. With a flourish he pulled out the cork and poured to the level indicated by MacFarlane, his broad two fingers held alongside the glass.

"I think I ought to go now," said Maisie.

"No, lass. Sit a while, I haven't finished yet." MacFarlane sipped from the glass. "Aye, that's better. Now, then, where was I?"

"Telling me you didn't have to inform me why you're here, or why you're interested in the case of Sebastian Babayoff."

"That I was. Now then, I am here with several things in mind. First, the question of refugees, of wrongdoing on the part of both the locals and those refugees and how that could affect the security of our great British Isles. And when I am in a British territory, or a protectorate or a colony, or whatever you care to call any place where the Union Jack flies, I am concerned with that little overlap between control of the criminal element and the more shadowy work of our brethren working in intelligence."

"Then what about the submarine?"

"You're sure it was a sub?"

Maisie nodded and sat back. "You knew already, didn't you?"

MacFarlane said nothing.

"Oh, for heaven's sake—" Maisie turned to gather her bag. "I'm fed up with cat and mouse. I have things to do today."

MacFarlane was about to respond when Salazar could be heard greeting another customer, with some enthusiasm. Maisie looked up. It was Professor Vallejo. His face was drawn, his eyes dull. Salazar's ebullient mood was replaced by a questioning look as he grasped the other man by the hand. Maisie strained to catch their conversation, but she could only hear Salazar repeating a single phrase—*Dios mio, Dios mio, Dios mio*—time and time again.

"What's going on over there?" asked MacFarlane, turning to follow Maisie's gaze.

"Shhh. I don't know. It's something serious, though."

At that point, Vallejo looked across the café, saw Maisie with Mac-Farlane, and turned to leave. Salazar held his hand to his heart and pressed a handkerchief to his eyes as he stepped back toward the bar. Maisie squeezed out from the banquette and approached Vallejo, stopping him at the door.

"Professor Vallejo, what is wrong? Why is Mr. Salazar so upset? And you're in shock—what has happened?" She laid a hand on his arm.

"It's only just coming in, the news—the tragedy."

"Tell me—what tragedy? What has happened?"

"In Guernica—close to France, in the north, a town in the Basque country. They've attacked, the Germans and the Italians—the Fascists. They've bombed the marketplace, killed men and women and children, little children, women, blown to pieces. The town is no more. They came yesterday, flying in and out and in and out, dropping their bombs. Those bastards were looking down, looking down at the market, at the people going about their business, and they killed them in cold blood."

Maisie held her hand to her mouth, feeling the nausea rise. "The bombers—they flew over Gibraltar, didn't they? They came in over here—I saw them."

"Then you saw the murderers of children, Miss Dobbs. The killers of little ones, of mothers who fell on top of their young to protect them, and fathers torn to shreds before their families. Women and children in the marketplace."

Maisie struggled to imagine such a scene. And when the picture flickered into her consciousness, she felt a searing pain, as if the scar had come alive.

"Maisie. Maisie, lass, sit down. You've lost your color." MacFarlane was at her side, his arm around her shoulders. He pulled out a seat for her, and as her feet became solid on the ground once more, the pain subsided. She sipped from a glass of water brought to her by Mr. Salazar, his eyes red.

"Where did the professor go?" asked Maisie.

"On his way, lass," replied MacFarlane. "He left after giving you the news."

And Maisie remembered, then, that it was as she felt the blackness encroach upon her vision, and as her knees began to fail her, that MacFarlane had come to her aid. Vallejo had looked up, nodded his acknowledgment toward her rescuer, and turned away. He'd walked out of the café, and was gone.

CHAPTER TEN

MacFarlane offered to accompany Maisie back to her lodging, but she declined. "I just want to take the air for a while, walk around," she said.

MacFarlane reached inside his pocket and took out a notebook and short pencil. He licked the end of the pencil, reminding Maisie of a tic-tac man at the races, pegging his prices and calculating a punter's winnings. He scribbled a telephone number.

"Salazar here has a telephone in his caff, so if you learn anything at all that you think I should know about, well, this is where you can find me. If I am not there, a man named David Shaw will take a message. No one but David Shaw."

Maisie nodded.

"And you've told me everything you know?"

"Yes," she replied, shivering.

"Terrible news, that—about the bombing," said MacFarlane, looking along Main Street toward Grand Casemates Square.

"Brings it all back, doesn't it?" said Maisie.

"Aye, it does that, lass. But we both came through it, that's the thing to remember—we came through it." He placed his hand on her shoulder. "And you'll get through this, Maisie, through your bereavement. You're made of stronger stuff than you will ever know." He cleared his throat. "There, you're making a wet rag of me, your ladyship." He gave a brief grin when Maisie shook her head, then was serious again. "I know you've kept a few things to yourself, but remember what I said, Maisie—this is not a game. Murder never is, and war definitely isn't, and when the two come together, we all have to look out for ourselves and the people we trust. Keep me informed, Maisie. I want to know what you're up to." He nodded, and walked away.

Maisie wasn't sure what she should do. Her plans, gathered in a neat mental list before she left Mrs. Bishop's, were now driven asunder, scattered across her mind like a fallen house of cards. At a slow walk she set off from Main Street in the direction of Governor's Parade and St. Andrew's Church, which with its no-nonsense solidity drew Maisie in. She felt at once a need to be tightly held and a desire to be alone, with just herself and her thoughts for company. Stepping from midday sunshine into the cool shadows of the building, she sat down in one of the pews.

The professor's description of the Guernica tragedy was alive in her mind's eye—the searing scenes of men, women, and children cut down, torn from limb to limb and from one another. These images of the terrors visited upon the Basque town mingled with memories of France and Flanders, of communities destroyed by shelling, innocents killed. *But they are all innocents,* she could hear Maurice saying. *They are all innocents.* She thought of the bombers attacking Guer-

nica, flown by men who'd descended low enough to gain a close view
of their quarry, men who had seen the children playing on market day
and then taken their lives. She wished she could ask Maurice, "Where
is the innocence now?" And he would no doubt have an answer. She
wished she knew what it was. Then, for the first time it occurred to
her that perhaps John Otterburn was right after all. Bombers were
the dark crows of death, sent out to lay their eggs on an unsuspecting
world. Perhaps a new, swift fighter aeroplane would destroy bombers
even before they could unleash their weapons. Perhaps, then, James
had not died in vain.

Maisie was aware that others were coming into the church to pray,
drawn into a place of worship by the news now spreading through the
community. She closed her eyes once more and tried to marshal her
thoughts. MacFarlane had given away little, and for her part she had
kept a few things to herself. She knew she wanted to find Babayoff's
killer on her own. In fact, if she were honest with herself, it was more
than something she wanted, it was a deep-rooted need. If she could
not attribute blame for her husband's death, by God she would bring
back the killer of a young man who had been—she had no doubt—
punching well above his weight.

She thought of Babayoff's photographs, and in particular the
image of Grillo's niece, clad in silk, her look sultry, her laugh wide,
drawing in the blond man as if she were a spider who had caught a fly
in her web. But Maisie was sure of one thing—the man was no help-
less insect. Everything about his stance, the lift of his chin, the swept-
back hair, the hand raised to make a point, the easy way he stood
before the young woman, spoke to a confidence that he would prevail
in anything he tried, whether it was his work or the art of seduction.
It was as if he knew he was engaged in a game, and it was one he was
playing on top form. She studied the photograph in her mind's eye

and considered the sport in progress—but who were the players, and what was the point?

Maisie raised her head and made ready to leave the church. She looked at the people around her, and then, as she glanced across the aisle, felt herself unable to take another step. A fair-haired man was sitting alone in the neighboring pew, staring in the direction of the altar, his face without expression, his gaze unblinking. Maisie looked away, then gathered her bag and stepped sideways along the pew to the aisle, where she bowed her head in respect and walked toward the door. She glanced back once, and at that moment, she noticed two things. One, that the man was now looking directly at her. Second, she could have sworn that the man sitting in the half-light at the back of the church was Robbie MacFarlane, yet his attention was not on Maisie—it was on the fair-haired man in the immaculate gray suit, his hair swept back from his blue eyes. He was the man in Sebastian Babayoff's photograph.

And as she stepped out once again into the hot sunshine, she realized that the man reminded her of James, though James, she knew, would have been praying for the souls of dead children and their grieving families. James had warmth and compassion. It would not surprise her had she been told that the man in the opposite pew was a man whose veins ran with cold blood.

Catalan Bay was warm by the time Maisie arrived. Fishermen were now working on their boats or talking in small groups. The scene reminded her of Hastings and Dungeness—it seemed to Maisie that women in fishing communities wore the same uniform, garbed in black. It was as if they expected disaster each time a boat with their menfolk aboard set out into the waves.

The women working on the nets informed her that Rosanna was probably at the market, or looking after her mother, who was unwell. No one offered to tell where the young woman lived, or to let her know that Maisie had come to see her, so Maisie turned away, prepared to come back another day. She tried to find shade as she walked—not at any speed, for she was weary. She was looking up to see if a cloud or two would lumber across the sky to offer respite, when she saw a man watching from the rocks above the beach ahead. She slowed, and squinted. If she were not mistaken, this was Arturo Kenyon—who was clearly not engaged in carpentry at the garrison.

Kenyon gave no indication that he had seen Maisie. His beige cotton trousers flapped in a breeze that had blown up, and his white shirt-sleeves were rolled to the elbows. He wore no jacket, though a fisherman's cap shielded his eyes from the sun. He brought down the binoculars, then looked out to sea and lifted them to his eyes again. Then, in a decisive movement, he lowered the binoculars, turned, and began walking away. Maisie scrambled up the rocks and set out on the path behind him, keeping well back so he would not see or hear her. He seemed intent upon making good time. Perhaps he knows I'm here, thought Maisie. Then she considered how strange it was that the man who had followed her, stalking her movements to report back to his Secret Service employers, was now being followed by his quarry.

Soon the path changed, becoming a narrower thoroughfare. Maisie realized this was not a route back into town, but was leading to another part of the looming rock that defined Gibraltar. Undergrowth increased, and it was not long before they were in an area of sandy brush land, populated by stunted trees as the path began an ascent. She could still see the white shirt ahead, though she kept well back. Just in time, Maisie stepped behind some bushes as Kenyon slowed

and looked around him. He seemed to be listening, his eyes searching the path he'd just walked. As he turned back to the path, Maisie
peered out from her hiding place. Instead of continuing, he extended
his hands in front of him, as if to grab something. She heard metal on
metal, and put her hand to her ear to try to distinguish the sound. The
noise changed: metal scraping across rock. Kenyon was no longer on
the path.

It was a risk, but she stepped out from her hiding place and slowly
crept toward the point where she had last seen Kenyon. Then she saw
it: a barred gate, looking as if it were the entrance to a prison cell. But
this gate led not to a gaol but to a cave—and it seemed that Arturo
Kenyon had vanished inside.

The rusty padlock was one of substance, and had she not taken
care, it would have clunked when she lifted it. She could see how a
man's hand could slip through the bars from inside the cave, to open
and close the padlock, as long as he had a key. She suspected, too,
that there were bolts on the inside—bolts that could be drawn back
from outside the gate only if a person knew where to place his hand to
wrench them free.

Maisie was thankful that sound echoes in a cave; she could hear
voices, coming closer. She turned and ran on tiptoe to her former
hiding place, crouching amid the low, leafy shrubbery. She heard the
scrape of bolts drawn back, the rattle of chain and padlock, followed
by the cast-iron gate screeching against the rock, a sound that set her
teeth on edge. The grating was repeated as the gate was closed and
secured again, and two people—or was it three?—walked along the
path flanking the place where she crouched to avoid detection.

She leaned forward to better identify who was there, when a sound
distracted her and she stumbled, cracking branches as she avoided falling onto the path. She closed her eyes and held her breath.

"What's that?" said Arturo Kenyon.

"Is anyone there? Show yourself, now—I've got a gun, and I know where the trigger is." It was a woman's voice.

At that point, two mischievous Barbary macaques scrambled past Maisie, jumping through the undergrowth and wrestling onto the path.

"Kill a harmless monkey, would you?" asked Kenyon of his companion.

The woman gave a half-laugh. "It's just as well I'm on my toes, Kenyon." Her voice had an authoritative tone, as if she were speaking with a subordinate. And perhaps she was, though until recently Maisie would never have taken Miriam Babayoff for a leader.

Maisie listened to the footsteps becoming more indistinct as the pair walked away, most likely, she thought, in the direction of town. The monkeys came back, rolling in the sandy path, then leapfrogging each other toward the gate. She was about to crawl from her hiding place when she heard a voice from behind the gate that led into the cave.

"Vete, alimana, vete." Go *away, vermin, go away.*

It was a man's voice, and the language was Spanish—Maisie knew just enough of the language to understand what he had said, and though he seemed annoyed by the monkeys rattling the gate, he was not distressed. It did not sound like a call for help, and Maisie imagined he had retreated inside the cavern.

The half-light of early evening cast shadows across whitewashed houses as Maisie walked along Main Street toward the series of narrow streets that would bring her to the door of Mrs. Bishop's guest house. People were beginning to make their way home or to a restaurant for supper. Two military policemen passed, walking toward Grand Casement Square. She watched as they approached a policeman of the local constabulary, who lifted his hand to his helmet, an acknowledgment—perhaps grudging—of a shared task: the keeping of peace and upholding of the law.

Her mind was blazing with questions. Who was the man in the cave? Had he been incarcerated against his will? Was he guarding something, perhaps? As she approached the heavy oak door that would lead to the welcoming courtyard of Mrs. Bishop's guest house, Maisie realized that when she had imagined a spider web earlier, perhaps it was because she now felt as if she were caught in its threads. She had only herself to blame—she'd clambered onto this web of her own volition.

THE TRAGEDY OF GUERNICA
TOWN DESTROYED IN AIR ATTACK
EYE-WITNESS'S ACCOUNT

From Our Special Correspondent
Bilbao, April 27th, 1937

> *Guernica, the most ancient town of the Basques and the centre of their cultural tradition, was completely destroyed yesterday afternoon by insurgent air raiders. The bombardment of this open town far behind the lines occupied precisely three hours and a quarter, during which a powerful fleet of aeroplanes consisting of three German types, Junkers and Henkel bombers, did not cease unloading on the town bombs weighing from 1,000lb. downwards and, it is calculated, more than 3,000 two-pounder aluminium incendiary projectiles. The fighters, meanwhile, plunged low from above the centre of the town to machinegun those of the civilian population who had taken refuge in the fields.*

M aisie sat in the guest-house courtyard, a pot of tea and a rack of toast in front of her, alongside a butter dish and a small glass bowl filled with homemade marmalade. Mrs. Bishop had prepared breakfast for her guest and then gone to the shops to buy groceries, so Maisie was alone. She only occasionally saw other guests, though she heard footsteps at night and in the morning; sightseers on their way out and returning after visiting one of the local restaurants, or bringing food back to eat in their rooms. Mrs. Bishop seemed easy with her customers, as long as they were no trouble to each other or the neighbors. Maisie suspected that no visitor had ever remained at the guest house for such a length of time, and having paid with cash in advance for a month-long sojourn. In another week she would pay for a further fortnight, perhaps more, and see where it went from there.

This morning, though, as she read the copy of the *Times* that Mrs. Bishop had left for her, she felt as if she had seen the bombers overhead once again, and felt a shiver when she recalled shadows the aircraft had created across the sands of Catalan Bay. What must it have been like to witness this murderous attack? And for what purpose was it mounted? Surely the world would not sit back and watch while Fascist Germany and Italy bombarded a civilian population?

She closed the newspaper and put it to one side. A shaft of sunshine had moved across the table, as if it were an ancient sundial. Maisie realized she was staring at the arrowlike shadow, struggling to plan her next steps. There were threads everywhere. She did not want to walk all the way to the fisherman's beach again, so instead mapped out another tack for her day—she would visit the Ridge Hotel, and then come back to Miriam Babayoff. She wanted to ask about Arturo Kenyon—or, as Mrs. Bishop would say, "little Artie Kenyon." It seemed to her that Gibraltar was large enough, with its transient population living alongside those who had spent their lives here, that people with disparate backgrounds might never know each other. She remembered growing up in Lambeth, where there were families living several streets away that she had never passed on the street. Yet in the village of Chelstone, so far from Lambeth's grime, everyone knew everyone else for miles around, and local gossip took a mere snap of the finger to whip from one end of the High Street to the other.

Maisie finished her tea, read the article again, and folded the newspaper. She looked at her watch, and collected up the crockery and remains of the toast. She had eaten only half a slice, all appetite gone in the wake of the news from Guernica. She stepped across the flagstones to the door that led into Mrs. Bishop's quarters, intending only to set down the tray on the kitchen table. It was as she was walking back out into the sunshine that she stopped to look at framed photographs on the wall of the narrow passageway. She had always liked to look at photographs, at happy scenes of family life, or a wedding in a long-gone era. She had visited so many people over the years, stepped into grand country mansions, Mayfair townhouses, and small terrace cottages in the damp streets of London's backwaters. She had looked at posed photographs and informal snaps, and taken her own with a camera bought in a pawn shop, framing her more successful photographs and putting them in pride of place on the wall, as if to create a family around her. Somewhere in her suitcase was the last photograph of her and James together, his arm around her, his hand atop her belly. She had been laughing. When she looked at that photograph for the first time, she had seen her own happiness and ease. It had all come right. And then it all went terribly wrong.

Mrs. Bishop and her husband made a handsome pair. There was a wedding photograph, and then one later—a professional photograph taken in a studio while on a holiday, she suspected—along with other family photographs. Without doubt, in her younger days the landlady had more of a Mediterranean look about her, even though now she appeared like so many British housewives of her generation. Maisie suspected that Mrs. Bishop had worked at the latter.

As Maisie walked toward the door leading out onto the courtyard, so the photographs took her back in time. There was Mr. Bishop in the uniform of a policeman—taken in London, it seemed, for Maisie was sure the door behind Bishop was an entrance into Scotland Yard. Then another of him with several uniformed colleagues, and finally a photograph in which he was still outside Scotland Yard, though he was in civilian clothes. And that is where Maisie stopped. The man with him was almost unrecognizable—he was younger, for a start, and there was a bit more hair atop his head. Maisie cast her eyes toward the photograph of policemen in uniform, then opened the door to shed more light along the passageway. There he was again, looking for all the world like a boy. Maisie wanted to laugh—she would love to bring this up in conversation. But for now she was concerned.

Hearing the heavy outer door whine its way open, Maisie stepped out onto the courtyard, closing Mrs. Bishop's door behind her.

"May I help you, Mrs. Bishop?" she asked the woman, who seemed to stagger in with her collection of hessian bags filled with groceries.

"Oh, you are a dear—here, if you could take these two, then I can balance again."

Maisie took two bags from the woman's right hand, allowing her to lead the way back into her quarters.

"I took my tray through, Mrs. Bishop—I hope that was all right."

"You needn't do that, Miss Dobbs—you're my paying guest, and you should be waited upon." The landlady bustled in, along the passageway and into the kitchen.

Maisie followed, setting the two bags on the table. "There. Now then, I'll be out most of the day, Mrs. Bishop, back late this afternoon."

"I'm making a fish stew this evening—you can have supper on a tray in your room, or join myself and a couple of other guests here in the courtyard—it should be a fine evening, but you might need a cardi."

"Right you are, Mrs. Bishop. I think I might remain in my room, if you don't mind—but I'll let you know."

"It doesn't do to lock yourself away on your own, Miss Dobbs. You've got to keep on living." Mrs. Bishop blushed as she finished the sentence, as if realizing she'd revealed that she knew more about her guest than she should.

"Well, this will never do," said Maisie. "I have things to get on with. I'll see you later, Mrs. Bishop." She smiled and turned away, trying not to walk too quickly out into the courtyard. She went up the stairs to her room, locked the door behind her, and leaned against it while she caught her breath.

Mrs. Bishop knew about her past. The woman knew she had been bereaved and that she had lost more than a husband; she was sure of it. But then, was it surprising, really? Though the light was poor and the photographs grainy, it was clear that Mr. Bishop had known Robert MacFarlane very well indeed. In fact, given the youth of the fresh-featured MacFarlane, the friendship was long-standing.

And Maisie was now convinced of something else. When she had made inquiries at the Ridge Hotel regarding small guest houses in Gibraltar, situated in easy walking distance of Main Street and Grand Casemates Square, Mrs. Bishop's name had been at the top of the list. At the time the clerk had smiled in a manner that unsettled Maisie, though she conceded that it did not take that much to unsettle her. But she wondered, now, whether Mrs. Bishop had been in touch with the hotel and asked them to give Miss Dobbs her name. If that were so, it meant that MacFarlane had been notified when she left the ship, and had guessed that she would not want to stay long in the luxurious hotel. That in turn meant she had been taken for a puppet on a string—and been followed for longer than she had at first thought.

As she made notes on the case map, she wondered how badly she had been manipulated. Was she *meant* to come across Babayoff's body almost immediately after the crime had taken place? Was she being directed into the case, or away from it, as MacFarlane maintained when he warned her that she should go home to England? Could she be a dispensable, and therefore useful, small player in a game she had yet to understand? Certainly MacFarlane did not appear to anticipate pressing her to take a significant role—he would have considered her too vulnerable and therefore too great a risk. Or was she just in the wrong place at the wrong time and therefore, with her background, a huge problem for the Secret Service—for whom MacFarlane was now working, as far as she knew?

She made some additional notations in her book, then folded the case map, hiding it in the chest of drawers underneath her clothing. It was time to leave, though given how much had happened, she thought she might drop in to Mr. Solomon's haberdashery shop. She wanted to talk to him about the lock on Miriam Babayoff's door.

CHAPTER ELEVEN

The Ridge Hotel was late-morning quiet when Maisie walked up the hill, cutting along a path that ran parallel to the hotel. She stopped twice to look out across the sea, then back toward the white building with its name emblazoned across its front in large modern letters. From a sailing boat, it must appear like a ship en route, plying the waves to cruise an exotic clime. It looked, well, *rich*, as if the only guests would be the well-heeled, those who wanted to rise above the ordinary people of the world, to be acknowledged at their elevated station. And that was why she had wanted to find another place to stay, one that did not demand that she be a certain person, to act in a given manner or have this attitude or that opinion. She'd never be invisible, staying at such a magnificent hotel—but had she made the right decision in going to Mrs. Bishop's guest house? Perhaps, from another perspective, she could have been less obvious among so many more people, even if they were different from her. There again, Maisie had to admit that she might be giving too much weight to that which separated her from others, rather than seeking out connections—but it had become her way, this retreat once again into the shell of aloneness. Solitude was her soul's hermitage.

Paths had been cut through the grounds to create places for guests to walk alongside rockeries, through arbors casting cool shadows, up steps, and around the perimeter of the hotel. Maisie wanted to talk to a clerk at the reception desk, but perhaps not someone she had spoken to before. She looked about her before entering the palatial main lobby, with columns seemingly plucked from a Greek temple, holding up the ceiling as Atlas supported the world on his shoulders. The floor appeared just-polished, gleaming under the lights. She had chosen her time well—there was no one else in the entrance hall, no guests rushing to check out or in, or inquiring where they might find a certain type of restaurant or a good sightseeing expedition. She suspected that some of the guests were wealthy Spaniards, at the hotel for an extended sojourn until they felt it safe to return home. The thought brought images of the Guernica tragedy to her mind, which she banished as she approached the clerk. The man looked up and smiled. She recognized him as the person who'd been on duty when she'd first arrived to register at the hotel, and also when she left for Mrs. Bishop's guest house. His jet-black hair was swept back and oiled, his skin seemed dark against the bright white of his collar, and his tie was knotted just so. He pulled at his shirt cuffs to adjust them as Maisie approached.

"It's Miss Dobbs, isn't it?"

"Oh, well done for recognizing me—though forgive me, I cannot remember your name."

"Mr. Santos, at your service. Will you be joining us here again, Miss Dobbs?" He flicked a page of the register, ready to check the availability of a room.

"Not quite yet, Mr. Santos. Perhaps I will come back for a few days before I leave Gibraltar. We'll see. In the meantime, I wonder if I could ask you about Mr. Babayoff, the photographer."

"Oh dear, yes, of course." Santos rubbed his forehead. "I had forgotten that it was you, poor lady, who discovered him following the terrible attack."

"Yes, it was me, and—"

"Miss Dobbs, I know why you are here—you are trying to put this terrible thing that you have seen behind you, to banish it to the past. If you wish, I will walk with you, if it makes you feel better." The man bore a look of genuine sympathy, his eyes glistening as if he shared her tears. "Goodness knows, Mr. Babayoff was known to everyone here, and we all liked him. A terrible, terrible thing."

"It was, yes. But please do not think of leaving your station here—I am perfectly at ease walking the paths on my own. I do, however, have a question, if you don't mind."

"Of course, Miss Dobbs—anything I can do to settle your heart." The clerk put a hand to his chest to demonstrate his compassion. "But I must warn you, we have been asked not to discuss the tragedy. It is for obvious reasons. We cannot have our guests disrupted by this event, and now the dust is settling upon it, we must let it rest. You understand?"

"I just wondered about a couple of things. If you prefer, we can move over here to the end of the desk, just in case someone comes along." She looked around. "It seems pretty quiet to me, and I'll soon be away for my walk."

The man's expression changed, and Maisie thought not for the better. His eyes lost their welcoming sparkle, and he seemed coated with indifference, his willingness to help diminished. Then he appeared to correct himself, and at once his smile was as warm as it had been when she first approached him.

"Please, continue. I will assist if I can."

"I know Mr. Babayoff came here to photograph parties, sometimes at the request of guests who wanted a photographer to record a special occasion, which accounts for his presence. However, I want to know—had you noticed any refugees loitering in the area?"

"Certainly I've seen a couple—there is wealth here, and many poor souls have flooded in with nothing, barely the clothes they stand up in. We've tried to deal with the situation with some delicacy—we do not want to seem harsh, in light of circumstances, but the well-being of our guests comes first." He paused. "I have heard that a couple of refugees were seen earlier, but sent on their way with some money to help them. They were asked not to return—after all, if summoned, the police would not be handing out gifts of coin."

"I see," said Maisie.

"Will that be all?"

"I have one more question. Before the attack, before Mr. Babayoff left the reception where he was working, he took one or two photographs of a man and woman talking—they certainly looked as if they were having a very nice time. The man was quite tall and had either blond or gray hair, though he wasn't old—probably in his thirties. He had quite sharp features, and his eyes—I would imagine they were blue or gray. He was with a woman—a very beautiful woman—with long, dark hair and dark features. Her hair was swept to one side. Do you happen to recall them? I remember you telling me you were working at the hotel that evening."

The man said nothing, then inclined his head. "May I ask how you know this, about the guests?"

Maisie hid her fluster—she had inadvertently given herself away. "Forgive me, I should have said—I recently met a couple of people, also guests of the hotel who had been at the party. I think they've left

Gibraltar now—in fact, didn't the SS *Beatrice* sail yesterday? So, yes, they've departed . . . but they mentioned seeing Mr. Babayoff, and that he took quite a few photographs of the couple. I simply wondered who they were—they might have observed someone following Mr. Babayoff from the hotel."

"Of course, I see now. But no, I don't remember any gentleman or woman such as those you describe. I'm not saying they were not there, but you will appreciate, as a member of staff when the hotel is busy—and I shouldn't admit this—one face looks much like another, after a while."

Maisie smiled and held out her hand. "Not to worry—it was just a thought. It's been bothering me, you see, that a man could be killed, leaving relatives to grieve his loss, yet with no knowledge of his attacker's identity. I wanted to see if I could find out anything."

"Best left to the police, Miss Dobbs." The man picked up his pen and smiled past Maisie. Two new guests were arriving, followed by a porter carrying their luggage.

"Yes, best left to the police," agreed Maisie.

She turned away and walked toward the doors, but before she reached them, she glanced back at the clerk. He had summoned a junior clerk and moved to use a telephone some distance from the new guests, who were loudly proclaiming their room preference. Maisie stepped around the edge of the entrance and moved with barely a sound in the direction of the far end of the desk where Santos was now dialing. The pillars were useful in hiding her approach, though he was looking down at a piece of paper he had unfolded and placed before him. Maisie positioned herself so that she could listen to the conversation, but not readily be seen. Santos continued to consult the note. Maisie strained to hear.

"Yes. Thank you. I can wait." There was a pause, then Santos gave a half-smile, as if greeting whoever was on the end of the line in person, rather than via telephone. "You were right. Yes, she came back. Yes. She asked about a man at the party, a man that Babayoff had paid some attention to with his camera—he was with a woman. No. She said she was told about them by another couple she'd met who were at the hotel when it happened—but apparently they've sailed now." He gave a half-laugh. "I thought so too, sir. Yes. Very well. Thank you, Mr. MacFarlane." He replaced the receiver on the cradle and turned toward the other clerk, who was smiling up at the new guests and telling them that of course they could have a room with the best view of the sea.

Maisie closed her eyes and shook her head, then slipped out of the hotel and back onto the path. She wanted to look at the place where Sebastian Babayoff had been killed. Just one more look.

She felt as if a cold blanket had enveloped her body as she walked along the path, closer to the place where she had discovered the mutilated body of Sebastian Babayoff. She recognized the exact point not by any sign of blood spilled, but by the very cleanliness of the area, as if acid had been poured liberally across the path, causing the ground to become almost white in places. She knelt down, touched the soil, and closed her eyes, reliving the evening she had first meandered along the path, soon after she had disembarked with no purpose but to become lost. She wanted nothing more than to slip away, as if she had never been known by anyone. Even that recollection grieved her now, because it was her father's face that came to mind as she stood in the bright sunshine, thinking of the terrible pain he would feel if he knew how she was enduring an existence rather than living a life. Soon she would have to square up to the business of sailing for England, if only to see the face she loved so very much behold her in return.

Breathing deeply, Maisie sat on the low wall that flanked the path. First she looked behind her at the bushes where she had discovered the Leica camera. Was she sorry she had not handed it over to the police? No, she wasn't. It would have been either destroyed or put away somewhere, never to be seen again. Not that she blamed the local police—far from it. She believed strings were being pulled to control their actions. It was a delicate time, after all, and they had enough on their plates, dealing with the local civilian consequences of a war too close for comfort.

It was while she was sitting in quiet contemplation, that she realized she had no idea what Babayoff looked like. When she encountered his body, it was twilight, a time when shadows crossed a grainy darkness, and even a silhouette seemed larger and without human form. She had taken his hand, felt the fading warmth as life ebbed from his body, and seen enough to know his face was bloody and bruised. A heavy weapon must have been used to beat him about the head, along with the knife used to run through his heart. The perpetrator had been intent upon his quest—which Maisie believed was not to rob, not to take money or valuables. Sebastian Babayoff was, she was sure, the intended target—there was no mistaken identity. She thought her investigation—if it could be termed such—revealed activities on the part of the photographer that were too unpredictable for her to take what she encountered of him at face value. His job was to see the world from a narrow perspective, to reveal smiles of joy, or a view of the ocean, or a landscape to be remembered. With his camera he laid down moments in time for posterity—images never to be forgotten because they were there forever, in black and white and shades of gray.

And as Maisie sifted through these thoughts, as she imagined Sebastian Babayoff, again, going about his work, she realized she could not search for the truth in black-and-white evidence, but in the grainy shadows, among the people who lurked there, hoping never to be seen. If that were so, then who was the man with the fair hair, photographed with Carlos Grillo's niece—who at the time bore little resemblance to the black-clad young woman from a family of Genoan fisherfolk? There was something so very blatant about his demeanor, as if he were afraid of no one.

She realized, then, that she didn't really want to come face-to-face with that man, though she anticipated it might well happen.

Jacob Solomon was behind the counter of his haberdashery shop when Maisie entered, the bell above the door clanging as she crossed the threshold. She quite liked the musty warmth in the store, as if particles of fabric had come together to reignite a childhood memory long forgotten. There had been a haberdashery shop not far from the small terrace house where she'd lived with her mother and father. She remembered being sent to the shop by her mother to buy a new transfer for her embroidery. There were many intricate designs, and Maisie knew that the greater the challenge, the more it might draw her mother's mind away from her pain. This was before her father had spent every penny he earned taking his wife to doctors he hoped might hold a cure. Maisie would step into the shop, the floorboards dark underfoot, flanked by chests of drawers full of all manner of linen and cotton goods, many wrapped in paper to protect the delicate materials from from damp and dust. The proprietor would bring out a selection of transfers for Maisie to pore over. There were flowers and paisleys, and embroidery transfers depicting Little Bo Peep and Jack and Jill. "Well, your mother will have her hands full with that one," the proprietor would say, and Maisie would nod and hand over the requisite number of pennies, telling the woman that she did not need silks; her mother had a basket full of thread in many colors. Maisie wondered, now, where all those squares of her mother's fine embroidery had gone. Had her father burned them in his grief? Or had they been given away, or sold to bring in a little more money? There was medicine to pay for, toward the end, medicine that took her mother into a netherworld, as if she were standing at a station in gauzy light, waiting to pass into another life, free from pain.

"Miss Dobbs. Miss Dobbs!"

Maisie looked up at Mr. Solomon. "I do beg your pardon—seeing all the beautiful embroidery reminded me of my mother, and I was just thinking of her."

Solomon smiled at Maisie and beckoned her closer. "Memories come out of nowhere, sometimes, don't they? Like a splinter long in the finger finally rises to the surface. Pluck it out, and the pain goes— and you realize there has been discomfort all along, but you have lived with it."

She was taken aback by Solomon's words, delivered with a quiet empathy as if he too knew the bittersweet melancholy encountered in recollections of someone much loved but now gone.

"And before I forget," he added, "the young couple were very, very grateful to you for the photograph. They wanted to meet you to express their gratitude, but I said I would pass on the message—I did not give your name, as you requested. I know you value privacy."

"Thank you, Mr. Solomon. Yes, I am grateful, and I'm glad the people have their portrait."

"What can I do for you, Miss Dobbs?"

Maisie looked behind her. She had walked into an empty shop, but it was her habit to double-check. She pointed to the sign on the door, which had been turned to inform passersby that the shop was open. "May I? Just for a moment?"

Solomon nodded, walked to the door, flipped the sign to Closed, and came back to the counter, where Maisie was standing. "This is about Sebastian?"

"In a way," said Maisie. "I wonder, how is Miss Babayoff now? She suffered quite a shock when someone tried to break into her house."

He sighed and nodded. "It was a great distress to her—more so than for her sister, who is bound to their home."

"Do you have any idea who might have done such a thing?"

He shrugged, reminding Maisie of a schoolboy reprimanded by his headmaster.

"Mr. Solomon?"

"If I were to guess, I would say that there is something in that house belonging to Sebastian that someone else wants—that is all. It might be a photograph revealing a man with a woman other than his wife, or a son at a party when he should have been at work. Sebastian was loose with that camera—if you don't already know that about him."

"I have seen an assortment of photographs he'd taken, and I understand what you mean." She paused, looking at an embroidered tablecloth laid across the counter. She took the fabric between thumb and forefinger and felt the soft linen against her skin. She looked up at Solomon. "Did you like Sebastian, Mr. Solomon? I've realized I don't know a lot about him—about what he was like, or who he was as a man. He was clearly a talented photographer, but—"

"People admired his work—myself included, as I told you before—but, if I am honest, he was no more talented than anyone else with a camera in his hand. Sebastian just wasn't afraid to look for the work, or put himself forward for a commission. He was always first to the ships when they came in, taking photographs of people to put on the mantelpiece when they return to their homes in dull places. No, if you want to know who has the talent in that family, you need look no further than

Miriam. Her embroidery stands out. Her paintings show such feeling, and if you put a camera in her hands, you will see something you would never see in Sebastian's work. And there she is, stuck with her sister upstairs, banging on the floor with her stick so Miriam can run up and down at her beck and call. Miriam could have been married one hundred times, I am sure, but Sebastian would not give his permission—he said he needed her at home. The last thing he wanted was to be left with Chana upstairs, summoned whenever she pounded the floor with her broom handle."

Maisie said nothing at first, taken aback by the passion in Solomon's voice.

"I had no idea," she said, at a point when to remain silent would have been ill-mannered. "It must have been very hard on Sebastian and Miriam, that their sister was cut down by such an illness."

"Cut down? You know what I think, Miss Dobbs?" Solomon took a step toward Maisie. She remained in place as he continued. "I think it's all up here." He tapped the side of his head. "As much as I feel sorry for her, I think that woman could move her legs as much as you or I, but she chooses not to. It's easier to lie in bed all day, painting and embroidering, than get up and do more. Look at poor Miriam, running backward and forward, doing everything that needs to be done—cooking, cleaning, looking after her brother and sister—and still she can embroider and paint and sell her work. Sebastian had her developing his film, running his errands, delivering to the hotels, back to the ships, bringing home the money, making sure he had supplies—and that wasn't easy, as you can imagine." He took a breath and rubbed his head. "The poor girl. She deserved more respect when he was alive, and she deserves better now."

Maisie cleared her throat. "You must have known the family your whole life, Mr. Solomon."

He nodded. "I am a little older than the three Babayoffs, but we all know each other here—in our community, among our people. And we know each other in Gibraltar—if not always by name, then by sight. Among all the visitors, the soldiers and sailors, you know who belongs."

"The men came to Miriam's aid very quickly, after the locks were broken."

"She is afraid, Miss Dobbs. I came directly I was summoned, and I brought in men to help. We went there without delay, and we made her house as secure as a fortress. We keep an eye on her—I am only a matter of yards away, and I will go to her at once if I am needed."

"You are a good neighbor, Mr. Solomon," said Maisie. She smiled at the man, but noticed he seemed pained by her words. She fingered the cloth once more, then looked up at Solomon. "May I ask, are you married? Do you have a wife at home?"

He shook his head. "No. I have family, but no wife."

"I believe I might have asked this question before, but some days have passed. Do you have any idea who might have killed Sebastian Babayoff? I am sure it was not a refugee."

"He probably annoyed someone. He could be very annoying, pestering. For all his so-called talent, he thought he was somebody. It would not surprise me to know that he was playing with fire, and he was burned by being too close to the flames."

"I see," said Maisie. "I thought I would call on Miss Babayoff today—I expect she's home."

Solomon shrugged.

"Tell me, Mr. Solomon, might you have seen Sebastian with a taller man, blond or gray hair, very sharp features? His hair is usually combed back from his face, and oiled, I would imagine. And I daresay he is well dressed, though I may be wrong."

164

Solomon looked at her, and after a few seconds shook his head. "No, I don't believe so—but there are many visitors here, it would be easy to miss someone. That's the enigma of this town, you know—we know each other, yet know so few people passing on the street, though that depends upon the time of year. As I said before—too many people passing through. And swept-back hair—you've surely seen the soldiers and sailors, they always look like they've doused their hair in brilliantine before they leave the barracks or their ship."

Maisie laughed. "I have noticed, Mr. Solomon—but they're only lads. They want to have some fun and look like matinee idols in their uniforms, I'm sure."

"Hmmph!" He looked at his watch.

"Yes, you'd better open up again—you should have a goodly number of visitors, Mr. Solomon. I think a ship docked today, and the passengers are probably ready to disembark and spend some money."

He gave a short bow, then held his hand towards the door. He flipped the sign, and opened the door for Maisie to leave. As they stepped out onto the street, they both looked in the direction of Mr. Salazar's café. Already the tables outside were busy, and more visitors were stopping to peer inside in search of a table.

"That's who'll be making the money today," said Solomon.

"He does a good trade, without doubt. But he's very personable, and he remembers people, which I think is a necessity in his line of work."

Solomon nodded. "Yes, he remembers people, Miss Dobbs. Perhaps Mr. Salazar can help you with your fair-haired man. I think he has quite a few German visitors."

Maisie turned up the street, setting out toward the house Miriam Babayoff shared with her sister. She would return to the café in time. As she walked along the narrow cobbled street, she knew she had much to think about. It had not occurred to her before, though it certainly did now, that Mr. Solomon was in love with Miriam, and perhaps more than a little protective of her. And there was something else. She had said nothing about the man with the oiled and swept back fair hair and fine features being German—in fact, she had never attributed a country of origin to him at all. Why, then, had Solomon assumed his nationality? And though these thoughts bothered her, it was true that she had come to the same conclusion herself.

CHAPTER TWELVE

Maisie strolled at a deliberate slow pace toward Miriam
Babayoff's house. She wanted to be alone with her thoughts
before a new conversation, and perhaps fresh ideas, cast
them into disarray. There were times she felt her energy rising, but
still, she was in the midst of a long physical and emotional recovery,
not over it by a long chalk—especially when it came to the renewal
of her spirit. After losing her new family in as long as it took for a
small aircraft—no bigger in the distant sky than a butterfly in her
hand—to fall to the earth, she had felt crushed in every part of her
being. Even after the necessary arrangements had been made with regard to her husband's remains, and even with Frankie and Brenda and
Lady Rowan at her bedside in the Toronto hospital, she had found it
hard to hold a thought in her mind for longer than it took another to
shatter it. Then, at her insistence, they had left, sailing for England
without her. And discharging herself from the hospital, she'd traveled
to Boston, hoping for the chance to claw back something of herself in

the company of people who knew she required a certain latitude, so that she might, perhaps, begin to fathom who she could possibly be in the world, if she made up her mind to be part of it once more. It was in the return to India that the soft healing of her soul had begun, and she could have remained there, easily. She could have lived in the bungalow set within the hills of Darjeeling for a long time. She might have stayed there forever. But Brenda had called her home.

Reflecting again, she acknowledged that it had been in the application of her mind that she had come through war's aftermath and the loss of Simon all those years ago. It was in *application* that she had risen from the ashes to become of some account to herself. And it was in getting to know the dead, especially, that she had tasked herself with witnessing the path through the myriad different responses that conspired to ignite terror—envy, greed, love, want, grief; they were many and powerful.

She knew very well that she had not given due consideration to her first lesson from Maurice. It had been issued on the very first day of her apprenticeship, when she accompanied him to the scene of a murder. He had taken time to inspect the body and, it seemed, to ask questions of the very air around him, both then and later in the day, when she assisted at the postmortem. "There is more to this than the wound that killed a human being, Maisie. We must spend time with the dead in silence, to try to hear them. Then we ask questions, not to gain an immediate answer but to let them know, even in their netherworld, that we care enough to give voice to our lack of understanding. We begin, Maisie, to study the dead not simply as a medical inquiry of the cadaver, but by applying the forensic science of the whole person. So I ask, who is this man? Who was he as a boy, and how did the child come to this? Who did he love? And who loved and hated him, perhaps in equal measure? There is never just one victim when a body is found—it is never singular. Who are the other victims, and which one has committed the crime of murder?"

At that moment she missed Billy Beale, her former assistant. Maurice had never quite approved of Billy, believing Maisie should have taken on someone with an intellect to match her own, or with some experience in their field of endeavor. But Maisie trusted Billy and knew he was a gem, often coming up with the right nugget of insight at the right time, and always without realizing his contribution. She stopped on the narrow cobbled street and leaned against a building in the shadows, remembering their conversations, and imagining what Billy might say about Babayoff.

"What I reckon, Miss, is that this 'ere Babayofff was a right dark 'orse." Billy's distinct accent was loud in her mind, and she smiled. "What you've got to remember is that he had it all his own way. Right, you've got a point, he had to look after them sisters, but they both pulled their weight, didn't they? And that younger one—well, I reckon she was the brains. I mean, look at her. Sharp? I bet she is too. And it wouldn't surprise me, Miss, if she weren't pulling the wool over our eyes. I'm not saying she is, but it wouldn't surprise me."

She listened to the voice in her imagination. The seagulls ceased to wheel overhead, and instead she could hear the clear yet gentle rustling leaves on the canopy of trees in Fitzroy Square.

"I think we should find out what else Babayoff was up to. You can't tell me he was going out on that boat to just take a few holiday snaps because he liked the water. No, Miss—people like him don't get murdered unless they're up to something. I mean, look at it—there's him and that girl, the fisherman's niece, both of them done up like two penn'orth of hambone at a party in a big hotel—especially her! She could've been a film star you see at the pictures, what with her standing there with that blond bloke, and him looking all Leslie Howard and smiling at her. If he's an Englishman, I'll eat my hat. No, Miss, we've got to dig a lot deeper into this one, or we'll never sort it all out. I mean, we make some guesses, as a rule, but you'd be the first to say we need more to go on before we stick our necks out."

"Oh, Billy," said Maisie to the air around her. "I could do with a dose of your solid feet on the ground next to me."

She knew she had been remiss. If Maurice, her dear mentor, were standing at her shoulder, he would be seconding Billy's comments and reminding her that if she'd learned so little about the dead man, how could she ever know enough to find and identify his killer? She had applied herself only enough to circle the field of tall grass that obscured the truth. Her case map resembled so many forays into the pasture and then out again, paths that led only a short distance, then to each other, and not to the center, to the essence of what had come to pass. Now it was time to stride in. It was long past time to bring her whole heart to the investigation, instead of leaving something of herself behind, curled up, lost, grieving, and afraid.

Miriam! Hello! It's Maisie Dobbs. I was passing and thought I would drop in to see you." Maisie waited while the bolts were drawn back and the chain released. As was her habit, Miriam looked both ways along the street before allowing herself to smile and welcome Maisie into the kitchen.

"How is your sister today, Miriam? I am sure it was good for her to get out into the sun the other day, even though the circumstances were horrible for you both." Her pause was brief, and only to catch her breath. "Look, I hope you don't mind, but I would like to see Sebastian's darkroom again—may I? And I want to know more about him." She stepped toward the door leading onto the landing.

Miriam folded a dress she had been in midst of repairing and nodded. "Yes, of course." She pulled aside the curtain, unlocked the door to the landing, and led Maisie down to the cellar. There she flicked a switch on the wall, casting weak light across the room. Maisie stepped toward the chest of drawers and looked back at Miriam.

"I'd like to look through Sebastian's photographs. Would you help me?"

Miriam shrugged. "If I can, though I must return to my work soon, Miss Dobbs—I have customers waiting."

"This shan't take long."

Maisie opened the first drawer, taking out a collection of prints, which she placed on the table in the center of the room, drawing an angle-poise lamp across to better see. She flicked through one photograph after another while Miriam stood beside her.

"Mr. Solomon tells me you're good with a camera too, Miriam," said Maisie, as if the question were off the cuff, something to be asked and forgotten in short order.

Miriam shrugged again. The shrug seemed to be a default mannerism for the young woman, as if she were shaking off a few raindrops. "Oh, I don't think Joseph Solomon would know a good photographer from a bad one. He's being kind."

Maisie smiled, still focusing on the photographs, in the main studio portraits, most likely taken in Solomon's shop. "He is very respectful of you, Miriam. It must be heartwarming to have such a caring neighbor just a few doors away."

The woman shifted her stance and tucked a loose tendril of hair behind her ear. "He has been very helpful. I sent a boy in the street to get him, after the business with the door. He gathered the other men, and soon it was repaired. Now everyone looks out for us."

"I'm glad. You have fine neighbors, Miriam." She paused, and lifted one of the prints. "You know, I never saw this one before, when we looked at your brother's work. Do you know this woman?"

Miriam blushed. "I have seen her before, yes."

"And you know who she is?"

"Yes, though she doesn't look like that every day."

"No, she doesn't. Why do you think she was photographed in such a manner?"

"It was probably Sebastian's idea—he liked to make people look different. Not in his studio work for customers, but in other photographs, the ones he took thinking he could sell them somewhere else."

"And what would you say about this woman?"

Miriam picked at a loose thread hanging from her cuff. "I would say that they loved each other. I knew it was so. I daresay this photograph was how he wanted to see her, and she went along with it."

Maisie nodded and placed the photographs back in the drawer.

"Miriam, are you acquainted with a man called Arturo Kenyon? He's from Gibraltar, and seems to be quite well known—he's a sort of odd-jobbing carpenter, as far as I know."

Maisie watched for some sign that Miriam was unsettled by the name, but observed nothing—no extra blink of the eye, no nervous touching of the hair or reaching for a handkerchief. Miriam's hands were steady and her manner indifferent, but not blasé.

"I've heard of him, and recently," said Miriam. "Someone suggested his name to me—the men did a good job with the repairs, but the door could be more secure, and Mr. Kenyon was mentioned as a good workman. But I could not possibly have him in our house, for he is not one of us."

"Yes, of course." Maisie nodded. "Here's what I know about your brother. That he was a good photographer, and that it had been his passion since he was given a camera as a boy. Over the years he built up this studio—and I am not sure whether he taught you, or whether you learned on your own, but you are also a worthy photographer, and you know how to process the film. Sebastian had two cameras—the larger camera used for professional work, and the smaller Leica. He would often use both on an assignment. He was carrying the larger camera—a Zeiss, I believe—when he was killed, and it remained with him. For some reason, as you know, the Leica was thrown into the shrubbery. The police have the Zeiss, and though I have not been able to confirm this, there is nothing on the camera to indicate that he pointed his lens anywhere it wasn't wanted. Not so the Leica, as we know—those photographs seem more off-the-cuff, don't they? More chancy, in my estimation. He knew that—and so did another person at the party."

"I don't know what you mean," said Miriam. "They seemed very ordinary to me."

Maisie reached into her large leather bag and pulled out the prints Miriam had developed for her. She laid them out and pointed to the face of Professor Vallejo.

"Do you know this man?"

"He seems a little familiar. Perhaps it's one of those faces one sees everywhere."

"Really? I have heard that said of a person so many times. I wonder if it's true, or if some people are very good at blending in with the scenery. To me, everyone is different—but that's just my way of seeing things." Maisie took a breath. She realized she was becoming impatient. "He is a professor of politics and philosophy at the University in Madrid, and he is also a Communist. I think he and Sebastian were acquainted."

"If he was a Communist, you may be right."

"Do you think Sebastian was only going out on the boat with

Carlos Grillo to take photographs of the clouds and the sunrise over the Rock?"

"Do you think he was doing anything more than that, Miss Dobbs? I may not leave my house often, and then only in the company of another woman to the shops, but even I have seen the number of gunboats and frigates and patrol vessels going back and forth in the Straits. What on earth do you think they could have done, without being seen by the British navy? To say nothing of the Americans, the Dutch, the Germans, Italians, Russians, and whoever else is sailing around keeping an eye on the war across the border, hoping it doesn't get any bigger or closer. Or perhaps they want it to. War is always about money and power."

"You're very well informed, Miriam."

"I pay attention, and I'm on my own for most of the day. I think about these things, and I worry about us." She pointed to the ceiling. "I have great responsibilities."

"Yes, I know." Maisie paused. "You've had a very difficult time, and it probably began long before your brother's death."

Miriam nodded.

"Let's go back upstairs to the kitchen, Miriam. Come on. I am sure your sister will be summoning you soon."

Miriam Babayoff looked at Maisie. "No, not today. I gave her a pill to help her sleep. She does not rest properly, even though she is in bed all day. It is a horrible life for her. She has only her imagination to take her beyond the walls of her room."

M aisie had not intended to show her hand, to let Miriam know she was acquainted with Arturo Kenyon. In one regard, it made sense—Communist sympathies would likely bring him into the same fold as the Babayoff family. And yet she wondered about Miriam and

Arturo, alone on a dusty path leading to a cave in the Rock. Surely that would not be an acceptable liaison in the eyes of her neighbors. Could they be lovers? Given her knowledge of Miriam thus far, she thought not. But who was the man she'd heard talking in the cave? She didn't think it was the man with swept-back blond hair—he didn't seem the type to be a willing captive. It might be someone working there temporarily, or guarding something valuable. But what? Could Miriam already know Vallejo? And what about *his* political sympathies?

As Maisie made her way along another alley, overhung by lines of freshly washed laundry, something else occurred to her—that the very broken, stilted English spoken by Miriam when they first met had given way to more articulate expression. Had this been a form of protection for Miriam, to conceal her linguistic skill at first? Perhaps now she had come to trust Maisie, she was letting down her guard. Or was she another who had cast out her line and hooked Maisie, and was now playing her for a fool?

Another question came to mind, one that she wanted to kick herself for not asking before—was it Miriam who had been burdened with the task of identifying her brother's dead body? Or had someone else stepped in to protect a vulnerable young woman from seeing Sebastian mortally wounded—perhaps a senior member of the hotel staff, or a neighbor? As Maisie passed Mr. Solomon's shop, she thought she might pop in and ask—one more question would not do any harm. But as she came alongside the entrance, she saw that the Closed sign was turned out for all to see. No one would be buying the Babayoff sisters' colorful embroidery today.

Maisie returned to the guest house. She did not want to cross paths with Mrs. Bishop—she still hadn't worked out what sort of com-

munication was going on between the landlady and Robert MacFarlane
—so she went to her room, placing a Do Not Disturb sign on the
door before closing and locking it behind her. She was tired. She just
wanted to lie on her bed for a while, and try to think of nothing.

To Maisie's surprise, almost as soon as her head touched the pillow
she fell into a deep, dreamless sleep. Wakefulness came to her slowly.
She struggled to become fully conscious, as if weights had been placed
on her eyelids. For a while she remained stretched out on the bed, her
neck damp with perspiration and her body languid with afternoon
fatigue. She was parched, her throat dry, so she lifted herself on one
elbow to pour a glass of water from the carafe on the bedside table. Her
thirst quenched, she forced herself to rise. A washbasin in the room
provided only cold water, but that was all Maisie needed to freshen
herself, splashing water on her face and neck time after time until she
felt her flesh tingle. She looked up into the mirror to wipe her skin dry
with a towel, and as she caught sight of her reflection, she said aloud, "I
am a widow." She said it again and again, not quite understanding why
she felt compelled to do so. But then she remembered Maurice telling
her that only by accepting the events of our lives can we go on—and
acceptance begins with admitting all that has come to pass.

"I am a widow, and my unborn child died."

Maisie didn't dwell on her declaration. Instead she thought of the
women and children of Guernica, of the suffering across the border in
so many towns and villages.

She turned from the mirror and opened the wardrobe door to
select fresh clothes. A black linen skirt, a white blouse, and a cream
linen jacket tailored to the hips caught her eye. She'd had the jacket
made in India, during her first sojourn in the country, before she had
given James her answer, that she would marry him. She had not worn
it for a long time, and felt defiant in bringing it out, as if she were gain-

ing purchase on another foothold out of the abyss. Putting on black sandals polished to remove scuffs and a hat and sunglasses to shield her eyes from the late-afternoon sun, she set off for the police station, where she would ask to see Inspector Marsh.

I t was a relief to be informed that Marsh was on duty when she arrived. She stated her business and was taken to a small room furnished with a table and two chairs to await the inspector. She did not have to linger in the soulless room for long.

"Miss Dobbs, a pleasure," said Marsh, beginning his greeting as he opened the door, so half of his words seemed directed along the corridor rather than at Maisie.

"Thank you for seeing me, Inspector Marsh. I appreciate your time." Maisie held out her hand, which he seemed to study before taking it in a less than firm shake.

Marsh was a tall, thin man, who Maisie estimated to be in his late thirties. It appeared his light woolen jacket may have been donned in a hurry—the cuffs of his shirt were not pulled down—and he seemed distracted.

"Well, then—what can I do for you?" he asked, indicating that she should take her seat once more. He sat down at the table opposite her.

"You've probably guessed it's about Mr. Babayoff, the photographer."

"Miss Dobbs—really, that case left my desk weeks ago. Do you have any idea what we are dealing with at the moment? Our resources are at their limit. Even though many refugees have gone back across the border, we still have a lot on our plates. Our population seems to change every day, and not always with an influx of the kind of people we would like to see on the streets. I really don't have the time to go back over old ground." He hit the table with his palm—not hard, but to make a point. "I told you when I took your statement that it was clear to us that Mr. Babayoff was—regrettably—the victim of an itinerant, someone looking for ready cash, and not a camera that would be hard to shift, hence leaving it behind. I do wish you would see this whole case from my point of view—it's so obvious, it beggars belief. Even MacFarlane thinks so."

"Ah, so you've met Mr. MacFarlane," said Maisie. She remained composed, her hands on her lap.

Marsh sighed. "Oh, please, Miss Dobbs. No cat and mouse—of course I've seen him. He was a senior Scotland Yard policeman, and he has contacts here, so we were his first stop when he came to Gibraltar. No surprises there, Miss Dobbs."

Maisie nodded. "Well, I've a simple question, Inspector. Can you tell me who identified Sebastian Babayoff's body?"

"I do wish you'd drop all this and either go home or enjoy your sojourn as a visitor to our town."

"As soon as you tell me, I promise I will not darken your door again, Inspector."

"I don't believe that for a minute, but I will tell you anyway. We prefer a body to be identified by the next of kin; after all, even if facial features have been . . . well, altered, there are other telling marks that a member of the family would be familiar with—a mole, a scar, a birthmark, that sort of thing. But Babayoff's wounds were quite distressing. He was beaten with metal of some sort—the pathologist suspected the perpetrator had both a knife and something pretty hefty, possibly a hammer, or a wrench, an iron pipe, something of that order. Given the degree of his wounds, we considered it too distressing for a woman. A man known to the family stepped forward, another Jew. He said it wasn't a woman's place to do the job. That seemed fair." Marsh sighed, pausing, as if still unsure as to whether he should reveal the information to Maisie. "His name is Solomon. He has that shop at the end of the street where the Babayoff sisters still live. Funny fellow, but serious, intent upon protecting Miriam Babayoff."

"Was he quick in his identification, or did he linger?"

"The thing is, he didn't identify the body after all—the sister was adamant. She said it was her brother, and only she could make that final decision. And she identified Babayoff by looking at his hands, both of them. Who am I to argue with that? She grew up with him. It took her barely any time at all—she wanted to be gone, and Solomon and the rabbi wanted her out of our hair and back into the bosom of the family. As soon as the paperwork was done, the body was released—it's their way, you know, to get the burial over and done with quickly."

"Yes, of course." She gathered her bag and came to her feet, pushing back the chair.

Marsh, who was now also standing, extended his hand, which Maisie took, smiling. "Thank you, Inspector. I appreciate your time and your willingness to speak to me about this matter."

"Miss Dobbs, a word of advice. Drop this matter, please. It's done. He's dead. I shall have to be honest with you and tell you that we do not have the time or the men to pursue the inquiry any longer. Leave well enough alone—and if you've any sense at all, leave Gibraltar. See a few sights, buy some trinkets, and go home." Marsh stepped back, opened the door, and held out his hand for Maisie to leave.

Maisie was loath to go back to her room. She waved to Mr. Salazar as she passed, but she wasn't in the mood for a drink, though she realized that she would rather like some company. Not the company of strangers, but of someone she knew, someone who knew her. She would love to be able to go to Priscilla's home, to be drawn into the Partridge enclave. She wondered how Priscilla's sons would approach her now—perhaps, mindful of her loss, not with their usual bubbling enthusiasm. The boys had loved James, had admired him not only for his exploits as a wartime aviator but because he was always ready to romp with them, whether they were flying kites on the Downs in Surrey or running along a beach, arms spread out, pretending to be aeroplanes.

"I sometimes think my husband is a very big child," said Maisie once, after she and James were married and before they left for Canada. They had taken a drive down to Camber Sands with the boys and Priscilla. Douglas was busy with an article for the *Manchester Guardian*, so he'd remained in town, but James was there to keep the younger ones amused, racing along the beach, throwing a rugby ball back and forth between them in teams of two.

"Oh, Maisie, they're all just big children, even my Douglas. Better that than a grumpy old man!"

And Maisie had laughed, loving James all the more as she watched him dive into a wave for the ball, at which point Thomas, Timothy, and Tarquin fell upon him, four boys soaking wet and wreathed in giggles.

Oh, she ached for so much. How angry she was at herself for dragging her feet before accepting James' proposal, for the time wasted. They could have had so much more fun together, if only she had not kept worrying about their courtship.

She realized that she had started to walk toward the village at Catalan Bay, and as she turned back, she stopped to look up at the Rock, at its magnificence, rearing up from the earth as if on course to touch the heavens. Clouds were gathering above the summit as the sun was going down, lending a glow that backlit the crags and ridges. She had heard about the many caves leading into the Rock of Gibraltar, both natural and man-made. Some were used to store munitions; others, it was said, tunneled right into the Rock's limestone core. A person could get lost inside forever, if they didn't know where they were going.

It was then that Maisie knew she would have to take a risk or two. She didn't care for caves or tunnels. Andrew Dene, the orthopedic surgeon she had courted years before, had once taken her up to the caves above the Old Town in Hastings. He told her that many of those caves incorporated smugglers' tunnels that led right down into the town, emerging in cellars under houses built in the fifteenth century. He'd teased her when she declined to venture farther, but added, "You're probably right, Maisie—I had to go into the caves once, to look at a child adventurer who'd fallen and broken his ankle. It was a dank place, dark and musty, and it made my skin crawl just being in there."

Despite her fear of being in a place that was dank, dark, and musty, Maisie knew she must return to the cave where she had seen Miriam Babayoff and Arturo Kenyon. If there was something untoward going on—and if nothing else, a man in a cave was untoward—then it would happen at night. It might not be this evening, but she would take a chance that at the very least, someone would have to come to the cave to bring sustenance for whoever was in there.

CHAPTER THIRTEEN

Before closing the door of her room at the guest house, Maisie hung the Do Not Disturb sign on the outer doorknob once more. She pulled out her leather case and carpetbag, and began to sort through the items she would need. First, her clothing—a pair of dark linen trousers and a navy-blue blouse. She unfolded her hemp knapsack and found a torch, which she switched on and off to ensure it worked—she would try not to use it, to avoid drawing attention to herself with a light. Setting her black beret, black socks, and leather walking shoes on the bed, she added her notebook and a pencil, her small binoculars, and the Victorinox knife Frankie had bought her so long ago. It still worked, though she had only used the larger blade to open letters in recent years. Finally, rooting through the carpetbag, she pulled out a wrap of dark aubergine wool. She stood for a moment, remembering. She had been alone on the veranda of her bungalow in Darjeeling late one evening, after her return from America. It was cold, though she felt nothing against her skin, and might have frozen had it not been for the boy, the one who swept the floors and brought water. He came onto the veranda and held out the shawl, bowing before her.

"For you not to catch your death, memsahib," he had said.

Maisie had taken the wrap, and remembered half-repeating his words. "For me not to catch my death." She had thanked him for his kindness and drawn the shawl around her. And she had wondered, then, what it might mean to catch death.

The shawl folded neatly into a small square, a shape that belied its ability to keep her warm. She knew she might need it, come nightfall.

Having checked each item as she placed it in her knapsack, and dressed in the clothing she had laid out, Maisie went to the window and looked out onto the cobbled street below. It appeared empty. She found her map of Gibraltar, put it in her pocket with some money, and glanced around the room. As an afterthought she pulled the bolster from underneath the pillows and laid it under the covers as if it were a body. The sign on the door would remain, and she would lock the door—the bolster in her place was only a precaution. She left the room.

Mrs. Bishop was out, probably shopping, so Maisie stepped into the kitchen to fill her water bottle and filch some bread and cheese from the larder. Now she was ready. Keeping away from Main Street as best she could, she was on her way, back through the town and then out onto the rocky paths that led up to the cave where she had seen Arturo Kenyon and Miriam Babayoff. Someone would have to bring food and water to the man incarcerated there.

She was confident that she would not see anyone during daylight, though once she had left the town's cobbled alleyways and flagstone streets, she took care to lighten her step and stop at intervals to check if anyone were following. She knew she would have to be patient, that waiting would be the name of the game—but she knew, too, that biding her time in silence was something at which she excelled.

Maisie chose a place among the scrubby trees that would camouflage her presence, yet at the same time offer a good sightline to the mouth of the cave and the path. The sun was lower in the sky now, though twilight was still a couple of hours away. She settled into a position with her legs crossed, as if she were with Khan. To bring silence to her mind and stillness to her body, she closed her eyes and began to take deep breaths, imagining she were in his room in the big house in Hampstead, the sheer white curtains billowing, caught like spinnakers in the city's summer breeze. Conscious thought was banished as she felt her mind separate from her physical self, yet she was still aware of seagulls overhead, of the chatter of birds and the soft movement of sand shifting across the rocky path.

She opened her eyes. At once her senses were alert, every sound audible, the slightest movement detected with ease. There were three people now—no, four—at the mouth of the cave, and they had brought handcarts with them. Two more approached, also pushing carts. Maisie's breath was shallow, almost as if her lungs would not fill. It was not dark, though it would be soon. Already her eyes were accustomed to the limited light. There were no lanterns along the approach to the mouth of the cave, though she could see shadows and beams within. Not a word was spoken. The six people moved as if well-orchestrated players on a familiar stage.

Maisie leaned forward and squinted. The handcarts were being loaded with boxes and, given the manner in which each box was lifted, she suspected the cargo was of some weight. She could not distinguish men from women, though she suspected two of the figures were female. She observed each person's movements, trying to identify a familiar gesture—shoulders held so, or a step taken in a certain manner. Soon she knew—Arturo Kenyon and Joseph Solomon were among the dark-clad coterie. And two women. Was Miriam Babayoff one of them? She waited.

The loading and checking did not take long—perhaps twenty minutes, half an hour? The gate to the cave clanged shut, and Maisie could hear the chain being pulled through the bars, and the padlock pushed home. The man locking the gate turned around and nodded. They were on their way—and Maisie suspected she knew their destination.

When the sound of the handcarts had faded, Maisie slipped from her hiding place. Her footfall was soft on the path, and with her keen ear she was able to keep the people and their cargo within her range of observation. If she thought she was gaining on them, she slowed her step. They were walking in the direction she had predicted—toward the fishing boats.

It was a rock on the path that caused her to stumble and lose her footing. As quickly as she could, she sought cover in the brush, as the caravan of handcarts and people ahead stopped. She heard voices for the first time since she had seen the group by the cave.

"What was that?" said a man—not Kenyon or Solomon, though Maisie thought the voice familiar—but then, perhaps not. Sound was altered in darkness.

There was silence. Maisie could feel tension in the air.

"Nothing. Probably a monkey. Vermin." It was a woman's voice, low, smooth—Rosanna Grillo.

"I'll go back, check," said a man.

"Don't be a fool—there's no time. They're waiting."

No one brooked the instruction. They continued on their way. Maisie drew herself out from under branches, feeling one score a graze across her cheekbone. She licked her fingers and wiped the blood from her face, then, turning her head to catch the sound of the handcarts, she stepped almost on tiptoe along the path.

Close to the village of Catalan Bay the group pushed their hand-carts onto the beach, where a fishing boat was waiting. Only one lantern guided them. Maisie found her way onto an outcrop of rock to watch the scene unfold before her. It was dark, and though she had become accustomed to the darkness, she had to squint to see, aided by the lantern, which flooded a person with light here, a handcart there. They loaded crates one by one onto the vessel, and when all was done, began to disperse, leaving two of the men on board.

"May God go with you," said Solomon, in a voice Maisie might not have associated with the quiet proprietor of a haberdashery shop.

"Tell them to make every bullet count, my friend," said another man.

Maisie watched as the boat was pushed into the water, soon catching the waves as she went on her way into the Straits of Gibraltar, where vessels patrolled bearing the flags of countries with a stake in the outcome of a terrible civil war. It was clear the fishermen knew where to set their course to avoid interception, but it was a journey not without risk. Nighttime fishing, but with a hold filled with weaponry and ammunition.

It was one thing to follow the group to the beach, yet quite another to retrace her steps. There was a greater likelihood of Maisie encountering one of the men and women making their separate ways home if she tried to return to the guest house under cover of darkness. Instead, she found shelter behind the rock, pulled the shawl around her, and took out her bread and cheese and water. Then she closed her eyes, and—to her surprise—dozed until just before daybreak, when she crept out from her shelter and walked back into town.

The banging began in her dream: a man with a mallet, thumping down hard on nails to secure a wooden crate—only as he wielded the tool, the crate became a coffin. Then she woke, coming back into morning consciousness by the sound of someone knocking on her door. It was not a light entreaty to greet the day but a sharp, insistent *rap-rap-rap* against the wood, as if the person on the other side had metal knuckles. Sunlight streamed across the rooftops and through her window—she had not even bothered to draw the curtains when she returned to her room. She shook her head and reached for the khaki linen dressing gown that lay across the foot of her bed. It had been made for a man, and had none of the lace or decoration of a woman's garment. It had belonged to her husband.

"All right, all right, I'm coming," she called out toward the closed door, rubbing her eyes and running her fingers through her hair.

"Miss Dobbs! It's me, Mrs. Bishop."

Maisie unlocked and opened the door. Her landlady stepped forward, but Maisie remained in place.

"What's the matter, Mrs. Bishop? You seem quite fraught."

"Well, there's a man downstairs to see you—the policeman."

Maisie felt herself become rooted. She would not be rushed, nor would she tolerate any more evasion from the guest-house proprietor.

"Mrs. Bishop, we both know his name—indeed, you've probably known Robert MacFarlane longer than I—so let's drop the pretense. I am afraid I have no patience for smoke and mirrors. Now then, let me get dressed, and in the meantime he will have to wait."

"He said it's urgent."

"Then I am sure it is, but will another five minutes hurt? I will be down shortly. Please give him a cup of your lovely coffee and tell him I am on my way."

She shook her head, turned back into the room, and closed the door behind her, leaning into the solid wood as the brass latch tongue released with an audible click.

A clean white linen blouse, a fresh walking skirt of heavy beige sailcloth, and her black sandals would be good enough for the day. She washed at the sink in her room, checking the graze across her cheekbone—there was nothing she could do about it, and it was superficial in any case. She dabbed some powder across the wound and, having applied a sweep of lipstick and placed her straw hat on her head, left the room, locking the door behind her.

MacFarlane was sitting at a table in the courtyard, mopping his brow with a handkerchief as she descended the stairs. He looked up.

"Ah, so the sleeping beauty wakes! Fine time of day for a working woman to rise from her slumber." MacFarlane rose from his chair as she approached.

"I'm on my own time, Robbie, not yours."

"Sit down, lass."

"What's going on? Why the urgent summons?"

"Walked into a door, did you?" MacFarlane pointed to her cheek.

"It seems to be my Achilles' heel—I managed to walk into a branch while meandering along one of the mountain paths. It hit me in exactly the same place where I sustained a graze falling in Hyde Park a few years ago."

"It'll not scar, I can see that."

"No, I know it won't—I've plenty of those to my name already. Anyway, you didn't have Mrs. Bishop bang at my door as if the world were ending just to while away the morning chatting with me."

"The morning's gone, lass—it's past noon." He paused. "Arturo Kenyon."

"Your lackey."

"Now, now, Maisie—sarcasm does not become you." He looked at her, sighing. "He seems to have vanished, and we—I—wondered if you knew anything about it. Thought you might have seen him on one of your walks."

"You know I've seen him—he was tasked with following me all over the place when I first arrived."

"Since then."

Maisie met MacFarlane's gaze. "I saw him last night. He was with others, on the beach at Catalan Bay."

"Did he know you were there?"

"Of course not."

"No? And why do you think he was there? And, more to the point, why were *you* there?"

Maisie allowed a long pause. "What's going on, Robbie? Why are you really here?"

"What *I* am doing here is between me and His Majesty's government. What *you* are doing here is my business."

"Here we go round the mulberry bush again. I am here because I realized I wasn't ready to return to England, and then a man named Sebastian Babayoff was ill-mannered enough to get himself murdered right in front of me—well, almost."

"Why were you at Catalan Bay?"

"I was there because I followed Arturo Kenyon, earlier."

MacFarlane shook his head. "I wish you'd take up knitting or something, Maisie, really I do."

"You're blowing hot and cold, Robbie. One minute you're confiding in me, and the next you want me to go home to my needles."

"Hmmph." MacFarlane looked away, folded his arms, and brought his attention back to Maisie. "Just tell me what you know."

"All right. I think Arturo Kenyon was engaged in smuggling. I cannot say for certain what he was smuggling, but I would guess armaments—and a fair stash at that. I last saw him on the beach at Catalan Bay. He might have left Gibraltar, MacFarlane. I believe he had Communist sympathies, and now he's gone."

"And where do you think he is now?"

Maisie shrugged. "Precisely? I have no idea, but I would guess it's across the border, then on to Madrid." She paused. "And that leads me to wonder—was he absconding with arms lifted from the garrison? Or was his cargo being shipped with an official nod and a wink?"

"We're not in the business of trading with Communists."

"And what about the Fascists?" She pointed up at the sky. "Sorry, but I couldn't help but notice the aircraft on their way to bomb Guernica. It appears they were given leave to fly over British sovereign territory—as they must have done on many an occasion to bomb men, women, and children who are fighting for nothing more than food in their bellies, books in their schools, and something of the life the gentry are leading."

"Don't go political on me, Maisie. Keep a level head, for goodness sake."

"But it's true, isn't it?"

"Arturo Kenyon," said MacFarlane, deflecting her question.

"What about him?"

"Foolish, foolish boy."

"There are always foolish boys in wartime, Robbie. I was married to one—and now he's dead." She pushed back her chair and stood up. "I have something to ask of you now."

"What can I do for you, lassie?" MacFarlane came to his feet alongside her.

"I want to talk to Marsh about Sebastian Babayoff."

MacFarlane laughed. "Oh, Maisie, what am I going to do with you? What do you want to know?"

"Specifically, I want to talk to him about Miriam Babayoff."

"Are you going to tell me why?"

Maisie tucked a lock of hair behind her right ear and squinted up into MacFarlane's eyes. "Just a feeling, that's all. I can't really say until I've spoken to him."

"All right, lass—and I'll be right there with you."

"Yes, I know—more's the pity." She met his eyes again. "What about Arturo Kenyon? What will you do about him?"

"I could wait until he turns up alive or I know he's dead, or I could send someone to intercept him—count on it being the latter. I don't want him to fall into the hands of Franco's boys, whether they're Spanish, German or Eye-ties, and I certainly don't want Stalin's mob to find him. Even tea boys know where the key to the office is."

"And as far as Spain's war is concerned, Gibraltar's Britain's guard-room, isn't it?"

"More like the entrance hall—we can see who goes in and comes out, and we keep an eye on all of them."

"I'll just get my bag," said Maisie.

Maisie waited while MacFarlane summoned Inspector Marsh. She had not missed the way in which MacFarlane was greeted at the police station. The constable on duty stood to attention, and there seemed to be a buzz about the place as soon as they entered the building. A small room was cleared for them to meet, and when Marsh appeared, MacFarlane had already taken the seat behind the desk, leaving Marsh to sit next to Maisie in front of him. He'd refused tea on behalf of himself and Maisie, whispering to her as the constable left, "We'll nip over to old Salazar's and have a decent cup of his coffee after this."

"Inspector Marsh," said MacFarlane, when they were all seated, "Miss Dobbs here has some questions for you, and I said you would be happy to assist her." He nodded at the other policeman to indicate that he was at liberty to answer.

"Miss Dobbs, how can I help you? I take it this is about the Babayoff murder. I think I explained that—regrettably—it was unlikely that his assailant would be found."

"Indeed, and I perfectly understand," said Maisie. "However, I'd like to go back to the time when Miriam Babayoff, the victim's sister, came to identify the body."

Marsh blew out his cheeks, suggesting this meeting was the most tedious thing he would have to deal with all day. It was clear from the way he crossed his legs at the ankle and wagged his foot back and forth, back and forth, that he could not wait for them to leave him alone.

"Inspector?" said MacFarlane.

Marsh uncrossed his legs so that both feet were firm on the floor. He placed his hands on his knees.

"It was fairly straightforward, as I said when I described the identification before. We'd sent a member of the Jewish police to—"

"Jewish police?" said Maisie.

MacFarlane interjected. "It was how things were done in the earlier days of the force here—there was a separate Jewish force to deal with matters arising among the Sephardic brethren. It's not formally organized like that anymore, but it's as well for people to receive bad news from a member of their own kind, so to speak." He looked at Marsh. "I assume you were about to allude to the fact that you sent one of the Jewish police to deliver news to the family about the man's death."

Marsh nodded, turning to Maisie. "It was the same with the Irish—they had their own police. Anyway, we sent one of our Jewish police to break the news to the sister—not the crippled one, but the younger one. He went to the house with the rabbi and a neighbor, a Mr. Solomon. They accompanied her to the mortuary to identify the body."

"Were you there?"

He nodded again. "I was in attendance, but not what you would call center stage—it would not be respectful of the deceased or the next-of-kin."

"What happened when she identified the body?" asked Maisie.

Marsh looked up at MacFarlane, who nodded for him to continue.

"Miss Dobbs, we've gone through all this. When you discovered the body, there was limited light. You were escorted from the scene; but when we brought in the pathologist and lights, we realized that Mr. Babayoff had received not only chest wounds but deep head and facial wounds. Miss Babayoff would not have been looking at the peaceful face of her brother, Miss Dobbs." He cleared his throat. "The rabbi had already been informed of this and had in turn explained the situation to Miss Babayoff. As I told you previously, Mr. Solomon was going to identify the body, to protect Miss Babayoff from even more distress. But she would not allow it."

"How did she identify the body?"

"She lifted the sheet close to his head, just enough to see his hair. Then she did the same to see his arm and inspected his fingers and she looked at his palm. She walked around the table to touch the other hand. Then she broke down. She wept almost uncontrollably, and said she wanted to leave. The rabbi consoled her. Solomon nodded to my colleague, and that was all we needed."

"I see. And was there any reason for you to doubt her?"

"Oh, no—she was distraught. In fact, as the rabbi guided her toward the door, she asked for some scissors. The pathologist handed her a pair, and she proceeded to snip a lock of her brother's hair, which she pressed into a locket she'd brought with her."

"And then they left."

Marsh shook his head. "Solomon remained. It is the tradition for a family member to remain in a sort of vigil, and in the absence of that family member, a person close to the deceased and the next-of-kin. We might be British here, but we're a mixed populace, and we try to respect one another's way of life."

Maisie nodded her understanding.

"The burial took place either the following day or the day after—I can check for you. As I said before, it is Jewish tradition to be respectful of the dead and those mourning by not waiting any longer than necessary to bury the deceased. We had no further need to retain the body, so it was released to the family."

"Of course," said Maisie. She glanced across at MacFarlane, who was frowning, then brought her attention back to Marsh. "That's all I needed to ask. I wanted to clarify what happened just once more. Thank you for your assistance, Inspector."

Marsh moved as if to stand, but MacFarlane remained seated.

"Miss Dobbs, I will see you in a little while," said MacFarlane. "I need to have a quick word with my colleague here."

Maisie smiled, shook hands with Marsh, who opened the door for her and called to a constable to escort her out. The door was closed behind her, and she heard nothing of the conversation between the two policemen.

She went on her way in the direction of Main Street and Mr. Salazar's café, where she was welcomed to her usual seat underneath the mural. She ordered a milky coffee and a *japonesa*. Though her eyes were heavy with fatigue, she felt something rising within her. It was the old energy, that feeling she'd have when working on a case, and it told her she was close, very close to peeling back the layers of lies and deception to reveal the truth.

CHAPTER FOURTEEN

M r. Salazar," said Maisie, when he stopped by her table to ask if she wanted more coffee, "have you seen Professor Vallejo in the past few days?"

Salazar shook his head, and as he did so, Maisie noticed a shift in his mood. He lowered his chin, cast his eyes across to the bar, and cleared his throat. "No, Miss Dobbs—he has not been in for a few days. But he is a busy man." He lifted the coffeepot and the jug that held warm milk. "Top-up, miss?"

Maisie looked at her watch. MacFarlane had indicated that they should meet at the café, but she had waited long enough.

"No, I think I've had my fill. But if you see Mr. MacFarlane—the tall man, with the . . ." She held her hand out in front of her to suggest someone who carried weight around the belly. "Could you tell him I had to leave? I have no doubt our paths will cross another time."

Salazar nodded and bowed as Maisie slipped coins into his hand, moved along the banquette, and stepped out from behind the table.

"And the professor—shall I tell him you asked after him, when he returns?"

Maisie gave a half smile and nodded. "Yes, please. Tell him I was asking after him."

On Main Street she checked Mr. Solomon's shop; the sign still informed shoppers that it was closed. More people were on the street now, and at once Maisie wanted to be in her room at the guest house, lying across her bed and staring at the cracks in the ceiling. Following those jagged lines seemed to calm her mind, and more than once had lulled her into a soft slumber, though one she would wake from with a sudden start, thirsty, her head seemingly filled with cotton wool. As she walked, she became more tired, yet she smiled again when she considered the conversation with Mr. Salazar. There was no doubt she liked the man, liked his honesty, even when he was trying to protect someone—as he had once protected her when she was being followed by Arturo Kenyon.

And where was Arturo Kenyon? Had he boarded the fishing boat, bound, she suspected, for a place along the Spanish coast where fighters loyal to the Republican army received the arms they so desperately needed? But where had those arms come from? They could not have come from the British, who—to all intents and purposes—were firm in their adherence to the non-intervention policy, and equally intent upon appeasing Fascist leaders in Germany and Italy. Or could Arturo Kenyon have acquired the arms from inside the garrison after all, perhaps with the help of sympathizers, or by greasing a few palms?

The thought of sympathizers brought Maisie back to the professor, and dear Mr. Salazar's question. *Shall I tell him you asked after him, when he returns?*

Returns from where? In her estimation there was only one place Vallejo might be at that moment, and that was Spain. Specifically,

Maisie suspected he had crossed the border and was in Madrid, likely as close to the front as he could get. But was he involved with Kenyon? Had he known Carlos Grillo? Of one thing, however, there was no doubt—the professor knew exactly who the blond man was, and so had Sebastian Babayoff and his lover, Rosanna Grillo. As Maisie walked, she recalled the moment when she saw the man in St. Andrew's Church—and just seconds afterward caught sight of MacFarlane, sitting in the shadows.

O h, Miss Dobbs—just a minute!" Mrs. Bishop came out of her quarters as Maisie began to climb the flagstone staircase to the guest rooms. Once more the house felt quiet, and Maisie wondered if other guests had left. Perhaps it was just the hiatus before more arrived to take up temporary residence.

The landlady flapped an envelope above her head. "Post for you, Miss Dobbs!"

Maisie turned and stepped down into the courtyard. "For me?" she asked, surprised. She had not told anyone of her specific whereabouts, though she had sent a telegram to Brenda the day after disembarking the ship, to let her know that she would be home in a month or so. Already her time on the Rock was extending into "or so."

"I had to go to the post office, and they asked me if I had a Miss Dobbs staying with me. The envelope was marked 'Poste Restante'—to be collected—and addressed to 'A Guest House,' with a note under the address to please deliver if possible. The staff in there know me, so they asked if you were one of my guests, and of course you are." She held out the envelope to Maisie and rested her hands on her hips. "Now you can tell your nearest and dearest where you are, can't you, dear?"

Maisie took the envelope and glanced at the return address—it was from Brenda, her stepmother. Considering the heft of it, she suspected it held not one but two letters. She sighed. *Priscilla.* It had to be her idea; sending the letters poste restante would not have occurred to Brenda.

"Thank you, Mrs. Bishop." Maisie tapped the envelope against her free hand. "Mrs. Bishop, I wonder if I could talk to you about something that's been bothering me a little."

"Why, of course, dear—let's sit down. Shall I bring us some wine? That would be lovely, wouldn't it?"

Mrs. Bishop hurried away before Maisie could answer. The landlady must have been so immersed in her adopted English culture during her marriage that she had taken on the self-important bustle of a London woman, one not living on the breadline but "comfortable"—not flush, and certainly not quite what was now termed middle class.

Maisie opened the letter to reveal two smaller envelopes inside. The one from Brenda was bulging, most likely filled with news of the village and of their new bungalow, and only at the end—lest it seem as if she were interfering in her stepdaughter's life—no doubt petitioning her husband's daughter to come home soon. Priscilla's would comprise two or three sheets of fine onionskin paper, covered with her expressive looping hand, giving the latest news of her boys, of life in London, of her husband's most recent published work. There might be a little gossip, too. With that out of the way, she would admonish Maisie, take her to task, threaten to come and get her. Such a threat should be taken seriously; Priscilla was more than capable of booking passage on the next sailing to Gibraltar and scouring the streets until she found her, after which she would not budge until Maisie—bullied and nagged—had agreed to return. Maisie smiled. Priscilla could go from being a feted socialite to a busybody in a second, and Maisie loved her for it.

"Here you are, dear." Mrs. Bishop set down a small carafe of white wine and two glasses. She poured for them both, then took her seat. "Chin-chin, my dear." She touched her glass to Maisie's, took a sip, and commented, "Letters from home?"

"Yes, it seems so." Maisie set down her glass, having toasted her companion. "Mrs. Bishop, as I said, I want to ask you something, if I may."

The woman pressed her lips into a smile and raised her eyebrows. "Fire away, my dear." She sipped again. "Fire away!"

"Mrs. Bishop, I think you have been somewhat—how can I put this—*cavalier* with the truth. And by that, I mean the truth about Mr. MacFarlane."

"Well, I'm sure I—"

Maisie raised her hand. "Let me finish." She paused for a few seconds. "You have acted as if Mr. MacFarlane was not known to you, as if you intuited by his very manner that he was with the police. You even said that you knew this because your husband was once with Scotland Yard, and therefore you could tell when a man was a policeman." Maisie sighed. "I could have said something before, but I chose not to—I wanted to see what might happen. But I have come to realize that Mr. MacFarlane was known to you for many years— the photographs in the passageway there attest to your acquaintance. And I suspect that MacFarlane—or one of his associates; goodness knows the web is complex enough here—sent you to the Ridge Hotel to ensure that they recommend your guest house to me when I inquired regarding accommodation that was a little less ostentatious. MacFarlane knows me well enough to understand my preference for simplicity." Another pause. "My question is—why, Mrs. Bishop, have you been lying to me?"

The woman took her time to respond. Finally she said, "Robbie

MacFarlane looked after me when my husband died. Bill was one of Robbie MacFarlane's men after he moved up the ranks—and Robbie moved fast; Scotland Yard was his life. When I was widowed, Robbie helped me get some money—a pension, you could call it. He said he never left his men high and dry, and that meant their families too. I'm not beholden to him, but I would do anything for that man, because he looks after his own." She looked at Maisie. "And if you didn't know that before, you know it now—that means you, too." She picked up her wineglass, took a hefty swig, and refilled it to the top.

"But why bother with all this maneuvering?"

"He wanted you kept an eye on for as long as possible without you knowing. Then he wanted you to know he was here before you actually saw him. He said that if he'd marched up to you without you having an inkling, that would be it—you'd take flight."

"He's probably right there." Maisie sipped her wine. The sun slanted across the courtyard now, so she moved her chair back into the shade. "But did he also add that he wanted to know what I had discovered about Sebastian Babayoff's death before he contacted me? Was that another reason?"

"It might have been. I'm no detective, Miss Dobbs—but I know how to keep an eye on things, and I know how to keep my mouth shut."

"And what about Arturo Kenyon?"

"What about him? I told you, I've known him since he was a little boy—lovely child, he was. I know almost nothing about him now."

Maisie nodded, swirled the wine around in the glass, and stood up. "Please, Mrs. Bishop, no more of this cloak-and-dagger business. As I said, MacFarlane knows I like simplicity. I particularly like it in the people I have to deal with every day." She smiled, as if to underline that there were no hard feelings. "Thank you for the wine—it was just what I needed. I've had a long day."

"And a long night, Miss Dobbs. No wonder you're looking so tired."
The two women regarded each other.

Maisie chose not to rise to the bait. "Indeed. If you have any soup on the stove, I'd love a bowl with bread in an hour or so. And perhaps another glass of wine too." She moved toward the staircase, and then turned back. "Oh, and if Mr. MacFarlane comes to see me, tell him it can wait until tomorrow morning."

I n her room, Maisie threw down her satchel, kicked off her sandals, poured herself a glass of water, and lay back on the bed, her head against the pillows. After some moments she sighed, sat up on the bed, and reached for the envelope bearing her stepmother's handwriting. She slipped her thumb into the edge of the sealed flap and tore the paper across the fold to reveal a letter comprising several pages.

Our dear Maisie,

Your father is sitting next to me as I write this letter to you, so it's not just from me, but both of us. First of all, we're both quite well, and your father's health is good for his years, though he had a nasty bout of bronchitis a month ago. Lady Rowan wanted to send him to the chest hospital, but he wanted to stay at home, so I nursed him through it and luckily it didn't run to pneumonia. Now, with the days getting longer and the weather brighter, we can get out into the garden a bit more and both feel the better for it.

Your father's rose garden is coming along. It's a lovely circle of different varieties in the middle of the lawn, and we've put a birdbath in the center. It tickles us to see the sparrows come down and have a flutter in the water. We also have a lovely song thrush who comes to the window every day for a few breadcrumbs. In fact, I think word has gone out that we have a bird table too, so we see them all—I don't like those starlings, though; bossy birds they are.

Lady Rowan keeps in touch, though I think she's trying not to come to the house as much as she did. When we go to the Dower House to keep it tidy, she will often walk across to see us. She's not the same woman, you know, Maisie. I don't want to go on about it, but she's broken, and so is Lord Julian. He always was a bit aloof, but you can see he's now a man whose heart has been taken from him. Sometimes I see them walking together, and it seems as if they're doing their level best to keep each other standing. You lost your dreams, Maisie, but so did they—they were so looking forward to being grandparents. I remember Lady Rowan saying to me, "I hope they come home, when the baby's born."

Your friend Priscilla is in touch a lot—I think she must telephone us every two days, asking after you. I sometimes wonder if it was a good idea, having that telephone put in, but your father said you'd want us to have one. I can't see the point in them, myself—nothing but trouble, and a postcard or a letter is just as good. People do natter on so. Anyway, I told her that I was taking a chance in sending you a letter, especially not knowing a definite address, and I offered to put one from her in the envelope, so she sent a letter on to me and I've enclosed it here. She told me about poste restante.

We hope you come home soon, Maisie. As I said before, you don't need to tell anyone you're here—we'll look after you. Your father misses you very much, you know.

With our love,
Your Father and Brenda

Maisie closed her eyes and pushed back the tears, remembering again—and it was a recollection that haunted her now—when she was a maid in the Ebury Place mansion. She had been walking from one room to the next, on an errand perhaps, or with her wooden box of dusters and polish in hand, and she had stopped when she heard singing coming from Lady Rowan's sitting room. She peered through the half-open door and saw James Compton in the uniform of the Royal Flying Corps, dancing with his mother, waltzing around the room together while he sang.

> He'd fly through the air with the greatest of ease,
> That daring young man on the flying trapeze.
> His movements were graceful, all girls he could please,
> And my love he purloined away.

Rowan had adored her son. Maisie discovered later, when so much had come to pass in her life, and when she and James had started tentatively courting, that an older sister had been lost in childhood. She had died while trying to save her brother's life at a woodland swimming hole on the estate. It was likely that Lady Rowan's strength of character and ebullient no-nonsense approach to life had carried the family until their grief subsided. Now there was little to encourage a woman who had lost both her children. It was clear Lady Rowan needed Maisie at home as much as, if not more than, Frankie Dobbs yearned to have his daughter back. As Maisie thought about Brenda's words, a feeling of responsibility settled upon her, but instead of willing her back to England, it weighed upon her. She feared that much would be expected of her, and she felt she had so little to give.

She picked up Priscilla's letter, her name written with such boldness on the front of the envelope:

Lady Margaret

Maisie rolled her eyes. She wished no one had ever known her real name. It was the housekeeper at Chelstone who had persuaded her to have the wedding announcement issued with the name on her birth certificate. It was a name never used, not even on her enlistment documents in the war. She had always been Maisie. Margaret was someone else, though she sometimes wondered if it might not suit her better. Maisie was, after all, girlish and carefree. It was strange that as she became more of a Maisie, so the name her mother chose for her had been revealed. And now Priscilla was using it, though she knew her friend's intention was not respect, or an idle tease. It was meant to goad her—into replying, if nothing else. Priscilla could be an annoying woman at times.

> *Dear Maisie,*
>
> *I, for once, do not know where to start. Of all the people in the world—well, in MY world—who I trusted never to do anything rash or worrisome, it was you. Miss Do Everything Right Dobbs. And now you are absolutely acting with no respect for your own safety, and thus (dare I say it) for the peace of mind of those who love you dearly. That includes me, and you know me—I'll be perfectly blunt, whereas your dear stepmother (and she is a dear) will probably dance around and not say right to your face (and I wish I could)—COME HOME NOW! What do you think you're doing, Maisie? It's one thing to want to go into hiding, and quite another to put yourself into a dangerous situation—and where you are right now is too close to someone else's war, for my comfort at least. I am a mother hen, Maisie, and I want all my chicks under my wing, even the big ones. You are my dearest friend, and I want you where I can see you. Apart from anything, you*

*cannot be well. How long did the doctors say it would take for you to
recover? Over a year, and that is just your body. I know Dr. Hayden
was very concerned when you left their home—I even placed an
international trunk call to them to talk about it. Thank heavens for the
telephone, that's all I can say!*

*When do you intend to grace all who love you with your presence?
I think an answer is deserved, if for no other reason than respect for
our deep sister-like friendship. If you don't want anyone to know you're
here apart from your parents and I (though I do think the Comptons
are entitled to know, and they will keep all others, including those
awful newspaper people, away from you), then I will collect you
from Southampton and drive you immediately to Dame Constance
at Camden Abbey. I have been in touch with her—though goodness
knows, she doesn't hold me in any high esteem—and she said you
would find comfort and healing if you sought refuge at the abbey. As
far as I'm concerned, the only Benedictine I want to have any proximity to is a drink, not a nun, but each to their own, and I think it
wouldn't be a bad thing, just for a little while, to rest at Camden as a
means of easing you into life in England again. You have gone through
so much, Maisie—do not deprive those who love you of the chance to
take care of you.*

Maisie put down the letter and pressed her fingers to her eyelids.
Perhaps it would be a good idea, when she returned, to go to Dame
Constance. She continued to read. There was news of Priscilla's sons
and her beloved husband, with tales of her middle son's sailing exploits, and her older son's pleas to be allowed to take flying lessons.
At this, Maisie shuddered. The younger son seemed happy to follow
the elder's lead, with Priscilla complaining that he rarely took off the
leather aviator's helmet he had been given by "Uncle" James. Priscilla

complained that informing her son that his hair would fall out hadn't had the slightest effect.

I suppose I should bring my diatribe to a close. I wanted to tell you that we saw the Otterburns a few days ago, at a dinner party—rather boring, actually. I tried to avoid them, but Lorraine took me aside when the ladies retired to the drawing room. She said they had worried about you very much, and that if I was in touch (and I would bet they know exactly where you are), then I was to tell you that John is at your service to send an aeroplane to bring you home to England at your convenience. I said I would convey the message if at some point I knew your address, but that you had been very unwell and you were now resting overseas. I can only say, Maisie, I hope you are bloody well resting! Oh, and one more snippet—that daughter of theirs, Elaine, is engaged to be married—rather soon, I believe. The gossip is that it's rather a "have to" marriage, and that sometime in December a birth announcement will be made and Lorraine will be talking about how they're so pleased that mother and "premature" baby are doing well. · Premature, my foot!

Maisie stood up and walked to the window, not bothering to read Priscilla's final signing-off, with much love expressed. A crushing weight of anger and grief was pressing down on her chest. So Elaine Otterburn—the dilettante daughter who should have been flying instead of James, but had instead been nursing a hangover—was to be married soon and was expecting a child. Maisie felt as if she were on the edge of the precipice again, looking down into the abyss, panicking, at once fearful of the slide and compelled to give in to it, as if to be buried were the very best thing that could happen to her.

She turned from the window, opened the wardrobe door, and was tugging at the straps of the leather suitcase, ready to reach inside for the bottle of pills—the small round white pills that would lift her up and take the pain away—when there was a knock at the door.

"Miss Dobbs! Miss Dobbs! Your supper!"

Maisie took a deep breath. Another knock at the door.

"Miss Dobbs? Are you there?"

She cleared her throat.

"Yes, Mrs. Bishop. Just a minute! I'm just washing my face. You can leave the tray there if you like."

"Right you are," called Mrs. Bishop. "Oh, and dear—can you hear me? Well, Mr. MacFarlane came again. I told him you were resting, and you'd see him tomorrow, in all likelihood."

Maisie had stepped across to the washbasin and was running water.

"Thank you! And thank you for the soup!"

"All right then. I'll put it down outside your door."

Maisie turned off the tap and heard the woman's steps as she descended to the courtyard. Only then did she turn on the tap again to splash water on her face. She looked at her reflection in the mirror. Her eyes were red-rimmed and her cheeks were hollow, despite having caught the sun in recent weeks. But there was something there in her eyes, something she recognized, as if it were an old friend to be welcomed. It was a certain resolve, a knowledge that the only way she could fight her way out of the abyss was to prove something to herself—that she could be brave, that she could survive and be strong. She had looked in the mirror so many times, hoping to see something of her former self.

She pushed the leather case back into the wardrobe and opened the door to the landing. She picked up the tray, brought it into the room, and set it on the table. Soup, fresh bread, a wedge of cheese, and a small carafe of wine. The food would comfort her, and the wine would lull her to sleep. Then tomorrow she would go to Mr. Salazar and ask him to send a message to Professor Vallejo. Her inquiry into the death of Sebastian Babayoff could wait a few days. Indeed, she had almost all the cards in her hand, ready to lay down. But there was something more important for her to do. A compulsion, she thought—if she had courage enough.

CHAPTER FIFTEEN

The day began with a soft humidity in the air, the sky overhead ashimmer as sun reflected through a fine silk-scarf layer of cloud. Maisie pulled out her knapsack and packed her wallet, plus a leftover piece of bread and cheese from the previous evening's supper wrapped in a clean handkerchief. She did not want to encounter her landlady, so she planned to stop at Mr. Salazar's café for a bottle of water. She had dressed in a linen walking skirt, her leather sandals, and a light cotton blouse of white broderie anglaise. She rubbed cold cream into the skin of her face and arms and placed a straw hat on her head. Last, but not least, she put on her sunglasses and cardigan. Doubtless she would soon be folding the cardigan into the knapsack, but she would benefit from it for the next hour.

Opening the door, she looked down the staircase and onto the silent courtyard below. She closed the door without a sound, and with a sure, soft step, made her way out onto the street. As far as she knew, she had not been seen. As far as she knew.

As she approached the café, Salazar was at the front of his premises, bidding good-morning to passersby—each one represented potential business—and either waving them on their way, or guiding them into the café. Then he returned to the street. When he saw Maisie walking toward the café, he raised his hand and set off toward her.

"Miss Dobbs! Miss Dobbs! Good morning to you, señora."

Señora. A married woman.

"Hello, Mr. Salazar—and a good morning to you, too," said Maisie.

"Will you come in for coffee, and a—what did you name it? Custard doughnut?"

Maisie laughed and shook her head. "Well, it was an apt description, was it not? And no, I cannot stop today, but I will buy a bottle of water from you, if I may."

"Buy water? Buy water? Since when is water for sale? I will *give* you a bottle of water, Miss Dobbs."

He led her into the café, where she sat on a stool at the bar while Salazar stepped behind the bar, filled a thick glass bottle with water, and stoppered it.

"There you are, Miss Dobbs." He looked around the restaurant and beckoned her closer. "I have a message for you, from the professor. He will meet you here later." Salazar looked behind him at the clock, then turned his attention to Maisie. "About two hours' time. Can you come?"

Maisie nodded. "Yes, of course." She paused. "Is he well? You seem concerned."

"The professor has become my friend. He is an honorable man, but a man who has taken risks for his beliefs. So, yes, señora—I worry about him."

Maisie placed the bottle in her knapsack. "Thank you, Mr.

Salazar—and tell the professor I will see him later. Around one." She slipped from the stool, smiled once more, and left the café. She did not look back, yet felt certain that Salazar had taken up his place outside the café, and was watching her until she was out of sight.

As she passed along the street, she noticed Solomon's haberdashery shop was still closed. She wondered how long the shopkeeper could afford to let business slip through his fingers.

Walking along Gibraltar's streets had, she thought, been good for her. At first she had felt the weakness in her body, as if the sadness had spread into every cell, every fiber and ligament, but as she stepped out along the road now, she felt stronger. Of course, when she put her idea to the professor, he might refuse her, but she'd made sure she was at least fitter in body and mind, thus less likely to represent a burden.

The village of Catalan Bay appeared picture-postcard perfect as Maisie rounded the curve of the path down to the beach. The sun was higher in the sky, and the morning coastal mist had burned off—she had shed her cardigan soon after leaving Main Street. She thought she might wander the streets of the village for a while, perhaps buy post-cards for Priscilla and Brenda. She'd send one to Billy and his family, too. There was nothing like a postcard of a sunnier clime to convey the idea of ease and enjoyment.

Once again the women were clustered in a circle close to the rocks, mending nets. Most of the fishing boats were in, lying on their sides like beached whales waiting for the tide to bring them breath and life. As Maisie walked toward the women, she noticed one of their number catch sight of her, and warn the others. A couple of the black-clad fishermen's wives looked around, and they seemed to cluster closer together, as if she were an interloper to be feared. And perhaps she was.

Maisie smiled as she continued on, and when she reached their circle, she sat down at the edge, leaning in as if she belonged.

"Good morning," she said. The women understood English, of that she was sure.

The women all nodded their acknowledgment at the same time, with the woman who had spotted her first replying, "Good morning" in heavily accented English. She set down her long thick needle, poking it through the net to mark her place.

"I wonder, do you know where I can find Rosanna?"

The woman laughed, and her companions giggled like nervous schoolgirls. She shrugged. "Not here, not today."

Maisie smiled again, inclining her head as she held the woman's gaze. "But you know where she is, don't you?"

The woman's face hardened. She shook her head and shrugged again. "She is a girl. She is late today—it will show her she should be working." The woman rubbed her finger and thumb together.

Maisie laughed. "Oh, she'll be sorry then."

The woman understood—and so did the others, their heads nodding in knowing accord.

"And you don't know where she's gone?" asked Maisie again.

The woman looked at her with the same stone-faced expression. "She is busy. That is all. She is busy." And with that comment, she looked out to sea.

Maisie followed her gaze and turned back to the woman, though this time she raised her chin, just a little, to show she understood. She thanked the women, who went on with their work and chatter, weaving their long, hooked needles in and out of the nets.

Maisie left the beach and, after wandering through the village and purchasing several postcards of Catalan Bay, began to make her way back toward Main Street.

So Rosanna Grillo was not among the women, had not been seen by them of late, and was—if that one glance across the sea could be taken as evidence—well away from home. But where was she? Could she have gone into hiding somewhere? Maisie had assumed she had remained after helping to load the boat in the dead of night—surely she would not have ventured into Spain.

Maisie wanted to go to the cave again, but having looked at her watch, she realized it was time to return to Mr. Salazar's café, and at a brisk clip, if she didn't want to miss Professor Vallejo.

The professor was waiting for her when she arrived, seated on the banquette underneath the mural depicting Gibraltar's history.

He stood as she approached. "Miss Dobbs."

Maisie was taken aback. Vallejo's eyelids were drooping with fatigue, and the fine skin above his cheekbones appeared dark and paper-thin. His lips barely moved as he spoke, as if he were trying to conserve whatever energy he had left.

"Professor, but why—"

"Sit down, Maisie." He paused. "May I call you Maisie? I fear I may have taken a liberty."

"Of course that's all right." She slid into the banquette.

"You need proper food." She looked around for Mr. Salazar.

"He's in the kitchen, making me something special to eat."

"Are you ill?"

Vallejo shook his head. "Just tired, Maisie. I have been busy."

"Across the border." It was not a question.

He nodded. "Yes. I was in Madrid, close to the front lines, in University City."

"You are helping the Republican Army?"

"Inasmuch as I am able. Not all fighting goes on in the trenches, but sometimes it is necessary to go to the edge of the terror."

"Madrid is being bombed almost daily—I know that much," said Maisie, looking back toward the kitchen again.

"Yet life goes on, in the strangest of ways. Franco is determined to take Madrid—it is the jewel in the crown of this war."

"Will you go back?"

Vallejo sighed. "In two days."

"Why, Professor? Why did you come here, anyway? Could you not have found rest in Spain, away from the fighting?"

"Questions I cannot answer, Maisie. I am a professor, but suffice it to say—" Vallejo shook his head and signaled toward the kitchen. Salazar was now approaching bearing a plate filled with food that Maisie would have been hard pushed to identify.

"Professor." Salazar set the plate before Vallejo and stepped back. "A glass of wine, perhaps? Something stronger? Have what you want."

Vallejo nodded. "I'll have a glass of rioja." He nodded in Maisie's direction.

"And for you, Miss Dobbs? Perhaps a tortilla?" Salazar laughed, noticing Maisie's expression. "Don't be afraid—it's just potato, sliced and cooked with eggs."

"Oh, sorry—of course, I've had it before. Yes, that would be lovely—and a glass of rioja for me too, please." She waited for Salazar to be beyond earshot, and turned back to Vallejo. "So you leave in two days."

Vallejo nodded.

"And you have no trouble going back and forth across the border?"

"I have the papers. I am welcome in both places, though there is another border within Spain to be negotiated."

"You must be a valuable person, Professor."

"To too many people, at times." He turned to his food again, slowing down only after three more mouthfuls.

Salazar approached with two glasses of rioja. He placed one each in front of Vallejo and Maisie. Vallejo, mouth full, nodded his thanks and reached for the glass.

"So, you leave in two days, perhaps three," repeated Maisie.

"As soon as I can, and as soon as I have had some—let us say, *conversations* with certain people."

Maisie nodded, then took a sip of the rich Spanish wine.

"I want to come with you."

Vallejo looked up, leaned back, and shook his head. "Don't be ridiculous. There might be your British fact-finding politicos over there, the well-meaning with socialist sympathies, but you don't know what it's like."

"I think I do, Professor. I do know what it's like. I would like to come with you."

"But you will need papers, and—"

"I do not envisage a problem, but perhaps you can help me." She paused, reaching into her knapsack for her passport, and placed it on the table in front of Salazar. "I have more than one legal name, and one carries more weight than the other at times like this. I read in the newspaper that the Duchess of Rathbone was visiting Madrid, along with other British women. If a duchess can be given leave to enter Spain, so can a lady."

Salazar approached the table with Maisie's freshly cooked tortilla and a basket of warm bread. They thanked the café owner, who left them to converse.

"You should eat up, Miss Dobbs."

Maisie met Vallejo's eyes, as if willing him to continue.

"You'll need your strength for Madrid." He took up her passport and placed it in the inside pocket of his jacket.

She smiled and raised her glass. Vallejo in turn lifted his glass and touched hers with an audible clink that caught the attention of other patrons. Vallejo sipped and set down his glass, pointing to her food with his fork.

"Eat, Miss Dobbs. An army always marches on its stomach."

Maisie cut into the tortilla and lifted a forkful, inhaling the the aroma of warm herbs and the promise of nourishment provided by the simple dish. In truth, she did not feel like eating, for her insides were turning with anticipation. She was choosing to walk into a war, onto a battlefield. Perhaps it was, after all, the only way to face down the dragon of memory. She had felt it rise up within her again at the very second she witnessed a small aeroplane tumble from the sky above an escarpment in Canada.

Twenty-four hours later, at the end of the working day, Maisie went to Mr. Salazar's café, where the proprietor handed her a small brown-paper-wrapped package. It contained her passport and the necessary paperwork. Facilitated by Vallejo's contacts, she had been given leave to depart for Spain at her earliest opportunity. She did not want MacFarlane to learn of her plans; with time, she knew someone, somewhere, would tell him. Vallejo had given Maisie exact instructions regarding where they should meet his driver, close to the border before sunrise the following morning. His note informed her that their journey would be circuitous. He would never take the same route to Madrid twice in a row, and care had to be taken to avoid Nationalist soldiers.

Maisie avoided crossing paths with MacFarlane, though she had received another message via Mrs. Bishop that he wanted to see her. And she had drawn back from further approaches to Miriam Babayoff and Mr. Solomon. As Billy would have said, she was laying low.

Following the meeting with Vallejo, Maisie had remained in the café stirring the dregs of her post-lunch coffee and staring into the grounds. Now, on the morning of her departure, in the darkness, she reflected upon a conversation she'd had with Mr. Salazar.

"There are those who can read the coffee grounds," said the café proprietor, standing alongside her with his coffeepot and jug of hot milk. "The future is not only written in English tea leaves, you know."

Maisie looked up into his eyes and saw there an understanding, as if he had intuited what had come to pass between two of his customers.

"Oh, I don't think I want to know, Mr. Salazar. The present is quite enough to deal with at times, without having to worry about what is coming around the corner. I've done my best not to be too afraid of the corners in life."

The proprietor nodded. "Yes, it is best to remain in this moment—you never know what might happen." He paused. "More coffee?"

Maisie looked at her watch. "I have much to do this evening, Mr. Salazar, so I had better get on. How much do I owe you?"

He shook his head. "On the house, Miss Dobbs."

"Oh, but Mr. Salazar—"

"Today you are my guest. I may not see you for a few days, eh, señora?"

Their eyes met.

"Perhaps not for a few days. But soon."

He sighed, nodding again. "Be careful, Miss Dobbs."

"I will. I am in safe hands," said Maisie as she moved along the banquette and stepped out from behind the table.

"There are places where not even God has safe hands, Miss Dobbs."

Salazar's ready smile seemed forced as he stepped back for Maisie to leave. "Take care, won't you, señora?"

She began walking along Main Street in the direction of Mrs. Bishop's guest house, but stopped and retraced her steps. The inside of St. Andrew's Church was cool as she entered. Though there was no one else there, she felt as if she could touch the prayers that had gone before, as if they were written on small squares of gossamer-thin tissue paper that lingered in the air above her, floating up into the rafters to be seen more clearly in heaven. She sat down and closed her eyes. She had rarely come to prayer in a house of worship, though she was no stranger to matters of the spirit. But in that moment she brought her hands together and whispered, "Be with me. Please. Be with me."

After packing a change of clothing into her carpet bag, along with a notebook and toiletries, Maisie went to bed. Anticipating her departure, she slept for only three or four hours before waking. Instead of tossing and turning, waiting for the hour when she would rise, she slipped from the bed, pulled a pillow onto the floorboards, and sat down with her legs crossed, her eyes almost closed, and her hands resting on her knees, thumb and forefinger just the width of one grain of rice apart.

In the hours of wakefulness, Maisie did not go back and question her motives. She accepted her decision: this journey was one she felt compelled to make. Then the hour came. She rose, and washed at the sink in the corner, then dressed in khaki linen trousers, a dark cotton blouse, and a linen jacket. She picked up her walking shoes, carpetbag, and satchel, and crept downstairs in her bare feet. Tiptoeing across the courtyard, she reached the door, which she unlatched with barely a sound. After stepping out onto the street, she closed it behind her and took a few paces before slipping on her socks and shoes and walking to the prearranged meeting place. A black motor car was idling in the gray light of early morning. Vallejo stepped out as she approached and held the door open for her. She slipped into the back seat, and Vallejo climbed in beside her.

"This is Raoul, the best driver on both sides of the border—eh, Raoul?" Vallejo tapped the driver on the shoulder.

Raoul turned to Maisie and smiled. His smile was broad but swift, as he turned and gave one nod of the head in greeting, then looked back at the road before him. He turned up the headlamps, and the motor car moved off. It was only a matter of yards to the border.

Maisie held her breath as the guard checked her passport and papers, shining a light on her face and then back onto the documents. A stamp came down with a thud. He seemed to know Vallejo, giving him back his papers and waving the car through. The sun was a mere red pinprick of light on the horizon as Raoul drove on.

At first Maisie was awake, taking account of the land around her. Sometimes it was arid, with low trees, and at other times it seemed as if they were driving through a primeval forest. Then the motor car slowed, moving at a crawl through a small village of rough stone houses, where a lone dog barked as they passed, and chickens crossed in front of the vehicle, hindering their progress. Then she slept, waking only when she heard Vallejo and Raoul in low conversation, discussing the route. Maisie was surprised—they must have stopped at some point, as Vallejo was now sitting alongside the driver. She had slept through the break in the journey. Having turned and noticed she was now awake, Vallejo gave her a brief smile.

"You slept for some time—it's good, for the route is longer than it might normally take. Raoul said he has made it from Gibraltar to Madrid in six and a half hours before, but for us, well, there are places we have to avoid. The Nationalists are concentrating their attention on the Madrid–Valencia road, but still, we had to weave well away from Malaga early on, and we must be careful to avoid pockets of fighting. Are you hungry? Do you need to stop?"

Maisie nodded. "I'm thirsty more than anything. And I'd certainly like to stretch my legs."

Vallejo smiled. He understood. "Raoul can pull over here if you need to go into the woods. There is nothing to fear in there—and it's private."

Maisie thanked Vallejo, who instructed Raoul to stop the car when it was convenient. The driver nodded, and a minute later maneuvered onto a dirt shoulder next to an area of dense woodland opposite a row of simple dwellings. There was no sign of human activity.

"No one can see you once you step in among the trees, and we have to study the map in any case."

Maisie stepped into the silent woodland, moving in for some yards to assure her privacy. It was as she was on her way out that she gasped and came to a sudden halt. She stepped behind a tree. The motor car was surrounded by three men in uniform, their rifles trained on Raoul in the driver's seat; another directed his weapon toward Vallejo, who was in conversation with a fifth soldier as he looked over their papers. She watched and waited, feeling her stomach muscles clench. Vallejo seemed calm, one hand in his pocket, one hand gesticulating, as if to underscore a point. He turned back to the motor car, leaned in through the window, and came out with the map in his hand. The soldier nodded. Maisie continued to watch, hardly allowing herself to breathe. Vallejo was talking them out of danger—she could see that in the way he had drawn the men into conversation. But who were the soldiers? Republican, or Franco's Nationalists? Were they Italians, brought in to support Franco's forces? Or German? Or perhaps members of the International Brigades?

The soldier speaking to Vallejo signaled his men to lower their rifles, and as Maisie watched, they gathered to one side. Raoul leaned from his window to offer cigarettes, which they took with gratitude, sharing a joke with the driver. Vallejo and the soldier had laid the map across the motor car bonnet, and she could see them marking out a route. Then it seemed as if everyone was more at ease. Vallejo rolled up the map and shook hands with the soldier, who touched his peaked cap and waved to his men to join him. They moved off, back along an alleyway between two rough sandstone buildings.

Vallejo watched them until they were out of sight, then turned and looked back into the woodland. He signaled. She stepped from her hiding place and ran to the motor car, where Vallejo was holding open the door ready for her. He closed the door, then moved to the front passenger seat.

"Get down, Maisie, just for a while. I'll tell you when you can sit up again."

From her cramped position, she saw both Raoul and Vallejo raise their hands, smile and wave at the soldiers, who had turned back to watch them depart. The motor car sped up.

"You can sit up now," said Vallejo, when some moments had passed.

"Who were they?"

"Russians—on our side, or at least, we think they are."

"What did they want with us?" asked Maisie.

"Just to find out who we were, and where we were going. The fact that I speak Russian helped," said Vallejo.

"Am I a liability on this journey?" She leaned forward to better be heard over the roar of the engine.

Vallejo shook his head. "When you get to Madrid, you will be surprised how many women have come into the city—women journalists, a photographer or two, a couple of your British politicians. There's that woman—Red Ellen. Red for Communist?"

"Ellen Wilkinson, in Madrid? She's called Red Ellen for the color of her hair, and she's a much-loved fighter for workers' rights in Britain."

"You approve of her?"

"I admire her—so yes, I approve, for what it's worth."

Vallejo nodded. "Anyway, no, you're not a liability—but you never know with Russians, which way they are going to go. They might not have been in proximity to a woman in a while, so it was best to be safe."

"Thank you." Maisie sat back, and then leaned forward again. "What is it like, in Madrid?"

"You'll see soon enough. Surprisingly normal, for a city being bombed almost every day. The Nationalists are trying very hard to take Madrid. Their plan is to encircle the city, so they have fought us in Jarama, where the International Brigades suffered terrible losses, and also in University City, where I was employed. It is now—more or less—the front, and they have been fighting within the buildings, with Italians taking one floor and the Republic another. We are holding the line, though, much to Franco's shock. He thought he could just walk in with his Nationalist soldiers, with his Moors from Africa and with the fascist Germans and Italians, but we are holding the line." He turned back to face the road again. "There are anti-Fascist Germans fighting for us, and the Garibaldi Battalion of sympathizing Italians. God bless them all. It is crazy."

Maisie nodded her understanding and looked out of the window. When she turned back, Vallejo's eyes were closed and his chin had slumped onto his chest; he was fast asleep. They drove through more villages, many with Republican slogans, where women pushed children into the shadows as the motor car went past. Maisie watched and wondered at the changing landscape as they neared the city, once again looping round to avoid the border between Nationalist and Republican armies. Still Vallejo slept, and for some moments Maisie looked at the man, at his olive skin and dark hair, gray at the temples. She suspected he was not as old as she had at first assumed. It was hard to say, given the lines across his forehead and at the corners of his eyes. And not for the first time, she wondered about the relationship between him, Babayoff, and Rosanna Grillo. In any time of war, she thought, there are alliances between those whose paths might never have crossed if the world were at peace.

CHAPTER SIXTEEN

S andbags, broken buildings like jagged teeth in the mouth of a
mad dog, and smoke rising up to block their way forward came
together to form Maisie's first impression of Madrid. She felt hot,
sticky, the leather seat adhering to her back, and when she leaned forward, she felt a rivulet of sweat run down the length of her spine. Her
palm was clammy when she brushed her hair from her forehead, and
she ran her parched tongue across her lips.

"I have made arrangements for you to stay at an hotel, Maisie. I
have lodgings nearby with a relative, but it is very small and not comfortable. Here is the address, should you need to be in touch in an
emergency. I will ensure your room is ready; then you'll be able to
rest for a few hours until suppertime. We can talk then about what,
precisely, you want to achieve while we're here. Raoul will be driving
back to Gibraltar in a few days—I'll let you know the arrangements for
your departure."

Maisie opened her mouth to counter his instruction—what if

she didn't want to leave when the time came? She decided it was not worth the discussion. Not yet, anyway. She wanted only to get to her room now, and then decide what exactly she wanted to do and see—to "achieve," as Vallejo put it.

The hotel on the Plaza de Callao was a bold square building, reminiscent of a large London hotel built during Queen Victoria's reign. There was a shabby grandeur about it; windows had been blown out and the marble facade exuded the air of an old lady under siege from a dark modernity never imagined when the hotel's first guests arrived in 1924. By the time Maisie was shown to her room, she could think of nothing she wanted more than to sink into a bathtub filled with cool water, and felt all the more selfish for her wanting.

Having bathed and washed her hair, she felt refreshed but still weary as she studied her face in the mirror. She secured her bathrobe tighter around her body—she would not chance it falling open, for fear of seeing her scar. Since losing the baby, she had avoided catching sight of her own body at any cost—she always undressed quickly, and looked away as she toweled her skin. And though the discomfort had lessened over recent days, she wondered how much she had held on to as a reminder, as if it was tantamount to abandonment to cast aside the pain, a betrayal of James and their child as she lived on without them.

She ran her fingers through her hair, and then, though she could not have explained at that moment why she did such a thing, she walked out of the bathroom and into the bedroom, took a small pair of scissors from her bag, and returned to stand before the mirror above the sink. Lifting up one clump of hair after another, she cut and cut and cut, not stopping until her hair lay like an elfin cap upon her head. And then she smiled, her cheekbones more pronounced and her eyes wide, as if encountering someone new in the reflection. A few strands of gray only pleased her the more, the visible signs of what had come to pass in her life. She looked at the scissors and ran a free hand through her boyish hair, beginning to laugh at her own audacity. She'd forgotten that there was another scar, from a shrapnel wound sustained in France some twenty years before. Though faint, it was still there, a line underneath her occipital bone for the sharp observer to see.

When she had washed her blouse and underclothes and hung them in the bathroom to dry, Maisie shook out her trousers and placed them on a hanger alongside the open window to air. She dressed in her linen skirt and a fresh white blouse and sandals and walked down to the bar, where she was supposed to meet Vallejo.

The bar was buzzing with people, many from overseas—British, American, a Russian, along with local men and women. She recognized a politician from London, though could not recall his name, and overheard two British nurses—volunteers—discussing their work at a hospital. She lingered for a while, eavesdropping, and learned that they were new in the country, and had been assigned—she was not sure by whom—to assist an American medical unit. They were working with a doctor they admired for his speed, operating on one man with devastating wounds after another. She was about to approach them—she had always felt a camaraderie among nurses, and though she'd last walked a ward some eighteen years before, she knew she only had to identify herself to be welcome among their number—when an American woman brandishing a camera broke into their conversation, introducing herself as an international correspondent for *Life* magazine and asking if she could interview them. Maisie turned away as one of the women exclaimed, "Well, we could always use more help— there's so much to do. And we're here in the city, where there's better organization—can you imagine what it's like outside, at some of the aid stations they've set up?"

Professor Vallejo was behind her. She wondered how long he might have been there, watching her.

"I did not recognize you at first. Your hair—well, it's like a man's." He paused, as if realizing his comment might have caused offense, and looked about him at the flurry of activity in the hotel. "Let's find somewhere quieter to talk. There's a small restaurant around the corner—I know the proprietor, and he remains open, come what may. I cannot bear this noise, or most of these people."

They walked along the rubble-strewn street in silence, entering the half-full restaurant.

"It's early yet," said Vallejo, pointing to a table in the corner.

The proprietor had raised his hand in a quick, economic wave as they entered—he had none of Mr. Salazar's ready ebullience—before pulling a bottle of red wine from the shelf and making his way between the tables toward them.

"Felipe," said Vallejo, "this is my friend, Miss Dobbs."

Felipe grunted his greeting as he poured wine into two glasses.

Maisie looked at Vallejo, unsure of how she should reply, then smiled and said, "How do you do," at once sensing the formality in her tone.

Felipe shrugged his shoulders, rolled his eyes at Vallejo, and moved away, having deposited the bottle of wine on the table.

"Felipe is not as friendly as our Mr. Salazar," said Vallejo. He drained his wine as if it were water, and began to speak as he lifted the bottle to refill his glass. "So you have two reasons for wanting to come to Madrid—perhaps three, though I think the third is the indulgence of a sudden desire to place yourself in an even more difficult situation than the one in which you found yourself in Gibraltar."

He sipped again, setting his glass on the table and raising his hand as Maisie opened her mouth to speak.

"Most people, upon discovering the body of a murdered man, would make their next port of call the shipping office, where they would book passage home to wherever home might be, on the next possible sailing. But you are different, aren't you? A murder is a question to be answered, a problem to be solved, and perhaps a tangle of wires to be unraveled. You are here now because your nose has followed a scent, but of course we know it might not be the right scent, and in your line of work there are as many fragrances as there are threads to be followed, and you are used to having a certain dogged endurance."

Maisie said nothing, but reached for her glass of wine.

"The second reason is allied to the first, in that this is one of your threads. You suspect—*something* is going on, so your nose is down and sniffing. You might be right, you might be wrong, but at least the stone has been turned. Still, perhaps you do not realize how broad is the stone, and how many pebbles lie underneath. In short, to be blunt, you stand little chance of finding what you are looking for."

"And what am I looking for?"

"Sebastian Babayoff."

"But Sebastian Babayoff is dead," she said, watching Vallejo's face.

"Oh, yes, he is indeed—we know that."

"Do we?"

"You discovered his body."

Maisie turned her wineglass by the stem, while Vallejo drained his glass again and poured more.

"And what's my third reason for being here?" she asked.

"War, Miss Dobbs. War is the antivenin for you, isn't it? Your losses can be attributed to war and the preparation for war, and you think you can rid yourself of whatever ails you—finally—by facing war again."

She brought her hand to her neck.

"And why did you cut your hair?" asked Vallejo.

"I was hot, the journey was dusty and long. I wanted to be free of the bother of it."

"You didn't cut it to punish yourself for the very act of living?"

Maisie smiled and shook her head, looking away as she did so. "How impertinent you are, Professor Vallejo. In some ways you remind me of someone I knew very well, though his honest appraisals were never so blunt."

"Ah, yes, Dr. Maurice Blanche."

Maisie reacted before she could disguise her shock. "You knew him?"

"I did indeed, Miss Dobbs. You were not the first of his students or those he took under his wing, though it is clear you were the most beloved. Put two and two together, Miss Dobbs; use that famous endurance. I am a professor of politics and philosophy, and I studied the latter under Maurice in France. Not for a long time, I'll admit, but enough to learn from his approach."

Maisie nodded. "Then we are like family."

"Yes. Family. And families have no secrets, do they?" There was a pause before Vallejo spoke again. "What do you want to know, Miss Dobbs? Now is the time to ask, though I cannot guarantee an answer. Then we will make our plans for the next two days—though all plans have to be malleable in Madrid."

At that moment Felipe came to take their order for supper. Again he did not speak, but stood beside the table and flicked over a page in his small notebook, licking the tip of his short pencil. Having taken their order for lamb with fried potatoes—*patatas*—he left the table, picking up the empty bottle and returning with another before the conversation resumed. The silence between Maisie and Vallejo gave her time to think, and the professor an opportunity to light a cigarette. He held up the packet to her, but she shook her head.

"Here's what I want to know—whether you can answer or not," said Maisie. "I want to know exactly what happened on the night I found the body of the man buried as Sebastian Babayoff on the path close to the Ridge Hotel. I'm not entirely sure it was the photographer, though I believe he had been foolish with his life for some time, taking actions well above his ability to deal with the outcome." She paused to observe Vallejo's response, but he only looked at her, one eye closed against the smoke from the cigarette as he exhaled, so she continued. "I'm curious to know how Arturo Kenyon, Miriam Babayoff, and Jacob Solomon fit together in this little tale of intrigue—"

"Oh, sarcasm, Miss Dobbs," Vallejo interrupted. "Do not give in to the whims of your wit."

Maisie paused and took a sip of her wine—her glass was still more than half full. "In addition, I believe those three, plus Rosanna Grillo and as many helpers as they have under their collective wings, have been arranging for arms to be brought to Spain for the Republican Army, perhaps to arm the International Brigades. Heaven knows how they managed to weave their way through the patrol vessels in the Straits."

"Where there's a will, there's a way." Vallejo stubbed the remains of the cigarette into the ashtray. "Go on."

"I want to know how you fit into all this—I know I have danced around the question before, but now I want to know the answer to all of these things."

"Is that it?" asked Vallejo.

"No. Not quite," answered Maisie. "I want to know what part I'm playing. I am a guest here, at your mercy. Frankly, I might have had my reasons for wanting to come, yet you must have had a reason for allowing me to accompany you. Perhaps you want truth to have a voice as much as I, and perhaps you're tired of the artifice." She took a deep breath and held it before exhaling slowly. She knew her frustration was visible in her heightened color; she could feel her cheeks redden. "And I want to know about that man with the fair hair who was at the party in the hotel—and in church on the day we found out about Guernica. Who is he, and what does he have to do with all this?"

Felipe returned bearing two plates, the aroma of roast lamb and *patatas* wafting across the table in a wave that rendered Maisie almost faint. Vallejo raised his hand just enough to signal his thanks.

"Gracias, señor," said Maisie. Felipe left with barely a nod of the head.

Vallejo looked at Maisie. "Eat, and then we'll talk some more."

When they had sated their immediate hunger, Vallejo leaned back in his chair.

"I feel more human already." He sighed. "Now then, let me see. Here's what I can tell you."

Maisie set down her knife and fork.

"After the Frenchman Léon Blum persuaded leaders of other countries to be part of the nonintervention pact in Spain's war, all arms shipments from those countries to the Republic—to the democratically elected leadership of this country—ceased. It ceased, though, with the exception of the Germans and Italians, who favor the Fascist Franco, and of course, as we have seen, they are not following any pacts with Britain, France, or the United States of America. So other ways of gathering necessary materiel had to be found, and as the British saying goes, 'Every little bit helps.' Now the Russians are offering arms, so there is less of a panic about it all, though with Russia, in particular, beware the hand that gives, for it will rip something away in return."

"And who supplied the arms kept in the cave in Gibraltar?"

Vallejo looked at her. "My, you have been stomping the path of investigation, haven't you? Let us just say that it was another route by which arms might be brought into Spain."

"And the people I've mentioned—Kenyon, the Babayoffs, Solomon, and Carlos Grillo and his niece—they were all part of this? Are they all Communists?"

Vallejo shook his head. "This is not black and white, Maisie—any more than those photographs you've studied. All people want here is a democracy, not a land steeped in the power of aristocracy, the robber industrialists, and the church—I'm not sure which has been the more complicit in keeping the common man in poverty. There are Communists fighting with the Republican armies, but certainly not all our soldiers are of that persuasion. Did you know, Maisie, that our citizenry here in Madrid are being trained to fight by Germans sympathetic to our cause? They fought one war and then saw the hand of Fascism come down on their own country; those seeking a democratic voice in Germany have been put in camps, beaten and starved. The Garibaldi Battalion is the same—Italians wanting the chance to fight Mussolini. And then we come again to your British." He paused and took another deep breath. "They are on the horns of a dilemma. They have an aristocracy to protect from the proletariat, and they want to appease Herr Hitler and keep his eye away from Britain. But there again, what he is doing here, in Spain, serves them well—the British are buying valuable ore from mines in areas now under Nationalist control. Oh, yes, the Nationalists want to exploit mineral wealth, and Britain is among the countries vying to buy—so your government's keeping its nest very well feathered and protected by not supporting the war for democracy here in Spain."

Maisie took up her water glass. She was feeling hot again, and wanted to be out in the fresh air.

"And just for the record, Miss Dobbs, had it not been for your secret service, Franco would not even be back in Spain. He had a little help along the way."

"Are you a Communist, Professor?"

Vallejo shook his head. "I am on the side of people having an opportunity to better themselves. The Republic gave our schools books and pencils they had never had before—an educated citizenry is a serious threat to a dictator." He paused. "Sadly, rabid communism poses an equal menace."

Maisie looked down at her plate and pushed it to the side.

"Felipe will be very upset. There are people who would love to get their teeth into what you've left on your plate." Vallejo pointed at Maisie's uneaten food.

She pulled the plate back and cut into the meat. "You're right."

"Now I will turn the tables, Miss Dobbs. You tell me the story as you see it, and I will tell you what I think of your summation. Let me be Maurice, for a moment or two."

Maisie laughed, and cut again into her meat, scooping some onto her fork with *patatas*. "There was only one Maurice, Professor Vallejo—don't flatter yourself." She took a few more bites, then pulled a handkerchief from her satchel and drew it across her lips. "Here's what I think so far. First, I believe Babayoff and Grillo saw something they either should not have seen or should not have been looking for one morning, early, while out on the boat. I believe they witnessed a submarine, and I believe the vessel had come to the surface either to allow someone to disembark, or to take someone on board. I think it was the former, but I could be wrong. And they were seen. I think Babayoff at least was identified, and the fact that he was a photographer sealed his fate. Carlos Grillo probably did have a heart attack, but he was a worried man, and he was fearful, without the youthful devil-may-care that marked Sebastian Babayoff. How am I doing so far?"

"Not bad, Miss Dobbs."

"Now, who was the man leaving the submarine? I have toyed with the idea that it was the blond man. And that he is German—though that would be obvious. But is he playing on two teams, or one? Is he going from place to place to stir up trouble, or to relay intelligence? Or is he agitating a situation and making it worse? I am not sure about him, though my gut tells me he is not just a pawn on the board." She looked up at Vallejo. "And you know very well who he is, because you tried to stop Babayoff taking his photograph. Rosanna Grillo was there, dressed like a picture-house siren—yet that was not her way, so I wonder about that. My guess is that she was the test, a lure of some sort. Her loyalty to Sebastian Babayoff knew no bounds, but I suspect he pushed her to play a part she was not quite at ease with."

Felipe came to clear the table. He did not utter a word. Instead, he nodded to both of them, as Vallejo made a mock scribble with his thumb and finger on the opposite palm, requesting the bill.

"Then we get to Miriam Babayoff and Jacob Solomon, who are in love. But something is not right there, so I will have to go farther along the plank in my speculation. I believe he may have asked her brother for her hand, but Babayoff laughed at him—in his manner if nothing else. Solomon at first seems like a nondescript soul, someone Babayoff might use, without setting any stock in his character. In fact, the more I speak of him, the more I find I am not sympathetic to Babayoff, though he was highly regarded. Perhaps I sense a selfishness that attends the artistic soul."

"Interesting, that you should think in such a way."

"I suspect he was frustrated by the endless round of portraits and tourist photographs, and was driven to take risks—being out on the boat in morning swells, or taking a photograph of a man he knew to be working in the shadows. Such people are dangerous, even when engaged in acts of intrigue for the common good."

"You should remember that, Miss Dobbs. But continue."

"At one point I suspected that Solomon had come to the Ridge Hotel that night to talk to Babayoff again, hoping perhaps to catch him as he walked along the path. It may seem wildly speculative now, in a different place, over a glass of wine and a good dinner, but it occurred to me that in the walk up to the hotel, in the dark, Solomon's emotions might have been compromised by his thoughts and what he held in his heart, so he became very angry with Babayoff. I mean, who was he to withhold consent from him, Jacob Solomon, a man with an established business, who was helping Babayoff by providing a studio for portrait work? Who was Babayoff to think his sister, Miriam, could do better for herself? Unless, that is, he was afraid his life would change if he were alone with crippled Chana upstairs in bed. I have gone over this in my mind, and it's a possibility that Solomon's temper boiled over on that path, so that when Babayoff came along . . . well, he attacked him."

"But didn't you just say you thought Babayoff was not dead?"

"Yes—though you have said he *is* dead. But let me finish. In this scenario, I think that if it *was* Solomon, then he attacked the wrong man. Though Solomon had not killed him, Babayoff, when he came along the path and discovered what had happened, perhaps saw an opportunity to vanish into obscurity for a while. If events indeed unfolded in this manner, I believe Babayoff instructed Solomon to leave. He threw his cameras to one side, changed his outer clothing with that of the unconscious man, and searched his pockets for identification. The man probably was a poor refugee, and perhaps a solitary ne'er-do-well into the bargain. Then he killed him, obliterating his face to make identification impossible."

"And why would he have done that?"

"Because he was afraid. Because you had warned him when you saw him taking the photograph of the blond man at the hotel. There was some threat there—he needed to escape. But now he had Solomon in his palm; now they needed each other. The only fly in the ointment was that he'd left his Leica. He heard footsteps on the path and could not waste time rooting around in the bushes, trying to locate it. Instead he put the Zeiss—which held nothing more than a few cocktail party photographs—around the dead man's neck."

"Miss Dobbs, this is an interesting story—but let me assure you, Sebastian Babayoff is dead."

As Maisie was about to respond, the door swung back with a thud, and a group of British and Americans came into the restaurant, laughing and back-slapping. Maisie thought they had the devil-may-care attitude she'd seen before in wartime, when death was so close his breath could be felt on the streets, yet at the same time, they were alive. Like a collie moving sheep, Felipe gathered them to a table and had them seated within a minute, bringing wine and bread to keep them occupied while they discussed the menu, such as it was. Maisie listened to their conversation, to the back-and-forth, the camaraderie and competitiveness between them.

Vallejo shrugged. "Journalists, coming to draw their conclusions and press their opinions onto the public at home. Each of them thinking this war will make them famous."

"And perhaps it will. Perhaps Sebastian Babayoff was one of their number, Professor Vallejo." She nodded in the direction of the group. "That one in the middle, with the dark hair. He's not a journalist—well, not a writer, anyway. He's a photographer—look at the two cameras he hasn't taken from his neck, even though he's not at work. His words are images. The others might be looking for the story that no one else has scooped—especially that woman there; she has more to prove—but that photographer, there's something in his manner, the way he is with his fellow storytellers. He would die for the very best photograph of this war." She sighed. "And if, as you say, Sebastian Babayoff is dead—well, I would hazard a guess that we're both right. I'm not sure he *was* killed on that night on a path close to the most famous hotel on the Rock of Gibraltar. But he might have been filled with enough hubris to think that he could continue to take chances and survive, perhaps here in Spain—and perhaps along with a consignment of arms, so he could come out with a picture well worth a thousand words. He wanted recognition so much, he would give his life for it."

Vallejo looked at Maisie, then glanced at the bill Felipe had brought to the table without being noticed by his guests. He pulled a handful of coins from his pocket and tossed them on the table. "Come. We'd better leave, Miss Dobbs. Tomorrow we go to the front, so you can look into the flames again and see if that burns out your terrible memories."

Maisie felt the sting of his words, but she would not be drawn. She had shot her own arrows across the bows of Vallejo's calm demeanor. Some had hit, and some—she understood—were off target, perhaps alarmingly so. But giving voice to her thoughts served to realign the evidence in her head. She ran her fingers through her short hair again, just to feel the freedom she'd given herself with a pair of scissors, and then pushed back her chair to leave. And as she stood up, the young man at the next table—the one she'd identified as a photographer— looked at her and smiled. She smiled in return. It was just a passing exchange; she might never see him again. But as she left the restaurant, and later, in her room, she reflected upon his face. He might only have been twenty-four, or twenty-five, yet she could see white hair threaded through the black already, and the lines around his eyes, likely from squinting into the viewfinder. It was as if the young man and the old resided within one body; the old had seen far too much in a short, young life. He had the look of one still searching for the one shot that would make his name. God willing, it would be from a camera and not a gun.

CHAPTER SEVENTEEN

Vallejo walked Maisie to the hotel, and after a brief instruction—
"Tomorrow morning—I'll see you at eight, in the dining
room"—he went on his way.

She did not linger. "See you then," she said, turning toward the
staircase. She went straight to her room. Locking the door behind her,
she leaned against it, closed her eyes, and sighed. She remained in that
position for some seconds, tired from her journey and from pent-up
anticipation about how she would react to being in a city under siege.

She stepped into the bathroom and washed her face, running her
wet fingers through the short hair again. Returning to the room, she
put away the aired trousers and sat on the edge of the bed, looking
out into the night. She kept the lights off, taking care not to violate
the blackout. In fact, she preferred to sit in darkness. She remembered
Maurice talking to her about the way being in a certain place changes
a person's perspective. On top of a hill or a tall building with a 360-
degree view seems to encourage the mind to look further than its

present circumstances. On the other hand, it's interesting to observe how clearly one can see through a difficult situation in darkness, when there is no distraction—though it is equally important to understand that the blackest hours before dawn are also when the mind can shift and, like a moon off-kilter, throw light in the wrong places, which in turn allows fear to take center stage.

She wondered if she had played too much of her hand over supper with Vallejo. Had she allowed him into her confidence to a greater degree than was wise, most crucially regarding Solomon and Babay-off, and her belief that there was a deep attachment between Miriam and the owner of the haberdashery shop? She thought it was the push Vallejo needed to confide in her, to make a confession on behalf of Babayoff. The ambiguity of his response troubled Maisie, leading her once again to wonder whether she was being played for a fool, a specu-lation that weighed on her mind. Yes, she had gone out on a limb to elicit a response, something concrete for her to peg her observations and "evidence" upon—but it wasn't an effective push, and it hadn't yielded any answers. She rubbed her eyes, then looked out again at the nighttime movement of people on the road below, as if they had become one with their shadows while negotiating their way in the dark. Questions continued to haunt her. Had she ignored Chana Babayoff in her room upstairs? And was she being naive about the siblings and indeed everyone else who'd crossed her path since she'd discovered Babayoff's body?

A few moments later, she stood up and pulled a pillow onto the floor. She had to still her mind and her heart. She knew only one way to exercise dominion over her brain, and that was to sit in silent medi-tation and bring her thoughts into alignment.

At first Maisie wondered what the sound was. A loud, relentless mechanical moaning filled the air, as if a giant hound constructed by the gods of iron and steel were baying at the moon. The air raid warning started, and then other sounds came—the whine of aircraft engines followed by the *crump, crump, crump* of bombs falling. Light flashed across the night sky as incendiaries enflamed buildings, and Maisie could hear screaming as men and women—perhaps returning from a restaurant or from work—ran for cover. She fell to her stomach and began crawling toward the bed, but was not fast enough to reach its shelter before the window shattered as if a cannonball had been launched through the glass. Shards and splinters sprayed across the floor as she continued to crawl, finally reaching safety under the bed. Bells tolled into the night, and with her eyes closed and her hands clamped over her ears, she felt surrounded by glass. She imagined the wounded bleeding, and the bereaved and shocked, out on the street and in their homes, men, women, and children, the life wrenched from their bodies by a killer swooping from above.

And then it stopped. Perhaps for a second. Two seconds? Time seemed to change shape in the silence, and then it changed again, and she could hear people below calling to one other. More bells tolled as ambulances raced to aid those caught in fire and falling masonry, and then another noise filled her head—an insistent pounding at the door.

"Señora! Señora! Come! Come!" The pounding continued. Maisie crawled from her refuge, trying to avoid glass strewn across the carpet. She reached for her shoes, shook the glass fragments out, and slipped them on; she felt the crunch underfoot as she stepped across to the door.

"I'm coming. I'm coming—don't worry, I'm all right."

She opened the door to see a hotel clerk standing before her. "Come downstairs, Miss Dobbs. Everyone is to come downstairs—we have to count, to make sure." He looked at her hair and squinted in the low light—there was still some illumination in the corridor. "Miss—your hair is filled with glass. Come. I will have a girl help you—no, don't touch it."

Maisie had instinctively raised her hand to feel her hair, but brought it to her side again.

The clerk led her to the lobby, along with other guests who followed as he guided them downstairs. At the reception desk another man was already checking the names of the guests lined up before him. Maisie joined the queue, looking around to see how many were there. She had no idea of the time, though she suspected it was still early, perhaps not even ten o'clock. Then she saw them, across the room, their heads close in conversation. It was Professor Vallejo and the blond man, though she realized now that he was not blond but gray. It was a strange gray, as if slate blended with silver. It did not suit him, for his face was that of a younger man, perhaps in his thirties. His physiognomy was still somewhat boyish—not ready for gray, she thought. She was already moving toward them when the hotel clerk who'd escorted her to the lobby tapped her on the shoulder. A young woman in the uniform of a maid stood beside him.

"Maria will help you with your hair. I have arranged for your belongings to be moved to another room. The hotel is quite safe now, but you need a room with a window in place. Fortunately, only two rooms were affected, though yours was one of them." He smiled, gave a short bow, then turned to another guest.

Maisie looked around. Vallejo and the man were gone.

"Señora? Miss?" The maid named Maria tapped Maisie on the shoulder. She smiled at her charge and, placing her gloved fingers on Maisie's hair with a gentle touch, spoke in halting English. "You have diamonds in your hair. Come. Let me take them out." And as they turned to leave, she saw the young photographer, the one with the dark hair and haunted eyes, pointing his camera toward them; he had snapped his shot at the moment Maria touched her hair with white-gloved fingers. Maisie looked down at the maid's hands, at the tiny splinters of glass catching light from the chandelier above.

M aisie fell asleep almost as soon as she lay down on the bed in her new room, with fresh linens and no sign that it was in an hotel in a city under attack. In the morning she shook out her clothing, inspecting it to ensure no slivers of glass remained, and dressed in the same blouse and trousers she had worn the night before. She laced her brown walking shoes and put on her linen jacket. Having run her fingers through her hair, she was ready to leave. She took her satchel, and left the room.

Entering the dining room—where Vallejo had suggested they meet—Maisie looked around for her traveling companion, but he had not yet arrived. She studied her watch—she was early. A waiter showed her to a small table. She ordered coffee and an egg and potato tortilla, some bread and jam, then sat back to wait for her breakfast.

The waiter approached an adjacent table. He was followed by two women, the British nurses she'd seen the day before. She had only guessed they were nurses from their conversation, for they were not in uniform. The tables were close, so the women acknowledged Maisie, bidding her good morning as the waiter held out seats for them. Both seemed to take a second look at her hair.

"Good morning." She smiled as she responded to their greeting.

"Are you new here?" asked the older one. Maisie thought the woman was in her early thirties, while the other was younger, perhaps twenty-four, twenty-five.

"I arrived yesterday. From Gibraltar." She turned her chair a little to face them. "You're nurses, aren't you? Where are you working?"

The older one laughed. "Are we so obvious? We came out a couple of weeks ago—we volunteered to assist at the hospital set up by an American medical unit. We wanted to get our feet wet before moving on. Very good doctors, you know." She held out her hand to the other woman. "This is my cousin, Freda Nicholls, and my name is Hattie Benson. Delighted to meet you."

"Maisie Dobbs. And I guessed you were nurses—I was a nurse too. Some years ago now, but still—"

"Have you come as a volunteer?" asked Freda.

Maisie took a second to answer. "No. No, I'm here for . . ." She stumbled on her words. How could she explain her presence in Madrid? "I'm here to assist someone with their work."

"Look, here comes your breakfast," said Hattie. "Would you like to join us? Come on, sit with us—it's no fun being on your own in a foreign hotel. Did you hear the bombs last night?"

Maisie nodded in reply, moving her chair while the waiter set her cutlery at the nurses' table before serving her breakfast.

"I've ordered exactly the same," said Hattie. "You can't beat those eggy tortillas."

"Where were you a nurse?" asked Freda.

"Well, I trained at the London Hospital—it was during the war—and then I went over to France, to a casualty clearing station. After the war I was eventually promoted to ward sister in a secure hospital, with shell-shocked men. It was just for another couple of years."

"Oh, my goodness. Then you know what it's like at the very sharp end, don't you?" Hattie moved her shoulder to allow the waiter to serve her breakfast. "We need people like you, you know."

Maisie shook her head. "Oh, no, you don't. I'm really quite rusty, I would imagine."

Hattie opened her mouth to make another comment, but was

interrupted by Freda. "Did you get married? Is that why you left nursing?"

"Freda!" said Hattie. "Your nose will get you into trouble."

"It's all right," said Maisie. She turned to the cousin. "No. I went back to continue my studies at university—I'd given up a scholarship to train as a nurse in 1915, so I thought I'd like to finish what I started. Then I went into a different line of work."

Maisie could see that Hattie wanted to find out what kind of work, but again Freda spoke up. "Well, *we're* going into a different line of work tomorrow—of a kind, and only for a day."

"What do you mean?" asked Maisie.

Hattie shook her head. "Freda's jumping the gun. We're going out to one of the villages tomorrow. It's just off the road to Valencia, along the Tajo River, and not terribly far from Jarama. There was a dreadful battle there earlier in the year. We've been told the people left behind in the village, mainly women and children, are living in simple cave dwellings for protection. Apparently there's a small makeshift hospital there with only one nurse—a nun—so our hospital sent word that we would come to help sort things out, but we can't be spared for longer than one day. And let me tell you, nuns are a bit persona non grata, what with all the trouble there's been with the church here. We've been told she's just exhausted and needs help—they are bringing in wounded fighters from the more rural areas for her to care for, so it's a bit like a casualty clearing station with a children's clinic thrown in for good measure. There's been a lot of skirmishing along the road with the Nationalist-held lands, but it's quieter at the moment. The local women are doing their best to help, but Sister Teresa needs some experienced assistance, so we thought we'd volunteer to do as much as we can for her, and see if we want to return for a longer period. We want to do our bit where it's needed most. Mind you, we're not used to that sort of knife-edge nursing. I think they're sending us to harden us up a bit."

Maisie set down her fork. "How are you getting there?"

Hattie shrugged. "Not sure yet—that's our problem. The driver we had lined up pulled out, and we've yet to find another driver willing to make the journey. It's safe enough—well, as safe as you could hope to be—because we'll be within the borders of Republican control, but still, you have to be careful."

"I might be able to help with the driver." Maisie looked around and saw Vallejo standing at the entrance of the restaurant. "Will you be here this evening?"

The two women nodded in unison. Maisie could see a likeness between them; both had brown eyes and hair, with a cowlick to the left of the forehead.

"Then I will see you in the bar. About seven?"

Hattie spoke first. "Yes, of course. Look here, thank you very much, Maisie. Most appreciated."

"Are you doing anything interesting today?" asked Freda.

Maisie stood up, collecting her bag and jacket. "Well, yes. I'm going closer to the front, at the university."

Hattie's eyes widened, while Freda remained unfazed. "Well, if you're prepared to do that, why don't you come with us tomorrow? I'm sure we could do with the help. That's if you've got nothing better to do."

Maisie looked around at Vallejo, who seemed agitated. He beckoned her to hurry. She turned back to the women.

"I'll let you know about the motor car this evening. The bar. At seven."

She looked back once as she made her way through the tables toward Vallejo. Both women were watching her leave. She waved.

Until that point, tomorrow had been a blank page, a sliver of time when she had nothing better to do.

R eady?" asked Vallejo as she joined him.

"Yes—is Raoul waiting?"

Vallejo nodded. "You've made some friends, I see."

"They're nurses. And they need a driver to take them out to a village south of Jarama, along the Tajo River, tomorrow. Can you spare Raoul? Or in any case, perhaps you can help me find a driver to take us?"

"You're going with them?"

"Why not? I have a day to spare before Raoul takes me back to Gibraltar, so I thought I could lend a hand. I'm rather out of practice when it comes to nursing, but I am assured it's like riding a bike. You never forget where the pedals are or how to steer."

They approached the black motor car. Raoul smiled at Maisie and opened the passenger door.

"Raoul, tomorrow you will be at the disposal of Miss Dobbs and her friends. It's just for one day. Then you will take her back to Gibraltar the following day."

Raoul nodded, then in his halting English said, "Just say me the time." He went to the driver's side of the motor car, took his seat, and started the engine. Vallejo sat next to Maisie in the back of the vehicle.

She had prepared herself for the journey to University City, to the front lines of the battle for Madrid being waged by the Nationalist armies of Franco and the Republican armies supported by International Brigades. But she realized, minutes into the journey, that nothing could have prepared her for the scenes of devastation as the motor car crawled along the streets. Yet still people went about their business. She could see women walking into a hairdressing salon. A bakery was open, and there were workers en route to offices and shops. The Telefonica building was standing and in operation, and though it crossed her mind that she could walk from the hotel along the Gran Via and send a wire to her father and to Priscilla, she also knew they would be horrified to learn that she was in Spain.

Raoul charted his route as if weaving a thread through cloth, around potholes, down narrow alleys just wide enough for a vehicle, and back and forth through streets to avoid devastation wrought by air raids. Soon they reached a point where men gathered in clusters, where sporadic gunfire peppered the air, though at the time no battle was raging. Maisie saw a low building in front of them, and held on to the leather strap above the door as the motor car swung into a courtyard and came to a halt outside a wooden door. The building was not old, in Maisie's estimation, but it seemed to mirror the fortunes of Madrid. University City had been constructed in 1927 to bring together the institutes of higher learning in Madrid, forming a center for intellectual inquiry, but because it was an ideal location for Nationalists to move across its flat terrain, march up Gran Via, and take the city, it was now the locus of battle. Here Spaniard fought Spaniard, and men—and women—from the nations of Europe took up arms against their own countryfolk in a battle between the forces of fascism and socialism. Maisie shivered when she reflected upon the scenes of devastation she had seen since crossing the border. Yet here, close to the front, she felt strangely safe.

She remembered, then, the feelings that assailed her while working in the casualty clearing station as a young woman. How old had she been then? Eighteen? Nineteen? At night, in their tent, as she talked with Iris in the darkness, it was as if they were in a private world, as if the fabric of the tent was made of wood and concrete, not canvas. Anyone passing could have heard them, yet they thought every word was oh so private. Then the following morning they walked out into the business of war, of men dying and wounds that bled more blood than she had ever seen in her life. Was there something about looking death in the eye every day that numbed the senses?

Vallejo led her into the building, then down a flight of stairs into a series of cellars. They must have been intended as storerooms, but now they were places of safe havens where Republican fighters rested, or took time to eat. A cluster of ten men passed, bandoliers across their chests and guns grasped in both hands, on their way back into the fight.

"This way, Maisie," said Vallejo.

They walked along a corridor, then stood outside another door. Vallejo knocked, and they walked in.

The man with gray hair was standing behind a desk, looking down at a sheaf of papers. To the side, against the wall, were wooden cases, open to reveal their contents: guns and ammunition.

"Comrade," said Vallejo.

The man looked up and smiled. It was a broad smile, without guile. He stepped from behind the desk and approached Maisie.

"Miss Dobbs, we meet at last." He reached out his hand.

"You know who I am, sir, so I think you might introduce yourself in return."

Vallejo spoke. "My apologies; I should have introduced you. In fact, I am remiss in not doing so earlier, but it would have compromised our security. So . . . Miss Maisie Dobbs." He paused, indicating the other man. "I would like to present Mr. Thomas Wright."

Wright gave a short bow, as if they were being introduced at a London supper party, not a battlefront. "My pleasure, Miss Dobbs."

Maisie nodded.

Vallejo pulled up two chairs in front of the desk, and Wright sat down to face them.

"Let me provide the missing pieces in your understanding of what I am doing, though I should add, Miss Dobbs, that you are not to divulge any of this. From the way in which you have immersed yourself in the minutiae of Sebastian Babayoff's death, it appeared I would have to take one of two measures—I would either have to ensure your lips were sealed by rather extreme means, or I would have to take you into our confidence. That would mean I'd have to trust you, and I do not extend my trust easily."

Maisie noticed that although the man spoke English without an accent, there was something almost too proper about it. He could have come from an aristocratic family, but she thought not. This was a man who could speak English perfectly because it was not his first language, though she was sure that if he were in England, people would guess his land of origin; his accent was too correct. But something about the way he held himself reminded her of Maurice—a man at home with whatever language he was speaking, but who seemed so very deliberate in his movements as each word was spoken.

"Do you have any idea what trouble you could have caused by putting your nose into matters that do not concern you?"

Maisie raised her eyebrows. "I think finding a man dead on a path makes it a matter of some concern to me."

"You could have left it to the police."

She shook her head. "No. I couldn't. They were too busy dealing with the number of people who had crossed the border and the problems caused by the human flood to pay attention to one man who had been killed by a refugee looking for money or something to sell."

"And if there was no killer to be found, why did you keep on searching?"

"Because there was something so very deliberate about it. And frankly, I didn't believe the story."

"What do you believe?"

Maisie allowed a moment to pass. She was being asked to extend her trust.

"I am missing many pieces in this puzzle, and I certainly don't know who you are, but I suspect you are moving between different factions, if I am to be honest. You speak good English—much better than an Englishman—but you are not from those shores. I believe you are Bavarian—I make the distinction because Germany is still a young country, and something in your bearing suggests a man at odds with his country but at the same time with great loyalty to his place of birth. Don't ask how I know that; I just have a feeling." She turned to Vallejo. "And you have tried to pull the wool over my eyes in a very strange way, Professor. You took me into your confidence, yet you bring me here, and I am told I should not have asked questions. Which leads me to one conclusion." She shifted her chair to face both men. "You want me here so you can tell me something. The fact that I came upon a man whose life had just been taken was an accident, but perhaps a fortuitous accident for you. You realized I was being followed by the British Secret Service. I assure you, any investigation into my presence in Gibraltar is purely personal; my family wanted to know of my whereabouts, and they have connections. But your curiosity was piqued, wasn't it, Professor Vallejo? Perhaps by Arturo Kenyon—and as for him, I suspect he was brought into your sphere of influence by Miriam Babayoff, though she is not in love with him, is she?"

"Well, you have been doing some thinking, Miss Dobbs."

"I've had time." She sat back in her chair, tired already, though it was barely half past ten. "Look, I think you're a very brave man—you're both brave. You, sir, are—I believe—working on both sides of the war."

Wright laughed. "More than two, Miss Dobbs."

"Yes, more than two. At first I thought you were a German spy, but that would have been too simple. The fact that you are here tells me that you are working against fascism, and if that means infiltrating the Russians and the Germans at the same time, so be it. And the British and French. Because everyone gets something out of this war, don't they? And you, I believe—because I am still here and not yet dead— want the people to get something for which they are fighting to the death." She turned to Vallejo. "And so do you."

"Thank you for believing me so gracious with my loyalties, Miss Dobbs," said Wright.

Maisie shook her head. "Gracious? It doesn't mean you would not kill to protect what you're doing here." She nodded toward the guns. "Are those the guns that came from Gibraltar? From the cave?"

"Perhaps some," said Vallejo. "We tend to make use of arms very quickly."

"There's more coming from Russia via a direct means now," said Wright.

"Ah, so not British, from the garrison?" asked Maisie.

Wright shook his head, laughing. "No, the British are straddling their options, trying to keep Herr Hitler happy. Though, as you may have heard, your politicians like to get their hands on our ore and minerals—and at a good price—from Franco. No one is clean in a time of war."

There was a pause. Each person in the room seemed to be waiting for another volley of questions. Wright and Vallejo did not have to wait long.

"Did you kill Sebastian Babayoff?" Maisie looked at Wright directly as she asked.

He shook his head. "Sebastian was a very enthusiastic supporter of our cause—as you know." He looked at Vallejo, as if to confirm the source of his information. "Sebastian was a Communist—as was his father before him—and so, by default, is his sister. They are supporters, and good Jews into the bargain."

"What did he do? Take too many photographs?" asked Maisie.

"That's exactly what he did. He took photographs of me." Wright looked at Maisie. His cool blue eyes seemed to threaten, negating the need for words. "I was engaged in very sensitive work at the time, and my means of entry into Gibraltar also rendered me somewhat vulnerable. But Sebastian could not hold back."

"The German submarine?" offered Maisie.

He ignored the question, instead continuing with his story. "Professor Vallejo has given me a briefing of your suspicions regarding the death of a man on the path by the hotel, and you—I must say—are almost correct in your assumptions. But here's what you do not yet know. Rosanna Grillo has returned to Gibraltar, to her life mending nets. For now. You will never at any point discuss this with her, or the fact that you saw a photograph in which she was presented in a—let's say, in a different light. Is that clear?" Wright did not wait for an answer. "She has been of great service to us, as was her uncle—who died of a heart attack, a loss indeed. And that is the truth. But now she must be left in safety. She will not be returning to any part of this work."

"What happened to Babayoff?"

"He is dead. He had become a liability, so we brought him from Gibraltar across the border. His enthusiasm—his passion, if you will—for our cause led him to be less than careful. Such passion has to be channeled. But there is something about the photographer, especially in this situation—he thought himself invincible because he looked through a lens, as if everything he observed was happening outside himself and not to himself. Do you understand?"

Maisie thought of the man she'd seen at the hotel—intense, as if he would go to the edge of the fire because he believed himself safe behind the camera. She nodded. "So he was killed while trying to take the best photograph of the civil war here in Spain."

Wright gave a barely perceptible nod.

"And Miriam?"

"Of course Miriam did not want her brother dead—she adored him. But she has always known his failings. She is more measured, but like Rosanna, it is time for her to become . . . settled."

"Solomon?"

"Ah, yes, plodding Solomon—always watch the plodders, Miss Dobbs. He was the tortoise to Babayoff's hare. Life will go on for all of them now. They have played a part, and now there are others in the fray. Arms are coming in, and Madrid is holding firm—at the moment, anyway." Wright paused. "Is there anything else you want to know from me, Miss Dobbs?"

"I am intrigued." She looked from one man to the other. "I am curious as to why you have indulged me."

"We have contacts, people known to us and to you, and some you have never encountered. We came to understand that you would never let go until you learned the truth."

"Contacts? Let me see—Brian Huntley, Robert MacFarlane, and perhaps even Dr. Francesca Thomas." Her gaze rested on Vallejo.

Vallejo opened his palms and shrugged, his mouth turned down as if to suggest there was no more he could say. The men exchanged smiles.

"And what of the dead man? The man who was not Babayoff, but who was buried with his name?"

Wright answered. "The policeman, Marsh—he was right. There was a refugee looking for someone to attack that evening, though this one was not as benign as some. He was a Nationalist spy. Gibraltar is an interesting place, Miss Dobbs—a place too valuable to be left unattended by your Secret Service. It is also never passed over by the eyes and ears of other powers. I am afraid it was I who took his life, and who arranged for Babayoff's immediate departure to Spain."

Silence enveloped the room for some seconds. Then Maisie spoke.

"And what about you, Mr. Wright? Although I am sure that isn't your real name. If I had to guess, it's something like Reiter. Am I correct?"

The man smiled, the skin at the corners of his eyes crinkling in a benevolent manner, though his blue eyes grew paler, like a robin's egg dusted with spring frost.

"I have work to do here, Miss Dobbs. Do not endeavor to attribute my endeavors to any single country—I am loyal to the people, not to a king or a president or a prime minister of any political entity. Yet I am affiliated with several, and though they might not trust me, they need me. I fight, and I keep the peace—both those things at the same time. As my friend here has indicated in your conversations—which he has graciously recounted for me—this is not just a battleground, here in Spain. It is a military and political exercise—peacocks fanning their tails while others watch and learn and make preparations. Do you understand, Miss Dobbs?"

Maisie nodded. Yes, she understood. She was in the company of a free agent, a man who manipulated those in power, who likely inspired the many who fought. A man who was answerable to no one, yet took orders at the highest level. And because of that, she suspected he must also be a marked man. The naive Babayoff must have rendered him more so, for a time.

"Now you are here, Miss Dobbs, what will we do with you?"

Maisie stood up. "I think I have seen enough, Mr. Wright. I have listened enough, too; through those walls, I can certainly hear enough of the battle. You need do nothing with me. I have plans of my own." She stepped forward and extended her hand. "We won't meet again, of that I am sure, though I am equally positive I'll cross paths with people of mutual acquaintance. Indeed, it would not surprise me to see Robert MacFarlane waiting for me on the other side of the border."

Vallejo exchanged nods with Wright. Maisie turned to leave.

"One moment, Miss Dobbs."

For the first time since Maisie had entered the room, she detected a certain reticence in Wright's demeanor. He clasped his hands, circling his thumbs around each other, then came to his feet.

"I am not sure how you will use this information, and I am in two minds as to whether to bring it to your attention. But John Otterburn is both your friend and your foe. He is too valuable to your country—and I have to say, ultimately, to peace—to render him anything other than untouchable. You do not have to nurture his friendship, Miss Dobbs, but you would do well not to put your hand near the hornets' nest. Remember how much you have witnessed of his activities; that renders you vulnerable too. In these times, as far as certain politicians in your country are concerned, he is a Goliath."

A rogue nerve in Maisie's eye twitched, and she wondered if Wright had noticed. "And we know what happened to Goliath. Don't we, Mr. Wright?"

CHAPTER EIGHTEEN

M aisie was silent on the way back to the hotel. The journey,
though not long, was slow, again snaking along roads all but
destroyed by the relentless bombing, past shattered houses
and offices with walls sheared off to reveal the contents of rooms, some
with furniture still standing, doors hanging off, beds still clothed and
pictures hanging askew on the walls, as if the sides had been taken
from a doll's house to reveal the normal life torn to shreds.

"You don't approve of our fight, do you, Miss Dobbs?" Vallejo did
not turn to face her as the motor car bumped down a narrow thoroughfare, past fractured concrete and fallen masonry.

She said nothing for a while, but continued looking out of the
window. It was as if every scene before her had been overlaid with
another image, the work of a clever photographer who had pointed his
camera at two subjects at once, and developed the film to reveal tragedy doubled—the ruins of a city, and a small aircraft spiraling down to
oblivion on an escarpment in Canada.

"It's not a question of approving or disapproving. I see how the gaping abyss between those who have much and those who have nothing can cause dangerous fractures in society. I see how power corrupts, how the people are manipulated and kept in their place. I see all of that, Professor Vallejo. But I am always left wondering if the fighting is worth so many dead. This country has been torn apart by authority-hungry men in all realms—in business, politics, and religion. It is the ordinary people who are crushed like ants underfoot. That is what happens. That is the only comment I have."

"And you think we're mad for trying to do something about it."

She felt Vallejo prodding her, and turned to face him. "No. Not at all. You and Wright are risking your lives, are standing up to be counted. You can call yourselves Communists, socialists, whatever you wish—but I can see you believe you are on the side of good. But at what point does being on the side of good lapse into thinking one is God? Where's the line? And again, what about the innocents?"

Vallejo nodded slowly. Maisie thought that the folds in his skin had become deeper since they first met. It was a moment before he spoke again, his voice edged with melancholy.

"You know, the Communists in Spain would never have become so powerful had not Germany and Italy sent their forces to join the Nationalists. The Moors from North Africa, especially, have been brutal, sweeping through the villages, tearing them apart, violating women and murdering them." Vallejo cleared his throat, as if he had realized his voice had become loud, almost as if he were trying to speak above music that had stopped without warning. "And you, what will you do, considering what you have seen, and what you now understand?"

Maisie looked out of the window once more, at a child with a bandage around her head helping a limping elderly man along the street. "Me? That remains to be seen, Professor Vallejo. It really remains to be seen."

At seven o'clock in the hotel bar, once again thronged by what Maisie thought of as "battle tourists," along with journalists, doctors, some soldiers, and minor politicians from other countries, she wove her way through the clusters of people to the two nurses who had claimed a small table at the far end of the room. They waved when they saw her.

"Do join us for a drink, Maisie," said Hattie.

Maisie shook her head. "Not for me—I'd like a hot soak while it's quiet, and while I can. I don't want to be caught in the bathtub during an air raid."

"Did you manage to help us with a motor car?" asked Freda.

"Yes. A man named Raoul will collect us at five o'clock tomorrow morning, and we'll get on our way. He's completely trustworthy. We'll have to begin our journey back to the hotel at about five, perhaps earlier—is that all right?"

Both women nodded.

"Right ho!" said Hattie. "Thank you very much, Maisie. A woman of connections! Not a bad thing, here."

"I suggest you don't wear your uniforms—just trousers and cotton blouses, though if you can acquire armbands with a red cross, that would be handy. And for Raoul and me too."

"It's as good as done. Five o'clock by the door, then?"

"Yes. I'll ask the clerk if we can have bottles of water and some sandwiches—or whatever looks like a sandwich here."

"You've done enough, Maisie—we'll bring food and water for the day, and we've medical supplies ready to take with us." She paused. "We're glad you're coming with us."

On the way to her room, Maisie stopped at the hotel clerk's desk and asked for a bowl of lemon chicken soup and some bread, to be brought to her quarters. Now she wanted to be alone. Now she wanted to think about James. She did not want to linger, this time, on the circumstances of his death. She wanted to sit and remember everything, from the first time he took her in his arms to the moment she came to him in his study at their apartment in Toronto, leaned into his neck, and told him he might have to move his papers and books to the box room, because the study was the best for conversion to a nursery. And before she had even slipped the key into the lock of her hotel room door, she felt again the tears of joy they'd shared, that their late union was to be so very blessed. Now she could feel herself slipping back, as if she had managed to climb almost to the top of grief's dark void, only to lose her strength, her fingernails ceasing to hold. She stood at her bedroom window and looked down at the damage wrought by battle, and at people on the streets—life going on. She stared at humanity enduring, then spoke in a soft voice.

"Don't worry, James, I will prevail. I am resilient too."

Raoul was waiting in front of the hotel, as arranged. By the time Maisie came down from her room, he was loading two boxes of medical supplies into the car boot as Freda pushed a bag made of sackcloth onto the back seat. It seemed as if sustenance for several days had been prepared, not just a few hours. Raoul nodded to Maisie as if pleased to see a familiar face, his usual taciturn manner replaced by gratitude that she was there to take charge, rather than allow him to be bossed by the two doughty British nurses.

Maisie approached and thanked him, slipping a note of currency into his palm, a promise that he would be well remunerated for his trouble. She took the seat next to him, while the cousins slid across the passenger seat, close to one another.

"Is bumpy," said Raoul, shaking his head up and down to demonstrate that the journey would not be an easy one.

"Oh, don't worry about us," said Hattie. "We're just grateful you can take us, Raoul—thank you. Bread and cheese, anyone?"

Maisie shook her head. "Perhaps later."

The nurses showed no fear as they made their way through the city and out onto the Valencia road. Maisie looked back once and saw a certain dullness in their eyes, as if their emotions had been anesthetized. It was a look she recognized, for she had seen it in herself once, a long time ago, when she was a young nurse in France. Compassion had not been lost, but it was on a leash. Nothing could hamper the work of a nurse; the time it took to brush away one tear could mean the difference between saving a soldier or laying him out after death.

Lulled by the motion of the motor car, even while negotiating the rough roads, Maisie dozed, sometimes half waking to hear the low mumble of the cousins talking, sometimes hearing nothing but Raoul rhythmically tapping his fingers on the steering wheel.

When the slowing car woke her again, the landscape outside had changed. Now they were surrounded by mountainous country, with rough hills and low vegetation. A series of sand-colored buildings were clustered around a church with a bell tower and spire. The heat seemed to glance off the walls where, in shallow shade, a couple of dogs lay back and yawned as the motor car came to a halt. Women scrubbing sheets in a series of barrels looked up at the same time as a small woman bustled from one of the buildings toward them, wiping her hands on a towel. She was not dressed like a nun—she wore a blouse and full skirt with a clean white apron, and her hair was secure under a scarf tied at the nape of her neck—but Maisie instinctively knew this was Sister Teresa. She spoke English very well.

"Are you the British nurses?" she asked, still approaching them, now raising a hand to her brow and squinting.

Maisie was surprised. Sister Teresa seemed much younger than she had at first imagined. About thirty years of age, she had a broad smile and a welcoming demeanor, though the deep lines around her eyes betrayed her. This was a woman burdened with constant worry.

"And we've brought another, with more experience of the front lines than us two," said Hattie.

Maisie stepped forward to greet the nun, who clasped her hands in both her own. "Much gratitude, much gratitude. You are most kind to be of service."

"I fear I might not live up to expectations, Sister Teresa. I was last a nurse some years ago, but I will do what I can to help."

"Good. That is good. I am very busy here, and our women help where they can. They believe the Republicans have made sure there are books in our schools, and pencils, paper, and teachers for the children, so we must do everything we can to help." She ushered them into the building as if she were a mother hen, arms wide, drawing the three women into a cluster.

Maisie looked back at Raoul, who had stepped out of the motor car and was watching the women talk, while also keeping an eye on the children gathered around the motor car. He pointed to the back of the building, to indicate that he would be leaving the vehicle there, in the shade and out of sight.

Inside the first building, Sister Teresa led her volunteer nurses into an anteroom that Maisie suspected should have been filled with medicines and bandages, with disinfectants and clean, sterilized equipment—but instead it was almost bare. Hattie and Freda lifted their boxes onto a table and looked at each other, then Maisie. Sister Teresa was swaying, as if she were unwell.

"You've been trying to do so much with so little, Sister," Maisie said. "You must need rest so very badly."

The nun shook her head. "I cannot, because—"

"Well, you can for a few hours. Just show us what's what, and we'll get stuck in," said Hattie.

Sister Teresa gestured for them to follow her through the anteroom. A heavy carved wooden door led into a long ward, set up with five beds on either side. Four were empty. She took the women to each bed and described the wounds suffered by the Republican fighters who had made their way to her makeshift hospital. In Maisie's estimation, every man could have been considered an acute case—and underneath the fumes left by disinfectant, she could smell the unmistakable odor of gangrene.

"There has been a lot of fighting in the hills these past few days, so I expect more to come in this evening. They often come after nightfall, when it is clear to move the wounded. I could send a message— one of the boys would take it—to say that it would be better to take the chance now."

Maisie glanced at the other two women and nodded, then turned back to the nun. "Do that, Sister. By the time the boy is back, we will be ready. First, though, let us get our supplies stored, the preparation room organized, and examine your patients here." She paused, not quite sure whether she should ask the question that seemed to linger on the lips of the three visitors. "Have you had medical training, Sister Teresa?"

The nun shook her head. "I was a teacher, but my father was a physician—not that it gives me any training, but I knew enough to at least try to help."

"You are here alone," said Maisie. "Where are the other nuns?"

Sister Teresa's eyes filled with tears. "There are those who no longer revere the church, and so they take vengeance on God. Our sisters have gone to safety, but I decided to remain here. Whatever army a man is with, if he needs care, I will provide it—though in our hills fighters are for the Republic. They know I will help them." She paused, wiping her brow and looking at her hand, and then focused on the women again. "Let me show you the other room—through here, to the right of the door that leads from the square. It's where we treat the wounded when they first come in."

She led the way through the preparation room to another oak door, which she opened into a stark whitewashed room with four scrubbed tables. Maisie saw Hattie and Freda exchange glances. The floor had been cleaned, but livid bloodstains remained across the tiles, as if red paint had been spilled. Someone had used a pick to create a makeshift gulley, so blood and water could be sluiced outside through a small hole in the wall where it met the floor. Beside each table, a smaller metal trolley had been situated, ready to hold the tools of surgery, water, bandages, swabs—the basic essentials required to tend a wounded fighter.

"We have everything but a doctor," said Sister Teresa.

"You have enough, Sister—and that is better than nothing," said Maisie. "We will prepare as quickly as we can." She looked at the cousins.

"You can bet on it," said Hattie.

Freda nodded, her face pale.

"Now then, you must go and rest—please, Sister," said Maisie. "We'll come for you if we need you, and definitely before we leave."

Sister Teresa nodded. As the three began walking toward the small preparation room, she called out to Maisie, "Does your driver chop wood?"

"I'm sure he can. What do you need?"

"The fire outside needs to be kept alight, to heat water for boiling bandages and cleaning wounds."

A DANGEROUS PLACE

"I'll see to it while Hattie and Freda sort out the supplies, and then we'll all get to work. Come, let me take you to your chamber—the least I can do is make sure you follow orders to rest."

Sister Teresa led Maisie through the church to another series of small rooms, set out in a square flanking a courtyard. One of the rooms was the nun's private cell. A narrow bed was set alongside the far wall, topped with a mattress so thin, Maisie wondered if she ever slept. A single sheet and blanket were folded at one end and it seemed undisturbed, as if unused for days. A small table positioned to the left, underneath an engraving of the Madonna, held a bowl and ewer half filled with water. Sister Teresa walked over to the bed. It was time to leave her alone with her prayers and—Maisie hoped—to sleep.

The women worked with speed, Maisie picking up her rhythm from Hattie and Freda. She had not hit her stride yet, but she understood what was required. Soon the preparation room was disinfected, its cupboards scrubbed and dried, and new supplies stored within easy reach. The surgical room was swabbed again, and necessary supplies placed on each of the trolleys.

"Now to the patients in the ward," announced Hattie.

Maisie took a large jug and left the building to go to the pump, to which a local woman had directed her earlier. She filled the jug and returned. The women had found cups, which had been washed and were now draining, so Maisie set them out and filled them, ready to be taken to the men once their examinations had been completed.

"We're in the deep end now, Maisie," said Hattie, looking at her watch. "We've got to get a lot done quickly. I'll take these two, Freda will take those two men and if you examine the pair at the end, we'll get it all finished in no time."

Maisie nodded. "Right you are," she said, taking up one of three trays, already prepared with swabs, bandages, scissors, scalpel, and a basin of water, plus disinfectant and—finally—morphia. She remembered her first day at the casualty clearing station in France, arriving with Iris and seeing approaching ambulances, rocking from side to side, as wounded were brought in from the battlefield. The screeching of shells falling assaulted her ears, the strange *crump, crump, crump* when they fell to earth to do their job—to kill. "You're in the deep end now," the nurse in charge had told them, before they had even caught their breath. *Death's deep end.*

Maisie greeted her first patient, a man with a bandaged shoulder. "Señor," she said, smiling before placing a white mask over her mouth and nose, "soy una enfermera." *I am a nurse.* She cleaned and dressed his wounds, a task that took longer than expected, due to his pain and the severity of the wound—they were saving as much morphia as they could for new patients. She was in the midst of caring for the second soldier when a boy of about ten years old came in, shouting.

"Los hombres heridos están llegando," he wailed.

Hattie looked up at Maisie, repeating in English, " 'The hurt men are coming'—some wounded are coming down from the hills."

Before another breath could be taken, the three women had rushed out to see eight men on makeshift stretchers being set down in the shade. The dogs were chivvied away, their noses following a trail of blood. Six other men, walking wounded, slumped, blood leaking from fabric torn from clothing and used to stem the flow from a forehead, an arm, a shoulder, a knee. Everywhere Maisie looked, it seemed that blood was seeping from a human being into the ground. The noise around her heightened, and she realized local women had come to help—grabbing bandages from washing lines flapping from tree to tree in the small square in front of the buildings. Soon Sister Teresa was among them.

"I could not sleep," she said, rolling up her sleeves.

"Come on, let's get on with it," said Maisie to Hattie and Freda, who were used to seeing patients after wounds had been treated and they'd passed through a dressing station. "I'll look at the wounds and tell Sister Teresa which order we should see them in, and make sure no one gets water by mouth yet. I think at least three need a surgeon, but we don't have one, so we'll have to do our best."

"Right you are. Come along, Freda," said Hattie. "Let's do as Maisie says, and get on with it."

Raoul helped Maisie bring in the wounded, one at a time, then returned to help Sister Teresa comfort the men who waited outside. A few moments later Maisie beckoned Raoul again. "Here, help me with this man—it's a nasty head wound, so let's get him in. I think I am going to have to be both doctor and nurse today."

Together they lifted the man onto a table in the surgical room. A large shrapnel splinter had entered his skull above the ear, and was partially embedded in flesh and bone.

"I don't think it's too deep," said Maisie. She looked up at Raoul, whose complexion had changed. "Step outside, Raoul—get some fresh air. Go back and help Sister Teresa."

"I can't hear very well, Nurse, and my head hurts," said the fighter.

Maisie was taken aback. "You're English."

"Well, there's a surprise—the nurse recognizes one of her own! Brian Smithers, at your service. Or should I say, at the service of my comrades."

"Hold still, Mr. Smithers. I want to look at this wound of yours."

"Will I live to tell the tale?"

"You might," said Maisie. "If you can just be quiet and not move."

She ascertained that the shrapnel had not penetrated too far, but internal bleeding and infection were her greatest fear. She began to cleanse the wound, using small swabs with disinfectant, working her way around the metal and across the skin.

"This isn't pleasant, Nurse," said the patient.

"No, I know. How brave do you feel, young man?" asked Maisie.

"I'm here, ain't I?" said Smithers. "Fighting away for the cause, so I reckon I'm brave enough."

"I have to remove a piece of shrapnel, and I have to do it quickly. I don't want to put you under to do this, so just hold still—now."

Not trusting the grip of forceps, she grasped the shrapnel with her gloved hand and pulled, ready with a swab to press against the wound. Smithers screamed, and Maisie could see he had willed himself not to move. Blood oozed through the swabs, which she replaced time and again, pressing against the wound. She looked up just as Freda returned to the room, having moved her patient to the ward, and making ready for another to be brought in.

"Freda, just one moment. Quick, hold this swab while I prepare a morphia injection."

"Not a bloody needle," said Smithers, who had begun to retch.

Maisie pushed the syringe into a bottle of morphia, measured enough to render Smithers pain-free, and lifted his arm. "Here we go—almost done."

Freda returned to her station, where Raoul was bringing in the next patient. Maisie finished dressing the wound and checked Smithers for more injuries. She knew he should be in a hospital, that the risk of infection was high—his face and head would be swollen like a football, come morning—but she had done all she could. She called Raoul to help her remove Smithers to the ward, where Sister Teresa was setting up mattresses on the floor.

Under the influence of morphia, Smithers was rambling, talking about going down to the pub later, taking out his girl to a picture, getting back to work on time.

"Why did you come here, Brian?" asked Maisie as she settled him on a mattress.

The man who had left his country to fight so far away giggled like a small child. "You can't let them Nationalists get away with it, can you? Us workers have got to stick together, wherever we're from."

F our hours later, all of the wounded had been tended, washed, and placed in a bed or on a straw mattress on the floor. Maisie, Hattie, and Freda, along with Sister Teresa and Raoul, were now slumped on the ground alongside the outside wall.

"I don't think I ever imagined I could learn Spanish so quickly," said Freda.

Hattie laughed—a short laugh, inspired not by humor but by irony. "I don't think that what you were speaking was anything like Spanish, but the men caught your drift."

"Now we've got to get them to a hospital," said Freda. "They can't all stay here. Some will be all right in a week or so, but there are others who won't make it another two days if they don't have vital operations."

Maisie leaned forward, her hands around her knees. "I'll talk to someone when I get back to the hotel, and make sure an ambulance comes." She turned to Raoul and, not letting the other women see her, rubbed her thumb and forefinger together. He nodded. Even if it was a makeshift ambulance in a cleaned-out lorry, transport would be found. She turned back to the two nurses and Sister Teresa. "It's as good as done—and they'll bring more supplies, Sister Teresa."

"It's quiet here, in the village," said Freda.

"It's time for the women to go to the hills, to the caves," said Sister Teresa. "That's where they sleep."

"And it's time for us to start sorting things out before we leave," said Hattie, coming to her feet.

The others followed her lead, brushing the dust from their clothing as they stood up. It was at that moment an older woman came toward them, leading another, much younger woman, who was clutching her swollen belly.

"Oh, no, I don't believe it—that woman's in labor!" said Freda.

"Dear Lord, I've never done midwifery—have you, Maisie?"

"Unless you count helping my father bring foals into the world, no, not me—but we're going to have to be quick about learning." She ran toward the women to help.

Sister Teresa shook her head, pointing to the church. "No, not with the men—she can't go in there. Take her into the church."

Soon a bed had been brought into the church. Maisie encouraged the woman to walk back and forth across the cool flagstones, flanked by herself and Sister Teresa.

"Isn't there a midwife in the village—a local woman who helps women with their babies?" she asked.

Sister Teresa shook her head. "There was, but she was killed in an air raid. And it's not as if the other women don't know how to usher in a new life, but now they come to me—and to God."

Maisie looked up at a statue of the Madonna, and silently petitioned her for help.

Hattie and Freda brought hot water and towels. It seemed to Maisie that they had stepped back from the task at hand.

"I suppose I impressed you with the foals, didn't I?" She turned to her patient. "I need to check the baby, señora." She pointed to her ear and then to the woman's belly, and the woman nodded. Hattie handed Maisie a stethoscope.

Having examined the mother-to-be and listened to the baby's heartbeat, Maisie turned to the other women. "It's not going to be long now. Hattie, you didn't happen to pack tea in that picnic bag of yours, did you?"

Hattie smiled. "I did, but I am not sure it's good for Mother."

Maisie looked up at her fellow nurse. "I wasn't actually thinking of the mother-to-be. I could really do with a cup."

The woman cried out, and Maisie urged her to push to bring her baby into the world. Time and again the scream came, and soon Maisie felt the infant's head against her fingers. "Again, señora, again now." Maisie blew out her cheeks to encourage the woman. "I have the shoulders."

"Now the hooves, eh?" said Freda, then muttered an apology when she saw the look on her cousin's face. "Just trying to lighten the moment."

"Uno more, señora. Uno. Just uno," said Maisie.

As the woman gave a final wail, Maisie supported her daughter's entry into the world. She felt her eyes fill with tears, her heart pounding as she held the baby in her hands, folding a soft sheet around the fragile body and allowing the tiny hand to clutch one of her fingers. Then she felt Sister Teresa's touch upon her back. "Give the child to her mother, Miss Maisie."

Maisie set the infant upon her mother's chest and took the scissors handed to her by Hattie.

"Well done, Maisie. I tell you, I could never have done that."

Maisie cut the baby's cord and ensured the delivery was complete. Freda held out her hand. "Stand up, Maisie. We'll do the rest. Then we have to get along before it's too late—now then, you go and have a wash."

But for a moment Maisie could not move. She stood looking down at the new mother and the way her lips brushed against the head of her infant daughter, her eyes closing as she smiled.

think I will sleep for a week after today," said Hattie.

"You slept for most of the journey back," Freda retorted.

"How about you, Maisie?" asked Hattie. "You were very quiet in the motor car. I bet you didn't think we'd get you into this amount of trouble, eh? . . . Patients with gangrene, wounded men coming in from the hills, and to cap it all, having to learn midwifery on the spot." She looked over toward the bar. "We could still get a drink, you know—I think we all deserve it."

"Oh, not me, thank you. That bathtub filled with hot water beckons." Maisie bid the women good night, and went to her room. But instead of falling asleep, she thought about the small hospital run by a single nun who barely slept, who feared for her life enough to cast aside her habit in favor of clothing that was little different from the women who helped her every day—washing bandages, cooking for the men, scrubbing floors of blood from battle and dust from the square outside. She thought of those same women taking refuge in the hills, and a newborn held close to her mother's heart. She replayed the moment outside the hotel, after Hattie and Freda had dragged their bags through the double doors, while she lingered to speak to Raoul. He would be there to collect her the following morning, before the sun rose over a battle-torn city—but in the meantime he would use the money Maisie had given him to find a driver and an ambulance to go to the village and bring back those men who could be moved, so that they might continue their treatment in the hospital.

In those dark hours, before fatigue claimed her, a plan began to form in her mind. And she admitted to herself that she had known what she must do from the moment she met Sister Teresa and witnessed her struggle. Perhaps it had come to her even before, as she watched warplanes flying low above her head.

CHAPTER NINETEEN

Maisie kept her eyes closed for much of the return journey to Gibraltar, and perhaps for that reason it seemed to take longer. She was not sleepy, but her eyes were heavy, though on occasion she would open them to see a village, always with the same pockmarked walls where bullets had struck, now a hallmark of so many buildings. Yet still women dressed in black would be going about their business, hanging laundry, calling children to them as the motor car drove past, standing to watch it disappear from view. Maisie wondered if they yearned to leave, then decided that, no, they only wanted days without fear to return.

As Raoul once again negotiated the often rough roads, Maisie considered the case of Sebastian Babayoff. She was uneasy with the outcome of her investigation, such as it was. Yes, she had come to conclusions and had put them to Vallejo and Wright, but she wondered if she had been directed in some way. Or had she only wanted an easy answer, when it came down to it, succumbing to the fatigue wrought by widowhood?

Widowhood. So short a time a wife, and then a widow. Had she inserted herself into the investigation because she wanted to judge someone guilty, wanted to point the finger of blame and say, "You shall pay"? Or did she simply wanted to see someone bear responsibility for the killing of Sebastian Babayoff, because she could never call anyone to account for James' death? Except, perhaps, James himself. Is that why she had failed to speak to Lord Julian and Lady Rowan about the memorial service? Had she needed to see someone plead guilty first? They had made one plan after another for the service, she knew, because they could not proceed without their son's wife present. But she knew that taking part in such a ritual would feel like walking the high wire without a safety net.

It was as the journey neared its close, after Raoul informed her that they were just twenty minutes from the border, that Maisie, reviewing the elements of Sebastian Babayoff's murder, thought back to the young photographer she had seen in the hotel. What was it she'd seen in him—a determination, yet a kind of recklessness? She recalled thinking that the camera itself might offer him a false sense of safety, that the lens between the photographer and his subject offered a perceived distance from the danger inherent in the moment. Did that happen? Or would he be haunted forever by his subject? Did he see the dead—and later, his black-and-white images of them—as a surgeon would view a human being he was about to cut into, or as a mechanic might look upon a motor car, an engine made of flesh and blood? Perhaps the detachment in that photographer's eyes was necessary—but she wondered if in the end it would be the death of him, as it had been the death of Babayoff.

They passed through the border with ease, showing their papers at the entry to the British garrison town. Raoul pulled over at the same place where he and Vallejo had met Maisie just days before, and she walked back along the quiet streets to Mrs. Bishop's guest house. She unlocked the outer door, stepped across the courtyard, and climbed up to her room, turning the second key to gain entry. Locking the door behind her, she leaned back once more, welcoming the comfort of wood against her spine. The room smelled of freshly laundered sheets; the window was open, the lace curtain flapping back and forth in a warm breeze. The white counterpane seemed even crisper; Mrs. Bishop must have been in to clean and polish. The scent of lavender beeswax reminded Maisie of Chelstone. Of home.

As she moved toward the bed, she saw an envelope on the small table, alongside the carafe of water and an upturned glass. It was addressed to Miss Maisie Dobbs.

MacFarlane. She sighed.

> *Dear Maisie,*
>
> *Well, lassie, you seem to have gone off adventuring. When you return to this little colonial outpost, perhaps you would be so kind as to send me a quick billy-do. Our mutual friend, Mr. Salazar will let me know next time you're in his establishment. I hope it's soon.*
>
> *Yours,*
>
> *MacFarlane*

"*Billy-do* indeed." She remembered once having tea with MacFarlane, when he referred to a plate of petits fours as "little fours." His deliberate impression of ignorance could be comic at times, yet at others it was like a needle under her skin.

Maisie bathed away the dust and sticky residue of travel and rested before leaving Mrs. Bishop's guest house. Dusk had not yet descended. She left a note for her landlady expressing thanks for keeping her room fresh and clean, and said she hoped all was well. She would be leaving for England soon, she noted, but would provide further details in good time—she would have to consult the shipping office first.

Mr. Salazar came to her with open arms, greeting her as if she had been gone for weeks, not days, and as if she were a customer of long standing, rather than one who had been in the town less than two months.

"Miss Dobbs, Miss Dobbs, Miss Dobbs!" he exclaimed. "I have missed you—come in, come in, come in." He pulled out a table so that she could sit with her back to the mural. "Now, some wine? You are hungry?"

Maisie nodded and asked for a glass of wine and a bowl of soup—if it was chicken and lemon soup, so much the better.

When Salazar returned, Maisie asked if MacFarlane had been in of late.

"Ah, yes, and he will be here soon, too—perhaps an hour? You will wait for him?"

Maisie shook her head. "No—I have had a long day, Mr. Salazar. Could you tell him I'll be here tomorrow morning? I have an errand first, and then I'll come at, say, half past eleven. Please pass on the message that I look forward to seeing him again."

Salazar frowned, but nodded. Maisie suspected that MacFarlane had asked him to keep Maisie in the café if she came in this evening, and her resolute alternative plan had rather unsettled the messenger.

The soup warmed her. When she'd finished, she pushed the bowl away and took a final sip of wine, leaving half the glass. It was time for her to go. She wanted to be alone now—she had seen life begin and life end since she was last in the café, and now she was ready for the day to be over, and to start again on the morrow. This evening, though, she would write four important letters.

M rs. Bishop made a fuss of Maisie when she emerged from her room the following morning, asking if she'd had a nice journey away from Gibraltar but not inquiring as to her exact whereabouts during her absence. The landlady offered to cook a "good English breakfast," but Maisie wanted only a cup of tea, which she would take back to her room. Today would be a busy one.

Her first stop was the shipping office, where she reserved passage for four days hence. Then she made her way to the Ridge Hotel, where she secured a room, arranging to move her belongings to the hotel the following day. She had no need to speak to Vallejo again, nor did she think she would see him, and she trusted that Raoul would be as good as his word.

Next, she would visit Miriam Babayoff.

O nce again, many locks had to be drawn back before Sebastian Babayoff's sister opened the door only enough for Maisie to see her face and part of her shoulder.

"Hello, Miss Babayoff—might you be able to spare me a few moments?"

Miriam closed the door, slipped the chain back, and opened the door just enough to let Maisie in. A pile of mending was on the table, a needlework box open.

"I can see you're hard at work. I won't keep you long, Miriam."

Miriam nodded and moved toward the stove. "Would you like tea?"

Maisie shook her head. "No, thank you. I shan't be staying too long. Is your sister here?"

Miriam looked at Maisie and shrugged. "She cannot move, Miss Dobbs—of course she is here." She held out a hand toward a chair and took her place again in front of her work. She picked up the fabric and began stitching where she had left off.

"I'd like to talk about Sebastian, Miss Babayoff."

The dead man's sister sighed deeply, her exasperation showing as she all but threw down the skirt she was hemming. "I thought I had answered every one of your questions. Too many questions. You are not the police, and my brother is dead. What do you think you are doing?"

Maisie softened her voice. "Yes, it does seem rather ill-mannered of me, but I am trying to get to the bottom of something. I have some answers, but not all. First of all, Miss Babayoff, would you mind describing for me what happened when you went to the mortuary, to identify your brother's body?"

Miriam Babayoff reached toward the garment she had been working on and picked at a thread. Her breath seemed to come faster, and she held her hands to her eyes. "It was terrible. Very terrible. I could not bear it."

"It is a hard thing to do—to know that one you love is gone, and have to look at his body. But you were not alone, were you?"

She shook her head. "Our rabbi and Mr. Solomon came with me— each a tower of strength. Mr. Solomon, especially, helped me so."

"He was there with you, a shoulder to lean on."

Miriam nodded. "I could not look at my brother's face—the rabbi told me not to—but I saw Sebastian's ring on his finger." She held up her left hand and moved her little finger. "It was my mother's wedding ring, though Sebastian wore it on his little finger—that's where it fitted him. He said he would wear it there until he found a bride."

"How very sad for you. Then of course you had to identify him."

She shook her head. "That was all I had. They said his face was—what did they say? Unrecognizable. I could bear to see no more after that. Once I'd told the policeman that it was Sebastian, Mr. Solomon led me to the door, and we were shown out. I was very upset."

"Miriam, I am very sorry to have to ask this—but did you look carefully at his hand?"

She nodded. "I turned away at first, and then I knew I had to hold his hand. So I did. And I asked for water, and I removed my mother's wedding ring." She stood and opened a cupboard next to the stove. Reaching for a small box on a high shelf, she took it down and set it on the table, opening the lid. A narrow band of rose gold sat in purple velvet.

"It's exquisite in its simplicity, isn't it?"

"It was the cheapest, I know—but my mother cherished it."

"It must have been difficult to remove, if Sebastian had pushed it onto his little finger."

Miriam smiled, a melancholy smile of remembrance. "Sebastian had narrow fingers, artists' fingers. He could work his fingers quickly with the camera—they were long fingers, almost like a pianist. When I saw him working, I thought it was like watching a maestro at the keys." She put her hands on the table, as if she were playing a piano. "But there was a—what do you call it?" She made a motion around her little finger with the fingers of her right hand.

"A ridge?"

"Yes, where he had worn it, and it was part of him."

"Is that so?"

The woman nodded.

"Tell me," said Maisie, "have you any doubt that the man you identified was your brother?"

Miriam Babayoff frowned. "I have held my brother's hand as a child and as a woman. I know his hands."

Maisie nodded. "Yes, I have no doubt that you do." She paused. "Tell me something else, then—and truthfully, Miriam. If nothing else, then please tell me the truth." Maisie looked at the needle threaded through the fabric of a skirt, waiting for Miriam to return to her work. She leaned forward, resting her elbows on the table. "I saw you at the cave. I know there was a man there. I know you went to the cave with Arturo Kenyon and that later, munitions were moved. They were loaded onto a fishing boat—perhaps two—and taken to arm the Republicans in Spain."

"It was Sebastian, he—"

Maisie held up her hand. "You can tell me that in a moment. I want to know who the man was—in the cave."

"Just a man. I knew him as Pedro. Arturo Kenyon brought him. He was paid to guard the cave, to watch, to report on anyone who came to search around."

"Was he from the garrison?"

She shrugged.

"It was not your brother."

"No—my brother was murdered, you know that. . . . Miss Dobbs, why are you asking me this?"

"I know he was murdered. But there are others who would have me think otherwise, and though I think I know why, I am looking a bit harder, for the moment."

Tears ran down Miriam Babayoff's face. Maisie reached to hold her hand. "So much of the story I have put together in my head is right—as far as I know. You said Sebastian had traveled into Spain before, at the outset of the war."

Miriam nodded. "As I told you, he went for a short time—enough to take photographs. He said it was an opportunity, you see. He wanted to be the first to send his photos to the Americans—the big ones, he said. He said life would be interested—I didn't quite understand, and he didn't explain."

"I think he meant *Life*—it's a publication in America, with lots of photographs. If he had sold his work to them, he would have become famous." She pulled a handkerchief from her leather satchel and gave it to Miriam. "Sebastian went to Spain, and I take it he came back with a greater feeling of injustice. Would that be fair to say?" She did not wait for a response. "He had taken photographs, and it was while developing them that he really began to look at what was on the other side of the camera. And he became more vociferous, more *angry*, about the injustice of it all. Was that the case?"

Miriam nodded, wiping her eyes and nose. "I told him it wasn't our battle, but then I saw his photos too, and I knew, *here*"—she pressed her hand to her chest—"that what he said was right. Our father believed in equality, and we believed in him. When Sebastian saw what Fascism was doing to the country just a few miles away, it changed him. It was as if he could be something like my father, as if he could honor him. And of course Carlos was our father's friend, and they had the same beliefs, so they felt outrage together—and it grows, in the way that coals together are a fire, but one alone is extinguished. See, the war changed Sebastian."

"That's when fate allowed him to photograph the German man—the man with the gray hair. He saw him in Spain, by chance, didn't he? And out on the boat with Carlos Grillo—using the binoculars—he thought he saw him being transferred to a German submarine. Then the man appeared again here in Gibraltar, and Sebastian wanted to photograph him and put his face in public—perhaps in a newspaper or even a pamphlet for the Ridge Hotel. And he asked Rosanna to help him."

There was silence, as if both women were weighing up how much truth the table between them could bear.

"He loved her, but not as much as she loved him," said Miriam. "She would have died for him. He asked her to dress as if she were a tourist—he took clothes . . ." She picked up a handful of the fabric in front of her and dropped it again. "Clothes that were here, waiting for me to mend and hem and add a tuck here and there. She dressed as a woman with money, to go to the party where he was taking photographs. I don't know how he knew the German would be there, but he did."

"And then, coincidentally, he was murdered."

Silence filled the space between Maisie and Miriam Babayoff, and this time Maisie made no attempt to take the woman's hand. It was as she had expected: the truth was being given voice. She had come close, when she had tackled Vallejo, but even then, her conclusions had taunted her, coming back time and again as if to ask, "Was it really so?"

"Who killed my brother, Miss Dobbs?" Miriam Babayoff looked away as she asked the question, unable to look at Maisie.

Maisie shook her head. "Sadly, after all this, I believe the police were correct. It was a refugee, possibly starving and rootless, perhaps himself haunted by what had come to pass in his country. Your brother paid the price." She leaned forward, closer to Miriam. "But know this—you have his legacy. You have his photographs, and if you trust me with those photographs, I will do everything I can to put them in the hands of people who will buy and print them for many, many others to see. Keep the negatives, make more prints, but I will take the best of them."

Miriam pressed her lips together to stem more tears. She spoke again, though her voice cracked. "A refugee, after all. You made all this effort, and only to find the police were right."

"I found out about Arturo Kenyon, though. I suppose he had seen Sebastian's photographs, and it inspired him to break the law."

"He is in Spain, you know, fighting in the International Brigades."

Maisie nodded. "Yes, I suspected as much." She pointed to the pile of clothing awaiting alteration on the table. "I must leave you to your work, Miss Babayoff—I have taken enough of your time. If you would like me to take some of Sebastian's photographs, get them ready for me as soon as you can. I'll come to see you again before I leave." Maisie stood, and smiled at Miriam. "One last thing—and forgive me for speaking out of turn—but if you are in love with Mr. Solomon, you must marry him. Do not wait, Miss Babayoff. Time isn't always on our side."

"But my sister, she's—"

Maisie reached for Miriam's hand. "Of course you cannot leave her, and of course you want her to be safe and cared for. But Mr. Solomon loves you, Miriam. And he would help you care for Chana too. Look how he was so gentle with her, on the day of the attempted break-in. I watched as he lifted her and carried her to her room. He did that for you, and he did that for her. Perhaps together you could get her out more, and she would be happier."

"But I don't want to upset her, Miss Dobbs. She can be very difficult when she's upset. Just the mention of trying to walk sends her into a tantrum—even my father could not tolerate it. She would be very troublesome if she knew I had accepted Mr. Solomon."

"I think she would get used to it—and probably used to the additional attention, too." Maisie stood up to leave. "Consider yourself, Miriam. You have given so much—not only to Sebastian and to Chana, but to the cause your family supported. It's time to honor your own dreams—and I believe doing so will benefit Chana, too."

Maisie bid Miriam farewell and left the Babayoff house, the sound of bolts being pushed home echoing as she turned away and started down the narrow street.

Maisie was not quite sure what she would say to MacFarlane, but she knew something had to be said. He would expect her to confront him with what she considered to be the truth. He would do nothing, but at least he would know that she knew what had happened. She had put her conclusions to Vallejo before they were settled in her mind, but it was her discomfort with the scenario she'd described that had made her think, and think again. It was as if she had something under her skin, a tiny splinter that festered. The professor's apparent agreement—as well as that of the German—served only to make her reflect on every piece of information she had gathered, every movement she had witnessed, every conversation memorized. There were those who wanted her to accept her unfinished deduction as the truth—though she thought that perhaps MacFarlane expected her to see through the layers of subterfuge.

Robert MacFarlane was sitting beneath the mural, sipping a cup of tea, when Maisie walked into the café. A glass with two fingers worth of single-malt whisky sat alongside his saucer, as if waiting for noon to strike. Maisie knew he generally did not drink in the morning, unless it was early morning, a continuation of the night before.

"So you're here again, Miss Maisie Dobbs." MacFarlane stood as Maisie approached, and Mr. Salazar rushed to pull out a chair. "Will you join me in a wee dram? The sun is over—"

"The yardarm somewhere across the Empire," said Maisie, mimicking his accent. "Not for me, thank you." She sat down and asked Mr. Salazar for a milky coffee.

"Very funny. So where have you been, your ladyship?"

Maisie shook her head. "Not now, MacFarlane. You know very well I do not use a title."

"It serves you well when it comes to getting papers to cross the border, and the like."

"Ah, I would be the first to admit one has to use the tools at one's disposal, but not every day."

"What were you doing in Madrid?"

"You know. I'm sure you're aware of my every movement. My question is, Why are you interested?"

"You need to be kept safe, Maisie Dobbs."

"What I really need, Robbie MacFarlane, is to know the truth."

"Didn't you already go over that with Professor Vallejo?"

"Your agent? He is, isn't he? An agent for the British government? That wasn't easy to work out. His beliefs don't quite mirror the government's with regard to the Spanish war, but I would imagine he's very useful all the same. Getting to the bottom of the mysterious Mr. Wright was another thing. It took me a while, though—"

MacFarlane raised a finger from the table as Salazar approached.

"Your coffee, madam. And your favorite *japonesa*, on the house."

"That's so kind," said Maisie. "Thank you very much, Mr. Salazar."

The proprietor gave a short bow and turned away to greet new customers.

"So what about the other man, Maisie? He's just a German fed up with Mr. Hitler and his big mouth, doing all he can to help the Republicans in Spain."

Maisie shook her head. "It's more than that, isn't it? The British government isn't interested in the Republicans—their sympathies are with the Nationalists. We've been through that. But Wright is a valuable man—he's moving between worlds. The Germans think he's working for them, the Republicans think he's on their side in Spain, and who's pulling the strings? From where I'm sitting, I would say it's him. But he's providing valuable information to the British government. He's a chameleon; he can hop from a German submarine to a cocktail party where some important people are sipping drinks and becoming a little loose-lipped, and then back to his bunker close to the trenches. He's a go-between, and he's very, very important to the government, though he also does not really exist. That is the world of the spy, the informer. The trouble was that Sebastian Babayoff, in his naïveté, thought he could reveal something and become important, perhaps by placing a photograph in a newspaper, or even an American weekly. He thought he'd bring our Mr. Wright out of the shadows and put him on center stage. So Babayoff had to go. But for someone like me, I believe it was a case of 'Let her think she's found something, and she'll go away.'"

MacFarlane sighed and looked at the clock above the door. He shook his head and picked up his malt whisky, downing it in one gulp.

"I'll not contradict you, Maisie. But I won't agree either. Babayoff was killed by a refugee. That's all that needs to be said."

"Yes, I'm sure it is. And that's what I have told his sister." Maisie paused. MacFarlane raised an eyebrow, and she continued. "But here's what else I have come to believe, amid all the lies and diversions—and I need to say it." Another pause. "Yes, Babayoff had become a security risk at a time when people such as Wright could ill afford exposure regarding their true work. Wright, of course, comes to mind, but there's Vallejo too. I do not for one moment believe the story I was told, that Babayoff was killed by a Nationalist spy. I do, however, believe he was attacked by a penniless refugee, likely primed by one of Wright's contacts, with a hint that a photographer with money in his pocket—cash payment for his work—was leaving the hotel." She ran her fingers through her cropped hair. "It was the refugee who was killed, not Babayoff, who was taken from the scene and told he was being moved to Spain for his safety. In his panic, he believed the story. He left the ring behind on the little finger of the dead refugee—probably chosen for his similarity to Babayoff. And of course, he knew Miriam would retrieve the ring.

"Yet when he was first set upon, before another man entered the scene to finish off the refugee and take Babayoff from the path to safety, he had panicked and thrown his Leica camera into the bushes. But he left behind the Zeiss. A refugee wanting instant money would not have taken a distinctive camera; a fist holding cash has more heft, after all." Maisie lifted her hand and rubbed it across her forehead. "I believe Babayoff was then taken into Spain, allowed to think it was for his own good—to document the war—and then conveniently killed in action. His sister, in her grief, recognized only the ring and the dark hair. She looked at the refugee's hands, but they were enough like Babayoff's so it did not alarm her. She buried her brother in the Jewish cemetery, and in the future she would have somewhere to go, a place of remembrance. But, knowing her brother's belief in the establishment of a republic for the people across the border, she wanted to continue his work. Thus she became acquainted with Arturo Kenyon, and of course, she knew Rosanna Grillo already. Now that she's done what she could—helping with a limited shipment of arms into Spain—such activities are behind her, though I believe part of her will never forgive her brother his reckless self-interest. She knew he upset people, and she was afraid for her own and Chana's personal security—the attempted break-in by one of Wright's people kept her in a state of fear. I do not believe either Miriam or Rosanna Grillo knew or had met

Wright before the day of the cocktail party and Sebastian's subsequent death, though they were acquainted with Vallejo.

"At the end of the day, it boils down to this: Sebastian Babayoff took chances without truly understanding the stakes, which in wartime are always high."

There was a brief silence, and then MacFarlane smiled. "Good work, Maisie. Very good work. Now then, go home."

"I'm not quite finished," said Maisie. "One thing continues to bother me. If Babayoff's activities presented a problem, why not just kill him on the path, and shore up the story that it was the act of a desperate refugee? That would have done the trick. But I think I know why the plan became so convoluted—it was all to buy time, to find out exactly what Babayoff knew, what photographs he had, what he had witnessed and how dangerous he was. Then, once in Spain, Wright just had to give him enough rope to hang himself—only it wasn't rope, it was opportunity. Sebastian Babayoff went off to photograph war. But he forgot that the camera is a flimsy thing. It is not a wall between the photographer and a bullet."

MacFarlane put down his empty glass. "You tell a good story, Maisie, I'll give you that."

"You're not going to say anything else, are you?" She reached for her satchel. "Well, you'll be pleased to hear I've booked my passage—though I bet you knew that already."

"I am pleased, and yes, I knew. You shouldn't be here. It's a dangerous place."

"I remained for the sake of Sebastian Babayoff and his sisters."

MacFarlane deflected her comment. "And I hear you're going up to stay among the rich people at the posh hotel for your last few days—I never thought you would do that, Maisie."

"It just makes it a little easier. I'll not enjoy saying good-bye to

Mrs. Bishop. She's a good egg." She paused again. "What happened to Arturo Kenyon?"

"Poor man was killed. A fine soldier, apparently."

"No doubt the agent took care of outstanding matters."

MacFarlane shrugged, then looked at Maisie. "This is how it is, Maisie. You know that very well. This is how people are kept safe—the sacrifice of others."

"I think I've had enough for one day, MacFarlane. I've had enough of the sacrifice of others. My husband was one of those others."

"I know that very well. And you've sacrificed enough, yourself."

"That's as may be. I'll go now. I have to pack my belongings, and I've a few things to do before I leave Gibraltar."

"I'll come to see you off. I'll be returning to the sunny skies of home soon myself."

"No need to wave from the dockside, MacFarlane." She stood up to leave.

"I'll see you in Blighty, then."

"Will you?"

MacFarlane nodded. "Most definitely. Along with my friend Brian Huntley."

Maisie met MacFarlane's gaze. And she heard again the words of Dr. Francesca Thomas, the Belgian agent she'd met while working undercover at a college in Cambridge.

They'll never let you go, you know. They'll never let you go.

CHAPTER TWENTY

M aisie pulled out her leather suitcase, her carpetbag, and her knapsack and repacked her clothing. She cleared her toiletries into a cotton drawstring bag and tucked it away in the carpetbag. As she did so, the vial of morphia tablets dropped out on the floor. She picked it up and looked at the label, realizing she'd not had cause to take a pill for a while. Perhaps focusing on something outside of herself had focused her immediate thoughts away from her wounds. The scar on her abdomen had become part of her. She felt comfort, now, because it marked the place where her tiny girl had lain within her, taking sustenance from her body. James, she held deep in her heart. She had wondered many times, during the war and then in the course of her work, how people could bear so much loss. She had met women who'd lost not just one son but two or three, and a husband. Like them, she had learned how to shoulder grief, and knew she would see a clear path ahead, in time.

A boy with a barrow was called to carry her luggage to the hotel, and she said her farewell to Mrs. Bishop. The woman encircled Maisie in her arms, and told her to take care of herself, and that she was welcome back to the guest house whenever she wanted.

"You like your privacy, and you keep yourself to yourself, Miss Dobbs, but some things are written on the heart, you know. You can see it in a person's eyes, and I've seen it in yours. I wish you well, my dear, and I hope the sun soon shines through the cloud that brought you here."

Maisie smiled, nodded, and left the guest house, accompanied by Mrs. Bishop as far as the street. She turned once as she walked away, to see the landlady standing, raising her hand to wave. She waved in return.

She stopped at the Babayoff house for as long as it took for Miriam to hand her an envelope, which she slipped into her satchel. The conversation between the two women was short, but enough time for thanks to be expressed, and a promise made that Maisie would do all she could to ensure the photographs were published.

Leaving Miriam's house, Maisie walked along to Jacob Solomon's shop. She bought a needlepoint cushion cover heavy with threads, with paper folded inside to bulk it out for display.

"Mr. Solomon, I wonder, might you have some brown paper for me to wrap this in? It's a gift for a friend, and I want to send it as soon as I can."

"I have some thick paper and string upstairs in the stockroom. Just a moment . . ."

As Maisie expected, Solomon left her alone in the shop. She pulled the envelope with Sebastian Babayoff's photographs from her bag and slipped it inside the cushion cover, together with three letter-size envelopes. Finding a pin on the counter, she used it to attach an envelope bearing Priscilla's name to the outside of the cushion cover. Solomon returned.

"I should remove the paper inside." Solomon held out his hand to take the cushion.

"Oh, not to worry. Look, I am sure you're really busy. If I might just stand at the end of the counter, I'll prepare the parcel. Thank you so much for the paper and string."

Solomon continued working on his accounts while Maisie wrapped the needlepoint cushion cover, secured the parcel with string, and addressed it to Mrs. Priscilla Partridge at her address in Holland Park. When she was finished, she held out her hand to Mr. Solomon.

"I hope you don't mind—I've used your shop as the return address. I'll be traveling a little, so I'll have no firm address as such, though I am sure it will reach its destination. May I prevail upon you to take it to the post office for me? I have the money for you here."

"It would be my pleasure."

They bid farewell, with no mention of Sebastian Babayoff, or the events of the past few weeks. As Maisie stepped out along Main Street, she heard the bell above Solomon's shop door clang. She turned in time to see him greeting the rabbi and a woman she assumed to be his wife, and together they began walking up the narrow alley toward Miriam Babayoff's house. Maisie hoped Jacob Solomon was about to offer his formal proposal of marriage. It was time.

Maisie set out again to walk to Catalan Bay, detouring to find the path that led to the cave where munitions had been stored before being taken by boat into Spain. She wondered how the fishermen ever managed to steer a course through the patrols—but then again, they had generations of navigation and knowledge to draw upon. Soon the path narrowed, and she reached the cave. She heard the chatter of monkeys close by, receding as they scampered farther up the rocks.

The iron gate was locked. She looked at it for some time, holding on to the rusty chain while peering into the depths beyond.

And she realized, then, that this was what it had felt like, after James had died, after their child was lost: she had gone into a dark cave, and the bars had clanged shut behind her. It had taken a death to open them again, just a little, enough space for faith to slip through. As she wiped away her tears, she looked down at her hands and saw that she had been gripping the chains.

"It's time to let go now, Maisie." She whispered the words to herself, but knew it was something that Maurice might have said. She turned away, wiping the rust from her fingers with a fresh handkerchief.

She did not go down to the beach, but looked across the sands from the road. The fishing boats were drawn up, some leaning to one side as if asleep, waiting for the tide to come in once more and set them upright, ready to sail. The women sat close together, mending nets. She did not know if Rosanna was with them, but in her heart she wished her well. She hoped that she would find contentment, if not happiness.

On her last night in the Ridge Hotel, Maisie set her alarm clock for three o'clock in the morning. To her surprise, she slept soundly, though she'd gone to bed at an earlier hour. She had enjoyed her sojourn in such luxurious accommodation more than she thought she might. There was no need to tiptoe along a stone corridor to the bathroom with her towel and soap, as she had at the guest house. Indeed, it seemed that there was always someone at her beck and call, whether she wanted a cup of tea, a three-course meal delivered to her room, or her clothing laundered and pressed.

Half an hour after waking, she was tiptoeing past a night watchman and out into the night. She carried only her carpetbag, knapsack and leather satchel. In her room she had left a note on her leather case, with instructions to have it shipped to an address in Holland Park, London. Sure that no one had seen her emerge from the hotel, she tried to keep her breath measured as she made her way alongside a low wall, but she walked faster when the headlights of a waiting motor car flashed once. Raoul had seen her. She was on her way.

They crossed the border into Spain long before the sun rose over the Rock of Gibraltar. Long before a maid discovered the note in Maisie's room, and hours before Robert MacFarlane received an urgent telephone call from the hotel: Miss Maisie Dobbs was gone.

Maisie remained awake for some time, then drifted into the dozing sleep that had marked her previous journeys. She was safe, for now, traveling through Republican held territory with no arms on board the motor car, and no other intention but to reach her destination. Soon enough the people she loved most in the world would know where she was. She trusted that Solomon would be true to his word and post the parcel, and she had no doubt that the letters would reach their respective destinations.

> *Dear Priscilla,*
>
> *If you are reading this letter, then I hope you don't fling down the needlepoint in disgust. I know it's not to your taste, but it was the best cover for this particular job. First of all, here's what I would like you to do with the enclosed photographs. Please ask Douglas to show them to his various editors. You will see the photographer's name printed on the back of each photograph, along with the name of his sister. His name is—was—Sebastian Babayoff, and he is now dead. You may say he was killed in the civil war raging in Spain. I hope you can find someone to take the photographs—his sister could do with the money, and it would be only right to see his memory honored.*

Would you please forward the letters I have enclosed to Mr. Klein, my father and Brenda, and Lady Rowan? By my reckoning, if this parcel goes out on the next ship, and you post the letters upon receipt, they will arrive at their destinations within a couple of weeks.

Priscilla, I can only apologize for not being in touch. One day we will sit down, you will pour us gin and tonics, and I will reveal all that is in my heart. I plan to return in just a few months—in time for Christmas, and to see in 1938. It's hard to believe next year will mark twenty years since the war ended, and here I am in a place where the memories have been brought back with such definition. I cannot speak of James in this letter—my spirit is still so wounded and raw—but I am better than I was. I know in the coming months I will grow much stronger, strong enough to face returning to England. It still seems to be such a dangerous place for my heart to reside, given all that has come to pass since James and I were married.

Please give my love to those toads of yours, and to Douglas—you are all so very dear to me. I will write again with news, though my letters might well take a while to reach you.

Until then. . .

With all my love,

Maisie

The letter to her father and Brenda was more difficult to compose; she tore up several versions before settling on her message.

My beloved Father and Brenda,

I know you must think me terribly selfish for not returning on the ship, and I hope you received my letter explaining why I could not come home at that particular juncture. As the ship sailed closer to

England, I was filled with trepidation every time I imagined my return to Chelstone. I am still afraid, if truth be told. But I have spent a while here in Gibraltar, and plan to return in time for Christmas. Perhaps we can spend it in London this year, at an hotel rather than home.

I will write you more about my current destination after I am settled, though I think it might be difficult for letters to go to and from England. Having said that, I have always found ways to transport my communications, whether by recognized means or not!

I miss you both very much, but before I return, there are some things I want to do. I have been working again, in a small way, and am on my way to another place, again to work. It is doing me good, I think, and in return I can do something of worth at the same time.

With all my love,
Your daughter,
Maisie

There were two more letters tucked away inside the cushion cover.

Dear Mr. Klein,

I sometimes think that Maurice landed you with more than you might have wanted to take on, when you became my solicitor. I trust my absence from England and the difficulty in reaching me has not been too troubling in the management of my affairs. In the years since Maurice passed away, you have given me such sterling guidance, and have become my most trusted adviser.

First of all, I will be sending a new address to you soon, though I should tell you that post is difficult in the region—but I have useful contacts. Thank you for your last letter, informing me that Sandra is still my tenant at the flat. I wish to confirm that I remain adamant that no rent should be charged, though if she continues to send you regular payments, then the funds must go toward costs for Maurice's medical clinics.

Thank you for confirming that the most recent lease on the Dower House will come to an end on December 31ˢᵗ. If the tenants wish to extend their stay to get them over the New Year, I have no objection. At this point, I do not plan to lease again, but I will advise you closer to the end of the year.

Now I must ask you to do the following: with monies from the Properties Account, I wish to fund the purchase of a fully kitted-out ambulance for use in Spain. I am not sure how one goes about this, but you can write to a Professor Vallejo, care of the address below. I believe an ambulance can be bought in France and then transported into Spain by road. It is to be used to take wounded men from a small hospital run by a nun named Sister Teresa in a hamlet—it is too small a community to be called a village—on the Tajo River. A driver should also be funded; Professor Vallejo will know how to find a suitable person to take on the job. I will be in a position to confirm purchase and use of the ambulance, though it will probably take a few weeks.

I expect to be in England again before year's end. I would be remiss if I did not mention my will. I have no changes to make at the present time. All beneficiaries remain the same, and in the event of my death, the Dower House should revert to the Chelstone estate, where it should once again become part of the Compton trust.

As always, my thanks for your wise counsel over the past few years, and particularly since my husband's sudden death. I expect to see you when I return.

Yours faithfully,

Maisie

She had lingered over the signature, but in the end used just her Christian name, though Klein would never have addressed her by anything other than her correct title, which was now somewhat grander than it had been when they first met.

Her final letter was addressed to Lady Rowan. She had gone back and forth over whether to send the letter to both in-laws, but decided, in the end, that her message would be more personal, a woman-to-woman communiqué.

> *Dear Lady Rowan . . .*

Again she had torn the paper into shreds and begun with a fresh sheet of vellum.

> *Dear Rowan,*
>
> *I can only apologize for not keeping in touch with any regularity. If I am to be perfectly honest—and it is my intention to do so in this letter—it is because not only did words fail me, but I have been in a very dark cave of sadness from which I have not really emerged, though I think I can see light at the end of the tunnel. You were so kind to me in Canada, so deeply understanding and compassionate at a time when your hearts were breaking. We all miss James so very much, don't we? And yet in my grief and shock I was unable to take the hands that were held out to me, so there was nothing to do but drift away from you all—even from my dear father.*
>
> *I appreciate Lord Julian's efforts to find me, and to keep an eye on me. But I am an investigator by training, so it was not long before I realized that I was the subject of some attention from men who could*

only have been working for Lord Julian's contacts in London. I would have done the same thing in his position.

We are all still so terribly stricken by the horror of losing James, but what I try to remember is that he died doing something he loved and believed in. He loved to fly. He loved the feeling of being aloft, above the earth and looking down upon all its goings-on, even though what he saw in the war grieved him. And that is what he was doing in Canada—he loved his country, and believed he was engaged in work that would ultimately be of service to her. Given what I have seen in Spain, I now believe him to have been right. I have been slow to come to that conclusion, and I will be honest, I still bear ill will toward John Otterburn, who persuaded him to come to Canada to undertake work that was fraught with danger. But I also have come to accept that James understood those dangers, and considered the cause to be worth such risk.

Rowan, I have felt the loss of James and our child so keenly. For a while I would have chosen death, and willed it to come to me so that I might join them. My experiences over the past month in particular—you doubtless know where I am, and where I have been—have made me realize that to make anything of my future, I must take a few steps back. When I was a girl, one of the first lessons Maurice taught me was to stand with my hands upturned as if to receive a most precious gift, and then ask, "How may I serve?" I have discovered the answer, for now at least. I have found a place where I may be of use, where my skills might save a life, so I must follow the voice of my heart. Dame Constance Charteris of Camden Abbey spoke to me of Saint Benedict once, and urged me to listen "with the ear of your heart." I have been trying hard to follow her counsel.

I will be in touch again soon with an address.

With my love and affection,

Maisie

W e're almost there, señora," said Raoul. "You have slept, no?"

Maisie rubbed her eyes. "I was dozing, not quite asleep." Looking out the window, she saw familiar buildings in the distance. "You made good time, Raoul."

Raoul smiled and patted the steering wheel. "She is good. Full of faith."

Maisie smiled. "Yes, a good faithful motor car."

As the motor car approached their destination, Raoul pumped the horn in a playful manner. *Parp-parp-pup-pup-parp*. . . . The sound brought children and dogs from the shadows and out into the square. As he maneuvered the vehicle in a circle and stopped in front of the church, women emerged from the houses and Sister Teresa came out of her hospital, wiping her hands on a cloth. Maisie stepped from the motor car, and the nun all but ran forward, dropping the cloth as she took Maisie's hands in her own, as she had at their first meeting.

"You kept your promise, Miss Maisie Dobbs. You returned to us."

"I didn't make a promise, Sister Teresa," said Maisie, giving a half-laugh at the error.

"Oh, yes, you did—it came from your heart. I saw it. God saw it."

Maisie nodded, feeling the itch of tears at the corners of her eyes. "Well, if you can't keep a promise, then you're in trouble, I think."

Sister Teresa laughed and wrapped her arms around Maisie. "I knew you would come back. I had faith."

Maisie and Sister Teresa drew apart as women and children clapped their hands. Sister Teresa announced that *efermera* Maisie—nurse Maisie—would be back in just a moment; she had to take her to her room. She turned and led Maisie through the church to the cloistered square where her own cell was situated. Maisie wondered how it might have been, when other nuns were present, their long habits brushing the ground, their hands clasped together in copious sleeves, heads bowed. Passing the nun's own quarters, they came to another door of dark oak, which opened into a simple room with a bed, a table, a washstand with a bowl and ewer, and a hand-plaited rug on the floor. A narrow window looked out onto the courtyard garden.

"It is very simple," said Sister Teresa.

"It is all I need," replied Maisie.

And it was. As she rested her carpetbag, knapsack, and satchel against the table, she looked around her. Yes, this was all she needed. She would do work she knew she was good at in the service of those who needed her. She knew she would grow strong here, putting others before herself. And because she had always worked, and accepted that working was part of who she was, she thought that in time, after she'd returned to England, she might even feel compelled to go back to her old business. But that was a few months away. Now there was a task before her, and she wanted to get on with it.

Sister Teresa walked with Maisie out to the front of the church. The women and children had remained, waiting, with one boy holding a pitcher of water for Maisie, another a plate with bread and sheep's milk cheese. Raoul had allowed children to take turns sitting in the motor car, but when he saw Maisie emerge from the church, he waved. She walked to the motor car and shook his hand.

"Gracias, Raoul. Gracias por su ayuda." *Thank you for your help.*

Raoul gave a short bow and said in halting English. "Look after you-self."

Maisie smiled as Raoul turned and told the children it was time to leave the motor car; because he wouldn't bring back stowaways.

It was as Raoul drove off, with a cloud of dust in his wake and everyone waving good-bye, that Maisie saw the young woman whose child she'd delivered walking toward them, carrying the infant wrapped in a cotton shawl. She stood in front of Maisie and held out her daughter.

"Oh, hasn't she grown, already—and she's still only days old!" said Maisie, reaching for the baby.

Sister Teresa translated, and the woman giggled and pointed to her lips, making a sucking sound.

"Ah, she feeds well." Maisie laughed along with the women as they applauded again. "What have you named her?" she asked, her words translated by Sister Teresa.

"Esperanza," replied the woman. She lifted her hands and brought them together in front of her lips, as if in prayer.

Maisie watched the nun, who nodded her understanding and turned to Maisie, resting her hand on the babe's head.

"It means 'hope.' Her name is Hope."

Maisie looked down at the child, at her tiny hand now wrapped around Maisie's little finger.

"Esperanza," she whispered. "*Hope.*"

ACKNOWLEDGMENTS

I t was during a trip to Gibraltar to visit my Cheef Resurcher (the misspelling is quite deliberate) that my interest in "The Rock" deepened. In the early years of the Maisie Dobbs series in particular, my esteemed researcher—"he who cannot be named"—provided a welcome helping hand, not only with his intimate knowledge of Scotland Yard, but with useful historic materials garnered from the Garrison Library. So thanks must go to my esteemed Cheef Resurcher, and of course also to the helpful staff at the Garrison Library, and to those at Gibraltar House in London for their assistance. Unforeseen errors and wide turns are all down to me.

Deepest gratitude to my fabulous editor, Jennifer Barth, to publisher Jonathan Burnham, and—as always—the wonderful team at HarperCollins, especially Katherine Beitner, Stephanie Cooper, and Josh Marwell.

The iconic cover designs for the Maisie Dobbs series are the result of collaboration between creative wizard Archie Ferguson, and the renowned artist and craftsman, Andrew Davidson—working with you both is a highlight of my year.

On the other side of the pond—many, many thanks must go to Susie Dunlop and the committed "Team Maisie" at Allison and Busby in London—you are all just terrific!

I consider myself blessed to have Amy Rennert in my corner, not only as my literary agent, but my friend.

And as always, last but never least, to John Morell—thanks, love, for being my #1 supporter.

ABOUT THE AUTHOR

JACQUELINE WINSPEAR is the author of the *New York Times* bestsellers *Leaving Everything Most Loved, Elegy for Eddie, A Lesson in Secrets, The Mapping of Love and Death, Among the Mad,* and *An Incomplete Revenge,* as well as four other national bestselling Maisie Dobbs novels. Her standalone novel, *The Care and Management of Lies,* was also a *New York Times* bestseller. She has won numerous awards for her work, including the Agatha, Alex, and Macavity awards for the first book in the series, *Maisie Dobbs,* which was also nominated for the Edgar Award for Best Novel and was a *New York Times* Notable Book. Originally from the United Kingdom, she now lives in California.